GEARS AND LEVERS 3

A Steampunk Anthology

Edited by

Phyllis Irene Radford

Sky Warrior Book Publishing, LLC

Published by Sky Warrior Book Publishing, LLC.
PO Box 99
Clinton, MT 59825
www.skywarriorbooks.com

Editor: Phyllis Irene Radford.
Cover: M. H. Bonham
Publisher: M. H. Bonham.
Printed in the United States of America
0   9 8 7 6 5 4 3 2 1

ACKNOWLEDGEMENTS

Kit Carson Versus the Toad Men of Rio Gila copyright © by David Boop 2013
New Lives copyright © by Nancy Jane Moore 2010, first published "Shadow Conspiracy" edited by Phyllis Irene Radford and Laura Anne Gilman, Book View Café
The Engineer copyright © by Bob Brown 2013
The Experiment copyright © by Cliff Winning 2013
Heart of Comstock copyright © Jennifer Rachel Baumer 2013
The Golden Larynx copyright © by Ellen Denham 2013
Ferrocararil's Honor copyright © by Sylvia Kelso 2013
Ragtime copyright © by T. Joseph Dunham 2013
Mine copyright © by Bryan Fields 2013
The Promise and the Reckoning copyright © by Andrew Knighton 2013

TABLE OF CONTENTS

KIT CARSON VERSUS THE TOAD MEN OF RIO GILA

David Boop

1866 Arizona, Territory:

Kit Carson held his hands up in surrender. It was far from the first time the former general and frontier tracker had been in such a predicament, but it was shaping up to be his last.

Toad men pointed the nefarious weapon known as *Professor Justin Jeremiah Janikowski's Amazing Nattling Gun* at him. The good professor lay on the ground, a dozen nails from his own invention sticking out of his left arm. The teenager, Will, tended to the professor's wounds, pulling nails out and wrapping the holes with pieces of cloth handed to him by his sweetheart, Sarah, as she torn them off her dress.

It struck Kit as ironic that this young lady happened to be one of the very people they'd come to save. The thought made him smirk, which in turn caused his captors to squint suspiciously at him. The strange, amphibian-like men didn't like him, nor his attempt to free their breeding stock from captivity.

And here he thought his reputation as a friend to all people; be they red, yellow, or, in this case, a lumpy-brownish, preceded him everywhere.

But then the Toad Men of Rio Gila were only concerned about three things: food, shelter, and mating.

The sound of the Nattling gun increased, and Kit knew he had only seconds before the gun recharged to full and would pummel his body with a hundred nails. Other toad warriors kept their guns trained on him, so Kit could make only the subtlest of moves.

He swallowed and thought of his wife and kids back on their farm in Colorado. Maybe he shouldn't have come to Arizona at the request of a good friend. Maybe he should have stayed retired as he was too old for adventures.

Maybe he desired to be the man in those damnable dime novels once more.

The whistling reached its peak. Kit said a small prayer and waited.

<>

Three Days Earlier:

Fourteen-year-old William Ragsdale couldn't reason how he'd lost track of his camp in the middle of a desert. Sure, it was late, but he'd only crossed two sand dunes to relieve himself. That being done, he'd returned the way he came.

Or had he? As he squatted, did he rotate to avoid a prairie cactus? Could he have gotten pointed in the wrong direction half-asleep? Still, at most he had to be only a couple hundred feet away from where he started. He should be able to see the cook's campfire from the top of a dune.

Scampering up a mound, Will scanned his surroundings. No smoke. No lights. No music or horses nickering. His parents, gone. The cute girl he'd had his eye on since leaving Kansas City, Sarah, vanished.

He had no provisions, barely any clothes, and certainly no weapon. Sunrise would come in six hours, give or take. He needed to find his way in the dark, as the Arizona desert had a reputation for being unforgiving to the lone traveler.

He tried to follow his original footsteps, but he'd crisscrossed them too many times in the sliver of moonlight. Instead, Will laid out a hunting pattern. Will's grandfather used to take him trapping up on Black Mountain, but then the Appalachians were much different from a desert at midnight.

Along the third path, he saw a glow warming the side of a hill and strands of music wafting in the air. Will didn't remember the hill when they'd set up camp, but who else would be out there this time of night?

He sprinted around the mound just as the music stopped. His heart stopped with it.

The light came not from a fire, but from a hundred little orbs that hung on the side of wagon. Built of wood, the wagon had enough elaborate carvings and designs to belong in a church. A side extended up to form a roof, showcasing the interior. Inside the wagon was a collage of little wooden musicians, each face and body carved with the minutest details. The band held intricately crafted instruments in their tiny hands that moved by rods and strings that disappeared out of view.

A blast of steam came from a stovepipe on the roof of the wagon and the music started up again; violinists bowed violins, trumpeters blew on trumpets and drummers drummed. Will counted two dozen musicians in all. The music came from somewhere inside the wagon, but the marionette men and women were choreographed perfectly to it.

He walked around the behemoth, but found neither his people hidden behind, nor an operator of the mystery machine. He did find two camels tied to a cactus nearby. They honked and spit on the ground as Will approached, to make sure he wasn't dreaming. Sure enough, two single-humped camels eyed him with detached resolve.

A curse erupted from inside the wagon and the music ground to a halt. A backdoor kicked open and a board slid out. With it came feet, then a waist and then a beard. And then even more beard. It was unlike any beard Will had ever seen. Golden, curly rings cascaded across the man's belly like Mississippi River rapids after a big storm. But not just ringlets, there were tools tied on the end of many strands of hair; small, precise screwdrivers and wrenches, and hammers and devices Will couldn't fathom a use for.

Instead of a tool belt, this man had a tool beard.

The board tilted until the end touched dirt and the owner of the beard pushed himself up and off of the ramp. He turned back toward the wagon and made an obscene gesture that made Will chuckle.

The man spun upon Will's laugh. At first, the anger at the wagon transferred to the new arrival, but then the man's eyes opened fully to take in the teen.

"Oh, my dear boy. I'm sorry. I didn't mean to give you such a fright. I obviously didn't hear your approach."

"No worries, sir. I didn't mean to sneak up on you like that. Just got myself turned around and I thought you were my people."

"People, you say? Are you part of a wagon train heading west?"

Will nodded, suspicion creeping into his mind. His pa told him to be wary of strangers asking too much about the caravan.

The man must be good at reading faces, for he said, "Oh, no. Don't you fret a bit. I'm no one to worry about." He stepped away from Will, motioning for the boy to follow. He reached to something on the top of the raised side panel and unfurled it. A sign dropped down:

Professor Justin Jeremiah Janikowski's Steam-powered Orchestra!

"I, my wayward lad, am a scientist and entertainer."

Will scratched his head. "You're both?"

The Professor sidled up to Will, slipping an arm around his shoulder and guiding him to a seat.

"A true performer must be a student of science. A lot goes into all those notes you hear, my boy. There're numbers on that sheet music for a reason. Calculations that go way beyond the understanding of non-musical types. It takes scientific artistry to make those instruments, too. One does not just make a Stradivarius the way one carves a whistle from a reed." The Professor waved with a flourish. "And this is my greatest musical invention!"

Will admitted it looked impressive.

"Like the player piano, I've built an automation that can play any song in the history of man; be it Mozart or hymnal. If there's sheet music to it, I can program it!" He held up a finger. "Let me show you. Pick a song, any song."

"Camptown races?" Will loved that song from his days at his grandfather's cabin.

"Just the song I was working on! Let me see if I can finish the brass section."

Professor Janikowski drew himself back into the machinery. Another string of curses erupted from its bowels, however, the good professor must have remembered he had an audience.

"Sorry!"

Will's nervousness increased. Surely, his parents must be wondering why he hadn't returned. Will craned his ear, yet he hadn't heard his name called. Just how far *had* he walked?

Steam belched forth and the music started again. Listening closer, Will could pick out the familiar tune. Will recognized it as the one playing when he arrived at the professor's camp. He just wasn't used to all the extra instruments. It sounded more like something sung in church than something sung around a campfire.

The Professor appeared beside him.

"You don't look happy. Is the brass section still amiss?"

"No. I should be getting back. I don't know how my camp disappeared so quickly."

Professor Janikowski opened his mouth to say something, frozen in mid-thought, and then looked slightly alarmed.

"Did you say 'disappeared'?"

When the teenager confirmed, the Professor closed up the wagon rapidly.

"Quick, my boy! Grab the camels. Hitch them up. Don't worry. They're docile."

"What? What's going on?"

Not waiting for an answer, Will hooked the animals to the front of the wagon, while Janikowski bounded up to the driver's seat. He reached his hand down indicating Will should join him.

"Please. Hurry. Your family may be in grave peril!"

While the professor prepared Will on the way over the dunes for what they might see, the young lad's heart broke at the reality of it. The camp had been destroyed, everything left in a state of disarray. Wagons tipped over, some still burned. Clothing and items strewn hither and yon. Horses missing. And, most disturbing, not a soul to be found anywhere.

Will's wagon stood intact, so he entered it in a rush, grabbing clothes and strapping on the six-gun his father had given him to his hip. Back outside, he spotted another gun; his mother's hold-out pistol. He smelled the end. It had been fired. Fighting back tears, he tucked the small gun in his boot.

He set about collecting other guns and ammo, whatever he could find. He'd need to arm them when he tracked them down.

The professor called out, "Will, my boy. You better come here."

With his heart in his throat, Will rushed over to where the old man's voice came from, only to discover the professor looking down at a pair of boots sticking straight up; boots with their owner still in them. The lad swallowed hard and approached to see who the dead man was.

<\>

Two Days Earlier:

Kit Carson hated Drowned Horse, Arizona. The place felt wrong. The whole area felt odd from the first time he'd explored it. He'd told the Army and anyone who'd listened not to build there. The Apache had legends about a great evil lurking in the red rocks that surrounded the valley. When he'd gotten word that a town had been built right where he said not to, he sighed and wondered why anyone ever asked his advice on anything.

His wife, Josefa, had been even more reluctant than usual letting him come back to Arizona. They had a farm to run, kids to raise, and he'd retired from the negotiator business.

"I can't tell you enough how much I appreciate this," Marshal Tucker Bandimere said for the third time that evening.

Tucker bought Kit's dinner, room and whiskey as a thank you. They leaned in camaraderie against the bar of the town's only saloon, *The Sagebrush*, but Tucker's gratitude grew quickly tedious.

"As I said, Tucker. I owed you. I never forget a debt. Plus, Indian negotiations are tough business, especially with the Apache."

Kit hoped his actions would help the U.S. Marshall establish himself in his new territory. Tucker stood a string bean of a man with a handlebar mustache. Kit remembered himfrom when he could barely grow one; a lad manning the walls of Fort Lupton. Those were dangerous times.

"Yes, but how you convinced the chief to turn his son in for the raid on that settlement? Well, that was pure artistry. Especially after you'd barely arrived from a week on the road."

"I've made the trip from Colorado to Arizona more times than I can count." Though, it took Kit a good deal longer than it ever had before; a product of his advancing age.

"Both sides were weary from all the fighting. It will strengthen the chief's son to do the time. When he gets out in a year, the situation will be different and the man will be a better example for his tribe."

A commotion rose up outside the saloon. Inside, the saloon goers heard hooves galloping in fast, but Kit's trained ear suggested they didn't belong to horses. Curiosity piqued, he made his way to the window where others had gathered to stare slack-jawed.

A wagon pulled into town drawn by two camels.

Kit looked again.

Two camels drew to a halt outside the sheriff's office; a man in the driver's seat with a beard so long and thick, he could wear it as clothing. Next to him sat a boy, no more than fourteen, a mixture of fear and anger evident on his face. On the roof, a body lay strapped down and blanketed, boots sticking straight up to heaven. A blood stained piece of cloth hung over the side.

Sheriff Levi Fossett, the local lawman, approached the wagon as the two men got down.

Don't get involved, Kit told himself.

Tucker left the saloon in a hurry to join the sheriff.

It has nothing to do with you, Kit reminded himself.

Tucker listened to the men intently, and then pointed toward the saloon as if he'd sent an arrow right at Kit.

You can leave out the back and be home in five days of hard riding, his mind pleaded with him. Kit's feet had other plans, though, as he walked out of the front.

<><>

Will couldn't believe that *the* Kit Carson actually sat across from him. The teen tried to act more mature around his idol, but the mix of grief from finding his family's camp raided and the discovery of the dead wagon master, left Will with uncontrollable emotions.

They sat in the local mortician's wake room. A coffin rested on a dais nearby, but it was thankfully unoccupied. Drowned Horse's sheriff directed them to the place, not because the wagon master's body needed to go there, which it did, but because it was the largest sitting room in town away from nosey people.

Will did his best not to stare at the legend. He practically tripped over himself saying hi.

"General Carson, sir? It's an honor to meet you. I've read all your books!"

General Carson kept an even expression as he moved past the teen to address the adults. "Don't believe anything you read and only half of what you see."

Will didn't register the brush off, so star-struck by Kit was he. He found it hard to focus on what Sheriff Fossett was saying.

"So, when you got back to the Ragsdale's camp, the wagons were there, but the people were missing?"

Professor Janikowski stroked his beard. "Yes, yes. All save for the body of the unfortunate wagon master, who as you saw, died of multiple nail wounds."

Tucker said, "About a hundred, give or take a nail or two. And this was caused by your invention?"

The Professor blushed, embarrassed. "I used to build forts before I retired and moved into the performance arts. I designed Fort Garland, a place the General should be familiar with."

Mr. Carson corrected him. "Just Mister, now."

"A loss for the Army," the professor promoted, "But even Ulysses had to go home eventually. Anyway, I invented a machine to save time. Professor Justin Jeremiah Janikowski's Nattling Gun." He beamed. "I used the principal of a Gatling gun, only made it smaller and fires nails."

Will heard all that on the ride to Drowned Horse, still finding it hard to believe something like the guns he'd seen mounted at forts could be made portable. Even harder to stomach was what came next.

"I headed to California to meet with an investor who wanted to reproduce them," Janikowski continued, "But on the way, I stopped by Rio Gila for a couple of nights to work on my orchestra." He leaned forward conspiratorial. "I saw their slanted, yellow eyes just outside my campfire. They were entranced by the music, barely able to breathe. I didn't know what to make of them as they approached."

"Toad Men," Fossett echoed the term Professor Janikowski used earlier.

"Hideous creatures! Flat faces covered with bumps and warts, hardly human. Webbed fingers, barely able to hold their weapons." He held up a finger. "Barely, but still able. I discovered this when the music irrevocably stopped and they grew angry. They took me hostage, collected my belongings. They wanted me to, um…"

The Professor looked at Will, seeming to not know what to say next. Will smiled.

"Oh, don't worry, Professor. Ain't nuthin' I haven't seen on a farm."

Still wary, Professor Janikowski chose his words carefully, "They're trying to breed the deformity out of them. From what I gathered, each generation looks less toad-like."

Fossett laughed, holding his gut. "You mean to say, they wanted you to lay with their toad women? Now I've heard it all!"

Will stood up. "They have my family! And… Well, others I care about. If the professor's right, they might kill them if they refuse. Or worse!"

The thought of the taken females brought somber reality to the group.

Mr. Carson asked, "How'd you escape?"

"I begged them to let me go back to my wagon. They'd taken the horses, so I couldn't leave. I managed to get the orchestra working, and while my guards were transfixed, I wacked them over the head. After days of walking, I saw the camels, at first thinking them a mirage. They are well trained. I led them back to the wagon and have been driving around Arizona for weeks, trying to figure out what my next move would be. Then I came across young Will here, or he, I."

Tucker's voice remained skeptical. "And you thought not to tell anyone?"

"Who in their right mind would believe me?"

Fossett cuffed the Marshal on the shoulder. "You've been here almost a year. You can't tell me this is the weirdest thing you've seen or heard?"

Sheepishly, Tucker agreed.

"Well, I've covered every inch of the Gila over the years," Mr. Carson challenged, "that's why Tucker pointed me out."

"Yes sir, Mr. Carson." Will couldn't stop himself, "First, you lead an expedition from California to the Colorado River, despite being attacked by a thousand Apaches warriors. Then, along with a division of Dragoons, you went down the Gila to get a message to the President during the Mexican-America—"

Mr. Carson harrumph, holding up a hand to cut him off. Will stopped his yammering, mortified.

"In all my trips, I certainly haven't seen a settlement of frog-like men."

"Toad."

The negotiator broke in his cool demeanor, but only slightly. "Frog. Toad. Lizard. Don't care if it's a thirty-foot python."

Fossett and Tucker shot a look at each other as if they shared a private joke.

"I'm just saying," he continued, "there isn't a place to hide a tribe of pioneer-stealing, lily-pad hopping, fly-eating, water-sucking monsters."

One Day Ago:

Kit Carson, Professor Janikowski and Will Ragsdale peered over a ledge and down into the river-worn canyon of Rio Gila.

There, in a secluded bend, roughly two dozen toad men, women, and children went about their daily business. They moved about simple huts, painted the colors of the red sandstone of the canyon walls, camouflaging them. Meanwhile, eight normal-looking, but unharmed people could be seen, captive in a prison carved out of rock opposite them.

Kit grumbled, "Exactly the reason I retired. Just when I think I've seen it all…"

"What was that, Mr. Carson?" the boy asked.

Kit couldn't decide what was more annoying; his inner-voice or the teenager who treated him as lord and savior. He wanted to leave Will back in town, but seeing as it *was* his family captured, the boy couldn't be discouraged.

"Nothin'. See those boulders there? Those had to have been loosened by a monsoon, or forcibly removed. That bend wasn't here when I went through with the Dragoons in '46."

"That's okay, sir. You couldn't have known."

"But I should have." Been too long away. What good am I as a tracker if I don't know the area I'm tracking? Bile rose in his throat.

"You can't be everywhere. You're an important man. The President—"

Kit's anger came as a hoarse whisper, but the emotion was clear to all.

"*Was* an important man. *Was*! Nobody calls on Kit Carson for matters of national importance anymore, kid. They put me out to pasture, like they do old horses. It's not like novels. Heroes don't always show up in time. And when they don't, people die. That's the truth of it."

The boy's father taught him right. Will didn't cry, even though it looked as if he wanted to. Instead, he walked over to the wagon.

"A little hard on the lad… and yourself… weren't you?"

"Sorry, professor, but the kid's got to grow up. This isn't a fairy tale."

The Professor stroked his beard. "True, true, but remember, those are his parents down there and a girl he fancies. Don't you have a son about that age? Do you talk to him like that?"

Didja fight Indians, pa? Were you outnumbered twenty to one?

Kit son's, Billy, became increasingly disheartened when Kit came home without new stories. He experienced his father going from war hero to messenger to farmer, losing more respect for him each time.

Is that why when a man pulled up in a camel-led wagon you leapt at it, Kit? To have a story to take home to your son? But it's not so easy anymore. The world changed around you and you're too old to change with it.

Kit looked over to where Will kicked some rocks. Was it better the boy understood sooner than later? Will glanced up and Kit saw eyes as disheartened as Billy's.

The Professor whispered, "Maybe talking about people dying right now isn't the best track. He needs to know there's a plan. Do you have one? How many toads do you count?"

They moved to join Will away from the cliff's edge.

Too many, Kit thought, but said "Thirty *if* you include the women and children."

"The women might fight," Professor Janikowski thought carefully, "but mostly to protect their children. They're the only ones they can count on to break the curse."

"Curse?" Will questioned, close enough to hear them.

"People don't turn into toads for nothing, my boy. Either they're diseased, or been cursed."

Kit raised a disbelieving eyebrow. "You call yourself a man of science and you believe in magic?"

"I found two camels wandering in the desert, General. How could I not?"

"It's mister," corrected Kit, "And those camels were part of a scheme gone bad. A guy brought them from Africa thinking they'd be the answer to desert travel. Turns out people prefer horses, so he just let them loose. There've been sightings of them for years."

"Yes, but to find two right when I needed them? That's the magic." The professor indicated his orchestra. "I make music that soothes savage beasts. I invent things no one has dreamed of..."

Kit interrupted, "One could say you dreamed of them."

The bearded man pinched his eyes at Kit. "Fine, *Mister* Sour-Puss, then I won't loan you any of my 'magic' to beat my *obviously* normal Nattling Gun."

Will spoke up, "You have something that will stop it?"

The professor held up his hands in mock protest. "I do, but if *Mister* Carson is too grounded in reality to use it, then I couldn't possibly..."

"Mister Carson, you've got to convince him to let you use it. Please, Mister Carson, Please!"

Will's pleading face made Kit laugh. Without Tucker or Fossett, they were outnumbered four to one. Kit held his hands up in mock-surrender. "I apologize, professor. You are a wizard of the first order and those are cursed toads down there. Lend me your magic so I may slay them."

Will chuckled and Kit tussled his hair.

"To be sure, I said a curse was *one* possibility." Professor Janikowski winked. "It's probably just a disease."

<<>>

Though he hadn't said so, Will knew his idol was sorry for his earlier words. Mr. Carson smiled reassuringly at him from time to time.

Professor Janikowski unloaded inventions. Will received a bandolier strap with several of the glowing orbs attached, unlit at the moment.

"We're approaching at night," the professor explained, "If you get caught, my boy, just pull this string." The string hung loosely over Will's shoulder and connected to the small batteries on his back. "The orbs will blaze to life, blinding your captors long enough for you to take action."

"Thanks, Professor. What does Mr. Carson's do?"

A square buckle replaced the one normally on Mr. Carson's belt, while wires ran around to his back to where a small canister was hooked.

The Professor held up a finger. "That's a surprise. Unfortunately, it's steam battery driven with only one use, or I'd demonstrate it. Let's hope we don't need it twice."

Will wondered how reliable any of the scientist's inventions were after seeing how much time he spent fixing the orchestra. The professor ran tubes from the wagon to the edge of the canyon. He didn't elaborate what they were for, either.

The plan Mister Carson thought up would take precise timing. Will's part would be to free the captives. All and all, not the easiest of tasks, but better than taking on the whole of the toad clan, which the professor and Mr. Carson planned to do. Will needed to climb down from above the prison cave, surprise the two guards and spring his people.

That part of the canyon wasn't deep, maybe a hundred feet at its farthest. Mr. Carson had pointed out the best place for Will to descend, showing him the ledges and handholds that he would use. The teenager memorized them until he pictured them with his eyes closed. The Professor secured a rope to a big, ol' cactus, bigger than any Will had seen on the trip west. The loose end ran through a box until the device held tight again the knot. Again, the rope went through the box hanging loose this time.

"*Professor Justin Jeremiah Janikowski's Incredible Recoiling Rope*," The Professor announced. "If you get in a bind, press this button and you'll find yourself wheeled back up."

Will thanked him and got into position. As the sun set, he waited for the signal. Upon receiving it, Will began the laborious climb down, careful not to send any loose rocks below. The wall had been worn raggedly, providing several adequate footholds. Will mis-stepped only once and slammed against the side. Worried he'd break the orbs, Will reversed the strap around his body so they were behind him.

Almost to the ledge above the cave, Will thanked the lord he'd had no problems. Two toads, younger and less toadish guarded the entrance to the cell. Will felt pretty confident he could get the drop on them. However, looking across the encampment, Will watched as two torches approach.

He didn't have time to finish his descent before he'd be spotted. Unhooking himself from the rope, Will dropped about ten feet to the ledge and ducked down. He drew his gun and waited.

<><>>

Two large toad men walked toward the prison. Kit held his breath as they got within visual range of Will.

Aiming his rifle, Kit would have a difficult shot in the near-dark. He doubted he'd get four shots off before others spotted his position near the encampment.

The two smaller guards moved aside to let the newcomers into the cell. Kit relaxed for the moment, figuring amphibian eyes must not be as good at night.

A young girl screamed while one of the toad men dragged her from the cave. A man, probably her father, protested and the other guard beat him to the ground. Kit's intuition flared.

"Oh, shit!"

Will cried out, "Sarah!" and leapt from the ledge. He landed on the toad man holding the girl, slamming its head to the dirt. The teen looked up just in time to avoid the butt end of a rifle swung at his head by another guard. He rolled off the one toad, drawing and firing at the same time. The shot was true and the guard dropped.

The younger pair of toads started crying out an alarm, though croaking might be a better description. They moved toward Will, and Kit took a shot. It wasn't a kill shot, but the gun arm of the leftmost toad was rendered useless.

More croaks sounded from the camp, and Kit caught movement in his peripheral vision. In amongst the toads, two carried a device that could only be the professor's Nattling gun. One carried the gun itself, several barrels strapped together and connected to a big stock. The second toad wore a pack on his back. He quickly pumped a lever on the side and Kit heard an increasing whine.

And then...

Toad people froze in their tracks as the orchestral sound of *Camptown Races* wafted through the canyon, piped in from the tubes the Professor had laid out. Kit looked up to where the Professor waved one of his glowing orbs.

However, be it that they were too far away or too focused, the toad Will faced still attacked him. Foregoing guns, they fought mono a mono. The former tracker ran to where the teens grasped each in mutual death grips.

"Use the orbs!" Kit called out as Will appeared to have forgotten all about them. Letting go with one hand, the teen pulled on the string.

White light blared in front of Kit. Everything lost detail and became a painful blur of black spots and rainbows. Kit brought his hands to his eyes, rubbing them. He blinked, trying his best to see something, anything, but he was effectively blind to the world.

Kit heard the thump of someone hitting the ground.

"Will? Will?"

"Oh, lord! Mr. Carson! I'm so sorry. I had to turn them—"

"Never mind! What happened to the guard?"

Will chuckled. "Sarah clocked him one over the head with his own rifle. He's out cold."

Kit felt Will take his arm and guide him over to a rock where the older man could sit.

"And the rest?"

"They're still swaying to the music. Like they ain't got a care in the world."

Vision slowly returning, Kit saw torches as flicking orange blurs.

"Where's the professor?"

"He's moving through the camp. He's almost to the toads that have his device."

And then… the music stopped.

<>>

Mr. Carson held his hands up in surrender. While Will knew

this wasn't the first time Kit had been in such a predicament, it looked to be his hero's last.

After the wagon broke down, the toad men sprung to life pretty fast. They surrounded Mr. Carson and Will before the older man's vision fully returned. The Professor, making a mad dash for the Nattling Gun, took a blast to the arm and lay bleeding on the ground. Their captors gathered the would-be rescuers together and planned to execute Kit, the one who looked the most dangerous and least useful for fathering children.

"I'm sorry, my boy," the professor said, "I guess I'm neither a good inventor nor entertainer. I've failed you and your lady here."

He looked as if he would weep, but Will patted his good arm reassuringly. "That's not true. Those orbs worked fine. Plus, Mr. Carson will think of something. He always does."

But Will wondered when he would as the whine of the Nattling Gun increased. A dozen toad men covered them with ordinary weapons. Sarah slid in close, wrapping herself around Will's arm. Even after days of captivity, she still was the prettiest woman he'd ever seen.

"Sarah, in case we don't make it out of here…"

She put a finger to his lips and nodded. She leaned forward to kiss him, but at that moment, the whining reaching its peak.

The Toad men's laugh was guttural and watery. One reached for the trigger and pulled.

Quicker than Will could see, Mr. Carson pressed a button on his buckle. An explosion of steam burst forth from the device on his back. Suddenly, metal blades unfolded from Kit's buckle. They sprang out like a woman's fan, growing bigger and bigger until they made a giant shield like a roman soldier's.

The nails launched from the professor's device, but bounced off the shield in a dozen directions, puncturing several of the surrounding toad men.

Will pulled his mom's two-shot hold out from his boot. He shot the toads holding the Nattling Gun. Mr. Carson grabbed a fallen pistol and took down several more armed creatures.

Gun fire sounded on the ridge and Will looked up to see

Marshal Tucker, Sheriff Fossett and a bunch of Indians on horseback. They rode down into the canyon and surrounded the whole toad clan. Will and Sarah helped the Professor to his feet, propping him up as the toad men laid down their weapons.

<><>

Families reunited, Kit felt he did really little to actually change the outcome of events and said as much. As expected, the boy disagreed.

"Sir, if it wasn't for you, I wouldn't have climbed down a cliff, faced a bunch of water-sucking toads without fear, nor seen my family again."

Will gazed lovingly at Sarah when he said "family" and Kit knew it wouldn't be long before those kids would need to get married. But a husband needs a job...

"Hey, Fossett. I noticed you didn't have a deputy. That right?"

Sheriff Fossett came over to where they stood. "You looking for a job, Kit?"

The tracker laughed. "Nope, but I know someone who'd make a fine one. Good in a fight. Thinks with his head. Well, most the time." Kit tussled Will's hair again. "He's old for his age. If his family settles in the area, I think he'd make a fine addition to your team. Plus, he already has a glimmer about how strange the territory is."

Fossett looked the lad over. "Can't make it legal until you're sixteen, but we could start you working around the office, teach you the ropes."

Will's eyes lit up. "Really! Thank you, Sheriff!" He turned to Kit. "And thank you, Mr. Carson." He offered his hand.

Kit drew him in for a hug, instead.

"It's Kit from now on. You earned it."

Stepping back, Kit said, "Now I got to get home, so as I can tell my son about Will Ragsdale and how he faced down a hundred lizardmen."

"Toad Men."

"Whatever."

The professor walked up, as Will and Sarah ran to talk to their parents. The bearded man escorted a toad woman with a slightly rounded belly.

"Seems my nights here, um, bore some fruit. I'm going to stick around and see if I can't help figure out what really happened to these people. Curse or science?" He winked at Kit. "I should be able to keep them out of trouble from now on. They seem more content to live *with* society as to attack it, now." He leaned toward the group and spoke in a stage whisper. "Plus, they love my music. Nothing like a captive audience."

"And maybe you can train them to build stuff... working stuff. Make a name for themselves." Marshal Tucker suggested. "Oh, and speaking of." He pulled an envelope from his pocket and handed it to Kit.

"Seems word that Kit Carson was in Arizona got out and this is for you, came before we left. Driver said it held a priority directive."

Kit turned it over and found the seal of the President of the United States on it. He looked up. Everyone smiled and the Professor prodded him to open it.

"It's a request to escort four Navaho Chiefs to Washington, D.C. to have a sit down with the President. He says I'm the only man he trusts for the job."

Tucker patted Kit on the shoulder.

"You better get going then. Don't want to keep President Johnson waiting."

The former general scratched his chin for a moment, eyes playing out a story in his mind and then he nodded decisively.

"He can wait. I want to see my family."

And so Kit Carson made the president wait for a week... and nine months later, welcomed a daughter to the world.

NEW LIVES

Nancy Jane Moore

Abigail Hancock held her breath as she removed the small silk sack from the tubing and carefully slit it open. Inside she found the cells had grown to form a spiral with a large rounded shape at its outer edge. It was virtually the same shape and size as the embryo she had taken from a mouse that was about seven days pregnant, but she had grown this one from fertilized mouse ovum in the little sack.

"Richard," she called to the man working at his own laboratory table on the other side of the basement room. "I think we have done it."

Richard hurried across the room and examined the embryo. "It appears to be developing normally. Maybe we have the right mixture of food this time. We might even get a mouse by the last one." He indicated the row of sacks, each set up in the same way as the one Abby had opened. They planned to open one per day, to see the progression.

"Even if we do not, we know we are right: embryos can be grown in an artificial environment. It is simply a matter of finding the right sustenance for nurturing them. And if we can do it with mice..."

"We will be able to do it with human beings," Richard said. He took hold of her slender white hands with his dark brown ones, then leaned over and kissed her on the forehead. "You are a genius, Abby."

"We are geniuses," she corrected. "This is our work. Never forget that, no matter how many people credit it only to me."

He kissed her forehead again.

From upstairs they heard a loud knocking at the door. "Who can that be?" Abby asked. She walked over to the wash basin and used the pitcher to pour water over her hands.

Richard bounded up the stairs two at a time. There was no one else to answer the door; Abby kept no servants, except a woman who came in twice weekly to do heavy cleaning and laundry. A fresh round of knocking came as he exited the basement.

Abby followed him at a more leisurely pace, drying her hands on her apron. As she entered the foyer, she could see several men in uniform standing on the stoop. Richard was holding the front door open.

"Miss Hancock," he said, acting the servant, "There are some policemen here to see you."

When Mary Somerville stood up to speak, the rustle of teacups and murmur of conversation stopped. The nine other women in the richly appointed drawing room knew they had not been invited simply to have tea.

Jane Freemantle sat alone, as she often did at these gatherings. She had spoken with most of the other women earlier, had paid her respects to Mrs. Somerville and to Mrs. Marcet, the oldest of the group, and had engaged in a lively discussion of mathematics with Ada King, the Countess of Lovelace, a woman about her own age. But while Jane corresponded with most of these women about natural philosophy and other subjects, and knew them socially through her guardian, the Hon. Elizabeth Freemantle, she also knew they were made uncomfortable by the dark color of her skin and her indigenous American birth.

Jane's people were dead, and she would have had no place of any kind in the world had not Elizabeth taken her in. Elizabeth had provided her not just with a home, but with a life of intellectual rigor, one she deeply enjoyed, but the price of that life was to always be the other, to never quite fit into any society. Sometimes this angered her; sometimes it merely made her sad.

Jane preferred to conduct most of her intercourse with the women here and the other natural philosophers of the time by letter, where the differences between them were not so obvious.

But Mrs. Somerville had been most insistent about her presence. "This is a matter of some urgency, and we have need of all the intelligent women we can muster. And we may have need of your other skills as well." Clearly the matter *was* of some urgency, since Mrs. Somerville had returned to London by airship from her current home in Italy to conduct this meeting.

And, indeed, it appeared that Mrs. Somerville had invited every significant woman of science living near enough to London to be able to make such a trip on short notice. Caroline Herschel was not there, of course; she was living in Hanover these days and too elderly to risk an airship trip. But she was the only notable not in attendance.

Despite being in her sixties, Mrs. Somerville conveyed the vigor of a much younger woman. Jane had first been presented to her at the ceremony in 1835 in which Mrs. Somerville had been made a special member of the Royal Astronomical Society with Miss Herschel—the first women so honored. It had been immediately obvious to Jane that Mrs. Somerville was a natural leader, a woman to be reckoned with, much like her own guardian. In a more equitable world, Mrs. Somerville would be in charge of the Astronomical Society instead of merely being admitted—in a condescending manner—to its meetings.

Of course, in a more equitable world, Jane would still be Tcax, living with her people in the bayou near New Orleans. And had the world been truly fair, perhaps Tcax could have studied the physics and mathematics that gave Jane's life meaning while still maintaining her place among her people.

But the world had never been fair.

All of the women in the smaller drawing room of Mrs. Somerville's London home sat quietly now, waiting to hear what had brought them together.

"I am sorry to inform you that our American colleague, Miss Abigail Hancock, has been arrested."

The room erupted into shocked murmurs. Jane corresponded regularly with Miss Hancock, and she thought most of the other women in the room did so as well. Her knowledge of the biological sciences was particularly respected; her late father had been a doctor and had taught her to be his assistant. A spinster of middle years, she made her living writing popular books on scientific subjects, work similar to that done by Jane Marcet.

"But why?" asked the Countess, speaking for them all.

"She is charged with helping women prevent conception," Mrs. Somerville said.

This was received with shocked silence. Mrs. Marcet finally broke it by asking, "And were there other charges?"

"No," said Mrs. Somerville. "But it appears that the authorities are also investigating her experiments. I have here a letter from one of her American supporters. This was sent to me in Italy via airship."

This evoked excited commentary, since the cost of airship mail rivalled that of actual travel and made clear the urgency of the situation.

The letter read:

My dear Mrs. Somerville:

I write with sad news. Miss Abigail Hancock, the well-known authoress of several popular books on natural history, has been arrested and charged with indecency for helping young women prevent childbirth.

Those of us active in the Baltimore Society for the Physical and Natural Sciences have established a fund for her defence and hired an attorney, but some of us despair that the legal process will be successful. A significant prison sentence is possible. It appears that the authorities think Miss Hancock is involved in a circle—indeed, for all that it is 1842 and the shameful history of witch trials is behind us, one might even say coven, given the official attitude—of women working to prevent the birth of children. They hint at more serious offenses related to that subject.

Further, we fear that the indecency charge may be only a ruse, and that the real intention of the authorities is to investigate and bring a halt to her biological experiments. This fear is not unfounded, as the police inspector in charge of the case has been interviewing many Society members and asking questions that go far afield of maternal issues. Since others in the Society are conducting related research, or investigating other areas that might not be approved by an over-orthodox civil establishment, some have expressed concern that the investigation may not stop with Miss Hancock. Indeed, some suspect that she was taken up as the most vulnerable among us, being a spinster without other family.

I am aware that Miss Hancock has many friends and correspondents in England and indeed in much of Europe as well, for all that she has never been able to travel across the ocean. It would be greatly appreciated if you would inform others of her circumstances, particularly Miss Herschel, Mrs. Marcet, and the Countess.

I do not know if there is any way that you may be of aid to her—unfortunately, the relations between our two countries remain somewhat strained, so I fear diplomatic efforts by some among your Royal Society would not be welcomed. But I thought it best to inform you regardless.

I remain your humble servant,

Mabel (Mrs. Henry) Johns.

The letter was met first with silence, and then with a murmur of discussion. Several of the women looked rather grim; Jane wondered if they disapproved of preventing childbirth, or if they knew more about Miss Hancock's research. She, herself, knew nothing of it; her correspondence with Miss Hancock had been limited to mathematical matters.

And so she asked, "Could someone tell us about Miss Hancock's experiments? I am not familiar with them." Several heads nodded at this; clearly, she was not the only one in ignorance.

"I understand," said Mrs. Somerville, "that she was working on the creation of life."

Several of the assembly gasped. Jane did not do so, but the expression on her face must have expressed a similar emotion, because several people looked from her to Mrs. Somerville. Her involvement with the downfall of the Prometheus was well known in this group.

"Oh, my dear Miss Freemantle, her work is not at all like

that with the Prometheus," Mrs. Somerville said. "She was solely working with the biological processes, not the transfer of life from one body to another. Her jail, as I understood it, was to find a way to create human life without women being forced to carry a child for nine months."

Mrs. Marcet spoke over the murmurs of both approval and disapproval that accompanied this announcement, "Her own mother died in childbirth when Miss Hancock was twelve. That tragedy has shaped her life."

The room grew quiet again. Jane suspected everyone there had lost a friend, a sister, a mother to childbirth.

"Her work builds on Von Baer's theories," a younger woman said. "It is pure biology; none of this move toward life by mechanical means. And of course, she is only working with mice at this point." The objection of Jane and her guardian to metalmen as well as to the Prometheus was well known.

"But even so, it is the sort of work frowned on by authorities, particularly when done by a woman," said Mrs. Somerville. "There are those who believe that matters of childbirth should not concern women."

This statement was met with the laughter that the speaker surely intended, though there was a bitter tone to it.

"It is my understanding," said Mrs. Marcet, "that any investigations into creation of life have been made illegal in the area where Miss Hancock resides."

"The state of Maryland," someone else said. "Founded by papists."

"The question before us," Mrs. Somerville said, "is 'what can we do to assist Miss Hancock?' That her innocent researches into biology may be considered a crime as well makes the whole situation more urgent."

This engendered a lively debate, beginning with discussion of the still-uncomfortable relations between the British Empire and its former colonies before moving on to outlining several schemes for raising money from gentlemen who might disapprove of Miss Hancock's efforts to prevent childbearing. The conversation was interspersed with several vigorous defences of biological research into reproductive matters.

By the end of the meeting, each woman there had contributed a modest amount and promised to provide additional funds from close friends in the next few days. Several had taken responsibility for obtaining funds from some of Miss Hancock's male correspondents and other scientists. It appeared likely that a substantial sum of money in aid of the defense would be raised forthwith.

As the women were leaving, Mrs. Somerville called Jane aside. "Miss Freemantle, I need to discuss something else with you. Can you remain for a few more minutes?"

She acquiesced, and stood aside as the others were shown out. When they were alone, Mrs. Somerville said, "Let us sit in my office. We will have something more fortifying than tea."

Mrs. Somerville's office was on an upper floor, and included a telescope mounted at the window. She noticed Jane looking at it. "That was my first one, and lacks the power of the one I keep in Italy. But I am sentimental about it, because I learned so much with it. I keep it here more to signify my work than to use, since it is virtually impossible to see the skies from London these days; if the fog is not too heavy, the gas streetlights are too bright."

The maid brought in a decanter of sherry and after each of them had taken a glass, Mrs. Somerville said, "Miss Freemantle, I am hoping that you will be willing to take the funds we raise to America."

Jane had been expecting something of the sort ever since Mrs. Somerville's mention of the need for her "other skills." In her life before she had become Jane Freemantle, she had been learning the path of the warrior, and she now at times taught defensive skills to other women. "I assume you want me to guard the money, and to keep it hidden from the authorities."

"I thought you would appreciate that point. But it is more than that. I believe that Mrs. Johns is correct when she despairs of a good outcome from the legal process. Though we make progress, for women such as you and I, the world is still arrayed against us. Miss Hancock, by offering up her medical knowledge to those of less education, has made herself vulnerable. It is unthinkable that she could go to prison, and yet it appears to be a very likely result."

"Are you asking me to help her escape from gaol?" Jane asked.

"Well, not precisely from gaol. I feel certain that, with the funds we raise and those raised in Baltimore and other places in the Americas, Miss Hancock will be released pending trial. What I want you to do is to get her out of the country, to bring her here where she can continue her work without persecution."

"Is not the offense she is charged with also a crime in England?"

"Yes, but I do not think our authorities will return her to the Americas, not with our patronage, not with the current relationship of the two countries. If she does not engage in such behavior here, she should be safe from any legal action. Her researches are not forbidden here.

"To this end, we must have someone help her leave the country without notice. And you are the appropriate person. You have been in America; in fact you are an American by birth."

"I do not think the authorities regard me as an American," Jane said. "And I know nothing of Baltimore. I have never been to any part of the country except Louisiana."

"I suppose that is true. But you do have other skills that might prove quite useful. Even if Miss Hancock is released, I am certain she will be watched. The woman who was able to destroy the Prometheus surely has the skills to help another leave the country by stealth."

Jane felt a pang at the mention of the Prometheus. True, she had followed Mary Shelley all the way to Galveston with the intention of killing the immortal monster described in such detail in Mrs. Shelley's famous "novel." But Jane had found no immortal monster, only Immanuel Dessins, a decent man saved from early death by the woman who loved him. After receiving assurances that the process that saved Mr. Dessins would never be used again, the three of them had faked the death of the mythical Prometheus.

If Mrs. Somerville had known the truth! But though she questioned whether she in fact had the necessary skills, Jane knew that none of the other women would be capable of such a feat. And, truth be told, much as she loved her researches into the physical sciences, she had developed a taste for adventure as well. She nodded in response.

"Are you willing to cross the Atlantic in an airship? I fear regular travel will be too slow."

Jane smiled. She had always wanted to do that.

"I have a pilot in mind," Mrs. Somerville went on. "She is something of a daredevil herself—a Danish girl. I believe she will be willing to fly Miss Hancock out as well, regardless of the legalities, assuming we pay her enough." The older woman wrinkled her nose. "She is unfortunately quite mercenary."

On her way home, Jane decided that she would not tell Elizabeth about the rescue effort, but only that she was being sent with the money. She sighed. She was becoming far too accomplished at lying to Elizabeth.

The policemen had tramped through Abby's house, taking private papers from her desk, disturbing the work in the laboratory, even removing some of the mice. Then they had escorted her off to the police headquarters, where she had been questioned by three different detectives, each of them asking the same questions in slightly different form.

It was only after an hour of questioning that she finally discovered the source of the indecency charge against her. It arose from her volunteer work at the charity clinic for women. Although Abby was not a doctor—no woman had yet been able to qualify for a medical license, though several had applied—she knew a great deal about medical matters. The clinic relied on her and on others with some experience of nursing, for few doctors would give them any assistance. It seemed that the husband of one woman she had counseled—a woman who had four children under the age of six—had discovered the sheep's gut barrier device Abby had given the woman to reduce the chances of another child. It was he who had complained to the police, after first beating his wife until she told him where she obtained it.

Abby found herself hard pressed to understand why a man who could not support the four children he already had would object to preventing the conception of more, but she did not say that to the policemen. What made the situation most frightening, though, was that it had never occurred to her that she might be arrested for such a thing. She did not even know it was illegal. Certainly she would have been much more careful had she realized she was transgressing; she had never intended to put her freedom at risk.

After some hours of questioning, the policemen had finally locked her up. The women's detention facility at the Baltimore City jail had ten bunks, but there were only six other women incarcerated there with Abby. Of these, two were Polish and spoke little English. One of the others was a recent Irish immigrant, by her accent; she was also about six months pregnant, Abby thought. Another was white of no obvious ancestry, and the remaining two were coloured. It surprised her a little that Baltimore did not keep a separate cell for colored women, given the official city attitude toward race mixing, but perhaps they never had enough women in custody to justify the expense.

All of them were considerably younger than Abby, who had recently reached the age of forty. The oldest might be just past twenty-five, and she doubted the Irish girl was even eighteen. All were in jail for prostitution, except for one of the colored women, who was charged with robbery.

Being in an all-female environment after hours of dealing with men was something of a relief, even if being locked up was itself quite terrifying. The only woman she had seen during the entire time she had been in custody was the matron who searched her—rather too thoroughly—before she was put in the cell.

The young women had been surprised to see someone of her age—and social class—put in with them. But they had been kind. And when they learned that she had been arrested for giving "marital advice"—as one policeman had delicately expressed it—they were outraged on her behalf. Of course, given the profession of most of them, they were very familiar with both effective and ineffective means of preventing childbirth.

All of the women had curled up in their bunks after the lights had been put out, but Abby was too worried to go to sleep. She was grateful they had not arrested Richard as well. They had looked at him, seen a young colored man in a household headed by a middle-aged spinster, and assumed him to be a servant. Or property. But if she were convicted of this supposed crime, what would happen to him? The household relied on her income from her books, and Richard would have no way of earning enough to keep things together on his own. While he had, in fact, done a great deal of work on the books, and was perfectly capable of writing others on his own, it was impossible that anyone would publish them. Had not the American publishers discovered that it was the fashion in England for ladies to write scientific books for children, Abby might not have been able to secure a publisher herself.

From one of the other bunks she heard someone crying. She wasn't the only person awake and worried. *I won't cry*, she told herself. But she felt tears well up in her eyes nonetheless.

With the next morning came inedible gruel and yet another session of interviews. Toward the end of the morning, one detective asked, "Miss Hancock, we found a number of vermin"—he wrinkled his nose—"In your basement, apparently being kept for the purpose of observation." His voice lilted up at that last word, making it almost a question.

"I am studying mice, yes."

"For what purpose, Miss Hancock?"

She thought furiously. Telling him that she was trying to understand reproduction clearly would not do. Perhaps if she told him that she was looking for ways to block the reproduction of "vermin"—no, that was uncomfortably close to the charge against her, for all that it was in mice. He might be intelligent enough to make the connection.

"For the sake of knowledge, sir," she said. "I study for the sake of knowledge."

"A fine activity for a woman," he said, his tone making it clear that he meant the exact opposite of his words.

Astrid Skytte was more than a daredevil, Jane decided; she was an Amazon, or, at least, what the Amazons would have looked like had they been fair-skinned Vikings rather than small dark Greeks. Miss Skytte was large, with a great mane of blond hair braided carelessly down her back. She laughed loudly, was frequently profane, and had demanded quite a lot money for this expedition. Jane concluded the best word for her was pirate.

Most interestingly, though, Miss Skytte—or Astrid, as she insisted on being called—did not react in the usual way of Europeans to Jane's appearance. "Good, someone who knows how to fight," was all she had said when they were introduced, shaking Jane's hand heartily.

Her airship reflected her personality. The gondola resembled a Viking ship, with a gilded image of the Goddess Freya as a figurehead. The huge air sack that allowed it to take to the skies was painted with ancient runes—"charms against bad weather," Astrid said. The inside of the gondola was furnished sparely, with bolted down cots for sleeping and a simple table with benches for eating or writing. But the pilot's compartment included the latest instrumentation, including a mercury barometer, a liquid compass (an improvement on Crow's invention), and one of William Herschel's smaller telescopes. Astrid could also control the amount of lifting gas pumped in or out of the air sack from her seat at the controls.

During the three-day flight, the two women had come to know each other rather well. Astrid had grown up in Greenland in a family of shippers, and, as the oldest child, had helped her mother run the business after her father had been murdered by pirates on one of his trips back to Denmark. Eventually one of her younger brothers had taken over the company, and Astrid had taken her share of the profits and purchased the airship.

She was fascinated by Jane's tales of her warrior training as a child and particularly thrilled with the tale of Jane's rescue of Elizabeth and their escape from the metalmen who had destroyed her village. But she thought it strange that Jane would have had to live as a man had she been able to remain in her native land. "Among my people, strong women have always had a place in society," she said. "You must come visit us in Greenland and see it for yourself."

The trip itself was uneventful, except for one four-hour period over the middle of the ocean, when they encountered a storm. Jane spent the duration sitting on the floor of the gondola, her head in her hands, trying not to be sick, but Astrid gloried in it, even as she cursed the weather forecasters. "Those damned bastards claim to be scientists, but they're not as good at predicting storms as a shaman up in some no name village around the Arctic Circle. 'No storms on the Atlantic for five days,' they said. Hah! Idiots. Sons of whores."

She steered the airship competently through the weather, even taking advantage of the high winds to subtract a few hours from the trip. Her understanding of the practical science of flying was substantial. But, alas, Jane found that Astrid was bored by more theoretical discussions; try as she might, she could not interest the Danish woman in a discussion of the workings of gravity or the implications of the speed of light.

"You can keep your philosophy," Astrid said. "I only care if it affects how my ship might fly."

They landed the ship on the peninsula jutting down between the ocean and the Chesapeake Bay, finding a deserted beach on the western part, near the small fishing and tobacco growing community of Rock Hall. Astrid had landed in this locale on earlier expeditions and knew some in the local fishing community. "I'm glad that this country is still so lightly settled," she told Jane. "We would be hard pressed to find an unnoticed landing place so close to London or Copenhagen."

Astrid negotiated storage for the airship in an isolated barn, and secured passage for them both on a boat bound for Baltimore, paying more than the usual rates, but not so much more that it would be a matter of wide discussion. The whole process confirmed Jane's suspicion that the Danish woman's endeavors often skirted the law.

Jane got off the boat near the official port of entry for Baltimore, so that she could mingle with those alighting from passenger ships and go through customs. Astrid was staying with the boat, and would get off when the fishermen docked to sell the fish and crabs they had caught in their trip across the bay. She would stay in a boarding house near Fell's Point and procure a boat for their return to Rock Hall, hopefully with Miss Hancock in tow.

While Jane would have preferred entering with Astrid, the official entry through customs was part of her protection. If she were stopped and questioned by police or any other officials, she might well be thrown in jail herself if she lacked documentation; her status as a "red Indian" made her even more suspect in America than in Britain. To that end, she carried not only her official passport from the United Kingdom and a letter to the Baltimore Society for the Physical and Natural Science from Mrs. Somerville, but also both a visa and a letter endorsing her trip "for scientific study" from the American Envoy to the Court of St. James, Edward Everett. Mrs. Somerville had been very thorough.

Indeed, that thoroughness paid off, because she moved smoothly through customs drawing nothing more than the occasional raised eyebrow, though she did hear one inspector mutter to another, "I do not know why the British aristocracy persist in adopting these savages."

Her reception at the home of Mrs. Johns on St. Paul Street was chillier than that of the American officials. The dark-skinned woman who answered the door said, "Don't you know enough to go to the back door?" and would have shut the door in her face if Jane had not stuck her bag in it.

"I am Miss Freemantle. Please tell Mrs. Johns that Mrs. Somerville has sent me from England to assist with the case of Miss Hancock."

The woman glared, but as Jane did not appear to be disposed

to remove her bag from the door, she shouted for someone to come. "Watch her," she told the young man who responded. He grinned at Jane as the woman stalked off. "Lilly knows what's proper, she does. Servants and tradesmen to the rear."

"I am neither," said Jane.

"Yeah, you're dressed like a white lady and you talk high class, but you don't look right to Lilly. Me, I'd let you in." He grinned again, this time more suggestively.

"Young man," Jane said, with steel in her voice. "I am old enough to be your mother. Mind your manners."

"You don't look that old," he said, not reproved in the slightest.

From behind him she heard a woman say, "For God's sake, bring her inside. What will the neighbors say if they see a savage on the doorstep? What can Mrs. Somerville have been thinking?"

Jane sighed and the young man said, "Looks like they going to let you in, but they ain't going to ask you to tea. When you get through talking to the mistress, come find me. I'll give you tea, or something better. I'm George."

He disappeared as Mrs. Johns opened the door widely. She was a short, stout woman with graying curls and a scowl on her face. "Please come in, Miss Freemantle. I apologize for the delay."

Jane was shown into the drawing room, and, as George had predicted, not offered tea.

"You were sent by Mrs. Somerville?"

"Yes. I have brought you funds for the defense of Miss Hancock." Jane handed a wallet to Mrs. Johns. It contained a substantial sum, though Jane had reserved rather more for her other purposes.

The woman took it and rifled through it. "Well, that will help. It was good of Mrs. Somerville to send someone with it, though I am sure a reputable air carrier could have been found."

"Mrs. Somerville also wanted me to check on the condition of Miss Hancock. Is she still confined to gaol?"

"No. Her attorney was able to convince a judge to release her to her home under house arrest." She shivered. "It was horrible, thinking of a respectable woman like that confined with all manner of common women."

"So she is at her home on West Fayette Street?"

"Yes, but you certainly cannot go to see her. You will just draw attention."

Jane had no intention of entering Miss Hancock's house through the front door if the police were watching it, but she said, "Mrs. Johns. While I have never met Miss Hancock in person, we have corresponded for several years on mathematical matters, and I am personally concerned—not merely concerned on Mrs. Somerville's behalf—about her welfare."

The woman looked flustered for the first time. "You, you study mathematics?"

"And the physical sciences. I am not greatly familiar with the biological ones. Is that your field?"

That seemed to make her even more uncomfortable. Perhaps she feared investigation by the police as well. "No, no. I primarily study astronomy."

"Of course. That is how you came to know Mrs. Somerville."

"Well, Miss Freemantle, I do not want to keep you...."

"I do need your assistance on one other matter," Jane said. "I do not have a place to stay in Baltimore." She paused for a moment, to allow Mrs. Johns time to fear that she might ask to stay in her house.

"Um."

"If you could introduce me to a respectable boarding house. My needs are very simple, but many doors will be closed to me." Mrs. Somerville had expected that one of the Society members would offer Jane a room, but clearly she had underestimated the prejudices of the Americans, which were, in fact, somewhat worse than those of the British, if Mrs. Johns was any indication.

"Um. Let me see. Mrs. Whitehead is still attached to the Society, though she has fallen on hard times since her husband passed on. It was he who was the member; she is not a scientist. She might be persuaded. Let me write her a note. I'll send George over to let her know you are coming."

And to let her know what I am, Jane thought. "Is her home

nearby?"

"Um. Some blocks. I—I will have my driver take you."

"Very kind."

The driver was, like George and Lilly, a black man. Apparently all of Mrs. Johns's servants were colored. It had been the same in Galveston, during her last trip to this side of the Atlantic. Jane wondered if they were slaves, but could think of no polite way to ask. The idea that some human beings were treated as property still horrified her, even though she was glad the servants were not metalmen. Metelmen, she had been given to understand, were illegal in Maryland.

Mrs. Whitehead resembled Mrs. Johns in that she was short, stout, and gray, but only in those superficial matters. "My dear Miss Freemantle. I am so glad you have come to help Miss Hancock, though I confess I do not know what any of us can do. Still, assistance from our colleagues across the Atlantic is very welcome."

"You are too kind."

Over dinner, Mrs. Whitehead gave Jane the latest information. "Miss Hancock was released from jail last Thursday"—it was now Tuesday—"but they have stationed a policeman in front of her home, and told her that she is not to leave for any reason except to come to court. She can have visitors, but, of course, their names are taken down and recorded. And, in fact, everyone who has visited has subsequently suffered an interview with the police. They have even questioned the woman who comes in to do the cleaning."

"So if I were to visit..."

"Miss Freemantle! You must not even consider it. I know you have the support of powerful people in England, but their influence will not help you with the Baltimore police. And I fear those policemen are shockingly prejudiced against Indians as well. Many people here have relatives out in the western regions who have suffered from Indian raids."

The raids were not all by one side, Jane thought, remembering the destruction of her people. But she said, "I understand. But how does Miss Hancock survive? She cannot be growing all her food in her home."

"Oh, her boy Dickie takes care of all that. He's really a most superior boy—quite able to handle her business."

"A child?" said Jane, deliberating misunderstanding.

"Oh, no. He's quite grown. A colored boy. Belonged to her family all his life."

So Miss Hancock owned a slave. Well, she would not be able to take him as her property to the United Kingdom. Slavery was now illegal there, for the most part. Jane reminded herself that her duty was to rescue Miss Hancock. She reminded herself that she had known the world was not fair for a long time. But the knowledge rankled her all the same.

Still, perhaps this man—she would not think of him as a boy—could prove useful. "Is he loyal to her?"

"Of course," said Mrs. Whitehead.

Jane rather suspected Mrs. Whitehead would not really know. But perhaps that young servant of Mrs. Johns might be of help.

<>>

Richard returned home rather later than Abby had expected. He brought the shopping into the kitchen, where Abby was putting together a light supper. They did their own cooking; it was one of the small economies that allowed them to focus most of their resources on their research.

"I was beginning to worry," Abby said, laying the table.

"I spent two hours being questioned by the police," he said.

She put her hand to her mouth. "Oh, Richard. Did they... did they hurt you?"

"No, nothing of that sort. They were rude and condescending, but they did not even bother to threaten me."

"What did they want to know?"

"They wanted to know what you were really doing with your research. They did not even bother to pretend that they were greatly concerned with your medical advice to young women. They asked me many questions about who came to call on you, and over and over they asked me if you were working on the creation of life."

"And what did you tell them?"

"I'se jus' a dumb darky, massa. I don't know nuthin' 'bout things like that. I barely know the ladies and gentlemen who call. I jus' clean things and do the errands and take care of Miz Abigail. She good to me, that all I know." The tone of his voice was bitter.

She put her arms around him. "Oh, I am so sorry you had to suffer through that, my dear."

"It is nothing to what you are facing, Abby. And barely worse than I am offered every day when I leave this house. But I think it does mean that they are serious in their requests for information from you about others engaged in research on the creation of life. Perhaps they are even telling the truth when they say they will dismiss the charges against you if you provide them with details of the work of others."

"Are you suggesting that I do that?"

"I am suggesting that you may have no choice but to do that."

She broke away from him. "No. I cannot. Not only would it be wrong—morally wrong, for I know of no one doing any researches that should be considered illegal—but it would be of no use. If I betrayed my colleagues, I would have no place, likely even no way to earn a living. Would our books be published if I were expelled from the Society?"

"Will our books be published if you go to prison?"

"Oh, this situation is intolerable. To be treated in this way because I was kind to the less fortunate, and because I want to expand knowledge."

"Yes, it is intolerable," said Richard. He took her hand. "But we must consider all our choices."

"I will not give information on others. I cannot. You understand that I cannot."

He nodded.

But what will become of you if I go to prison? Abby thought. Do I have the right to take the moral high ground when my own are threatened? She knew she should discuss this with Richard, but could not bring herself to say the words out loud.

<<>>

Jane was in luck: George came the next morning to deliver a letter to Mrs. Whitehead. Jane caught up with him as he left by the kitchen door. "Excuse me."

"Ah, it's the savage lady. I reckon Miz Whitehead's treating you good, but I'd still take you for that tea you didn't get at our place."

"I do not need tea, but I would like some information, Mr.— what is your surname?"

"Johns. Everybody at our place is Johns."

"Mr. Johns."

He laughed. "Ain't nobody ever called me that. I don't know if I like it or not."

"Formal is always better in business matters," Jane said.

"What kind of business?"

"I would like to meet the gentleman who works for Miss Hancock. And I would like to do so without drawing the attention of the police."

"The gentleman? You mean Dickie? Oh, right enough. That can be arranged. The police ain't paying much attention to him. We'd need a place, though. Miz Whitehead would probably find it funny if I brought him here to see you. In fact, she's going to find it funny you talking to me."

"I'm just thanking you for assisting me the other day at Mrs. Johns."

"You got a gift for sneaking around, I can see that. I know a place. There's a colored lady who does sewing for people. You could go there, like you was getting stuff made. I could tell Dickie to act like he had an errand for Miss Hancock. You could probably talk in private. Might take a little money to set up."

"Money is not a consideration."

"Money is always a consideration, Miss Freemantle. I'll let you know tomorrow."

"Thank you, Mr. Johns. Oh, and one other thing. You know this man. Is he loyal to Miss Hancock, or does he only work for her?"

"I'm pretty sure he'd die for her, ma'am. I don't know what it is about them, but it's not the same like it is at our place. Any of us, you give us half a chance we'd be gone and good riddance. But not him. Oh, and since you like to be formal and all, I think his name is Hancock, too."

<>

George Johns must have told Mrs. Simmons the seamstress all about her, because Jane detected no reaction when she came for her appointment to have an afternoon dress made. "It is warmer here in September than it is in London," she explained. "Perhaps something in linen?"

The woman took her measurements, and as they were discussing colors, a man about Jane's age entered the shop. His skin was the color of tea with milk—not the dark brown she had imagined. "Mr. Hancock?" she asked.

"Yes. I am glad to meet you, Miss Freemantle." He gave her a polite bow.

Mrs. Simmons suddenly remembered an errand she needed to take care of. "I'll be back in ten minutes, Miss Freemantle. I hope you don't mind waiting."

"Not at all, Mrs. Simmons," Jane said.

They sat on two straight back chairs in the workroom. "I represent a group of natural philosophers in England who want to help Miss Hancock. She is well known there for her books and through her correspondence with many leading thinkers."

"Yes, Miss Freemantle. I recognize your name. Your latest letter on Feodor Deahna's theorem was quite impressive."

Jane tried to hide the surprise she felt. "So you, too, are a natural philosopher?"

"I work with Miss Hancock."

This man was not at all what she had been led to expect. *A superior boy indeed*, she thought, remembering Mrs. Whitehead's words; *in a society that considers him to be property he has managed to become a scientist.*

"Some in the group I represent fear Miss Hancock stands little chance in the legal system."

He sighed. "I have heard some of her discussions with her attorney. There is some concern that if she does not plead guilty quickly, they will charge her with helping young women who are already in a family way put an end to that situation. She tells me that she did not do that, but it seems the authorities are determined to make an example of her one way or another.

"But in truth, I believe that the police are more interested in her research than they are in the marital matters. I am given to understand that if she will explain her research and, more significantly, if she will provide them with information about the research of others who are investigating the creation of life— both real and artificial—they will forget the other matters."

Jane sighed. "We feared as much."

"She remains unwilling to give information about others."

"That is admirable of her."

"But you said you had come to help; how do you propose to do that?"

"I have an airship and pilot who can fly her out of the country, if we can remove her from your house without being seen by the police. I gather that may be somewhat difficult."

"Yes, but not impossible. She and I have discussed several possibilities, but as we could not think of any place we could reach where we would be safe, we have not acted upon them. But with an airship...." He smiled for the first time since he had entered the room. "I think, perhaps, you need to talk with her."

"Yes, but how do I enter your house without being seen by the police?"

"I have an idea," he said, "if you would not object to pretending to be enamored of a colored man."

And so it was on the next night that Dickie Hancock was seen leaving his home dressed as a man going out on the town. He returned several hours later with a woman on his arm.

Jane had not had a great deal of time to design a disguise,

but she had acquired a large bonnet that hid most of her face. In dim light, the dark color of her skin would let the typical observer assume she was a colored woman.

Jane laughed rather loudly as they approached the back door of the Hancock home. "Shh. I don't want the Missus to hear us," he said. "Or the nosy neighbors." He led her inside.

Miss Hancock was waiting for them in the kitchen. "My dear Miss Freemantle, thank you so much for coming. Richard, do you think you were successful in deceiving the police."

"I believe so. They did not seem overly interested in us."

They sat in a small parlor, and Miss Hancock poured tea. Jane noted that Dickie—or Richard, as he seemed to be called inside the home—sat with them and was served a cup by his mistress. A very curious situation.

"Richard says that you can help us leave the country."

"Yes," Jane said, and explained about Astrid Skytte and her airship. "Mrs. Somerville was looking into arrangements to house you when I left. And there are publishers interested in your books. I believe you could establish yourself so that you could continue your research."

"I do not suppose we could take the mice along, could we, Richard? We will have to start again. But we have made progress. The police invasion stopped our last experiment, but not before we had seen some small success."

"Did you intend to bring Mr. Hancock with you? Forgive me, but you are aware, are you not, of the differing legal situation in the United Kingdom. Ownership of a person..."

"Richard is not a slave, Miss Freemantle."

"Oh, I most humbly beg your pardon. I was told that he was, and saw no reason to doubt it, since such seems to be the custom in this country."

"No, of course, you would not know. We let it appear so. But I feel I can be frank with you. Obviously, your own situation is not the usual one."

"No," Jane said, and explained about her relationship with Elizabeth.

"And are you accepted by these people, Miss Freemantle? I

know your work; it is excellent. But do the others there consider you one of their own?"

Jane knew she was being asked an important question. "They accept me, within limitations, because I am the ward of Elizabeth Freemantle, and she is a well-off and charismatic woman. If I did not have her patronage, the others would not consider me as part of their society. My situation is most unusual."

"Would they accept Richard? He is a scientist, you know, every bit as able as I. My books, my research, all of it is a collaboration. But he has never been able to receive any credit. I would like very much for him to be a recognized partner in all this work."

He spoke for the first time. "Abby, that is not important."

"Yes, it is."

Jane hesitated. But she had spent too much time in upper class British drawing rooms. "No, I do not believe they would accept him."

"So if we go to England, our situation is the same as it is here."

"The world is not a fair place, Miss Hancock."

"No." Her tone was bitter. "No. Even biology betrays us. You are probably wondering why it matters so much if Richard comes. Indeed, you probably wonder how it is that he came to work with me."

"I assumed you recognized his abilities."

"That is a kind way of putting it. But it is more than that. Richard is my brother, Miss Freemantle."

Jane looked at the two of them then, and saw the resemblance; for all that the man's skin was dark where the woman's was fair, his hair tightly curled where hers waved gently. The eyes, the curve of the jaw, the expression on their faces when both were speaking seriously, those were the same.

"My mother was partly of African heritage, though like me, she did not appear so. I did not know it. My father did not know it. But when Richard was born, the truth was obvious.

"Oh, not obvious to my father, who maintained until his dying day that she must have betrayed him with a servant.

My father, who turned away from her as she lay dying after childbirth. But obvious to the servants, to the midwife who attended her, to me. She told me the truth then, before she died. And I knew Richard and I were the same, but due to the vagaries of our biology, we did not look it. It is why I never married.

"My father was not so cruel as to throw a newborn out of our home, but he gave Richard to a maid to raise and never acknowledged him. I, though, spent all the time I could with him. After our father died, I was able to educate him in earnest. But of course, he had to learn early to lie about who he was."

"As Miss Freemantle said, Abby: the world is not fair."

"But if we are to uproot our lives, to change our circumstances, I want to end the lie," Miss Hancock said. "I want to live openly, to say, 'this is my brother,' to put his name with mine on the books, on the research." There was a pleading tone in her voice.

Jane shook her head. "If you did that, I fear you would lose your patronage, and perhaps even a chance at publication. There is no slavery in Britain, but it is not a paradise where all persons are considered equal."

Mr. Hancock said, "Abby, we cannot turn down this offer. You cannot go to prison. We have never expected a fair life; why ask for one now when we are in such dire circumstances?"

"If we are going to change our lives, Richard, why not change them in all ways? And I am certainly not rejecting this offer. But must we go to England? Would your people be offended if we went elsewhere?"

They probably would be, Jane thought. She said, "I am sure our pilot would be glad to fly you anywhere you might choose to go. And the funds we have raised are yours to do with as you please. They might provide a start in some new place, though I do not think you can expect any other assistance from our people if you do not go to England. We might, perhaps, still arrange a publisher, if your urge for honesty did not extend to telling them things they would not be able to see for themselves."

"How delicately you put things."

"Where would you go?"

"We had thought about the northwestern area of this continent. Perhaps in a frontier environment, things that matter very much here will not be so important."

"But will you be able to work there?"

"If we can take some of the equipment," she said. "We do not need a great deal. But the police are watching my every move. How are we to leave the house?"

Jane had been giving this matter quite a lot of consideration. "We need someone to create a disturbance in the street. Perhaps Mr. Johns can help."

"Mr. Johns is a very respectable gentleman," Abby said. "I do not think he will be willing to cause a disturbance of any kind."

"She means George the slave, not Mr. Henry Johns," Richard said. He turned to Jane. "But you cannot ask him to do this. Do you have any idea what would happen to Negroes who rioted in the streets?"

In her mind's eye, Jane saw a row of gibbets. "I am so sorry, Mr. Hancock. I did not think." She paused for a moment. "What we really need is a mob of people upset by Miss Hancock's contraceptive advice. If someone could start a rumor with the man who first brought charges against you... perhaps some young man affiliated with the scientific community?"

"I doubt any of them would take the risk," Richard said.

"Dr. Barrett might," Abby said. "His researches are similar to ours. Should I be forced to talk, he is at great risk."

"I will approach him," Jane said. And she began to lay her plans.

Jane called on Dr. Barrett the next day, announcing herself as representing Mrs. Somerville. "I understand that you have made great strides in your study of the origins of life," she told him.

He was obviously pleased to hear the compliment, but turned pale when she told him her informant was Miss Hancock. "I... I am very concerned about what may become of Miss Hancock. Her situation...."

"It is about her situation that I have come."

Once he realized that his assistance might help get Miss Hancock out of the country, Dr. Barrett became eager to help. As a physician who did some charity work, he travelled in some low circles. "I might know someone."

Jane also hired the services of George Johns. Mrs. Johns had been loath to let him go, but a bit of genteel blackmail— It seemed that her husband was another who might be at risk should Miss Hancock talk—led her to accept the arrangement, though she charged a pretty penny for it.

George was eager to help; like far too many foolish young men, he craved adventures. "I bet I can take any of those fat old policemen," he said.

"All I need you to do is to escort Miss and Mr. Hancock down to Fell's Point once we have distracted the police."

"Where you gonna be?"

"Making certain that the police follow the wrong person."

"I can help with that," he said again.

Jane pictured him lying dead in the street and shuddered. "I have no one else I can trust to make certain they get away safely," she said, and that appeased him.

To the police, it likely appeared that Richard had a regular woman, because he brought Jane back to the house almost every evening. One evening as Richard and Jane walked in the back door, they heard one of the guards say, "That boy must have figured out his mistress don't count for much anymore, the way he carries on."

In this way, the two of them were able to smuggle the Hancocks' most valuable possessions—a few clothes, jewelry and other valuables that could be converted into dollars, and as much of the laboratory equipment and lab records as they could manage—out of the house. George carried them down to Fell's Point.

Late on a Saturday afternoon, a crowd of young men gathered in the street outside the Hancock home. They carried signs calling Abby Hancock a whore and worse, and their leaders screamed speeches demanding that she be tarred and feathered or thrown back in jail. Jane, watching from inside the house, noted that, despite their outrage, no one ever said exactly what it was she had done.

The police guards soon had their hands full trying to contain the crowd, which, while it only included a dozen or so men, was quite unruly. Even the guards from the alley came to the front to help keep the peace and one policeman was sent off for reinforcements.

A sharp whistle announced the arrival of additional policemen, and Jane—dressed in Abby Hancock's clothes, including a hat with a veil and white gloves—chose that moment to slip out the back door. There were no guards there, but as she rounded the corner toward the street, someone screamed out, "She's getting away."

An alert policeman looked away from the riot, saw her, and yelled to the others to follow him. But in the confusion caused by the rioters, Jane managed to gain nearly a block on her pursuers before the chase started in earnest.

She wore trousers under her skirt. Now she ripped it off and began to run full out. It had been more than fifteen years since she had been Tcax, the girl running through the woods, but she had not lost her stride nor her speed. The policemen—there were at least six behind her—were not closing the distance.

As Jane ran, Abby and Richard walked boldly out the back door, Abby dressed in the clothes Jane had worn in her role as Richard's woman. But there were no policemen there to view them. Two blocks away, a coach driven by George Johns pulled up, and both got in quickly.

Twilight was now coming on, making it harder to see. George drove the coach south on Charles Street, and turned to the east on Lombard. At Market Street he stopped the coach; he and Jane had arranged a rendezvous at that point.

Straining his eyes in the growing darkness, George saw her running from the direction of Water Street, but he also saw, as she could not, a policeman running up Lombard from the west, moving quite as fast as Jane. Obviously he had anticipated where she might run and was hoping to cut her off. He spotted no other officers.

George jumped down from the seat and stood behind the coach. The policeman came running up just as Jane reached the intersection, but as he ran past the coach, George tackled him from behind, pinning his arms to his chest.

"Let go of me in the name of the law," the officer yelled. Jane came running up. She took one look at the situation and immediately punched the policeman in the chest, causing him drop his head forward. She then clipped him on the back of the head, knocking him unconscious.

George let the man drop, and jumped back up to the driver's seat. Jane climbed in the coach with the Hancocks, and they made it the rest of the way to Fell's Point without incident.

Astrid Skytte awaited them at the dock with a small boat. "Your baggage is already loaded," she said, welcoming the Hancocks aboard. She professed herself delighted at the change in plans. "I have never seen the northwest of this country," she told them.

Jane changed her clothes inside the coach as George returned it to the hire place. He then followed her—playing the servant all the way—back to her lodging with Mrs. Whitehead.

"I thank you for your assistance, Mr. Johns," she told him as they reached her door.

"My pleasure. I might never get me another chance to attack a policeman without something bad coming of it."

Jane nodded. She handed him a purse.

"You don't owe me nothing."

"I owe you a great deal and so do the Hancocks. And you should have some resources of your own. I have heard it is possible for a slave to buy his freedom."

George's hands trembled after he opened the bag and realized the amount within. "God bless you," he said. There was none of the joking demeanor he had shown up to then. "God bless you," he repeated. "This may be enough to free my mother as well."

He clasped her hands once, then ran off down the street. Jane felt her eyes fill with tears. "I wish you luck," she called after him.

Jane, who embarked shortly thereafter on a ship bound for England, found herself wondering if the Hancocks had made the right choice. Would they truly be able to live as brother and sister in the wilderness? Their medical training might make them of use, but would they be able to continue their studies, their research?

At the same time, Jane rather envied them. Perhaps they would find a place where they could be their true selves. She though, would always be other. There was no right place for her.

THE ENGINEER

Bob Brown

I knew the man was crazy. You don't serve up ale without being able to see it. I'd known it from the time I stepped over him, and spilling not a drop mind you, after old Angus threw him across the table. He lay there, flat on his back still trying to explain the wisdom of using machines to mine coal.

Angus, with a leap that looked impossible for his square frame, was now perched atop the table, preparing to finish the issue.

"Angus!" I called loud enough to be heard over a room full of drunken miners.

He didn't respond and the fallen engineer continued to blather about man hours and productivity.

"Angus!" I shouted again and gave the edge of the table a kick. Angus wobbled with the table. I had his attention.

"Patience, my dear lassie," his Scottish tongue sounded thick to my Welsh ears, every time I heard it. He wasn't the only Scot in Wales. The colliers attracted them like flies to a wound. But he was the foreman at the pit and the coal miners loved him. "You need to stay out of this."

"You know the rules Angus. If you're going to kill each other, you do it in the road. You don't break my bowls." I pointed to the broken dishes at his feet.

"If I don't do it, somebody else will." He pointed down at the man on the floor, now up on his elbows, his eyes averted. There are vantages from which a kilt should not be viewed. "He'd have us all put out of the mines. All so his machines will put out more coal and Mr. Soulbender won't have to pay a man's wages."

"You really like breaking your back every day." The engineer was now sitting.

"A man that ain't breaking his back ain't getting paid."

"Better machines won't put anybody out of work," said the Engineer.

"They told that to the drovers when the steam trolley started pulling the barges." Angus held up his hands and turned in a circle on the table. Shouts of acknowledgment rose from the crowd. "And do you see any drovers in here?" The ale mugs rose in a resounding shout of "NO."

"That ain't fair Angus," I shouted over the crowd. "You know full well why there ain't no drover's come in here." The crowd quieted to hear my response. "After a day smelling horse shit, they can't stand to be around miners." I did my own play on the crowd. "They say it smells too much like work."

"Give it up Angus," came a shout from the back. "You'll never top Patience." The room laughed and men returned to their seats. The mood was broken.

Angus pointed a thick hairy finger at the engineer. "Just don't be coming in no more spouting your fancy words." And with a scream and a whoop as loud as any savage from the colonies, he leaped off the table. His boots hit the oak floor hard enough to crack wood.

I held out a hand to pull the engineer to his feet. "Now you be for getting out of here afore Old Angus breaks something that'd get him in trouble. I can't afford it if he stopped drinking."

The engineer muttered his thanks and left and old Angus broke into his silver to pay for a table's worth of spilt ale and new bowls of Hattie's mutton stew. The bread was picked up and wiped off. We were a miner's pub. The pit gates were a five minute walk down the lane and this was the first place to get ale that didn't serve up sluts as well.

Because of that, wives allowed their men to come here.

A married man coming out of the Boars Belly, a low hall located toward the mine with baths in the back and slattern girls upstairs, was likely to find coal dust in his tommy box instead of the dried cod and onions he might otherwise expect.

Rosey's was no such place. For that I was grateful. The ladies in town might stare down their noses at me, but I could stare right back. I never had been, and, bless the Virgin, never would be, one of those girls climbing those worn stairs, tugging wearily on the hard heavy hands of the miners. Taking them beyond the filthy curtains where they were groped and piled on. No, Rosey's was a nice place.

The engineer arrived at the pub the next morning as soon as the doors were open. He wore a suit, probably second hand and a bit overly large, but it was still a suit.

It isn't that there weren't men in suits at the mine; they just never got their faces black. Except for old Angus. He wore his suit the way a pig wore a dress, I'd seen him make a dress kilt into high fashion, but you couldn't buy a suit that would fit the square-bodied old Scot.

The engineer was different. From the look of his freshly scrubbed hands and nails, he'd never seen the inside of a mine, or a shovel, or field or anything outside of the worlds of paper and pen.

Today Rosey's smelled of sweet lye and flowers. One of the kitchen boys—and knowing what he and the other boys are said to do, I use the term loosely, but they do put on a good show on Saturday nights, dressing up and all—had brought in a bundle of Iris that I put in a flagon on the short bar.

With all the windows open, those flowers on the counter, and it being spring and all, Rosey's smelled pretty good as long the breeze went toward, and not from, the privy out back. Otherwise no amount of cleaning, sunshine, or flowery smells could make it smell like anything more than what we all know has been going into the hole under the boards.

The Engineer had a bruise on one side of his face. Old Angus must've got a couple of solid smacks in before I stopped him.

"You got bollocks coming in here after last night."

He ignored my comment. "You got something to drink? Water?"

"Water?" I asked.

"Yes, I believe that is what I said." And with that he sat at the bench by the table he'd been on the floor next to last night. I resisted the urge to put him there again.

When he saw I wasn't moving, he gave the table top a slap. "A bit of water isn't too much for you is it?"

It took me only a second to pull the flowers free of the flagon and slam it on the table in front of him. He glared up for a moment and then mumbled something that sounded like "pardons," and drank deeply from the water. He forced a swallow and said, "I hope the ale's better."

"It's a tuppence to know." I said and pulled the flagon from the table and refilled it with water from the pump. "And it's better for you." The flowers could wait.

"I'll take the ale." He said. I stood and looked at him. He looked back, his face blank. Finally he got my point and spun a coin on the table top.

It was still spinning when I snagged it and pulled him ale.

"Thank you," he mumbled and returned his focus to the table.

"You'll be wanting food?"

I saw his glance and the cold hearth where last night's stew still sat in the pot.

"You have anything warm?"

"You want hot food, come back tonight. Makes it too hot in here, summer coming and all."

"You need a smaller fire," he said.

I ignored him, but he looked at the fire place again. I went back to cleaning and when I looked up, he was gone.

When I showed the next day, he was waiting, perched on the red stone wall, peeling back a rose blossom. He had a canvas bag at his feet.

"Patience," he nodded in greeting.

I returned the nod and opened the door.

Without invite, he followed me in. He was still wearing the suit. The bruise on his face showed worse than before.

"You took a walloping."

"Somebody had to."

"What?" I asked.

"There were only two of us. Somebody had to take it. In a room full of drunken miners, it seemed like the best option."

I snorted. He ignored it.

"You really make machines?"

He nodded. "And more. He pulled a green glass jar from the canvas bag.

"What's that?"

"I call it mine oil. I made it from coal. It is a boon to the frugal. It's economical and it burns in lamps, like whale oil. Only better."

He set the bottle down and went to the hearth. As usual the remains of last night's stew lined the pot. We'd serve it cold with a slab of bread for a noon meal before we'd scrape the pot and make the night's.

He pulled a string out of his pocket and pulled it across the width of the hearth making a series of measurements.

"Best be for taking care. You think old Angus is tough; you mess with Hattie's pot, you're liable to be in it.

"I don't think I have to fear the wrath of your cook." He paused to peer into the pot. "Unless I'm forced to eat this."

I heard the kitchen door swing, but when I looked, no one was there. Hattie's nature was not to forgive, but she likely had things to do that were of more import than playing a ladle off of the engineer's already bruised head.

Unaware of his close brush, the engineer left.

Two days later he was again sitting on the sandstone wall by the roses, whistling a tune. He carried the same canvas bag, this time looped over his shoulder. He still wore the suit, freshly brushed this time.

"Good morning Patience."

I nodded.

He reached into his bag and pulled out a small wrap of flowers.

"You had to throw yours out." His face at this point was of sufficient earnestness that I stopped my tongue before it loosed. He raised the flowers again, a queer sense of sincerity.

I took the flowers. "They're not as nice as the ones I had to throw out on your account. But they'll do." They were actually quite nice, a bouquet of pink thrifts, like my granny grew in her garden. I pulled water from the pump, added a dab of ale to keep the flowers fresh, and set them on the end of the short bar so they'd be near the door.

Noise from the kitchen told me old Hattie was in. Didn't know why except she most always was. I could hear the sound of kitchen steel being sharpened. Likely a sheep about to get foisted onto a hook. Many a local farmer'd let no one but Hattie carve a sheep. I didn't really care what she did in the back, it was her domain.

I heard footsteps behind me and turned. It was the old miners, Dylan, Reece, and Berwyn. I smiled in turn to each and they each, in turn, nodded back.

"We saw the door was open," said Dylan. Reece and Berwyn each nodded, affirming they had indeed seen the open door. All of them paused long enough to look at the engineer before passing into the pub where they vanished into the darkness, their presence marked only by the sounds of dice.

The engineer ignored the glares and went to the hearth.

He pulled a small contraption of brightly hammered brass out of the bag and held it up against the hearth as if he were sizing a seam. Satisfied, he knelt, his black suit made blacker from the soot. He grasped the hearth brush gingerly, pausing long enough to push the bleached white cuffs of his suit higher on his forearms, exposing the pale whiteness of his thickly haired skin.

He found the brush inadequate and reached for the shovel and began to move aside the ashes. I pushed the ash bucket in his direction.

"If you be doing it, then do it."

He looked at me in confusion for a moment and then looked at the small scoop in his hand, at the hearth, and then at the ash bucket.

He nodded and scooped the ash into the bucket until he had cleared the area under Hattie's cauldron.

He pushed the bucket aside and picked up his device. It was odd. It looked like a lamp but with a tube formed into a circle that ran across the top, welded to where the wick on a right-made lamp would be. The metal tube had small holes around the top in a neat even circle. None of the holes were bigger than a straw of grass. Otherwise it looked like a lamp, the base likely had been a lamp with engraved silver filigree on each of the delicate legs it perched on.

He took out the same glass bottle he'd shown me two days prior, pulled the stopper and filled the base of his odd little lamp. It smelled foul.

Dylan, Reece, and Berwyn still sat at the rear of the bar, but the sounds of the dice were gone.

At the hearth, the engineer slid the contraption under the kettle. A rustle of skirts told me Hattie had ventured forth from the kitchen and stooped just a bit more than normal to watch, her beady black eyes looking over the hooked nose taking in every detail. Her briar pipe was held solidly by her ox-hide tough gums.

Even though the cauldron was in the front of the pub, she still considered it hers. The engineer was treading on dangerous ground. I looked and saw that no kitchen steel showed in Hattie's hands, though such could appear in a moment.

The engineer continued to adjust the device, the soldered welds still silvery fresh, bright against the hammered brass. He muttered to himself and adjusted the device until, finally satisfied, he leaned back, his narrow bum settled in on his heels. "A match."

Quicker than I could reach the bar, Old Hattie pulled a short length of wood through the striking cloth and held the blazing splinter, first to her pipe, and then to him. He took it without question and held it to the top of the small ring atop the device. Flames spread in a circle, centered under the cauldron. Blue flames. A faint hiss came with it. He adjusted a small wheel and the flames rose and fell.

Old Hattie, using a boney elbow into my ribs, pushed me aside. I looked again for steel and there was none so I let her be. She put a hand on the engineer's shoulder and leaned in.

Her nose wrinkled with a sniff and she pulled her pipe free and glared at the flame and then at the engineer. With no hint of her intent, she, with the pipe in one hand slid the other around his neck and placed a full kiss on his cheek and with what sounded like a cackle, scampered back to the kitchen. She returned in minutes with buckets of what I recognized as the leavings from the night's plates, but I said nothing as I watched her empty each into the kettle.

That was how it began.

The engineer became common, each day, lighter by the normal tuppence, the engineer sat at his now normal spot at the first table drinking his ale while the smell of cooking filled the room. Old Hattie made frequent trips from the kitchen with bowls of bits. She would, on occasion, wordlessly put a fresh pasty on the table by the engineer.

The Engineer was now part of the odd regular, in that he joined Dylan, Reece, and Berwyn. They in turn cursed the ground he walked on, even so far as to go next door to the smithy to curse the mining machine that was taking shape. Each afternoon, I was treated to the cackling laughter as they discussed the various aspects of the machine's shortcomings, failures, and uselessness. The Engineer stayed clear on evenings. He was smart enough to not play the fool for Angus again.

He studied the pub. He watched everything as if it were an invitation to intervene. Old Hattie had chased him out of the kitchen so many times they had achieved a treaty of sorts. He didn't speak or touch and she didn't poke at him with the long thin knives she seemed to spend endless hours sharpening.

My only day away from the pub was Sunday and it was on such a Sunday afternoon when the trio, Dylan, Reece, and Berwyn were sitting on the stoop of my flat when I returned from services. "Boys," I said. I didn't comment on their lack of attendance at services.

"Miss Patience."

They all stood together. "He's at the pub, Miss Patience." Dylan, the spokesman for the group held his hat in his hands. His chorus nodded their assent. "There is some fierce pounding. He's got the Smith boy in there with him. A terrible racket."

I looked at my garden with a bit a longing, let go a sigh, and put my feet in motion toward the pub, followed by the three. At each step I was assured by Dylan that they could take care of any trouble and I needn't worry for my safety.

They were right about the clanging. I could hear it a hundred yards away. The front door stood open. I was used to such noise from the smithy, but not in the pub.

I stepped through the doorway and almost tripped over the kettle.

The Engineer lay on his back in the hearth, not wearing his suit, but swinging a hammer over his head. He didn't notice me. I kicked him. Twice.

"What the hell." He stopped pounding and looked up. "Oh shit," he said.

"You'll be just that and more if you don't put this back right now. Hattie will be boiling your liver with jiboons." I looked to where the Smith boy stood, his leather apron covered with soot and ash. "And yours too." The tables had been pushed aside to make room. "What in the name of Saint David are you doing? And on the Sabbath as well."

A metal frame had been fitted tightly into the fire place.

"And what the bloody hell is that contraption." I pointed.

"Mr. Soulbender said it would be okay."

"Well Mr. Soulbender may own the mine and half the buildings in the town, but here the lease is paid and you'll be for putting Hattie's pot back on the hanger."

"Mister Soulben—"

I kicked him again. It felt just as good the second time.

"Was Mr. Soulbender here to keep Old Angus from throwing you across the tables?"

"No, but—"

"Do you think he'll come by and explain this to Hattie?" I cut him off.

He started to answer. I kicked him again.

"What the hell! Stop kicking me."

"Just fix it."

The sound of Dylan clearing his throat interrupted my thoughts of kicking the engineer one more time.

"So long as we're here, Miss Patience." His eyes went to

the keg of ale.

"Oh bloody hell." I muttered. "Why the hell not?"

The trio settled in at their table, each with a pint.

The Engineer began to pound again.

The Smith boy looked at me and back to the keg.

"You're with him." I pointed at the Engineer. It's a tuppence on his account."

"Make it two," came the muffled shout.

"Three," I said.

"Now watch," said the engineer. He pulled on a metal bar. The kettle hook slid out the front of the fireplace bringing the kettle with it. He pushed the lever back. The kettle, with a slight sway, followed the hook back into the fireplace.

The kitchen door opened. Hattie, a bloody knife in one hand, a sheep's foot in the other took in the view. The fine white hair of her head stood out in all directions and the small beady eyes scanned every person in the room, finally coming to rest on the hearth.

She slid across the room. The Smith boy crossed himself and stepped back. A bit late, I thought, this being the Sabbath and all.

She stopped and peered into the hearth. Finally she slipped the bloody knife into her apron and worked the lever, moving the kettle in and out of the hearth.

She reached into her apron and the knife appeared. She tapped the kettle hook.

"Inch higher. You'll burn my stew."

In the smithy, work on the machine continued. It was two days later three wagons loaded with men and gear pulled to the far side of the smithy.

The engineer was in his normal place, setting on the red rock wall by the roses. He didn't notice me; his focus was on the wagons.

"You have help." My gaze pointed up the road where Old Angus shouted instructions to the work crew.

"A test," he said. His voice lacked the usual enthusiasm.

"Of what? Seeing if Old Angus can keep his hands off your

throat?"

"My invention."

"You lack interest and enthusiasm."

He looked at me queerly. "I have built the most advanced mining machine in existence." He gestured toward the road. "Every day men trek down that road. They crawl down into the mine and with pick and bucket, remove the coal. Twenty years ago we stopped using horses to draw the mine barges, we use rail mounted steam engines to take coal to port. We use machines to load and unload. We use machines to crush the coal. But in the mine, in the blessed mine, we put men on the coal face with picks and shovels to haul out the coal, one bucket at a time."

He spoke like a peddler now. Full of notions and ideas.

"They crawl into the ground where the roof can collapse any time; where air is scarce and gas will kill them. Do they fear that? No, the Tommy Knocker's will protect them. Leave a pasty in your tommy box and it'll all be OK. This mine killed a dozen men in the last year. But do they fear the mine? No. I come to them with a machine that can move as much coal in an hour as they can in a week. Who do they fear? Me of course."

I touched his arm. "The men say the machine burned the Gurdy boy so bad he's still growing the skin back."

"There are accidents."

"Accidents," muttered Dylan as he Reece and Berwyn walked past us into the pub. Dylan turned, "It's an abomination." He spit on the ground and each of the others spit in turn and went to their dice.

The Engineer looked down at the ground and his shoulders slumped. "That was a terrible thing. He will recover. But he's not got a crushed leg and he can still breathe." He waved a loose hand toward the smithy. "There will be machines. Miners will operate them. I should be pushing my engine into a seam of coal, not defending a fool miner getting hurt who doesn't know right from left when turning a valve."

"So it was the boy's fault."

He looked at me, his eyes filled with pain. "No, it was my fault. I shouldn't have let him operate the machine." He took a deep breath. "One steam burn doesn't change the future. Machines, operated by men, will be in the mines."

"So what's this to do with why you're here?" I asked. I was not willing to look into those hazel eyes filled with pain. Hell if he didn't have nice eyes.

"Mr. Soulbender is not a country farmer. He knows that machines are coming and the mines with the best machines will make the most money."

"And you will build those machines?"

"Yes," he answered.

Shouts from the wagons made him look past me to where men were gathered around the wagons unloading gear.

"Speaking of machines," he said. "I have one to assemble." He touched my hand. I didn't pull away. "Would you like to see it?" Yes, I realized. I would like to. And with that realization the world suddenly got small. I ran a pub and made enough money to eat meat when I wanted it. I didn't need to wrapped up in this any further. With the realization, I drew a quick breath and pulled my hand away. Mumbling about the need to make ready, I opened the door and left him standing by the roses.

Old Hattie already stood in the room, lit only by the engineer's small device under the kettle, already smells of cooked food filled the room with the gentle smell of last night's plate scrapings turned today's meal.

She smiled a knowing toothless smile and turned back to the kettle.

Each day for the next week he met me by the roses. A shared greeting and then me into the tavern to face Old Hattie, each day a broader smile, and him off to his work. Usually muttering curses about Angus. Each noon hour he would settle into his chair and the work crew would grin through broken teeth and wait as I served up the savory remains from the Hattie's kettle. The Smith boy even seemed to have become a part of the crew. We spoke little.

Angus, being the crew boss, limited his men to two pints, but we never denied a man his due. The occasional extra pint made its way.

It was a Saturday and the spring was inching toward summer and the end of a solid week of courteous greetings when the engineer greeted me at the door, as usual. But he wore his suit again today. And there was the buggy. I recognized it as belonging to one of Mr. Soulbender's partners in the mine. He lived at the east end of the village.

"Patience," he said. The suit was brushed.

I realized at that point I had no name for him. "Sir." I responded, my first such response where I acknowledge him as aught but a customer or as, we all did, The Engineer.

"Miles," he said.

"Miles," I responded, it was a nice name. I sensed a blush.

"I have a carriage."

"Yes." I said.

"I thought I might yet show you my machine." He gestured the quarter mile down the road where the wagons gathered on the other side of the smithy.

"It is not so far as to be beyond a walk." I couldn't believe my words. I walked further to gather eggs.

"But further than a gentleman should expect a lady to walk."

I reached for the door to the tavern. "I've work to—"

"God help me girl," came old Hattie's voice from behind the door. "Mount the carriage before I do." A cackle followed and for a moment I thought I detected a blush from Miles.

I had never before been on such a delicate transport. Freight wagons a many, but they scarcely moved when I boarded. This light surrey dipped visibly with my weight. The padded seats were dyed leather. Miles provided a gentle assist, and then joined me. I could feel his leg against mine. We rode in brief silence until we stopped beside the wagons.

The steam drill was smaller than I expected; no bigger than a pony. Three long steel lances protruded from the front and it sat on a two wheeled caisson with a wagon tongue behind that the men used to maneuver the beast. It smelled of hot grease and burning coal.

The machine sat at the bottom of a wide flat trench, the deep end deeper than any cellar in the village and the last 10 feet were carved out of the sand stone that lined the undersurface of the world in Wales.

He walked me the last 100 feet to the lip of the pit. A ladder led to the bottom. A raised platform with several out of place chairs pushed close to the edge. Right now it also held a half dozen dented tommy boxes from the miners below. A dog that I knew Old Hattie was prone to throw scraps to when she thought nobody knew, lay on the platform, his nose strategically pointed at the clustered collection of food.

Miles gestured to the chairs. "Would you care to sit?" He held out a hand and I took it. This time I didn't pull away, he was no schoolmaster and I felt a blush. He must have felt something similar because he turned quickly to the crew.

"Ready up boys."

"We know how to run the bloody machine," responded Old Angus. He saw me and paused, "Miss Patience." And with that, the crew began to pump the bellows and smoke poured out of a short stack. The three lances on the front of the machine slowly began to move.

Machines did not draw the attention they once did. This one might re-kindle that interest. It was large, but no more than the surrey I'd been delivered on. The great spears of iron protruded from the front, each thicker than my wrist. They pushed forward in turn, slowly now, measurably faster as the rhythm of the belching machine increased. The machine was beautiful, a plated mixture of copper and iron. Bars of beaten red gleamed where they covered the curved, dull black iron plates that made up the body of the machine. Tubes and gauges completed the elegant dance of form and function that filled a half box on the back of the machine. Wheeled valves and levers awaited an operator.

I watched. The Engineer now stood on the ground pointing and shouting, his words lost over the noise. Old Angus himself stood on the flat platform pulling the levers and turning the valves. A flat belt beneath the pushing shafts began to move in cross pattern to the shafts. Two men on the ground slowly turned a wheel that looked s if it were set to steer a ship and the machine inched forward until the iron shafts touched the surface of the sandstone wall. The stone fell in fist sized pieces and landed on the flexible belt and carried it to a waiting Irishman with a wheelbarrow, and then quicker than you could say God bless the Queen, another hopped in place pushing a new barrow forward. Another and another. The barrows were emptied into a flat wagon.

"My God." I turned to see Dylan, Reece, and Berwyn standing beside the platform staring into the pit. Berwyn crossed himself. Their eyes were glued to the steady stream of falling stones from the driving spikes carving a slow trench across the stone face. I knew little of mining but I knew that stones falling at the speed I was seeing was the work of dozens of men.

No wonder the miners hated the very idea of the machine. I looked again at Dylan, Reece, and Berwyn. These were not the faces of men who saw their children freed of the pick and shovel, but men who saw them enslaved to a great black machine.

As quickly as it started, it was done. The wagon was full. Another engine at the top of the trench began to steam and soon the loaded wagon was pulled to the surface.

The engineer did not look up, but busily crawled over the platform, shouting commands. He had forgotten me in the moment.

"Come along boys." I said to Dylan, Reece, and Berwyn. "I believe I can pull you each an ale without worry this morning." They ceased their dark looks at the engine long enough to come to a silent agreement and we walked in silence back to Rosey's. The dog stayed, its nose closer by an inch to the bottom of the miner's lunches.

The engineer did not come back that day. The test had gone even better the second try, this time with Mr. Soulbender and his partners sitting in soft chairs on the little raised platform.

I scarce had time to worry about the engineer or how his touch felt. The miners that packed the pub that night were in a dark mood. There was talk of little else but the machine. And it was angry talk. The room buzzed with it.

"They're breaking the infernal machine." A miner stood in the open door, backlit by torches and lamps. There was a moment of silence and I heard shouts from the miners outside. In the distance, I heard pounding. The room emptied. A good many mugs walked out the door.

The sun had been up for several hours when I got to the open trench. The small platform was no longer there. It lay in splinters at the bottom of the trench. I found four mugs lying on the ground near where it had sat. I added them to the six I'd found on the road, only slightly chipped, it made the walk worth it. The Engineer, Miles now, sat on the edge, looking into the trench. I sat beside him, took his hand, and leaned into him.

The huge spikes that had cut the furrow in the rock wall had been torn free. One impaled the boiler, sticking straight out the side of the engine. The others had been used to bend the great guide wheels. The bright streaks of copper that had marked the seams were peeled loose and littered the ground. The morning sun glinted on them. The bright gauges were bent handfuls of metal pounded into scrap by the miner's hammers and picks. The metal belt that moved the coal was torn free and the wooden slats splintered and cracked.

Miles' eyes were red, either from lack of sleep or tears. It didn't matter which. We sat in silence until the mine whistle shattered the moment.

Three sharp blasts. Repeated three times. *Cave in*!

We were among the first to arrive at the mine, but were quickly joined by the wives who quickly settled into a tight knot of women who'd husbands were not on the surface.

By noon the worst was confirmed. The portion of the mine leading toward the village was cutoff. Thirty-two men were trapped or dead.

Mr. Soulbender, his face gray, summoned Miles, Angus, and others of import into the mine offices. No one seemed to notice as I accompanied. A large board covering an entire wall showed a map of the mine and Old Angus used a broom handle to point as he explained the situation.

"The cave in is here." He pointed to a large open area that connected to the entrance by the main tunnel." He pointed to one of a dozen shafts that led off of the open area. He traced a circle where the mine showed an area dotted with Xs. "Those are the pillars where the collapse happened. There've been Tommy knockers in the area for weeks." Tommy knockers I knew were the wee folk of the mines that warned miners, with creaks and knocks, of unstable rock. You couldn't work the pub without hearing the tales.

"This tunnel," he tapped the one on the left, "is completely lost." He spoke briskly of the thirty two men. "If they were where they were supposed be, they are still down there."

"What does this mean?" asked Mr. Soulbender.

"It means thirty two men dying in the dark, thirsty and hungry, knowing their wives and children won't ever see them again."

He reached his broom handle up at the map. "That is unless we can dig through this rubble."

"Can we?" asked Mr. Soulbender.

"No." Miles stepped away from me and toward the map.

Mr. Soulbender turned to Miles. His eyes paused on me and his eyebrows rose, but his attention turned quickly back to Miles.

"Trying to dig a shaft through the cave in," said Miles, "is pointless." He consulted some figures he had scrawled on a small paper. "That will take more than three weeks."

Mr. Soulbender looked to Angus and the other men in the room. They all looked at the floor.

"Then we tunnel for three days, hope for a miracle, and tell the families we did what we could." Soulbender said the words flatly with a look of finality. He looked over at a man with thick glasses. "We'll need to do something for the families of course."

Old Angus looked ready to shrivel into nothingness, as did almost every man in the room.

"We have an option," said Miles. He took the broom handle from Angus and tapped the far end of the isolated shaft. "We come in from the other direction."

Angus looked at the map. "That'd be two weeks of digging. We'd never make it. You'd be digging 400 feet through solid stone."

"My machine—"

"Your machine is broken," said Angus. "Besides, men dig mines, not machines."

"My machine can be fixed. Nothing broken that can't be fixed by tomorrow morning."

Mr. Soulbender looked a Miles. "You really think so?"

"Yes, Sir. I do." He looked at Angus. "With the right crew. She can be done."

Angus looked at the floor for a long minute and then raised his head. "If that infernal machine of yours will get those miners out, then I don't give a care."

The sound of hammers sounded through the night from the smithy. The pub stayed open. The new tunnel would start right behind Rosey's. Mr. Soulbender himself commandeered the table close to the fire and made it clear in a loud voice that he would pay for the food and drink.

At one point he found himself fidgeting with the engineer's Kettle Swing as we had taken to calling it. It earned him a thwacking from Old Hattie.

Once the Engineer came in, he put a lamp up to the wall and pointed at a half dozen metal shapes and men attacked the wall and pulled them off, carrying them to the shop.

"My apologies" was all he said and disappeared out the door.

The machine started up at dawn. The tables inside Rosey's were all lined with slender ribbons of dirt fallen from between the ceiling boards from the steady vibration of the machine. There seemed to be an endless supply.

The rest of the story has become mine lore. The machine worked and newer better versions of it pull coal deeper than ever imagined. The engineer's mine oil is used in Buckingham Palace.

But not all is spoke of with fond memories. The miners had been reached. It was three rain-soaked days, almost to the hour from when the triple whistles sounded to when the machine broke through. Water, food and light were passed around the machine. The machine had to be removed, to let the miners escape. They were, to the man, alive. They pushed and the donkey engine pulled and I'm told the mining machine literally flew back up the tunnel. Perhaps too fast when it became wedged near the entrance.

The privy was sadly close to the shaft.

I was perched in the warm rain, listening to the curses and groans the people tried in vain to pull the machine clear.

Picks were handed down and Old Angus himself positioned himself to take the first swing.

The miners took a chant and blow after blow fell, chipping away at the stone until the pick punched through the stone wedging the machine in place. It had barely moved a foot when screams of the miners could be heard as the rain soaked privy released its thirty year load into the mine shaft.

The curses turned to laughter as man after man came out of the shaft and families gathered their men in the warm summer rain.

But each man patted the machine with affection, or gratitude as he passed.

As I patted the arm of the Engineer with gratitude... and affection until he placed said arm firmly around my shoulders.

THE EXPERIMENT

Cliff Winnig

Professor Edwards treated me to a withering look, one that said quite clearly my uncle must have been suffering a brain fever to have sent me to him.

"An aetheric integrator, Hodgins. Do keep up."

I hadn't been. In fact, I had no comprehension whatsoever of the strange contraption that hissed and rumbled on the workbench in front of me. Just then, it gave off a small jet of steam. It seemed to me a reproachful sigh from the device itself for my failure to grasp its workings on even the coarsest level.

Edwards wiped his brow, despite the cold Martian air, and stuffed his handkerchief back in his coat pocket. Beyond him, the too-small sun was setting over the rusty horizon, its reflection pale in the water of the canals. "Look here, Hodgins. What night is it, on Earth I mean?"

I relaxed, happy to get a question I could actually answer. "Why Hallowe'en night, sir." I glanced at my wrist chronometer. It had two dials, one for New London and one for Greenwich Mean Time. "In London as we speak."

"Yes, of course in London. Well, that makes it Hallowe'en in New London too, doesn't it?"

"Yes, sir. I fancy it does, sir. I don't hold with all that talk about adopting the calendar of the natives, despite their obvious astronomical sophistication."

Edwards waved a dismissive hand. "Witch doctors and dunderheaded priests. You know how superstitious those Martians are. I'm talking *science*."

"Yes, Professor. Of course you are."

"Damned certain I am. Now, where was I? Ah yes, Hallowe'en. I have taken measurements for the last fifteen years—proper Earth years, you understand—and I can demonstrate conclusively that the aetheric index rises significantly on All Hallows' Eve. In fact, my measurements here on Mars have shown this to be the case as well. This device...." He patted the contraption, part of which accordioned shut at his touch, springing up again when he removed his hand. "This device will boost that already strong signal to previously unachieved heights."

"Aetheric index, Professor?"

"Yes, lad. You know that aether fills the space between worlds, right?"

"Of course, sir. I flew through it to get here."

"So you did, though I daresay the voyage has profited you little thus far." He grabbed the lapels of his jacket and drew himself up. "'Tis my solemn duty to reverse that trend, for your uncle's sake." He nodded once, then adopted a more informal pose. "In any case, that same medium separates us from the world beyond, the other side, if you like. In fact, the beings of that world are composed of the stuff."

"I'm not really into spiritualism, sir. So I fail to see...."

He jabbed me with his index finger, his face reddening. "Yes, Hodgins, you fail to see. You fail to see everything! I'm not some charlatan medium, here to commune with your Great Aunt Elizabeth, poorly played by a boy crouching under the table. No! I'm going to solve the Redchapel murders by speaking with one of the victims."

The Redchapel murders! That nasty business had occurred a year ago here in New London, Martian time, on this very evening. The crime had captured the imagination not only of Mars but also of the public back on Earth. No one knew what conspiracy—for it could not have been the work of one man, not twenty-three murders in a single night—could have underlain those foul deeds, or who could have profited by it. The victims had been ladies of the night, and the killings had all taken place in the hours before dawn. No witness had come forward. The bricks of Redchapel had failed to divulge their mysteries, even to the most scrupulous of police and private detectives. A pair had flown through the aether all the way from London and back without solving the case. And here my uncle's friend would put them all to shame. It was a dizzying prospect, and I said so.

"At last!" Edwards stepped back and smiled. "You begin at least to appreciate the scope of our endeavor tonight. Now, let me show you your role in operating the device. You don't need to understand their purpose to pull these levers here and monitor this dial."

We spent the next hour busying ourselves with the final preparations for the experiment. It would be, I learned, the first time he would be operating the device at full strength.

By the time he pronounced us ready to begin, the sky had darkened to black. Bright stars shone through the thin Martian atmosphere in achingly familiar constellations, for they looked the same from Earth. The Earth itself crossed over the tower of Big Bertha, which struck the nine o'clock hour. That edifice had been quite a controversy, calibrated as it was to the slightly longer Martian day rather than Earth's.

With a flourish, Edwards wound the crank that caused the machine to stir, until it came fully to life. Gears turned. The device emitted a low hum, rising gradually in volume as the professor made adjustments to various knobs and switches. Steam burst forth from a long iron tube at regular intervals.

The oil lamp that provided the main illumination in the laboratory flickered out, no doubt the result of some stray draft set in motion by Edwards' aetheric integrator. Yet Phobos and Deimos had risen, and I could see by their cold light that my part of the experimental run was proceeding apace. Gradually the room began to brighten, and I saw my shadow cast over the dial. Automatically, I moved so as to view it better, but then I realized that the moonlight originated in front of me, and this new light came from behind.

I spun around then, driven by a sudden fear, and gasped at the glowing shape in the center of the room, gradually taking on human form.

"Professor!" I shouted.

"Not now, Hodgins. I'm making the final adjustments."

"But Professor...." I could see the form more clearly now and, in sudden panic, I averted my eyes.

"Aw," said a lady's voice in a Redchapel accent. "Ain't that a darling sight. Never seen a lady's undergarments, has he?"

At this utterance Edwards ceased his efforts and turned to face our Hallowe'en visitor. I saw a look of triumph on his face.

"Professor Edwards," said the woman. "Lovely to see you again."

At this familiarity Edwards blushed, then paled. "Madam, I believe you have the better of me."

"Oh, don't be coy, Harry. And tell your young friend to stop hiding from me. I don't bite, at least not anymore."

"Hodgins," Edwards said in a stern voice. "I need you alert and taking notes concerning this apparition. You can't do that if you're looking at me."

Reluctantly, I fetched a pen and notepad, then began jotting down what I saw: a young woman, fair-haired, manifesting in the middle of the room. I couldn't tell her eye or hair color exactly, for she glowed with a ghostly white light, and she was semitransparent to begin with. Her form seemed solid enough otherwise, though her feet tapered into smoke. At least I couldn't see her ankles. She'd spared me that scandal. Judging from her clothes and demeanor, her profession had been one where she'd regularly showed them to all sorts of men. And Professor Edwards had known her. Did he have an interest in this case beyond pure science?

"Madam," began the professor.

"Oh, you can call me Rose, Harry. You did when I was alive."

"Madam," said Edwards. "I did not know which victim would be called up by my aetheric integrator."

"That's what you call it, eh? You do say the sweetest things to a girl. Still, cute little bugger, innit? Like a tiny steam engine."

Edwards sighed. "We have little time."

Rose smiled, sadly it seemed to me. (I jotted that detail down.) "Aye, I know. It being All Hallows' Eve an' all, plus a Martian year since the murders, though that bit's just icing on the cake, innit love?"

"For the sake of justice, we must know who did it. Did you

get a good look at your assailant?"

Just then, a knock came at the door.

"Hellfire and damnation! Hodgins, go see who it is."

I gratefully turned from the underdressed young woman and went to the door. Upon opening it, I saw a miniature Martian princess—judging from the apparel over greasepaint and papier-mâché horns—and a ghost. The latter looked nothing like Rose, his costume being a white sheet with holes cut in it for eyes.

"Sorry t'be disturbing you and the professor, kind sir," said the girl, who looked to be a year older than the ghost boy. "But would you be having any candies about the place, or other such treats?"

I grinned, for I recognized both her Irish accent from a happy year spent in Dublin and the custom she was enacting. I'd never seen it practiced in England, but it had been popular in Ireland. Clearly, the waves of Irish workers had transported the custom to Mars.

"Professor Edwards," I shouted. "It's children come guising."

"What? We've important work to do, Hodgins."

"Hey!" shouted the boy. "What's that light?"

Before I could stop him, he ran round me to the main room beyond. "Ellie!" he shouted back. "A real ghost—a lady!"

"Quit making things up!" But she followed him to the doorway and stood gaping.

"Fantastic Hallowe'en t'you both!" said the real ghost.

The boy just stood there, but the girl curtsied. "Good evening, ma'am. Not disturbing you, are we?"

"Not at all," said Rose. "But you've other homes to visit, no doubt. Harr ... Professor Edwards, why not give the children apples from your tree in the greenhouse. Such wonderful costumes, an' all."

"How'd you know I had...."

"Fresh apples!" cried the children. "Oh please, sir. 'Twould be lovely, it would," added the girl. "We hardly ever get them."

I expected Edwards to snap at them and go on about how little time he had, but instead a broad and seemingly genuine smile spread across his countenance. "Now I know you: Ellie and Jim, as I live and breathe!"

"And as I don't," added Rose.

"Hodgins, get the children some apples, and let them each have a sweet roll as well."

I did, and the children ate their sweet rolls, pocketed their apples, and bade us all a good evening.

"Be sure to tell your father that my aetheric integrator worked just as I told him it would. We'll soon have solid information on that matter he and I discussed."

The children nodded solemnly and said they would. Then they ran out the door into the night, eager to find their next victim.

"They're O'Flaherty's children," Edwards said by way of explanation, once I'd returned to the laboratory and again taken up my pen and notebook.

"Ah, the chief of police." I remembered the name from an article I'd read.

"Quite so. Lives in the neighborhood."

That didn't surprise me. The professor lived in an area mixing middle-class English with well-to-do Irish. No Martians, of course. They all lived outside the city proper, even their royalty.

"Which brings us," Edwards added, "to the task at hand."

"'Twas a foul business, was that night," said Rose.

"I know," Edwards said, with surprising gentleness. "But those children's father will sort it out for us, if we can point him to sufficient evidence."

"Indeed he will, but he won't like doing it. Not as long as that windbag's still Lord Mayor."

I smiled at her description, having briefly met the man upon my arrival, but I stifled it when Edwards threw me a reproachful look.

"He's best friends with O'Flaherty," said Edwards. "He stands to gain from solving these crimes. Trust me, he'll throw the full weight of his office behind our investigation."

"I bet he won't," said Rose. "You see, it's him what had us

all done in, me and twenty-two other girls that night."

"What!" Edwards and I exclaimed in unison.

"Aye," said Rose, fixing us with a bold stare. "He didn't do it himself, mind you, but he hired the hands that held the knives, sure enough."

"But why?" I asked.

"Oh it served him well enough, on two fronts: gave him the excuse he wanted to crack down on us Redchapel professionals, and it brought more curiosity seekers to Mars than ever before. Boosted the local economy for months, it did."

My mind balked at the prospect at first, but as I thought about it, I realized it made an odd sort of sense. "That's ghastly!" I said at last.

"That's politics." Rose was clearly sharper than her manner of dress implied. She had thorns.

"You have evidence?" Edwards asked. "We can't go to O'Flaherty on the word of a ghost, however trustworthy." He said the last word with a note of doubt, but I could tell he too had come to believe her accusation.

"O'course, love. Them men the Lord Mayor hired were good, but they left a stray bit of evidence here, a bit there. An' all that don't hold a candle to what I could show you, having personally haunted the mayoral mansion many a night. I seen what he wrote down and where he put what he wrote. You'll prove he done it. Safe as houses."

"We must handle this very delicately," said Edwards.

Outside Phobos and Deimos arced across the sky. The night would not last forever. Rose pointed this out.

"Of course," said Edwards. "Hodgins, take careful notes."

So I did. Rose talked until Hallowe'en ended and the rosy dawn began. The last of her light faded with the first of the sun's. Bleary-eyed, I looked over the many pages I'd written. Her observations had been very specific. Taken together, the clues would form a trail of breadcrumbs that could not be ignored. It would be hard work, but I had no doubt that, along with O'Flaherty and his men, we could do it.

"Well, Professor, I'd say your experiment was a roaring

success." I felt happy, but exhausted.

"What? Oh, yes. Terrible business, those murders. Terrible things will come to light. Still, we did our part for science, eh?" He treated me to a weary smile. "Good work, Hodgins." It was the nicest thing he'd ever said to me.

Edwards went off to his chambers to catch a little rest, and I set out for my room in a nearby neighborhood. As I walked, I felt a pair of eyes upon me, but not unfriendly ones.

"Will I see you again, Rose?" I asked the empty street. In the course of our long night, I'd grown rather fonder and less shy of the sad young woman.

"Aye," came a faint voice that might simply have been the wind, blowing thinly through the empty streets. "Visit you next Hallowe'en, I might. I'm all light and shadow now, but I can speak of better things than murder."

"I'd like that," I said, and went home to sleep.

HEART OF COMSTOCK

Jennifer Rachel Baumer

Overhead the Nevada sky was the deep forever blue of high desert. Underfoot the ground was trampled muddy, colored with a combination of blue veins of silver and the ruddy red of blood.

Two bodies lay head facing head, hands stretching out as if they had died trying to touch. Two men, each holding a Colt revolver. If they'd been trying to reach each other, it was only to inflict more damage.

Nell sighed and stood. She'd written this one up so many times she could rerun the article and just change the names. She turned off the small recording device, a gift from her inventor uncle, and skirted the small group of people as she crossed to where Charles stood with the lone camera that made him a star. No array of black accordion boxes and umbrellas and tripods. Just Charles and his special dry plate method. A twist of lips within chestnut whiskers said he was no more excited about the story than she was.

Charles could capture images much faster than any other photographer and their newspaper was lucky to have him, even if Nell didn't understand how he did what he did. Might as well ask her to explain how her heart worked.

Though of course no one would do that. Those who loved her steered clear of the topic. To the rest, she was a freak.

She started toward him but had to step back out of the way of the Virginia City sheriff.

Marvin Clyde was taking his own notes, asking for witnesses, treating this as if it were the first time in summer 1864 that two men had fought and died over the same stretch of silver.

Nell gave him room. She gave everyone room. She took up more than her fair share of space with the heavy baroque canister on her back. It was beautiful, ornate, golden with copper tracings forming a pattern, a tapered lid with the apparatus inside. It was a lovely piece of metal work. It was the thin flexible tubes of light silvery metal that ran from the canister and disappeared under the neckline of her dress that made it a burden and made Nell a freak.

Freak or not, it kept her alive. A metal coil inside the canister kept the saltwater hot and the steam powering the gears inside the tank. From there compressed air was forced into one of the silvery tubes that snaked beneath her skin, forcing her sluggish heart to send oxygenated blood through her body. The other tube vented impurities and byproducts.

"I am taking names of witnesses and will need to speak to each of you in turn," Sheriff Clyde said. He was a large man, handsome if one ignored the barley concealed anger in him. Nell had. The sheriff had lost his wife three years earlier to an unsolved murder. He was the sheriff. If he couldn't solve it, no one could.

No point in asking the sheriff what had happened. Martin Clyde didn't believe in the media. Newspapers were beneath his contempt.

Most people and things were.

Nell definitely was.

"The undersheriff will meet you at the office in ten minutes." Charles moved closer to her and aimed the camera at the sheriff, a sure way to get the man to go somewhere else.

It worked. Martin Clyde turned to signal the wagon that would cart the bodies away and to start taking the younger, prettier witnesses with him to give statements first.

Nell glowered after him. Once he'd been the answer to her prayers, but then her heart had failed and her father's money and her uncle's experiments had saved her.

She couldn't be heartbroken now. It would go on beating; a combination of heated salt water, pulleys and the apparatus that functioned like bellows that utilized the thin silvery tubes to keep oxygen and blood flowing to her heart and away made certain of that.

And besides, Martin Clyde had married, loved (for all intents and purposes) and lost his wife. Nell on the other hand– Nell was still alive. Reporter for her father's newspaper, who sometimes stepped out of an evening with Charles because people wondered why he'd never wed and because tongues wagged a little less obtrusively when Nell was sometimes seen in public. Acting normal, wearing her heart not on her sleeve but attached to her back.

I don't care, Nell thought at the sheriff's retreating back. It had been years since the death of the sheriff's wife and Nell had come to believe that had he tried to come back to her after Mary died she would have scorned and refused him.

She was completely able to believe this, as sheriff Martin Clyde hadn't tested her resolve even once.

Murder, she reminded herself, his wife was murdered and Clyde wasn't investigated because he was the sheriff. Even if she were stupid enough–and if he were at all apt to ask–just imagine how easy it would be for a man to move on without suspicion after the death of a wife with a steampowered heart.

Almost as easy as determining the story of the two men face down in the Nevada dirt. More than one miner had died of heartbreak on the Comstock.

Charles went with her when she went to the Sheriff's Office. Probably he was afraid she'd run into Martin Clyde. Unlikely– some of the potential witnesses had been quite attractive.

Undersheriff Ben Dawson opened the door of the sheriff's office as they approached, pulled them both inside and slammed the door in one fluid movement. He was a carroty-haired man, small, wiry and nervous, which Nell thought wasn't a bad trait for someone working directly under Martin Clyde. More like a survival skill.

Charles, fetched up hard against the wall, panted. "Is there a problem?"

Dawson, staring out the window, most of his body pressed against the interior wall, nodded. "Could be. Probably is. Why I ast you to come."

Nell frowned. She couldn't see anything past him on the

street. "We thought it was in regards to the murder on C Street."

Dawson favored her with a look long enough to convey the idiocy of her statement, the wrongness of her assumption, that he'd expected better and that with that thing on her back and the leads going under her dress, she was a freak.

"Anything out there you can't understand from what you already seen?"

Charles laughed and tried unsuccessfully to turn it into a cough. Nell glared at him and shrugged.

"So, that's not why I ast you here," Dawson said, and finally moved away from the window, convinced the street was empty.

They sat in the tiny parlor behind the sheriff's office and jail, and Dawson produced a decent cup of tea. Nell sat primly on the edge of her chair, her attention fixed on the clock.

The fact of her steampowered heart meant that Nell had limited time between refills of water going into the canister and that she sat very primly with posture that often hurt her back.

Dawson didn't seem to notice.

She hadn't been gone that long but ought to keep her eye on the time. When a story snagged her attention, she'd been known to forget to take kettles form the fire, eat or refill the water in her canister.

"Miss Osborne," undersheriff Dawson said, when the tea had been poured and pleasantries observed. Dawson's manners were fit more to Boston than Virginia City.

"Nell," she said automatically. The undersheriff was friendly and good looking and so bent on propriety they weren't ever going to get to the point if she didn't help things along.

"You're a newspaper woman and you know some things about the world so I'm hoping you won't be upset by what I'm about to tell you."

Across the round lace-covered table from Nell Charles made a sound that could easily be interpreted as a choked off laugh. She raised her eyes in a ladylike glower and turned her attention to the undersheriff.

"Mr. Dawson, I just came here from a crime scene in which two men are lying dead in blood, mud and silver. Please don't try to spare my feminine sensibilities. If there is a story, I want it."

Dawson's eyes widened slightly. He glanced back toward the sheriff's office but the bell over the door hadn't rung and the sheriff was no doubt still questioning the more attractive witnesses while the older, less attractive witnesses fidgeted.

"All right, Miss–Nell." He cleared his throat, took a sip of tea and about the time Nell was beginning to appreciate that the canister on her back protected her from a pounding heartbeat of impatience, he said, "There have been a number of young women found dead in the last three years in our territory."

Nell and Charles both abandoned their tea cups with a clatter and sat forward–in Nell's case, nearly leaving the edge of her seat she currently claimed–their attention riveted on the ginger haired undersheriff.

"I know as newspaper folk you'd likely have heard of them, but these particular killings have been–'erm." He stopped and took a sip of tea. Nell eyed the clock and wondered what hot tea would do for the steampowered heart because she wasn't leaving and Dawson wasn't going very fast.

"Gruesome," Dawson said at the end of his sip of tea. He seemed to take courage either from the tea or the fact neither of them bolted from the table. He began talking very fast. Nell, not caught unawares, began writing as he spoke, her fountain pen dashing.

"It's been kept quiet, of course. For three years. Because the sheriff's the one doing investigating and he didn't think it would benefit the town any if people were afraid to come here and by people I mean women, because the murders–there have been an even baker's dozen, ma'am–sir, I'm sorry if this offends, but there've been 13 good women gone to their reward and the sheriff no closer to solving the case. You can see his success rate on everything else, he'll figure out what happened on C Street today–"

"*I* figured out what happened on C Street today," Charles muttered and Nell glanced at him but the interruption didn't phase Dawson who continued.

"Thirteen women and begging your pardon, ma'am, but a

township like this, we need women to come here, teach the kids, marry the miners, bake the bread and–" He stopped again and this time colored an unattractive fuchsia to the very start of his carroty hair. "Well. To put it indelicately, to entertain the men what aren't married."

Nell made a series of dashed questions down the side of one page, and said, "Mr. Dawson, if it's not too indelicate to inquire, were the women who have been murdered–" She liked that word so much better than simply *killed* which could happen by one of the wild camels trampling someone or a miner losing his temper–"Were they of the teaching our children and baking our bread variety or of the keeping the men entertained persuasion?"

Dawson nodded, as if this was how he meant to answer, and Nell convinced herself not to stab him with her fountain pen, as that would make the ink glob and the pen perform poorly.

"They were more the latter sort, Miss," Dawson said.

Thirteen prostitutes murdered in the last three years, Nell thought. "And nothing has been said on the sheriff's behest?"

Dawson nodded. "Only ones that know't are myself, the sheriff, the doc and the undertaker." He glanced at their faces and nodded. "The sheriff's got his reasons, and in the long and short of it they do make sense." He stood, moving to the pump at the sink to refill the kettle.

"But it's murder," Nell said softly.

Charles stood, brushing down his waistcoat. His boots still bore traces of mud from C Street. He was caught up in the story, Nell thought, or he'd have been wild to go clean his clothing.

"Why tell us now?" Charles asked and Nell thought he was just about desperate to have a camera in his hands, to document everything. She herself had switched on the recording device.

At the same time, she glanced at the clock again. Two hours before she absolutely needed to go and change out the canister, filling it with the boiling concoction of salt water.

She was alive because of it. The fact made her dependence on it no less frustrating.

Dawson turned back from the sink, the kettle still in his hands. He placed it absently on the top of the pot belly stove.

"Because it's not being solved," he said, and as if the admission freed him somehow, he crossed the room and sat down at the table with them again, his long fingered freckled hands moving expressively. "It makes sense to wait until we know something. There's no point scaring people and yes, sir, we do need ladies of all descriptions to move here, same as we need a doc and a sheriff and an undertaker and a good many folks to run the saloons."

He paused, took a breath. "But nothing's being done. I'm the sheriff's right hand, so if something *was* being done, I'd know it. Damn all, 'cuse me miss, like as not I'd be the one doing it."

Nell frowned at her notebook because she didn't want to frown at Dawson. "So no one has checked any of these out? The sheriff?" And she stopped talking, just looking at her notebook, trying hard not to look at Charles because she already knew exactly what Charles was thinking.

She looked up at Dawson, instead, and had the unpleasant notion she knew exactly what Dawson was thinking, also.

"Tell me about them," and to the shocked expression he gave her, she summoned all 61 inches of height, tried to somehow imagine away the blond ringlets and look serious and staid as one of those females brought into the territory to teach.

Probably didn't work, but he answered her.

"First one three years ago this month." He looked for an instant like he was going to apologize to her again for his upsetting remarks, and then he glanced toward the street, at the clock, and began: "If you count the sheriff's wife. And then there was the girl from San Francisco, maybe had her heart broke there. Working girl, why'd she want to leave gold country to come here? Life's a lot easier there. But she'd come our way and showed interest of maybe changing her ways. Hard to say because she never got the chance. Found behind the Ponderosa, face real white because she didn't have any blood left. Someone must have dragged her up there. She put up a fight, but she was a tiny thing like you, Miss–'er, Nell."

Silence for a minute and she didn't look up, used the time to catch up her notes and only looked up shocked when Dawson said in a flat cold voice: "He cut out her heart."

Charles held on to her elbow like he thought she needed support, solicitous and somewhat irritating, and she let him do it because evening was coming on and it was more proper for her to be seen in the company of a young man who was escorting her proper, and because Charles seemed to need it.

She certainly wasn't going to admit that she needed it, or that her stomach shook with nerves or that her heart, if it could have, would have pounded hard against her ribs. She was a newspaper woman, and this was a story.

She wouldn't let it be anything else.

Thirteen victims. Thirteen hearts. Cut out of victims and left crushed in pools of blood throughout Virginia City. Thirteen victims, the sheriff's wife and then 12 ladies of the night, good girls gone hungry or maybe looking to make some money quick as the men folk do and a man who's just struck a nice vein of silver can make a good companion for a night or two if a girl's not fussy. Thirteen girls, each one tiny as Nell, blond and hopeful and found dead with their hearts cut out.

First one just about three years ago, Dawson had said, and hadn't looked at a calendar of late, because it wasn't just about. It was three years ago. April 4, the snows still lingering on the Comstock, blood and mud and ice mingling with the clay of the mountain range and the muck that silver mining kicked up.

Three years ago, April 4, when Nell's father first brought her back from her uncle's house, alive but changed, the canister now a part of her life and Sheriff Martin Clyde not.

They'd had a year of courtship, of picnic dinners and horseback rides and leaked information because her father's newspaper quailed before the might of the Territorial Enterprise when that paper made its move from Genoa to Virginia City in 1860. A year when Martin Clyde's enormous shoulders and hands made her feel safe.

Then her heart had failed, the winter before their wedding,

and when Nell's father had brought her back from her uncle's house, alive but too entirely changed, Sheriff Martin Clyde was already married.

His wife had been found murdered on April 4. The day Nell would have married.

Three years ago.

Nell shuddered.

Charles took a more firm hold of her elbow and guided her past her own modest front door and into the newspaper offices two blocks away.

"Nelly, girl, your copy is late." Frank Osborne, striding through his offices, landed a kiss on her forehead and gave Charles the sort of uncertain smile he often favored the photographer with.

"You'll have it tomorrow morning, daddy," she said and headed for the kitchen in the back. As she heated salt water and reached cautiously back to disconnect the thin silver tubes and ease the canister and its straps from her shoulders, she could hear the two men in the newspaper offices, their voices rising and falling. Charles would tell her father about the sheriff on scene. He wouldn't mention a word of the rest until the two of them had proof.

She was grateful to the bottom of her little steampowered heart. Whatever else the sheriff might have done, he'd broken the heart of Frank Osborne's daughter. Nell needed proof that Martin Clyde had done anything worse than that, more proof than the coincidence of dates, and she didn't need her father in the middle of it.

Or her steampowered heart. For a few minutes a few times a day she could be without the weight of the canister on her shoulders, without the straps digging into her flesh. Her uncle had said her own heart might grow stronger with the assistance. So far, she'd been too afraid to test it.

Too afraid to be without the constant reminder of the device that kept her alive and kept Martin Clyde away from her.

Something started to make sense to her just then and Nell went still, vision blurring as she tried to chase down the thought.

But her real heart bumped unhappily and the water on the stove was at a boil. From the newspaper offices her father called goodbye and Charles was headed back her way. Nell let it go.

Darkness fell early in the Virginia City foothills in April. Outside dusk was heavy and gray as Nell finished her article. The names of the two men were still withheld because no one had given them to her yet, but the sheriff had come by briefly to make a statement so she wouldn't get it wrong. He didn't look at Nell but stared more or less at Charles' left knee while he stated the obvious: The two men, both in their 20s. A falling-out over a claim. An argument. A few shots of bourbon followed by two shots, one each, and each hit home.

"*That* quote I won't use," Nell said as the sheriff closed the door behind him and Charles, who refused to leave her alone with Clyde, grunted a vague response before he headed into his darkroom. His technique allowed him to leave the portable dark room on newspaper premises and create his images once they were back in the office.

Nell rolled a sheet of paper into the typing machine and pounded out the story of the miners on C Street. Even as she wrote, her mind refused to settle, fluttering from topic to topic, the waste of the young men who shot each other over a vein of silver when the next rich find might be right next to the one in contention, from that to the wasted lives of the young girls just trying to get ahead and survive any way they could, who sold their favors for enough money to live and eat (and here she thought Charles would snort derisively and point out a good many of those women made more money and lived better than either Nell or Charles).

And then she'd think again of what her future could have been if not for the rheumatic fever that had damaged her heart and she moved too fast and clanged the canister against the chair back.

For a few minutes then she didn't think of much of anything

at all, just watched out of the front window of the newspaper offices over the wooden sidewalks into the heavy, falling dusk, and wished.

<<>>

"You should put your canister back on," Charles said. His dark hair and eyes in the lamplight were warm and familiar. Sometimes Nell could almost imagine the two of them staying this way forever.

But she'd wanted more. A family. She didn't think Charles favored women.

"It's all right. I have time."

She glanced away from him, out the office window at the dark street. "I can't imagine being out there, alone, no one else to depend on. That would be enough without–"

She let the sentence drift away. It was Charles, characteristically blunt, who steered her back from suppositions about the poor lonely women and into the facts.

"You think it's the sheriff, don't you?"

Nell smiled slightly. She never had to pretend with Charles. "The murders started the day we would have wed, April 4. He was married before I came back to Virginia City–" She paused and simply waved her hand at the canister she hadn't reattached yet. "And his wife died–" *Under mysterious circumstances*, she wanted to say but didn't, and Charles knew it as well as she did anyway–"On the day that would have been our anniversary. The women are found with their hearts cut out." She stopped, and shrugged, though it didn't come off very well.

Charles gestured. "Please put it back on. I worry the whole time it's off."

Nell gave him a rueful smile. "I do have some time. It's all right. But I can. I will." And because it was Charles, she pulled the tank on, the elaborate baroque design only an irritant now. All the things her uncle could do–the recording devices so small that trapped human voices, the special press that combined typing machine with glass to project the page before it was typed.

But he couldn't *fix* her heart. Only augment it.

When she returned to the kitchen from assuming the canister, Charles met her eyes across the table, one hand stroking his goatee.

"You know what you're suggesting," he said, trying to make a statement, but it came out a question. No doubt the underlying question was, *Are you crazy?* Because nobody in Virginia City voluntarily took on Sheriff Martin Clyde.

Nell pursed her lips. "Just thinking through what Dawson said."

Charles was quiet then. He stood up and took his plate over to the sink. Nell, her stomach hot with nerves, abandoned her own plate and headed for the front office. She thought her heart might be beating faster. Despite the fact that it couldn't.

"It's a bad idea," Charles said, following her. Nell stood staring out at what was now uncompromisingly night.

"It's not an idea yet," she returned and he went away.

Thirteen girls in three years. It wasn't just the suspicions circumstances Mrs. Clyde had expired from. It was something about Martin Clyde himself.

"Even if you prove it, who are you going to prove it *to*?"

"U.S. Marshals," she said without turning from the window, as if she'd thought it though or discussed it with Dawson.

"Of course," Charles said, and disappeared into the darkroom again. Nell sighed and started making tea again, partly to top off her canister with hot water and partly because he'd be back momentarily: he'd already developed all the film for at least the last month.

"It's not at all a good plan, Nellie," he said when he poured the tea.

"It's not a plan," Nell said. "Just a general wondering. *Do* sit down to drink that, you're going to spill."

Charles, distracted, sat, then put the teacup down and sat staring at it. "We could photograph the two of you."

She didn't notice the sidelong look in time. "Exactly!" she said, and then, backtracking much too late, "Who said that I–"

"And use your uncle's invention to capture your conversation."

He leaned his cheek against one hand, watching her across the table.

"You're assuming that I–"

"Wear your heart on your sleeve," Charles said, with compassion in his voice that made her nervous.

"On my back, actually," Nell said, and saw Charles's expression change fast.

The U.S. Marshal Service in Carson City was manned by Rick Harding, tall, affable, fast on the draw. He had a relationship with the Osbornes because of the newspaper, and because he and Henry played chess when circumstances allowed.

He was also plainspoken. When she telegraphed the plan he sent back adamant refusal, questioned her sanity and threatened to tell her father.

"Running out of time," she sent. "Already April. Our wedding would have been April 4."

Long silence before the machine rattled a reply. "When and where?"

The weather turned overnight, a not-at-all-unnatural occurrence in Northern Nevada. Nell woke on April 4 panicky about what the day would bring and more panicky that it wouldn't. Spring meant drunk miners and drunk miners meant busy lawmen. If the sheriff couldn't meet her, the whole plan fell apart.

Not that there was much of a plan. Nell had sent a message to the sheriff, one so full of promises and suggestions it sounded as though Nell had joined the ranks of entertaining ladies. But she had to get him there somehow, long enough for him to see her.

"I don't get it," Charles had said the night before. "I'm sorry, Nell, but he left you and he's shown no interest in coming back." He looked earnest and guilty as if somehow responsible for this fact.

"You're right," she said, though her heart ached to say it. Martin Clyde wasn't the man she'd thought he was. But being thrown over because of her illness hurt her heart.

A tiny corner of Nell, one she'd never admit to, still hoped somehow that Martin Clyde would eventually see the girl with the steampowered heart was the girl he had loved.

She didn't look past that scenario, didn't admit the sheriff scared her now and that her wish was for him to come back was only because—

"I want to win," Nell said.

April 4 Nell left the newspaper offices just before noon. Outside the sky was endless and blue and the sun sharp on the melting slush that lined the streets. People brushed by her, a few friends and her great aunt, and none of them looked twice at her. Without the canister strapped to her back, she went unrecognized.

She felt light as a feather. She wore one of her beautiful older dresses, without the double button holes sewn carefully into the left breast to allow the silver tubes to snake out and back to the canister. The tubes she'd detached; there were only small silver connectors flush against her skin, barely a ripple under her blue calico dress.

She felt new and even the errand in front of her didn't daunt her until she drew close to the restaurant.

And then, as the restaurant appeared in front of her, the plate glass windows needing washing and the sun shining bright off them, the gingham curtains inside flung wide, her heart began to pound wildly and Nell stopped, leaning one hand against the support to the awning that covered the wooden sidewalk.

Flooded with dizziness, she stood uncertainly. Three years her heart had been controlled by the metal canister. She'd forgotten what it was like to feel so vulnerable.

But she'd reached the restaurant. Charles would be installed at a window table and if he saw her out here, leaning, panting, he'd be out the door before he even realized he'd ruined–well, what little plan they had.

She straightened. The dizziness backed down a little though not far. Nell took a moment to check her little round wrist bag, sliding her hand inside to wind the gear-driven recording device. The thing was tiny, and took impressions on thin sheets of hard beeswax inside. Once activated, she'd have very little time to capture the sounds around her.

Charles would be there, ready to get several pictures of Nell and the sheriff with a handheld camera.

The first would be the most important–the sheriff as yet unawares–but they'd all matter. Then the U.S. Marshal would step in, take the sheriff into custody and install Ben Dawson in his place.

It was the best plan they'd come up with. If only, Nell thought, she'd been able to figure out anything to say past, "Why did you kill all those women?"

Because the bad thing was the second half of that sentence was, "Who looked just like me."

Sheriff Martin Clyde sat toward the back of the restaurant with his back to the wall. A glance showed Nell a number of people having lunch, very few empty tables, Charles at a table alongside a window, one that allowed him to look over both south and west onto C Street and the east/west cross street. He'd no doubt seen her pause so she met his eyes and raised her head, all the while trying to keep the sheriff from noticing, though likely he had and come to think of it, wasn't it more strange if she didn't? She raised a hand to Charles, then made her way to Martin Clyde.

He stood to greet her, and Nell drew in a breath. She'd forgotten how tall he was, how broad and how frightening.

She'd forgotten the pleasure of watching his face when she walked into the room, the way his features just lit up, the way he watched her move, as if everything she did was just for him.

Sunlight coming in through the windows fell just short of the table where Clyde sat. When she stepped out of it she felt chilled.

The smile he greeted her with was purely predatory.

When she sat down across from him, it was the look in his eye that chilled her.

"Miss Osborne," he said, leaning forward as if he meant to take her hand. "Ne–" And broke off. He'd noticed. '

Her irresponsible heart began to pound.

He can't have missed that. I had it on yesterday.

The look in his eyes when she found the courage to meet them, said, *Nell. My Nell.*

That scared her more than anything.

From where Nell sat, Charles was slightly behind her. As she sat, she watched him in her peripheral vision.

He was, very slowly, making very, very tiny movements with his head.

Shaking his head.

Nell paused. Only for a fraction of a second, but Clyde would notice it. Clyde had always noticed everything.

She managed not to look directly from Charles to Clyde, to study the table briefly as if missing something. Her left hand stayed on her lap, fingers nervously running around the outside of the bag she held.

"How have you been, Sheriff Clyde?"

He gave her a self-deprecating smile. "Please, Nell, we were engaged."

"All right," she said. "Martin."

But what was Charles trying to tell her? And where was the U.S. Marshal who should have been there?

Heat ran up her back as those two questions met and connected. He hadn't come. Charles must have gotten word just before lunch, and Nell had been too busy with her preparations to check the telegraph machine.

One of the identical Morris girls came out of the back, carrying bowls of steaming stew, followed by her mother with beer and water and Nell chose the former. She couldn't quite get past the idea the water in Virginia City was full of things it shouldn't be, from the mining, or from the people or the plants or something. Her uncle was working on a system to filter large quantities, but until then she avoided the water unless it was boiled.

She had access to enough boiled water, anyway, and she put a hand up to her chest, not quite touching, but aware of her freedom from the tank, the straps, the connections.

The incredible weight of the steampowered heart.

"How have you been?" she asked Martin as the Morris's moved away.

He didn't answer. Instead he said, "It's good to see you, Nell," and sounded like he meant it. "You're looking–well." The pause gave her time to explain what had happened if she wanted to.

She didn't take it.

"And you," she said.

Martin looked around the room for a minute and Nell knew he already had pinpointed the position of everyone in the restaurant. Most especially Charles.

When he looked back at her, his face had gone hard. Nell slid her fingers inside her bag, found the switch on the recording device and pressed it.

The tiniest of metal snicks sounded as the gears met and began to pulse, sending messages to it to create a record on the sheets of wax.

"Why did you ask me to meet you here?"

That was the most obvious question and the one she hadn't been able to establish a rational answer for.

Except suddenly she did, and looked down at her bag, pulled it to table level, shoving her stew aside. The notebook, pen and ink came out. She left the bag on the table, closer to the sheriff.

"I need your help," she said, fountain pen poised over a sheet of paper. "Ever since the Territorial Enterprise came here with Twain writing his pieces which I swear are half lies–"

"Tales," the sheriff said. His voice was polite, light. His eyes were cold and dark.

Nell shrugged, showing disregard for the correction and showing off her canister-free shoulders. "My father's paper has been losing readers. I've been feeling so much better. I wanted to take on a project for our newspaper." She gazed at him. Did he know where she was going? "I was hoping you might have more information about the murders that you could share with me."

She looked very deliberately down at her food, because Martin Clyde had gone dangerously still as a sullen sky before the first lightning strike.

"Are you referring to the two gentlemen on C Street?" he asked in a voice that was careful and cold and offered no encouragement to anyone fond of living.

Nell waved a careless hand. It only trembled a little. If she wanted to get anything of value recorded, she had to make him angry.

It hadn't been that difficult to do in the past.

Perhaps she should have worn the canister after all.

"I'm sure everyone who has been in town for a day knows what that was about. No, I'm talking about the murder of the girl found behind the newspaper offices along the railroad tracks."

Behind her the door opened, cold spring air coming in and the sound of horses going by, and then it closed again. Clyde's eyes followed it, tracking the newcomer. Nell frowned at him, trying to convey an irritated newspaper writer after the sheriff's attention and a story, but she was relieved to see the gangling figure of the newcomer who sat down across the table from Charles.

Only Martin Clyde tracked it too. Harding was no stranger.

His attention turned back to Nell, too fully. "I gave your newspaper a statement on that case. The girl was–" He stumbled, and she imagined what he wanted to say but he almost covered, would have if she hadn't known him. "She was a young woman of ill repute. It is unfortunate that some women feel this is the only means they have to make their way in the world, but that is the truth of the matter."

It seemed to be the end of the matter too, because he turned his gaze to her again, looking down at her shoulders and nodding.

"You do look better, Miss Nell. Has there been some improvement?"

Would you want me back if there had been? She wondered, and was relieved to find the question was full of anger, not longing. When it came to her human heart, it was hard to predict what silly notions it might embrace. "Things have been going very well for me," she said, noncommittal, and then, because things had reached a turning point where they could either have lunch at the expense of everyone else's time and money, or she could press forward with what she thought she knew.

"The girl," she said, and saw his lips fold, thin with irritation. The subject was supposed to be closed. "She looked rather a lot like me. I'm sure you can understand how–"

"Yes," Martin Clyde said and looked at the U.S. Marshal sitting with Charles, apparently not listening to Nell and Martin.

Nell took a breath, noticed that her heart was beating much too quick and fast. Her freedom from the canister wouldn't last much longer. "What about the others?" Her hand was still poised over the paper she'd yet to make a single mark on.

"Did the others also look like me?"

The rage climbed up his face fast. His fists balled beside his plate. He leaned toward her, his eyes furious and, she thought, not quite sane.

"What. Do. You. Know?"

She flinched back away from him, but answered. "I know 13 women have died in three years. I know that your wife was the first and that no one in the territory has heard about the 11 between your wife and this woman."

She stopped and swallowed. Across the table from her Martin Clyde was a summer storm ready to strike.

"I know the murders haven't been reported. The undersheriff said it was because we need women to feel safe in Virginia City."

She looked hard at him. "That isn't the reason, is it?"

He got his breathing under control faster than she expected him to, but his hands remained fisted. He didn't lean back. His face filled her world. "Where is your heart, you freak? I fell in love with a lady who was not human and you dare to ask me what *I* have done?"

For the record, she felt like agreeing. And for the edification of the gentleman sitting with Charles over there.

Neither of them had stood but they were no longer looking away from Nell and the sheriff.

"What did you hope to gain from begging me to meet you, Miss Osborne? A story? A reconciliation? Did you think that coming here without that contraption I would be smitten anew?" He leaned farther across the table to her, enough for other diners to start to turn. "Did you think that you were the first?"

Nell sucked in a breath and coughed, a splintered feeling in her throat. Her heart still beat, too quick and hard, but comfortingly there. From across the saloon, she heard the sound of Charles' camera, documenting.

Clyde grinned at her and finally drew back across the table. People around them relaxed. Nell did not. She waited, trying to find a moment when she could stand, excuse herself and get away.

Martin Clyde stood first. His chair clattered over behind him. His revolver was in his hand.

Marshal Harding was on his feet. Charles had made it halfway across to her in a couple bounds.

Martin Clyde waved the pistol at both of them without bothering to look. "Sit down," he said. "Unless you want to get a photograph of this freak's innards now."

To Nell he said, "I cannot believe you would do this."

She closed her eyes. She couldn't believe what she was doing had gone so terribly wrong.

A wave of dizziness swept over her.

Not now.

"Get up," he told her and rounded the table to take her arm and drag her to her feet. "We're going for a walk. You wanted a story, and I am going to give you one."

Her heart lurched, like a trout on a line, and black spots filled her vision. Not now, she thought frantically, and scrabbled at the sheriff's arm to keep herself upright.

"I'm walking out of here," Clyde said. "If you want her to live, keep away from us."

It won't matter, Nell thought. It's me he's been killing and now he has access to the original.

All the access he could desire, to the heart he so hated.

He forced her onto the first stagecoach on the street, his gun shoving into her back as she scrambled from wheel axel across the driver's box up to the top. When the driver appeared, waving his arms, shouting at them both to stop, Clyde shot the man in the shoulder. Charles and the marshal had barely reached the door of the saloon when Clyde stung the horses into a gallop.

"Please," she said thickly. She lay sprawled across the luggage bar atop the stagecoach, panting from the climb, unable to quite sit up. Her damned heart wasn't steampowered. That's just what everyone thought, steampowered heart, toy girl, something unnatural. Her heart was flesh and blood muscle that no one could fix, a muscle damaged by rheumatic fever the winter before she would have wed. She was damaged. But she was human. Human enough that her heart had broken and all the steam power that pumped the blood and augmented her own failing heart couldn't change that.

Now that heart pounded in fear as Clyde whipped the horses, driving them hard. They cleared the edge of the city in minutes, heading for Gold Hill. He'd drive straight through it. Even if someone telegraphed ahead, no law would stop the sheriff of Virginia City.

Charles and the Marshal were behind them. Clyde had shot a man to steal his coach. She couldn't let Charles and Harding catch up. Through the dust behind the coach she could just glimpse them, some distance back, lost to sight as the dirt road twisted through Sierra foothills.

Her heart pounded, but the black spots had gone from her vision. Her breathing was no longer labored. Her fingertips didn't tingle from poor circulation.

For a breath Nell forgot about the sheriff and his murders, about Charles and the U.S. Marshal following. She forgot about the Colt revolver her ex-fiancé held. She marveled at her human heart, beating on its own.

It had before her uncle's invention, of course. But more weakly. Erratic.

She smiled. He'd told her maybe, if she was lucky, the steam canister might not just keep her alive. It might make her stronger.

Not free, maybe, but to spend time away from the canister, to sleep through a night without it attached? To be held, with no straps, no connectors, no leads?

Nell saw a future.

She wanted it.

Martin Clyde was going to kill her. He was going to kill Charles, who she loved and he was going to kill Nell, who suddenly thought she had a future even more worth struggling for.

She sat up. Behind them the dust clouds were mingling as the horses caught up with the coach.

She moved before she could think.

He'd thrown her across the top of the stagecoach and now he hovered over the driver's box, legs braced in the foot well as he drove the horses faster.

He hadn't noticed when she sat up.

Nell gripped the rail along the top of the coach, started wildly at the road and sage-covered hills, the sharp drops down to the mines. The landscape seemed to careen wildly toward them, as if the stagecoach wasn't moving but the land was. They hit a rock, and bounced, and she clung to the metal railing meant for lashing packages and luggage to.

Not now. She wasn't going to fall now.

The only weapon was the sheriff's gun, holstered as he

whipped the galloping horses.

Nell stared around in a frenzy, and her gaze went back to the sheriff and her breathing calmed again.

She couldn't get to the sheriff's pistol. But she could get to the sheriff.

And? Nell asked herself.

The only weapons available were the sheriff's pistol. And the ground.

He'll kill you, she thought. But that's what he meant to do, cut out her heart, because its failure had betrayed him.

As would its owner.

Ahead of them the rocky road curved sharply right. She saw Clyde brace himself, leaning back to the left. She launched herself, as if about to fly, and hit him from behind on the left side, coming at him where he didn't expect force.

For a sickening instant he didn't move though she could feel the shock and rage travel fast through his muscles, and then he tipped, started to catch himself, turned toward her and overbalanced. He'd spun until he faced her, falling backward, his legs catching the lip of the foot well. His fingertips just grazed the shoulders of her dress. If she'd worn the canister he'd have caught the straps and pulled her with him.

As it was, he grabbed her bag, buying another couple seconds until the ribbon that held the drawstring taut snapped from her wrist and the bag flew at him, along with the recording device and the beeswax record of what he'd done.

His mouth opened but he only made one short sharp sound of shock. The lip of the stagecoach caught him just below the knee. Nell caught her breath, because he balanced, impossible, for a long moment.

And then Sheriff Martin Clyde fell away.

She imagined she heard his neck break but she couldn't have, not over the pounding of the horses, the thunder of the wheels or the sounds of the men behind her catching up.

Not over the thundering of her own human heart.

Charles caught her as she jumped down from the stagecoach and found her liberty sharply curtailed. The black spots were back. Her legs went weak. She barely protested when her best friend kissed her.

She touched his face and waited for the world to fade.

It didn't.

<><>

Undersheriff Ben Dawson met them on the road back to Virginia City. He led a team of men and horses to bring back a body. The fact that the body was the sheriff's made him happy.

Charles rode back into town with Nell pressed against his chest on the horse. Her skin had gone pale but when she touched the pulse at her throat her heart beat steadily, only a few quick stray beats thrown in.

She was willing to bet those were on account of Charles.

In the kitchen behind the newspaper offices she heated water and once it boiled, sat staring with loathing at the canister and leads.

"Come on," Charles said. "You need to get back into it."

Nell looked at him. "I'm fine." She took a deep breath to prove it. If only she could stay this way. Human. Not a freak. If only—

"I think I can—"

Charles nodded, long brown hair and big brown eyes and every bit of him watching her. "You can. You will again. Just not right now. Now you let the steampowered heart do its work. We can listen to the recording if it still works." He held up her bag. "Your father will be back soon. I'm sure word has reached him."

That made Nell swallow. Father would not be pleased at such exploits.

"And I've seen you in your steampowered heart for years." He stood, drawing her up with him into his arms. "I'm not offended by it. You wear your heart on your back. I wear mine on my sleeve."

When she met his gaze, he kissed her, and Nell saw the future she'd fought for full of stories and printing presses, a steampowered heart, and Charles.

THE GOLDEN LARYNX

Ellen Denham

When my voice teacher, Melisande Rossi, died of a fever, the devotees of the Vyenne Opera were devastated, none more than myself. I was sixteen, and I must have cried every day for weeks. Never again would she perform the roles she had made famous: the exiled Queen of Athilan, the leopard-headed Goddess Nilah, the consumptive courtesan Maline, or the madwoman Carlotta.

She breathed her last on the very day she was to have originally appeared in the first opera to use the latest technology— the thunder run had been converted to steam power in order to increase the number of cannon balls that would run the length of the proscenium to produce sound for the storm scene. Her personal physician, Dr. Dulcamara, claimed he would preserve her larynx so that another generation of opera devotees might enjoy her dulcet tones. Though he had collaborated with Kapellmeister Heinz on building a steam-powered pipe organ, making a dead larynx sing was entirely different. Surely his scheme was an empty boast.

My mother was a costumer at the opera house, her eyes nearly gone bad from all the hand stitching until they bought her a new lockstitch machine from America. Mother had been close to Madame Rossi, which is probably the only reason the great diva had accepted me as a student. I was mediocre at best, with a smallish voice, but I had big dreams. My teacher was kind. When I asked if she thought I had the talent to be an opera singer, she always said, "We shall see, dear. The voice is still growing." She would purse her full lips and study me as if I were a painting on an easel. I always wished for lips like hers. "You do have a good sense of pitch. If you practice hard at reading music, you may be ready to sing for Herr Schmied this autumn. Perhaps he could use another soprano in the chorus. A couple of the ladies are getting on in years. Can you dance?"

To my young mind, this meant I was surely her anointed successor. I dreamed of having her teach me to perform that heart-wrenching operatic scream in Carlotta's death scene, just the way she had. I was almost as tall as Rossi, and found myself imitating her mannerisms. I began wearing my hair swept up and swathing my throat in gauzy scarves in imitation of my famous teacher, when I should have paid more attention to what she tried to teach me.

About a month after Madame Rossi's death, when the spring leaves were just beginning to show on the great plane trees outside the opera house's colonnade, my mother came home all a-twitter to tell me that Dr. Dulcamara would be performing a demonstration of his new invention that very evening for a select audience of patrons and financiers. He'd done it—he claimed that Rossi's voice would be heard again! I might have wondered if it was right to make a dead voice box sing, or perhaps I didn't think of it at all, caught up in ghoulish fascination. Mother and I rushed to the theatre and spied from the wings.

Several important-looking personages stood upon a bare stage, talking in low murmurs. Monsieur Chauvin, the old impresario who had run the opera house since my mother was young, said a few words, and the guests applauded politely. The doctor, a slight man with an impressive moustache, wheeled a golden cart onto the stage. Two people followed. First was Hans Braun, the symphony's timpanist, balding and red-faced. He winked at me. Second came Annelise Silber, who had been the first trombonist until a jaw injury from a carriage accident rendered her incapable of playing. Though she was a striking woman, her smile was now crooked.

Dr. Dulcamara spoke for a while, but I didn't listen. Madame Silber and Herr Braun stood a couple of steps behind him, looking important, though I hadn't guessed their purpose. I couldn't take my eyes off the golden cart. What did a larynx look like? I placed a hand upon my own throat and felt the bump of cartilage. How strange to think that part of Melisande Rossi was there, underneath the velvet cloth. If she were in heaven looking down, or a ghost floating about the opera house, what would she think?

"... encased, ladies and gentlemen, in a thin, flexible layer of pure gold, all except the vocal folds themselves, which must remain well-oiled..." The doctor removed the cloth with a flourish.

I leaned as close as I dared. A small, roughly triangular object of gleaming gold perched inside a glass canister with a tube descending from it into the cart. A bell, like a French horn's, made of rubbery-looking material extended from the top of the canister. I swallowed, aware of my own larynx as it bobbed up and down. A woman in the crowd fainted in a rustle of skirts and had to be carried past us by her escort.

"Miraculous!" My mother whispered, clutching my arm.

"... Herr Braun and Madame Silber have worked together all week to learn to operate this magnificent voice, and I think you will be pleased with the results." The doctor nodded, as if in agreement with himself. "As they continue their work, they will be able to perform more challenging pieces. But for today's demonstration, they will assist Madame Rossi in a performance of 'The First Blush of Springtime.'"

"Assist Madame Rossi?" my mother said. "How dare he—" She choked off the last word, silencing herself by force. Her fingernails bit into my arm. I knew what she must have been thinking. That golden object was not Madame Rossi. Imagining the doctor cutting into her throat, I felt a momentary wave of nausea and closed my eyes until it passed. Nevertheless, I wanted to hear the voice. I wanted it more than anything.

Herr Braun gripped a bellows on the side of the cart, and Madame Silber placed one hand on the bell. She was doing something with her other hand, perhaps manipulating tiny levers, but I wasn't close enough to tell. Their heads moved in time to an unseen beat, and then the first sound came forth, the lovely ascending scale I knew so well. "The First Blush of Springtime" was one of the first songs Madame Rossi had assigned to me. The voice sang without words, mostly on an "ah" vowel, though sometimes when Madame Silber squeezed the bell, it came out more like an "oo." The sound was unmistakably human, and sent the same vibrations through me that Melisande Rossi's voice had done when alive. I am certain that I wept. We all did, to hear a sound that might have been lost forever.

As mother and I clutched each other and dabbed our eyes with handkerchiefs, the doctor posed beside his invention for a photographer, a wide grin etched upon his narrow face. The acrid smoke of the magnesium flash drifted upward through the catwalks above the stage. The invited guests began to leave, murmuring excitedly. Franco Tomasi, the flamboyant tenor who had often performed opposite Madame Rossi, stormed past us, his coat extending on either side like bats' wings. "They've turned her into an organ pipe," he said to his companion. "I'm seeing my lawyer right now to make sure I sing my last note when I'm still alive."

I pulled my shawl around my shoulders, my desire to hear the voice now seeming morbid. The doctor had claimed that Rossi consented to this on her deathbed, but now I wondered. Would she really have wanted this? Would anyone?

Melisande Rossi's first role after her death was the one that had made her famous—the queen of Athilan; exiled for her dead husband's crime, though she herself was innocent. Opening night sold out within hours. The stagehands were used to having me watch from the wings, as long as I stayed out of their way. I had thought maybe they would dress an actress up to mime the role of the queen, while Herr Braun and Madame Silber rolled the cart behind her. But the cart itself was swathed in royal purple, and rolled about to the places on stage where Madame Rossi would have stood. Hans Braun simply wore his tails, and Annelise Silber, her black concert gown.

In the opening scene, when the maidens bring flowers to the queen, the cart was rolled center stage. All the chorus women curtsied before it, leaving silk blossoms at its wheels. Everyone sang and interacted with the cart as if it were a person. The sound that came from the golden larynx, though quite lovely, lacked the warmth and emotion for which Madame Rossi had been known. I missed hearing the words. Yet I supposed it was better than nothing, better than having that voice silent forever. I could imagine what she looked like singing the role—her tall figure robed in rich purple, her elaborate eye make-up, the sympathetic curve of her smile as she embraced the maidens. I had seen it many times, and had hoped to learn the role myself. No, that was frivolous dreaming. My high notes would never come close to the beautiful shimmering quality of hers. Finally, I closed my eyes and tried to see her in my mind as I listened.

"You must wonder how it works," a tobacco-scented voice whispered at my ear.

I opened my eyes to see Dr. Dulcamara standing beside me, his dark hair and moustache oiled.

"Are you an aspiring singer?" he asked.

"Yes," I said, and instantly thought I should have said no. "I mean, I had some lessons. With Madame Rossi."

"Splendid." He placed his hands together with the fingers steepled. "Then you will understand. Hans there controls the air pressure with the bellows. It's a difficult task. He can't just pump away like a choirboy at the pipe organ, but must deliver the precise amount of pressure at the right time. Like a singer would with his or her diaphragm. Do you follow me?"

He pressed a hand against my stomach, as Madame Rossi had often done when instructing me on breath control, but with him it felt much more awkward.

"Could it be controlled by steam power?" I asked, more to change the subject than out of curiosity. The steam-powered thunder run was not to be unveiled yet, so as not to compete with the doctor's marvelous machine.

"Of course not." Dr. Dulcamara removed his hand from my stomach. "A steam-powered organ works because the pressure is constant. Could you make a steam-powered tuba? No. It could not control the pressure as precisely as a player. At least not yet. Maybe someday."

Our conversation paused as we both listened to the climactic notes of the Queen's aria, after which the audience cheered and applauded vigorously. The curtain fell, and Herr Braun and Madame Silber rolled the cart past us offstage. The doctor took my arm and escorted me away from the stage, to make room for the scene change.

"A little more oil, there, Anna," Dr. Dulcamara said, as stagehands bustled past us wheeling the parts of the castle offstage and trees onstage for the forest scene. "The last note sounded a bit dry." He turned back to me with an exaggerated smile, revealing horse-like teeth. "Can you understand what Anna does with the bell?"

I pondered this. I had seen her use her hand to manipulate the flexible bell coming from the larynx, as one might change the shape of one's own mouth to alter the tone color.

"Placement of the tone," I replied.

"Very good," the Doctor said. "What about her other hand?"

I thought about it, but had to confess I did not know.

"I didn't expect you would," he replied. "Most singers have little idea what goes on inside their throats. She manipulates the tension of the vocal folds, using specially designed slides to change the position of the cartilages. This controls the pitch."

I nodded. "That's a little like what she used to do with her trombone," I said.

"Clever girl!" Dr. Dulcamara took my hand and pumped it up and down excitedly. "If you don't succeed in singing, I may have a job for you, later on. The great singers can't live forever. Don't you think Franz is looking a little peaked?"

Herr Franz was the baritone, famous for playing villains like the Queen's deceitful older brother. He stood in the wings downstage from us, bouncing on the balls of his feet with his arms clasped behind him as he waited for his entrance. Though well into his sixties, he looked perfectly vigorous to me. My skin prickled as I understood what the doctor was suggesting. Perhaps I didn't have the talent to be a singer, but I might yet have a stage career, pulling slides and playing someone else's voice.

I drew myself up to my full height, almost even with the

doctor, and did my best imitation of Madame Rossi's haughty glare. "I aspire to be a singer."

"Do you, now." The doctor looked me up and down through narrowed eyes, as if taking my measure for a dress. "A thought just occurred to me..." He waggled a finger at me, mouth open as if intending to say more, but just then, the whir of a pulley signaled the curtain rising on scene two. The orchestra launched into the villainous brother's theme. The doctor rested a hairy hand briefly upon my arm. "I must get Madame Rossi ready for her next scene. Find me in the green room at intermission."

I tried to tell myself that I was silly to be afraid of Dr. Dulcamara, but I couldn't help imagining him with Madame Rossi's dead body, cutting into that white throat. Still, I was curious enough to seek him out. The green room was full of black-clad orchestra players clumped in groups like crows, and the chorus of soldiers, cheeks rouged, some still waiting to be wigged. My mother would usually have been in Madame Rossi's dressing room changing her costume, but I wasn't sure where she was now. Dr. Dulcamara stood in the corner with his back to me, talking to Monsieur Chauvin. The impresario was a little man, stooped with age, but his piercing blue eyes missed nothing. I was still half afraid of him since he had caught me climbing on the tower from the Act I set of "The Prophetess." That had been years ago; I wondered if he remembered.

"You mean Leonora's girl, don't you?" Monsieur Chauvin said to Dr. Dulcamara.

Leonora was my mother. I didn't catch the doctor's reply. I shrank back a step.

"She has the height and the coloring," Monsieur Chauvin said, "but I wonder, can she handle—" his eyes fell on me. "Lilli, come here. We were just talking about you."

He remembered my name! I approached, timidly. "Hello, sir."

"You studied with Madame Rossi, is that correct?" he asked.

"Yes sir."

"Stand up straight, girl, and let me look at you!"

I did, and he adjusted his spectacles on his beak of a nose and squinted up to look at me. When had I gotten so tall?

Dr. Dulcamara's lips twitched up beneath his moustache. "Didn't I tell you? Tall as Rossi, and since she studied with her, she could certainly copy some of her mannerisms."

Monsieur Chauvin snapped his gnarled fingers at me. "Cast your eyes heavenward, and place a hand on your bosom, like Rossi as Maline."

Maline was one of the roles I longed to perform, with the sustained high note at the end, just before the courtesan succumbed to her illness. I did my best impression.

"Good. Now, the queen ordering her maidservants away. No, extend your arm more forcefully. There. That's it."

The old man put me through a few more poses, then chortled like a little boy and clapped his hands together. "Marvelous! I think I can use you. See me tomorrow morning to discuss the terms of the contract."

"Thank you, sir," I said to his back as he and the doctor walked away, through the sea of instrumentalists. Dr. Dulcamara turned and winked at me.

"But," I said to no one, "you haven't heard me sing."

Of course they didn't want me to sing. At first, I didn't want any part of it. But my mother "talked sense into me," as she called it, and coached me so I knew what to ask for when negotiating the contract.

"Think of it as an opportunity to learn the business," she said. "Make sure you get voice lessons as part of the deal. If you can already act the roles, you can keep working on learning how to sing them."

Mother insisted on coming with me. She was dressed far too flamboyantly, in a ruffled purple gown and matching hat, and had me wear a blue silk gown that had belonged to Madame Rossi.

It was way too loose, but she'd taken in the bodice and added one of the new exaggerated bustles to round out my adolescent figure. I wore my hair piled high on my head, like the great diva herself.

My footsteps and my mother's were silent upon the plush rug in Monsieur Chauvin's upstairs office. Though I'd practically grown up in the opera house, I'd never been inside this room. One wall was nearly filled with tall windows, letting in the morning sun to make sharp angles on the floor. Bookshelves filled the opposite wall, above which hung paintings of the earlier opera stars and daguerreotypes of the more recent ones, like Rossi. The impresario sat behind a massive mahogany desk; Dr. Dulcamara sat in a straight chair to his right. I wished the doctor wasn't there. Perhaps he expected a commission for discovering me.

"It's good to see you." The skin around Monsieur Chauvin's eyes crinkled into tiny pleats as he stood to take my hand. "We'll go over the contract, and I think you will be pleased."

I sat with my hands in my lap and listened as he read the terms. I'd be an apprentice artist for two months, paid at the usual rate, and given instruction in dance as well as private coachings with Monsieur Chauvin himself, to learn to act the roles Madame Rossi had performed. If I proved satisfactory, I'd be hired on as a regular company member, though paid at the rate of comprimaria rather than lead roles.

"This seems fair," Monsieur Chauvin said, "as you will not actually be singing the roles."

"She will need voice lessons," my mother chimed in before I could speak.

"You understand," Dr. Dulcamara enunciated as if explaining to someone who was stupid, "that she won't be singing the roles?"

"If I am to mime the roles, I need to be able to sing them," I said, surprising myself with the firmness in my voice. "I need to know how much breath each phrase takes, and how to shape the vowels, to better look as if I am singing."

Dr. Dulcamara grinned like a shark. "Didn't I tell you she was clever? Of course she should have voice lessons. Do you suppose Madame Abendroth might come out of retirement to teach her, considering the unusual circumstances?"

I gasped. Madame Abendroth had been Rossi's own teacher, a formidable woman known mostly as the composer of "Lady of Sorrows," about the heroine Carlotta's descent into madness. Carlotta was Rossi's first leading role.

The doctor leaned expectantly toward the impresario, eyebrows raised. I wasn't sure why he had taken such an interest. Having me mime the roles would take attention away from his invention, wouldn't it?

Monsieur Chauvin drummed his fingers upon the table, his mouth pressed into a flat line. "The circumstances are unusual, to be sure. I will speak with Madame Abendroth."

Not a week later, everything was arranged. I'd never before been so fussed-over: private coachings with Monsieur Chauvin, daily ballet lessons (I was terribly inflexible, but was told I "moved well"), and lessons with Madame Abendroth on Tuesdays and Thursdays. She terrified me.

Dr. Dulcamara escorted me in his own carriage to my first lesson with her. I wanted to flinch from his hand on my arm, but I didn't dare. I prayed that he wouldn't try to take any indecent liberties, and wondered what on earth I would do if he did. Thus far, he had been a gentleman, but I still didn't relish being alone with him.

A maid let us in. Madame Abendroth's drawing room was filled with ancient, yellowed lace, adorning the mantel and the piano. Small, round doilies draped over the backs of chairs. The grand dame hefted her considerable bulk from an upholstered chair to cross the room. She peered at me through small spectacles. Her face wasn't as lined as I would have expected of a woman who had to be at least seventy.

"Hmm, well. What have you prepared, child?"

"I can sing 'The First Blush of Springtime,'" I said.

"Very well," she said, gliding to the piano bench. I had

never seen such a large woman move with such grace.

My voice shook as I sang for her. I was constantly aware of the doctor's gaze. He sat, chin in hand, his eyes intent, examining me like a specimen.

"It's not much of a voice," Madame Abendroth said as soon as I stopped singing. "But your intonation is good. That is something to work with."

Dr. Dulcamara practically leapt from his chair. "No need to worry about the tone quality, Madame. Work with her on placement and support, and the tone will take care of itself."

She peered at him over her spectacles. "I believe I know more about vocal technique than you, young man."

I nearly snickered to hear her call him "young."

"Please keep quiet while we work, or you may wait outside."

Dr. Dulcamara kept very quiet after that. The first thing Madame Abendroth did was to make me hold a rope with both hands while I vocalized. "Plant your feet, girl, and don't move." She pulled the other end, hard, and I nearly lost my balance. "Hmmm. Melisande didn't teach you a thing about support, did she?"

After two months of hard work, Monsieur Chauvin deemed me ready to perform the role of Carlotta. "You have that desperate, mad look down so well. Never forget how much one can convey with the eyes." He tapped a finger to the wrinkled bag beneath his own eye.

I found it fitting I should perform Rossi's first leading role, but I'd always hoped to sing it, not simply mime and mouth the words with her larynx traveling behind me on the stage. Not that acting the role wasn't challenging—I had never realized how much went into an opera besides singing. I couldn't let my concentration slip for an instant.

I was nervous before my first entrance, when Carlotta is seen visiting her mother's grave. But once I got out on stage, I relaxed into the role, moving to the sound of Madame Rossi's voice behind me. Yes, the cart was still quite visible on stage, which must have pleased Dr. Dulcamara, but his reasoning made sense. Herr Braun and Madame Silber needed to see my movements in order to coordinate the sound. I had grown accustomed to taking exaggerated breaths that they could see, as if I were really about to sing. The storm at the end of scene one shook the stage with the rumble of cannon balls traversing the thunder run overhead. The steam power had at least doubled the effect, making the audience murmur and gasp. I did not have to pretend to be frightened when the storm scares Carlotta away from the grave—I half expected a bolt of lightening to split the stage.

In the last scene of the opera, wig disheveled and my body draped in artfully arranged burlap, I mimed and mouthed the lyrics to Carlotta's last aria. I longed so much to sing along with Madame Rossi's larynx that I think I did sing a few notes, very softly, an octave lower, before I caught myself. As the last note died away, I held aloft the shining knife to plunge it into my midsection. The knife, of course, retracted—simply an illusion. My tears were real. I had performed my first leading role in an opera, without singing a note.

My performance, along with that of Madame Rossi's larynx, received rave reviews. I couldn't have been more miserable, though perhaps I should have appreciated the opportunity for what it was. I was determined to prove to Monsieur Chauvin that I could sing the roles. Even if I wasn't ready to sing Carlotta, or the Queen, surely I could be the maid who sings a short aria in Act I of "The Exile of Athilan." It didn't go too high.

For an entire season, I mimed the roles that Madame Rossi had sung. People came from all over to see the performances, though I knew they weren't coming to see me. Everyone was curious about Madame Rossi's larynx, singing on after her death. I was just window-dressing. Spring became summer, and then the leaves on the plane trees at last began to wither as autumn breezes came from the mountains. I sang on my own time and during my lessons with Madame Abendroth.

Dr. Dulcamara often accompanied me to my lessons, and encouraged me even when Madame didn't. Quite possibly, I had misjudged him. I begged him to speak to Monsieur Chauvin on my behalf, to arrange for me to sing for the impresario. At last, Chauvin agreed.

Madame Abendroth was skeptical. "I'm not sure you're ready."

"When do you think I'll be ready?" I asked.

She pursed her lips, considering. "Well, frankly, never. I suppose now is as good a time as any."

Her words stung, but I was determined to prove her wrong. I could sing, and I knew it.

Dr. Dulcamara came with me the morning of my audition, offering words of encouragement before I walked out onto the empty stage. I was nervous, but by then I'd learned how to appear calm. Herr Schmied accompanied me on the piano. Monsieur Chauvin and Dr. Dulcamara sat a few rows back, to hear how my voice handled the acoustics. Only a few lamps burned, so I couldn't even see them.

"You may begin," Chauvin's voice boomed from the darkness.

I sang the maid's aria, which suited my voice "as well as anything," Madame Abendroth had said. "Though you're too tall for the soubrette roles," she always added. I sang my heart out, concentrating on everything I had learned. When I finished, the sound of one person applauding filled the empty house. I imagined it was Dr. Dulcamara and not Monsieur Chauvin. I waited on the stage until both of them came up to greet me.

"Marvelous!" Dr. Dulcamara approached first, across the bare stage, waving his hands in the air, as he did when excited. "You're supporting the sound much better now." He flashed a toothy grin.

Monsieur Chauvin followed behind, frowning, looking more stooped than ever. I hadn't impressed him.

"Are you sure you're ready for this?" he asked.

"Of course she's ready," Dr. Dulcamara said, taking my arm. "We can proceed as planned, can't we?" He squeezed my arm, hard.

"Yes," I said, unsure what I was agreeing to.

Chauvin's eyes narrowed. "She doesn't know. You haven't told her, have you?"

"We have an agreement," Dr. Dulcamara said. "You can see how hard she's worked for this. She'll be able to support it now."

My stomach sank. Dulcamara's grip on my arm was so firm I was sure he'd leave bruises. What was I missing?

"Come along, Lilli," Dr. Dulcamara said. He turned me, firmly, and we began to walk into the wings.

"Wait," I said, but he only walked faster, and I stumbled along beside him.

"Don't destroy everything we've worked for," Monsieur Chauvin called after us. "The operation is far too risky."

I grew cold all over, and swallowing, felt my larynx move.

"Meddling old fool," Dulcamara said, practically dragging me. "If you trust me, you'll have the career you've always wanted."

But he had lied to me. Now he meant to... Holy Mother of God, he was going to implant Rossi's larynx into me!

"No," I said with all the force of my training with Madame Abendroth. I spun counterclockwise and lurched away. He pitched forward, losing his balance as he lost his grip on my arm. I ran down the stairs, into my dressing room, and shut and locked the door behind me. Panting, I lit a lamp with shaking hands. The gaslight illuminated all the accoutrements of my profession—my make-up kit sitting beneath the mirror; all the costumes for the role of Maline hanging on a rack, from the opulent Act I dress to the Act III plain dressing gown; faded flowers and notes from admirers; a few photographs of me with the other cast members—the real singers. Madame Rossi's larynx had its own dressing room, next to mine, but a drawing of her in full leopard make-up for the role of Nilah hung above my mirror. Nilah would be my next role, in the spring. How I longed to put on the leopard headdress and sing—

And sing. My hands trembled as I raised them to my throat. Chauvin would never let me sing the role with my own voice. Perhaps with Rossi's larynx, I could. My breathing quickened; I sank into my chair. I closed my eyes and tried to imagine her voice coming out of my mouth. All along, I'd emulated Rossi. Could I turn down a chance to become her?

The key turned in the lock. Damnation! The doctor had a key to Rossi's dressing room; it must fit my lock as well. I saw him in the mirror even before I had the chance to turn around.

"Ah, Lilli, I thought I'd find you here." He stood in the doorway, all smiles, one arm behind his back. "Can't we talk about this?"

I rose from the chair. I wanted to tell him I'd think about it, maybe ask a question about whether it was safe, but I knew what he'd reply.

"I need to talk to my mother," I said, pushing past him.

He seized me and pressed a strong-smelling cloth to my face. I thought I'd suffocate. I struggled for a moment to stay conscious, tried to plead, but to no avail. He'd never intended to give me a choice. My last half-formed thought as I lost consciousness was a goodbye to everything I had known. I didn't expect to survive the operation.

The next thing I knew, I was lying down, groggy, with a head that felt swollen as a balloon. My fingers brushed the surface of plush upholstery beneath me. The memory of what had transpired crept slowly into my consciousness, and I raised a hand to my throat. Nothing seemed amiss. I cleared my throat and hummed a soft note. No, my voice was my own.

"She's awake!" My mother's voice.

I opened gummy eyes to see her approach and take my hand. Monsieur Chauvin sat in a dark velvet chair at my feet. Waning light made narrow rectangles on the floor. I recognized the room—I lay stretched out upon the couch in Chauvin's office.

Mother clasped my hand and kissed it, and began to sob quietly.

"What happened?" I asked.

Monsieur Chauvin replied. "I was afraid he would try to force you. Tomasi was just arriving for a wig fitting, and I enlisted his help. When the doctor tried to carry you from the opera house, Tomasi was waiting. He overpowered the doctor and brought you here."

The tenor was a big man; I could easily imagine him besting the doctor. I hoped Tomasi had punched him in that ugly grin. I wished I had done so myself.

"Will the doctor be arrested?" Mother asked.

"No," Chauvin replied. "I don't want to involve the police."

I pushed my mother's hand away and sat up, which made me dizzy. "You knew what he was planning." I stabbed a finger in Chauvin's direction.

He spread his hands. "I owe you an apology. I knew, but I had cautioned him against it. I was afraid it could damage both Madame Rossi's glorious instrument, and of course, you. I thought you wouldn't consent, and didn't expect he would force you, unwilling."

I sighed and sank back down upon the couch. Mother brushed my hair from my forehead. "What now?" I asked.

"I'm afraid I have to let you go," Chauvin said, his brow furrowed. "I'm sorry."

I clenched my hands into unladylike fists. He'd let me go, but he'd keep Dulcamara and his cursed invention, because that sold tickets.

"What am I to do now?" I asked. To my shame, tears welled up in my eyes. I turned my face to the wall.

"Your voice is really too small for opera," Monsieur Chauvin said. He rested a hand on his chin, considering. "You might be an actress. You have a real talent for interpreting a role."

"No," I replied. I'd been to the theatre once, and it bored me. I had no interest in people walking about on stage and gesticulating at each other, their voices unmelodic rather than soaring above a full orchestra. This was what I loved most of all: the sound I'd taken for granted for most of my life. And now I had to leave it.

I began to weep in earnest. Monsieur Chauvin politely left me alone with my mother until I felt well enough to go home.

It's been ten years since I left the opera house, vowing never to return. I married a wealthy dairy farmer who was enchanted by my brief celebrity. We live in a remote, mountainous province, and I never accompany him when business takes him into Vyenne. The people in the village believe I was a famous singer, no matter how many times I've told them I didn't actually sing the roles. Finally, I stopped trying to explain. After many pleas, I began to sing in the parish choir. The Kapellmeister never complains that my voice is too small. Village women bring their daughters to me to teach. My studio has photographs on the wall of me in costume as the Queen of Athilan, Carlotta, and the other roles I mimed but never sang. I do my best to teach the girls what I learned from Madame Rossi and Madame Abendroth. A few of them are doing quite well. I've even begun to compose an opera of my own, though I don't know if I'll ever show it to anyone.

Madame Rossi's larynx had a short career. The day after I left the opera house for good, a fire in Rossi's dressing room destroyed Dulcamara's invention. Mother discovered the fire. No one suspected that she had set it, or that she did so in order to cover up another crime. The larynx was presumed destroyed, but it actually left the opera house at the same time I did, concealed in a hat. If the key to Rossi's room fit mine, I reasoned correctly that the opposite must be true. I intended at the time to sneak out some night and bury the larynx with the rest of her, where it belonged, but, strange as it may sound, I can't bear to part with it.

If given a choice, I think I would have ultimately rejected the surgery. The risk was too great. How ironic that even now,

I can't escape the lie I lived for a few months in my youth. "There's Lilli Bourdon, the famous singer!" Sometimes I wish I hadn't been rescued. If I were going to be known as a singer anyway, regardless of anything else I ever do, shouldn't I have enjoyed a real singing career? Every now and then, I close my eyes and imagine her voice coming out of my mouth, and I want it more than I've ever wanted anything.

Now, Mother says, the same people who crowded the opera house to hear Madame Rossi's larynx say that what the doctor did was monstrous and should never have been permitted. Monsieur Chauvin died of pneumonia that winter, and the new director insists that any singer performing a role must be alive and intact. Dr. Dulcamara left the country, and the last anyone heard, he was working on an invention he called an "extra lung," for singers to tap into when they ran out of breath.

I keep the larynx in a mahogany jewelry box with a découpage photograph of Rossi on the lid. The gold leaf is mostly worn off the voice box now. Sometimes I take the miraculous relic out and hold it. I don't dare manipulate the fragile cartilages to change the pitch, but if I blow through it, the larynx still emits a faint sound, like a dying whimper. For good or ill, I feel eternally linked to this remnant of my great teacher. I'll never know who I really am, or who I might have become.

THE HONOR OF THE FERROCARRIL

Sylvia Kelso

As the *Internationale* pulled out of La Paz station, the man at the window beside Concepçion Gonzaga leant over and made a proposition that took her breath away.

"Beautiful senora, permit my little bat to share your room tonight, and I will see you attain immortality."

The locomotive blew pressure for the first zigzag up to El Alto, a blast of steam that blotted the view and drowned human chatter; but not his urgently muttering voice.

"A very little bat, senora, his wings cannot span my forearm, very rare and very precious. He came to me on the Altiplano, alone, solitary, unique. I must carry him safe to Arequipa. If you permit him in your cabin, senora, only tonight..."

Concepçion got out the first word she found.

"What?"

"My bat, senora. My little, little, precious bat." Anxious eyes squinted down at her from a seamed, Indian-dark face. Full Aymara, or even Uro, she classified automatically, from round Lake Titicaca. Guaqui, by the colors in his serape. "Only the one night, I swear to you." His hair trailed lankly over a high forehead sheened with oil or sweat. "And I promise, I promise, immortality–" The reek of coca leaves breathed through his yellowed teeth.

Concepçion withdrew her head and said crisply, "My soul is already immortal, if I heed the priest. But what is this of the bat?"

The locomotive braked to reverse for the switch-point to the zigzag's second leg. The man looming over her wrung his hands.

"They will not permit him in the carriages, senora, and I cannot uncage him in the luggage van. He must stretch his wings, could you travel five hundred miles with your arms bound down? You are a great lady, I hear them speak of you. The Cuzco line-chief's wife, good-hearted as her husband, and he the best foreman on the Ferrocarril. The governor has a stateroom. El Presidente del Ferrocarril has a stateroom, all the honorable senores of La Paz have staterooms. And you, you have a stateroom. Of your mercy, this one small favour. Only this one night."

He was tall for an Indian, almost skeletal under the serape. Concepçion stared up at him and saw instead Edouard's narrow black eyes, his sudden smile, the deceptively flamboyant sweep of his moustache. Yes, she thought. After thirty years, Senor Meiggs' Southern Peru Railway is finally open, clear from La Paz to the sea. For this inaugural journey, I have first class passage, in honor of Edouard. Who, on the face of those perfidious Andes just below La Raya, was kind once too often. And some lazy, stupid ganger's mistake cost him his life.

But if Edouard had been kind, he was also nobody's fool.

"Senor," she said, "it is true, all the fine senores of La Paz have staterooms. For such a recompense one will doubtless favor you. I am a widow, of no great rank. But my honor demands that, even for immortality, such an offer I must decline."

She stepped back, past his shoulder, away from the window where the hewn side of the second incline was sliding past, and without looking the other way to the magnificent vista of green-patterned La Paz valley, with the white city at its heart and Illimani's sugar-crystal snows above, she went into the stateroom Edouard had earned her, and closed the door.

Four hours later she stopped staring at the bleak tan and treeless vistas of the Altiplano, and began to doff her good navy suit. As the first twilight dimmed Sorata and Illimani's receding peaks, the major domo, murmuring mechanically, "An honor," ushered her into the dining car. Eyeing the vista of glistening silver, crystal and white tablecloth beyond him, she braced herself for the doubtless endless orations ahead.

Her three table-companions bowed her into a chair and forgot about her. Upper-level office people, she judged, from Lima, perhaps. Criollos, by their almost arrogant confidence, maybe with an actual Spanish Peninsular ancestor only a generation back. But they mentioned Don Enrique Meiggs with nostalgic approval too. They even drank an impromptu toast as Lake Titicaca glinted briefly under a sunset-filled sky. "A man whose visions endure, five years into this new century. And humane beyond parallel!"

Too humane, Concepçion retorted silently, smoothing the high lace tucker of her best grey silk. If Don Enrique knew enough to hire Edouard, he was far too gentle with those Chilean rotos, not to mention Chinese coolies, that he used to build his tracks. Whose clumsy stupidity at a landslide–

She stopped herself with the harshness of long experience. Now the others were laughing about the "loco hombre Indios."

"Special, precious, unique, forsooth! If 'tis so small, the thing is only another vampire bat! Found it battening on his cattle, and persuaded himself t'is a hudu–or a brujo itself!"

"Ha ha! And how does he think to feed it, on such a train as this? A freight now, with a couple of cattle-cars–"

"Oh, have no concern, senores. He will call manna from heaven–thus anyone kind enough to house his bat is sure of immortality!"

The locomotive whistled for a siding, a long, long, wail that rose to an ear-shrilling scream. As points clacked and whitewashed adobe houses slid past Concepçion said carefully, "So, senores. Did all decline his offer, then?"

They met her eyes from sheer surprise. Then all three pomaded, mustachioed, evening-dressed dandies seemed to lose their tongues. Not merely embarrassed, or surprised, or even scandalized. Perhaps, she wondered, a touch of fear?

So the Indian had disturbed them too.

Then the man opposite exclaimed, "Dios mios, did you hear that whistle? One of the new Baldwin locomotives. Eight drivers, amazing traction. And the whistle, it was never done before–the whistle climbs a scale!"

"Never before, probably never after." The man beside Concepçion laughed. "Though they say its top note outdoes La Melba's best–"–"No, no, La Melba is a lyric soprano, amazing high range, but this whistle can span *six octaves!*" But the first speaker had risen at the official table, and Concepçion braced herself.

When she felt it acceptable to slip away, the third speaker had concluded, and the dining car was a glittering bubble afloat on the Altiplano's dark. Easing into the dimmed connection-tube, she chided herself: you are the widow of a line foreman, gone these twenty years. Why should these *manos blancos* recall a forty-year-old relict like you?

So how, she wondered suddenly, did the Indian know?

She released the Patent Steam-Pressure Door Seal Don Enrique had required for all his trains. *Powered by steam, yes,* Edward fulminated in her ear, *but what when the steam stops?* Then she stepped into the first-class car and voices hissed, "Senora, por favor!"–"Senora Gonzaga, venga por aqui!"

Only the shadowy blue of Southern Peru Rail uniforms persuaded her to comply. They were huddled at the further car end, and the closer she came, the more their postures, their anxious dancing motions, alarmed her in turn. Halting short of the last stateroom, she said, "Senores?"

Their stances relaxed. They came to her with careful celerity. "Senora," the taller one bowed hurriedly, "as a favor, we ask, we beg for your advice."

"There is a–a situation." The shorter man gestured back up the train. "All the Ferrocarril officers are at dinner, the guard, the major domo, are inside or beyond the dining car–but something must be done!"

"Why," Concepçion asked blankly, "come to me?"

"But senora!!" Hands flew up. "You are of the Ferrocarril–Senor Gonzaga's wife! And he said, he always said, his wife was very–very wise."

In the half-light Concepçion could barely catch the liquid glint of eyes, but something about their manner, the entire situation, prickled her spine. Why should she be counted wise?

Did they believe she was like her grandmother?

"Senores," she said abruptly, "do you think me a bruja?"

"No, no, senora, never, never, we crave your pardon, no-one thought of such a thing. But Edouard–Senor Gonzaga always said–you were very wise."

They stared then in a silence that drove her brain into its highest gear. A situation, what situation would leave seasoned rail-crew paralyzed? What situation could demand a higher ranking decision, from anyone who would serve to make it–even a dead foreman's wife they half-feared was a witch?

The train blew for a crossing and the rumble of tracks jerked her back to life. They were approaching Guaqui. The rising panic in the men's movements insisted on action, now, but it need only be a stop-gap, until the station, until someone else could take command.

"Show me," she said.

The body lay on its back in the second-class galley entrance, sprawled like a broken sack of potatoes. Loose trousers, fawn workman's shirt, a disordered serape. Second or third-class passenger, Concepçion guessed; young, by the shape. The arms had fallen wide, one leg was drawn up. She had time to see the black substance pooling widely round the left shoulder before the stench struck.

"Phew!"

Concepçion had been at deathbeds, had coped with the details dramatic novels carefully left out. But no deathbed had brought a stench like this.

Then she identified its source.

"What is that round him? That black stuff?"

"We do not know, senora!" Both men recoiled from her. "We have never seen such, such... But senora." The taller man produced a cumbrous electric torch, almost as long as his arm. "That is not–all."

The light flowed up over the body. Boots, legs, torso, chest, the serape dragged aside, the shirt torn or opened loose, the throat.

"Madre de Dios." Concepçion had crossed herself before she thought.

The wounds were shadowed deep as bullet-holes in the slanted glare. Two of them: perhaps the size of a peso, her appalled mind assessed, ragged-edged and sunken each side the jugular vein, as if some giant beast had bitten and sucked–

A giant version, some tiny crazy voice commented, of the bites left on a cow's skin by a vampire bat.

How does he think to feed it, on such a train as this?

Concepçion shook herself all over and administered the mental equivalent of a ringing slap.

"Get a blanket. A tablecloth. Something. Cover him up." First makeshift measures, to keep unexpected witnesses under control. "At Guaqui, someone must–see to this."

The train called another crossing, wailing like a sundered spirit, crossing with a jolt and shudder over points. At her side the two men wavered but did not move. When Concepçion turned in surprise one jerked into speech.

"Senora, he is only a, a peon, a third-class passenger, we thought–perhaps–for the honor of the Ferrocarril..." The torch wobbled. "We are not yet in the town. If he were lost. If he fell from the door. From a window."

"No-one may know him," the other chimed in. "No-one would think: the train. Nothing would involve the *Internationale*–"

Something fiery rose behind Concepçion's eyes. The words were in her mouth before she thought. "*This* you call the honor of the Ferrocarril?"

Both of them flinched.

"Put that away." The torch went hastily off. "Get a blanket. One of you stay here to keep–others out. If they leave the dining car before Guaqui, advise the major domo. The guard. Otherwise, at the station. The *honor* of the Ferrocarril demands that this be explained."

<>

Eduoard would never have permitted it, Concepçion fumed, bundling her belongings for transfer to the Titicaca ferry. Not the merest peon would he see shuffled off like rubbish, with such a calamity unexamined, such a threat to others left untouched. Honor of the Ferrocarril, hah!

And why do we not disembark?

The Guaqui platform stretched left and right, stark in electric glare, desolate. New passengers boarded at the ferry-wharf, but station and engine crew should have been swarming to collect luggage, tend the locomotive, meet passengers pouring bee-like from the train itself.

You have done what you could, Concepçion argued, perching at the stateroom window with a book. Doubtless they signaled ahead, once senior officials heard. The porters will have been kept back, the train attendants stopping passengers on board. They will be waiting for the Guardia Civiles, a doctor, to examine the dead. Edouard had been a rapacious reader on his rare leaves, delighting in the exploits of the English detective, Sherlock Holmes. She knew all about murder procedures, in theory at least.

Two minutes later she put the book down. It can do no harm, she told herself, to look.

The first-class exit was indeed guarded, but Concepçion was going past. Lights glared from the second-class galley-car, daubing the platform beyond the open exit door. She heard the clash of voices from the connection-tube, even before she emerged upon a wall of backs.

"... should have been put overboard at the first!"

"And I tell you again, it is too late!"

"Imbeciles! Idiots! Had you acted with initiative–"

"Forget *then*–we must do something now!"

"Then do it! Get the thing away–a laundry basket, a wine-carrier–Get it off the train! Get the passengers out of here before worse comes–"

"*Nom' de Dios*, what is going on?"

The new voice bellowed at Concepçion's own back. A blast of Havana cigar smoke wreathed her ears, a bulky body shouldered past and clove like a bull into the press. By sheer instinct she pushed in its wake.

"Senor!" Consternation rang in the shout. "Senor el Jefe!"

"Senor el Jefe, it is nothing, a small problem, we will have it settled immediately—"

"Is that a body?"

The cigar shot out like a gun. From his other elbow-point, Concepçion recognized the luxuriant goatee, the broad face and even broader neck. Don Jose Menendez, the Ferrocarril President himself.

The man confronting him stammered, "A third-class passenger, a—"

"Get the blanket off."

The rustle of wool was louder than wind in the hush.

Possibly to his credit, Don Jose did not flinch. He did draw hard on the cigar and expel a blast of smoke that almost worsted the stench.

"Cordon off the car. Start disembarkation elsewhere. You, you, you—where are the first-class stewards? Move those passengers now. The rest of you arrange the others. We have had a delay. You do not know what. You, you, get rid of this."

He made to step back. Concepçion sidled past. Beyond the corpse the two men she had first met stood open-mouthed with fear and absolute bewilderment.

"But, but, Senor el Jefe—how?"

The cigar flapped. *"Nom' de Dios,* use your wits!"

Concepçion's voice came out louder than an alarm bell and entirely without her choice.

"Should the body not be left where it is—to show the Guardia Civiles?"

Every face in the crowd turned. Don Jose was so close she almost recoiled at his stare's impact. She could see the bloodshot whites of his eyes, taste the smoke and cognac on his breath.

Then he swung his head and rapped at the men opposite him, "Take it away!"

Rage overran Concepçion so fast her voice bounced off the roof. "This man died by violence, by some unknown means!

Investigations must be made!"

Don Jose turned his shoulder, all of a piece like a wagon swinging, and took a step away.

Concepçion lowered her voice. It hissed like a drawn dagger and she meant it as a blow. "Would Don *Enrique* have let this pass? On *his* Ferrocarril?"

Don Jose stopped. The silence shuddered with the stink of sweat and human panic, cigar smoke and the stench of untoward death.

Then Don Jose half-turned about. She saw the livid color in his face as he ground out, "Fetch the Guardia Civiles."

<\<\>>

"Senora Gonzaga, you have hindered me."

Concepçion shot upright in her bunk. Through the bulkhead beside her the steamer engines throbbed. The *Internationale* had reached Guaqui at eight, the *Inca* should have sailed by nine. Argument, waiting for the Guardia Civiles, had taken till eleven. Disbelief at their perfunctory examination, the spluttering and muttering and breast-crossing, then the hasty verdict that "the man died by misadventure. Remove the body. Do not hinder the Ferrocarril!" and the certainty of pesos sliding from Don Jose to ready Guardia palms had gagged Concepçion until the *Inca* finally sailed, around half past two.

Her porthole was closed. Though she did not think she had slept, the icy beginnings of dawn over miles of open water glimmered through the glass, silver-bleak. It could not wholly clear the cabin's Stygian black.

But for first-class passengers the *Inca* sported a light-switch by the bunk.

The cabin burst into light. Something gave a furious hiss. Black flashed through Concepçion's clearing vision, black velvet in an old-fashioned cutaway coat beneath a thin but pristine white stock. A small shape, but upright and elegant as a rapier. Tiny black goatee and moustache, back-slicked black hair, black brows high and crooked as a devil's knife over deep-hooded black eyes.

Concepçion wrenched her gaze down. Never look at a brujo, her grandmother had said most often of all, eye to eye.

"Who are you?" She managed not to gasp. "What are you doing in here?"

"Put out the light." Like the "z" in "Gonzaga," the one in "luz" had the pure Castilian lisp.

"No! How did you get in here?"

Blackness advanced a soundless step. The fastidiously thin lips parted. Teeth shone in the gap, white, glistening. Two overlarge front teeth.

"You," the drawling hiss repeated, "have hindered me." A long-drawn, almost snoring breath. "You have exposed an–accident. Raised a commotion. Disturbed the Guard. This will cease."

"Commotion? *Accident*?" Outrage fired Concepçion's wits. "What do you mean, hinder you?"

The upper lip rose. Concepçion's back hair rose too and her hand flew to the other first-class passenger's recourse.

"One more step and I pull the alarm!"

Blackness froze. Another vicious hiss.

Concepçion clutched the bell-pull for dear life. The arrogance of the intruder's bearing outdid Criollo bluster; every movement spoke birth, rank, privilege. Yet the skin was just too dark, the nose just too heavily arched, for a true Peninsular.

"Who are you? *What* are you –" She amended the question. "What were you doing on the train?"

The lips curled in a sneer. Concepçion tweaked the bell-pull. There was another furious hiss.

"Baseborn putana. I travel to Arequipa."

I must carry him safe to Arequipa.

Concepçion's heart jumped in her chest. She blurted, "Why?"

The slender body seemed to coil. She could feel the glare. She fixed her own gaze grimly on the mouth, the two anomalously protuberant teeth.

"That is no concern of *thine*." The "tua" dripped contempt.

Then the stiffness became a sudden, lethal fluidity. "I came to warn thee." Now it was a purr. "Not to cross my path again. That no longer matters. So now I tell thee: I go to Arequipa to feed."

"To–what?"

"There is little choice on the Altiplano. Shepherds, herders, railway gangs. But Arequipa is a city. A choice of plenitude. Now thy–ferrocarril–has taught my–food–to travel, I shall travel too."

Food, Concepçion's brain repeated stupidly. Shepherds, herders...

Found it battening on his cattle, and persuaded himself 'tis a hudu–or a brujo in its own right!

Her free hand was driven against her breast, to stop the heart jumping clear out of her throat.

"You killed that man."

The devil's eyebrows tilted. The sneer was the devil's own smile.

"You are a cannibal."

The smile vanished. A feline hiss.

"Am I a pig, to gorge on flesh?"

Two huge holes in a man's throat. Puncture wounds, pale, ragged, where the killer sucked.

"You..." Concepçion fought down shudders. "How did you *get* on the train?"

Affront mutated to a mocking half-bow. "My estimable Jesus, senora. My servant. My slave. Discovered on the Altiplano. Carrier of baggage, disposer of–arrangements. Eternally dependable."

He came to me on the Altiplano, alone, solitary, unique.

"Though growing past his best, I fear."

Concepçion's backbone cringed. She could just whisper. "What will happen to him?"

A tiny shrug. A hand-wave, the turn of the wrist, the fingers' droop, eloquent of hidalgos, princes, antique courtesy of a status Concepçion had never dreamed.

"He will be discarded. Eventually."

Concepçion tried not to gulp.

"But thou–" The purr altered. "Thou art a woman, true; a

mere castiza. But hast some qualities. Perhaps..."

She saw the velvet shoulders firm. Then her heart jerked at the rasping whisper. "Look at me."

Concepçion shook her head furiously. She could not speak, but she gripped the cord and would not raise her eyes.

"Fool woman! Serve me, and become immortal!"

And was that what you promised Jesus?

Concepçion kept her face down and shook her head again.

A long-drawn hiss. "Dirt-bred mestiza..."

At that Concepçion's head flew up despite herself. "Do not thou call *me* mestizo!"

The slender figure went taut as a drawn rapier. The whisper scorched. "*Thou* art the get of a Chilean *roto* and an Aymara slut. *I* am Don Sebastian de la Vega y Vargas, son of an Inca's grandchild and a Conquistador."

Concepçion gasped in utter disbelief for a split second too long. Blackness loomed suddenly to the roof above her, spread, and swooped. She saw the dead man on the galley floor and in sheer reflex her hand flew to the only recourse she had left.

"Madre de Dios, ayudame!"

Her fingers snatched the pure Potosi-silver crucifix that had been Edouard's wedding gift.

Concepçion sat shaking in the *Inca*'s first-class passenger saloon, ears still ringing to the crescendo of the intruder's final shriek. The thud of the cabin door reverberated in her memory, and thought-shards ricocheted in her brain.

A Conquistador's son. Routed by a crucifix. *Jesus, my slave.* On the Altiplano. *I promise you will attain immortality.* A feeder on humans. Old enough to seem immortal. Four hundred years old. On a train. Then in my cabin. The clothes. The teeth. The protuberant front teeth. *My precious, precious bat.* The Indian, in the corridor. *Just another vampire bat... A brujo in its own right!*

Madre de Dios, what *is* that thing?

And as Edouard had armed her for survival, Edouard offered the vital clue: Edouard smiling over a lurid book cover, exclaiming, "What a brujo, this Dracula!"

The shards collapsed into intelligible shapes. Dracula, the novelist's legendary monster: a vampire. Blood-drinker, walker by night. Sleeper by day, enslaving human servants. Travelling in his coffin, going abroad in human form. Or as a bat.

A vampire bat.

Half-hysterical laughter clogged Concepçion's throat. Ah, but here in South America, we have the reality. With the habits, the size, the teeth... oh, to see that haughty Conquistador's descendant penned among the luggage, upside down in a cage!

Then comprehension drenched her, colder than Titicaca's waves. He would not be in the cage. Jesus had released him. He had reached her cabin in the night. Had killed in the night. Now it was day. Somewhere, as bat or human, like Dracula, "Don Sebastian" had found another shelter for his sleep.

She never isolated the moment decision emerged from that understanding's depth. It was simply there, setting her teeth, stiffening her back. The murdered man, Jesus, my daughters in Potosi, in Arequipa, all that unsuspecting population: they matter, yes. But that–creature–is using the Ferrocarril. Truly dishonoring the Ferrocarril. Don Enrique's Ferrocarril, Edouard's Ferrocarril.

She heard again the editorials and encomiums as Don Enrique's projects dazzled Peru. Edouard, on leave but still ablaze too: "Querida, Don Enrique is beyond amazing. The Challape bridge! The Cacray zigzag! The Galera tunnel–a tunnel, at fifteen thousand feet! This Ferrocarril will upturn the world!"

And it killed them, some bitter second voice interposed. Edouard in a rock fall, Don Enrique in the national bankruptcy. Ten thousand others with them, on the Central Line alone. In its way, the Ferrocarril is a greater blood-sucker than Don Sebastian. Why should its honor be saved?

At last, the first voice replied.

Don Enrique, it said, was a Yanqui, a speculator, a money-maker, but he was a magnificent engineer. Only a magnificent engineer could master the Andes' seaward face.

Edouard understood that, it went on. Edouard used, Edouard gave his life for that. Will you let old bitterness shame them both?

No, she said at last, answering both voices. I will not leave their work a means to that thing's filthy ends.

She settled back in the gilt-edged chair. The Ferrocarril gave me a cause, she thought. Edouard has named the enemy. But only grandmamma knew how to handle a brujo.

<<>>

She allowed time for breakfast to be served and cleared away. Then she rang her stateroom bell, and asked the attendant the question on which her whole plan relied.

"Does the crew from La Paz stay with the *Internationale* all the way?"

When he nodded, she took the first, irretrievable step. "Senor, the two men who found the–body–before Guaqui. Will you ask them to attend me here?"

"Senores," she said, when they arrived, "in the confusion, last night, I never heard your names."

The taller one was Ramon Flores, the shorter Esteban Gamarra. She acknowledged their half-bows and said, "I request you in good faith, senores, to come within here. And close the door."

They both hesitated. She held her head up as if at Mass. They took heart at such respectability.

"Senores," she said, as they stood crowded by the bunk, "in the matter of the dead man on the train." Their stances shot from nervous to alarmed attention. "I have found what killed him. It was a brujo."

Before the consternation could burgeon she added a counterblow. "It is on this ship."

"I saw it," she went on, when their outcry, irrepressible even for seasoned railway crew, had begun to abate. "Last night."

And with their eyes and mouths gone even wider, she

forestalled the obvious question. "It could not abide my crucifix."

She watched the sequence of shocks level into a first tinge of relief. "Either the crucifix," she amended, "or that it was silver. In either case, senores, we are not unarmed."

She let the full significance of that "we" sink in. Then she said softly, "This creature has killed. And it has dishonored–abused– the Ferrocarril. I seek your help, in finding–in encountering–in removing it." She held their eyes and let her own feelings into her voice. "Yes. I intend to remove it. I have, senores, a plan."

The engines throbbed vaguely under them. Someone clattered past in the corridor. Their eyes told her they believed her; because they still thought her a bruja as well.

Then Ramon Flores tucked his chin down, and straightened the cap under his arm.

"Senora," he sounded only moderately shaky. "Remove it... how?"

Concepçion released a breath that seemed to have strained her stay laces. "Senores," she said, "do you both possess a crucifix?"

Grandmama never said it would be easy, Concepçion fumed. Aloud she said, "Senores, no-one could ask you to search a first-class cabin, naturally. And yes, something so small as a bat might be anywhere. Nevertheless, we must still find it. And before tonight."

Both men shuddered. Both right hands clamped tightly round a crucifix, one silver, the other tied to a silver medal of St. Christopher.

"It was necessary to search. To eliminate what places we could." But, she realized with relief, one other certain clue remained.

"Senores, the Indian. Jesus, the brujo's slave. We must watch for him at Puno, when we disembark. The brujo may evade us. Jesus, we will see."

Ramon Flores took the lead as usual. "And–then, senora?"

Concepçion's brain ratcheted like a runaway windlass. "Then we find means to–dispose of it. But first we watch: I at the passengers' gangway. Senor Flores, the luggage? And you, Senor Gamarra, if you watch the ticket-checkers?"

Esteban Gamarra licked his lips. "And if one of us sees?"

"We follow. We find where he settles himself. He must have baggage." One way or another, Don Sebastian had to leave the ship, and by day, Jesus would have to carry him. A coffin like Dracula's would be impossibly conspicuous. He would have to be in bat shape. "Do not approach him! Only come to report. We will meet on the Puno platform. While the train loads."

<></>

"Senora! Senora!" Esteban Gamarra's voice overrode the din at the station entry, as Concepçion struggled to keep her footing in the crowd. "Senora, the train is not going to load!"

Concepçion hauled herself round, to find his eyes staring wide. "The engineer says the descent to Arequipa is too dangerous in the dark–"

"But surely, we could advance to Juliaca?"

"Senora, Juliaca has no hotel! Nor enough room for half these." His gesture flashed about the hallway, first, second, third class passengers entangled in protest and demand. "The train must stay at Puno. First-class passengers at the hotel, billets for the others. Senor el Jefe is, ah, very angry. But the engineer will not budge."

My fault. Concepçion felt her ears burn with shame. Single-handed, I delayed the *Inca* at Guaqui, and for nothing of use. Now Don Jose will be rabid. And his wrath will fall on this one honest man.

"Yes, have someone take my baggage," she cut into Esteban's next outburst. "But I must see the engineer."

At the very least, she told herself, I must explain. Take the blame. Apologize.

Not surprisingly, the engineer was by his locomotive. Evidently he had prevailed, for the boiler was uncompromisingly cold. Underlings ran about with oilcans, tools and water buckets, but the engineer himself was tapping the left-hand drivers with a small hammer, wheel by wheel. Painted black like all Southern Rail engines, the locomotive loomed in the twilit station-shed like some great machine demon, the arrogant jut of funnel, the long prow of the cow-catcher, the squared lines of cabin and tender only emphasizing the breadth of the massive, glistening boiler's flank.

Under that wall of weight and power, against the serried rank of pilot and driver and trailing wheels, the man looked insignificant. Yet it is he who controls all this in motion, Concepçion thought. He who, for conscience' sake, has brought the whole enterprise to a halt.

Esteban coughed. "Senor Vivanco?"

The engineer straightened. Concepçion met grave dark eyes in a rawboned face. The bones were uncompromising as the look. A gravel-rough voice said, "Yes?"

Mestizo, she thought. Castizo, one mixed-blood parent, as I have, but Indian blood somewhere close. "I am Concepçion Gonzaga," she said. "Edouard's widow. I am also the person who delayed the *Inca* at Guaqui. Since this has caused such trouble, I have come to apologize."

For Don Jose's undoubted demands, curses, threats of dismissal, and at the least, copious abuse, all directed at this man. Both of them knew what she meant.

Vivanco examined her for another unblinking half-second. Then, briefly and slightly, inclined his head.

"Edouard's widow," he said.

Concepçion inclined her head in turn.

"The delay. It was then for good cause?"

Concepçion blinked. *Edouard,* she said silently, *what a reputation you left.* "Senor, you are of the Ferrocarril. A person of reason. Rationality. Science. But not all things, yet, can be explained by science."

Vivanco's silence answered, *Go on.*

"A man died on the train, outside Guaqui. Senor Gamarra here can attest: something bit his throat and drained his blood."

Vivanco glanced at Gamarra and back to her.

"I wished, I demanded that the Guardia Civiles investigate. They did not find the killer. On the steamer, I learned that–it was a brujo."

Someone on the boiler housing overhead banged metal on metal with a vicious clang. The iron roof reverberated. Unmoved, the locomotive towered over them, black in the dimness as the vampire himself.

"It feeds on human blood," Concepçion said. "It means to go to Arequipa, to find more people. It told me this. When it tried to enslave me, on the steamer last night."

She could feel Esteban Gamarra's gasp. Vivanco merely shifted the hammer to his other hand. Stared another endless moment. And said, "So it will try to board this train?"

Concepçion tried not to babble in relief. "Senor, I fear so. I mean to–remove it. With Senor Esteban here. And another. We will try to find it, here in Puno. But if we cannot..."

Gamarra flinched. Vivanco lowered his head a little, looking up under his brows. Then he said, with a new, harsher grate in his voice. "Senora, whatever you ask, tomorrow, the engine crew will attempt."

"Senora, I swear, we have looked everywhere! The steamer, the wharf–I examined every piece of baggage, Esteban saw all who passed the ticket-office. We cannot find either of them!"

Ramon Flores was almost inarticulate with terror and frustration. And fear learnt from a bad master, Concepçion thought. Well, Edouard always said, action wrecks every plan. "I could have missed them, at the gangplank," she said, "in the station. The streets."

Would I had this brujo's art, querida, Edouard chuckled in her ear, to wile men and pass invisible. How I would shake those idle gangers of mine!

If this one has such an art, she asked herself, how will it help to search?

How will it help, to say that now?

"Senores," she said firmly, "tonight, they may be anywhere. Tomorrow, they must be on the train. We must watch straitly, on the platform, so we cannot miss Jesus. After that, it is a matter of patience. Remember, by daylight, the other must be asleep."

They looked back at her, half credulous, half uncertain. I must be confident, she told herself, as a foreman, as Edouard would be. I must bolster, not destroy their trust.

"Remember, if you do encounter the brujo, hold fast to your cross. Pray to Mary, to Pachamama of the Indians–so you believe, no matter which. And do not–do not! look into its eyes."

The hotel was thin-walled, rackety with drinkers and others working off their impatience, her bed lumpy. None of it would have mattered, Concepçion knew as she tossed, had there been any form of surety in her mind.

The vampire must be on the train when we leave, she told herself for the fortieth time. His slave must carry him. His slave we can find.

Or might he board in the darkness, in human form? If he could reach my cabin unnoticed, escape unnoticed, can he pass locked doors and conceal himself somewhere we never imagined? In the coal, under the carriage floors, on the roof?

When the faintest hint of grey paled the window she could bear no more. Fifteen minutes later, in her warmer shirtwaist, skirt and shawl, she was in the street.

I can scan the alleyways, she told herself, on chance of sighting Jesus. Go down to the station, patrol around the train, till dawn.

Puno's ragged main thoroughfare stretched ghost-misty between blots of building to the paling stars. Any street lamps had gone out. Under building eaves deeper shadow blotches marked the poorest travelers, swathed in a blanket or serape, emitting a faint undertow of sound. Grunts, sighs, snores. Somewhere in a distant back street a dog was barking. Somewhere else, cold and bitter as the air, a cock crowed for the approaching dawn.

Concepçion paced half a block, another. The station façade coalesced before her, its broad arch identifiable even in the gelid dark. Then in the maw of an alleyway, a boot clicked on wood. A man half-grunted, half-gulped. Something hissed.

Concepçion's heart stood still in her breast.

Then her hands flew to her reticule, to the crucifix about her neck. She whipped the chain over her head and about her fingers and with miraculous deftness wrenched out her brand-new Ladies' Magnesium-Powered Personal Illuminator. She took three long strides into the darkness' maw and scrabbled for the switch.

Light blazed. The darkness snarled like a furious cat. White brilliance drove the picture into memory indelibly as a lightning strike.

A man jammed against the boarded alley wall, head back in a parody of ecstasy, bulging eyes, gaping mouth. Dangling hands, a mass of shadow folds from the upthrust serape, the black shape of the vampire pressed beneath, head fastened like a tick's to the naked throat.

One hand gripped the man's jaw, forcing his head up, holding him in place. The other made a white blot at the vampire's groin. The black velvet trousers gaped. He held himself as at a urinal, and something streamed down against the other man's leg, thick and black as tar, with a throat-stopping stench.

Concepçion cried, "Madre de Dios!" and swung the cross.

The light snuffed. She heard the vampire curse. Something thumped, something flew by so close she staggered as from the passage of a train. Then the shuddering dimness held only stench, and the victim's body, settling amid a slow rustle of garments like a just-felled tree.

Concepçion managed not to actually fall out of the alley mouth. She laced her stays looser than most, but they cut breathing so she could only scurry, eyes clinging desperately to the fitful black blur ahead. Making for the station. Mother of God, let me not lose it! It must be going to the train...

Blackness flitted across the station façade and vanished in the entry arch. Lungs bursting, Concepçion rushed through onto the platform. Men criss-crossed under the coldly glaring lights, train, engine, station crew. Nobody staring, nobody shouting. Oh, Dios, did no-one see where it went?

Sheer instinct sent her to the locomotive: the train's head, its motive force, the province of the man who had kept it here. "Senor Vivanco!" she gasped.

And as by magic he was beside her, saying sharply, "Senora, what is wrong?"

"The brujo." Concepçion coughed in the raw Altiplano air. "I saw him in the street. I think he came to the train."

She felt rather than saw Vivanco spring alert. Then he shouted, "Roberto!" over a shoulder. And to her, brusquely, "What do we seek?"

"A man–small, very upright, a high mestizo. Black old-fashioned coat. A face like an Inca. Proud. Proud as Pizarro. But if you see him, do not approach! He will spell you with his eyes."

She heard the sharp intake of breath and caught his sleeve. "Or else..."

"Or else?"

She tried not to make her voice small. "Look for a bat. A vampire bat."

"Senores, I most sincerely ask your pardon." Concepçion bit her lip. "I have taken you all from your work. Disrupted the station. Perhaps delayed the *Internationale*. But there is a man, a, a creature. Involved with the murder, in Guaqui. We must find him! Because one way or another, he *will* be on this train."

The assembled men's silence was its own reply. They think me hysterical, if not crazy. But if I tell them the truth?

Vivanco was abruptly again beside her, saying loudly, "Dismiss. We must finish the work." Drawing her into the half-arches behind the platform, he kept hold of her elbow, eyes scanning her face. As abruptly he said, "What will you do?"

Concepçion's tears burnt away. Her spine stiffened. "My helpers and I must check the passengers. The brujo may be on board, but his servant is not. If we can find, we can follow him."

Vivanco's eyes narrowed. *You will not,* that look asked, *give up?*

"Senor, I delayed the train at Guaqui, so you were forced to hold it here. There is a man dead, back down the street, because this–brujo–was delayed too." She saw the sudden appalled guilt in his face. "Senor, you are blameless. But I let even the dead lie, to follow this creature. While I may stop it, I will not give up."

For an instant he was silent. Then he touched right hand to temple as if saluting Don Jose. "Send," he said, "if you have need."

<><>

"Senora, senora!" Ramon Flores all but fell into Concepçion's sleeper, exclaiming at the top of his lungs. "We found him, we found him after all!"

Concepçion nearly fell off the bunk herself. "Madre de Dios! How? Where?"

"I remembered what you told us." Flores grabbed the door jamb giddily. "Pray if you meet him, to Mary or Pachamama. And we had not found them–the train loaded, pulled out, there was no stop before Juliaca." He was too overstrung in the wake of desperation to laugh, even in joy. "So I prayed, senora! Pachamama, I begged. Show me. Just show me, where... Oh senora! It was as if my eyes cleared, and there he was! Rolled in his serape, under the provision shelf in the second-class galley, the door was open, I looked straight in!"

"Blessed Pachamama!" At that moment Concepçion could have kissed him. "But he, did he see you?"

"No, no, senora! His head was down, as if he slept." He danced on the shuddering floor as the train rattled down a slope. "Now, senora, now what do we do?"

"Find the brujo." Concepçion hardly had to think. "He must be close. And in bat form, or they had seen him, in the earlier search. Quick, Senor Flores, back to second class. Pray to Pachamama as we look." With a faint pang, she wished that she, too, could invoke grandmama's Aymara earth goddess. "I will call on Mary myself."

The vampire was in the galley too. Above the range-hood, a rod spanned the car to hold up pots and pans. The vampire was still little more than a black smear among the utensils, but it was there. The long-handled hook for fetching pans down leant beside the range. Concepçion stared up, clutching her crucifix, prayer ebbing on her lips. We have found him. Now, what do we do?

"First, we get the Indian out." Ramon Flores was still jittering beside her. "I can bring a conductor. If I pray to Pachamama, he should see too. That one should not be in the galley, and be sure, he has only a third-class ticket. We can take him all the way down there."

"Yes." Whatever noise Jesus made, the vampire would not wake. With Jesus out of earshot, what could they not do?

Grandmama's permanent remedies for a brujo were close to Stoker's for Dracula: stake the sleeper's heart with hawthorn wood. Cut off the head, fill the mouth with garlic. Expose all to the sun, and let it burn up the undead flesh. But how do I behead a vampire bat?

Superimposed ran pictures of Don Sebastian in her cabin, rapier upright, ancient as Pizarro, haughty as a hidalgo, immaculate in white stock and black velvet coat. Whatever horrors he had wrought, his presence demanded a death with dignity.

However undignified the death he dealt. The lightning-etched scene in the alleyway flashed past her too. Dios, how he must hate that. Why, in heaven's name, must even a Dracula piss when he feeds?

The train noises blanked. Instead she heard her brother, dead of fever these seven years, laughing in her ear beside her grandfather's herd-fire, hissing, "Cepcion, 'Cepcion, come and see!"

Dragging her to the recumbent, slumbering cow, to crouch, stifling giggles, as the small black shape of a vampire bat planed to earth, to waddle, on its wingtips, to the cow's side. Scale a shoulder, bare the two razor-sharp front teeth, and bend to feed.

And begin to urinate, a bare minute after it drank.

Concepçion gasped. So this one is truly a vampire-bat?

Then the other memory overrode everything, grandmama by her hearth, smiling as Roberto closed his shrilling narrative. "Abuela, it started to *pee!*" And adding lore of her own. Yes, vampires walked rather than risk rousing prey by a direct landing. And did Roberto know the secret of how they flew?

"Oh. Oh, Dios."

Ramon Flores stopped babbling and stared at her. Stared harder as she took her hands from her cheeks and twitched like a crazy woman and demanded, "How far is it to Juliaca? Quick!"

The *Internationale* slid majestically up to the platform in Juliaca. Brakes squealed, the locomotive let out a bullfrog roar of steam. More steam wreathed the driving wheels as Concepçion cascaded inelegantly from the first-class doorway and tried to run among the station scrimmage to the cabin side.

"Senor Vivanco!"

The engineer came down in a leap. "You have found it," he said.

"I have found it, por Dios. And I think I know how to deal with it. Senor, only tell me: is this engine a Baldwin too?"

He looked at her almost as Ramon Flores had. But he nodded immediately.

"Truly, thank God." For what seemed the first time in minutes, Concepçion breathed. "One favor, then, senor. On the down grades, after Crucero Alto–maybe over Colca Canyon–I mean to pull the emergency cord."

Vivanco nearly reared back like a horse. "Senora!"

"And then I want you to blow the whistle. As hard, as high

as it will go, so long as the steam lasts. Or until I pull the cord again."

"What?"

"Then, please God, we will be rid of our brujo." She could feel the flush of mad inspiration, of madder excitement, in her cheeks. "Por favor, senor. This once, ignore the regulations. The train will take no harm, and nor will any other passenger. A great many people will be saved... if you can do this one thing."

Vivanco stared as if she had grown the devil's horns. Then, slowly, his face changed. Abruptly, he made a little half-bow. "When you pull the cord," he said, "the whistle will blow."

<><>

Concepçion stood in the second-class galley door, pot-hook in hand and mouth oven-dry. By the connection tube, Ramon Flores gripped the red emergency-stop handle, eyes locked on her. At the car's end, she knew Esteban Gamarra waited, clutching his crucifix, to block off entry from third-class.

Two and a half eternal hours ago, the *Internationale* had pulled out of Juliaca, to thread its way over the Altiplano, along Lagunilles lake, past endless vistas where only a herd of lama or alpaca or a one-room farmhouse broke the emptiness. Half an hour since, they had taken coal and water at Crucero Alto. Now the locomotive was braking, easing the train into the steepest section of the descent.

Her head still ached from the height of Crucero Alto's fifteen thousand feet. The landscape had gone to glaring, pallid blues and browns, mountain on mountain with the snake track of Don Enrique's rails, Edouard's tunnels and bridges, stretched piecemeal behind. Now the vista changed to roaring dark. She glanced at Edouard's personal altimeter, his one everyday possession she had kept, worn like a watch about her neck. The dial read, five thousand feet. Within minutes this tunnel would open on the wall of Colca canyon, its floor four thousand feet below.

She licked her lips and launched one final prayer.

The door panel blazed with light. She hauled open the screeching galley window. Squinted upward, hitched the pothook round a bat-leg and gave one fierce jerk.

The vampire landed on the floor in front of her and she could not restrain one frantic leap. Ramon Flores yelped. Somewhere along the train another man screamed.

"Jesu Maria, senora, that was the Indian. Quick!"

Concepçion flung the hook aside and snatched the pot-holder, clapping it round velvet black fur, flinching from the twisting, hairless cat-head, the hissing, the bared incisor teeth. Staggering for the window she shrieked, "Now!"

Ramon Flores yanked the emergency stop.

Wheels, rails, frames and girders screamed as every driver locked. Despite its slowed speed the whole train slid under her and Concepçion had time to thank heaven she had not chosen to do this on the actual bridge.

Then the whistle began.

In seconds its normal hollow roar crescendoed, climbing in pitch and volume like an insane opera singer until she thought her ears would burst. She staggered for the galley window, twisting the pot-holder into a bundle, stretching to the best angle for a throw.

Human shrieks pierced the whistle scream. A body hurtled round the galley jamb and crashed into her, serape flying, hands thrashing, Jesus' voice caterwauling, "My bat, my bat! You will damage, you will hurt him, strega, bruja, malevola, let him go, let him go!"

Concepçion thrust herself back at the window and threw.

The bundle sailed straight out, pot-holder unrolling to leave the bat-shape black and clear on colorless sky. The pot-holder arced toward the miniature brown mazes of canyon below. Above it, Concepçion saw the bat wings open. Beat convulsively. The steam-whistle reached a high A like a soul in torment and the black crescent staggered sidelong. Then, like a small black leaf, it began to fall.

A battering ram hurled Concepçion against the range. Jesus screamed too, louder than the steam-whistle, and flung himself head-first through the window-gap.

Human body-weight carried him downward far faster than the bat. Mesmerized, Concepçion saw him strike the canyon side, a silent puff of dust. Then the body rebounded, over and over, vanishing into the depths.

A great distance off, the steam-whistle was still shrieking. Someone made a gesture. Ramon Flores yanked the stop handle again.

After another eternity, the whistle scaled down and stopped.

"My *abuela*, senores." Ramon and Esteban goggled. Concepçion rested her aching head against the galley wall. "She knew much about bats. When I was a child, she told me they steered by the noise of things around them. I heard the engine, the other Baldwin engine, whistle on the way to Guaqui. If we only threw it–him–out, it–he–might have flown away. But if the whistle deafened him–then he could not steer himself."

The hush revealed uproar beyond them, shouts and outcries, pounding feet. In a moment the wrath of the Ferrocarril will burst upon us, she thought. And poor Jesus. Immortality. How long did he serve, on the Altiplano? How many times did that emaciation nourish his master? Final obscenity, that his death will serve his master's destroyers, even as that master stole his life.

Something banged ferociously on the exit door.

They all jumped a measurable foot. Then Esteban peered out and suddenly began to yank at the handle, crying, "Senor Vivanco!"

Glowering, the engineer balanced below them on sleeper ends. "Give me a hand up!"

Crazy laughter burst in Concepçion's lungs. She thrust the pot-hook at Esteban. "Use this!"

One pull to reach the foot-plate and Vivanco had doubled himself over and in the door. Demanding almost before he uncoiled, "Did you get it or not?"

"Yes." Concepçion felt her voice shake. "The brujo is gone."

Vivanco made a noise like a boiling tea-kettle. "And how will you explain this–this –"

"A man fell from the window." I can explain the bat later. "He was acting very strangely. Perhaps he chewed too much coca.. He screamed that his master had gone out the window, he must follow. We could not control him, and he jumped."

She stared limpidly into Vivanco's eyes. He was turning an odd color, like a half-bleached aubergine. "So," she aimed to sound both virtuous and shaken, "this helpful employee pulled the emergency stop."

Vivanco's jaw moved. Word-fragments percolated. Then the champing stopped.

"You." It was more than half a growl. "At Puno, I thought you a remarkable woman. Now, I am sure Edouard knew what he was about, to marry you."

Concepçion felt her eyes start. Vivanco stepped forward, giving her a full-scale bow.

"Ma Generale, permit me to introduce myself. I am Miguel Vivanco, senior engineer on the Ferrocarril del Sur del Peru, and I humbly request to know your direction. Because in La Paz or elsewhere, I intend to call on you."

Vaguely Concepçion saw Ramon and Esteban suddenly beaming like god-parents at a christening. Far too certainly she felt her whole face crimson in a blush.

Then at Vivanco's back the connecting door crashed open and Don Jose burst through like a cannonball, bawling, *"Nom' de Dios*, what is *this*! Sixteen hours behind, and now an emergency stop! No word, no explanation, no attendant, and then all the doors stuck fast! I will dismiss, I will jail every man who connived at this!"

Faster than the vampire, Vivanco turned on him.

"Do not disturb yourself, Senor Jefe. This was a matter concerning only the honor of the Ferrocarril. And it has already been resolved."

RAGTIME

T. Joseph Dunham

The Preacher declared that the Hun be destroyed and the German nation be wiped from the earth. Nameless workers toiled in the London steel mills, their names appropriated by the state when their status changed. Mined coal and iron from deep in the barren earth, mixed with their blood in the coke. They hammered steel into steamflies for sky-flight and they filled machine bellies with bombs and copies of the Testament carved onto steel sheets to survive the conflagration.

Eyes will burn. And they will at last see. We save them all.

The Preacher promised his people in the land-that-forgot-its-name that no enemy ship would chug over their cities. They would be protected.

Doctor Faust remembered that last speech over the wireless, as he sat in the Pink Lion Pub, sipping a glass of moonshine and clutching the notice-of-death telegram in his hand. Explosions rattled the building. He covered his drink to keep it free of falling dust. He didn't recall his walk from the Whitehall or even entering the cabaret.

Poison Sumac leaned over the table, posed a cigarette holder pertly in his painted rosy lips. He leaned his leg on the table side, exposed through the split in his midnight satin gown, showing his garter strap.

"Got a light, Doctor?" Sumac asked.

Dr. Faust scanned the showroom of the humble club. On the wall hung a defaced grainy poster of The Preacher and David Lloyd George shaking hands. Red lipstick painted their eyes. The tables waited empty, their candles dead. Only he, the drag queen, and the record player patronized the cabaret. The third guest sang Marlene Dietrich in a dull drone, skipping on the record scratches.

The mechanism in Faust's mechanical leg wheezed, playing background to Marlene. He'd lost the limb in the early bombings of the war.

Never releasing the sallow telegram, Doctor Faust turned the crank on the side of his gas lighter, held the silver flare to the performer's smoke.

"I adore a gentleman," the drag queen said, sucking in the miasma then blowing the acrid smoke in a thin spout from his puckered lips. Faust's stomach twisted from the ersatz cigarette, rife with chemicals, sulfur, tar, maybe a hint of tobacco.

"I don't know how you managed to get tobacco with a war on," Doctor Faust said.

"A lady has her ways," Sumac said.

The high notes of his feminine voice dropped at the end of his sentence, reflecting the deep roots of his vocal cords.

The showroom of the Pink Lion trembled after another detonation. Photos of guests and previous drag queens who once graced the stage rattled, some slipping from their nails and cracking on the floor. The pink flame from the gas spouts flickered.

"All my lovely boys are at the front," the transvestite said. "My lovely, lovely Tommies coming back missing bits and pieces, limbs blown up, stumps and gouges. Still my lovely lovely boys."

He paused for another explosion to play out, this time closer. They listened to the grumbling of a low-flying steamfly. Its boiler sputtered and chugged.

"I had such a fine man, you know," Sumac said, putting his leg up on a chair and leaning on his knee. Leg stubble grew back up his shin, piercing the worn, white stockings. Everyone had to make do. "My man is coming home, stomach full of lead, won't open his eyes. Not much good now."

Poison Sumac blew another smoke stream into Doctor Faust's austere mug—skin so tight down his forehead and cheeks, it looked ready to split. In the dull, gas lighting of the club, his eyes drained of any color, all the life long-since fled. He removed his spectacles and rubbed the lenses with a handkerchief. He sipped his drink.

"My son comes home today," Doctor Faust said. "He so wanted me to be proud."

His mechanical leg sputtered. He reached below the table, pulled up his pant leg and tightened a copper coil. A vapor stream released from the exhaust pipe, burning his palm. He didn't flinch, didn't pull his hand back by reflex. It felt like a tale of pain told to him by a stranger.

"Coming home by ship?" Sumac asked.

"In a box."

"He has my congratulations," Poison Sumac said, pulling up his stockings. Their thin fabric couldn't conceal the masculine design of his thigh muscles. His short dress bounced. "He's won. Victorious. Gone and gone. No more pain for him. Isn't that the purse? The kitty?"

Doctor Faust slurped the rest of his drink then slammed it down on the table, cracking the crystal.

"You must break the rigor mortis," Sumac said. "Don't you see? It's all a comedy. This war will never end. Our fearless leader lives by this war. To make peace would be to die."

Doctor Faust searched the room to ensure they were alone. Such words would quickly have them both sucking down volts in a static throne.

"He sorted paperwork at the Ministry of War, exempt from conscription," he said. "Only joined the army because I told him it was his duty. Guard the empire. Rule Britannia. Kill the Hun. I couldn't tell him how proud I was. I always made him fight for my approval, held it over his head just out of reach."

Sumac set his leg down, leaned over and kissed Doctor Faust, clutching his jowls in gloved hands. Sumac tasted of skunk, the residual smoke flowing into Faust's mouth.

"You are a skilled surgeon from what I read before your disgrace," Sumac said, still holding his cheeks. Sumac's furry, left eyebrow slipped its glue and dangled from his forehead. "Why not sew up all the holes, make your son all pretty?"

"No animation. No life. He is not a ragdoll. Not a toy."

"Life is merely a little extra spice. He's better off without it."

The walls shook from more local explosions.

"I cannot think," Doctor Faust said.

Visions of his son invaded the clarity of the doctor's cogitations: Wilhelm's body shredded by shrapnel, burned by poison gas. The body sinks into the mud, forgotten. A flock of doves land in the trench and peck and chew at his flesh. The vision shattered his mind.

"Darling, come with me." Poison Sumac extended his gloved hand. Weak in will, an evaporating oil puddle, Doctor Faust took it. Sumac led him through the torn, burgundy curtains hanging over the small stage to a backroom of ropes, curtains, pyramid props from previous shows.

Poison Sumac took off his wig of silvery curls, revealing his shaved head. Without the wig, his feminine delusion thinned with the evidence of his angular nose and stern brow.

"You need a little ragtime, darling," Sumac said. "You'll be dead when you're still sucking down oxygen. Makes you so cold you strip down naked to banish any heat."

Sumac wrapped his arms around the old Doctor's shoulders, pressed him down on his knees, rubbing the worn tweed on his knees further into holes. Sumac tapped on his head.

"Don't go away now," he said. Sumac swayed off then returned pushing a cart, ferrying a child's coffin. It looked miniaturized, like comedy prop; a coffin from a little world. He set it on the floor in front of him and opened the latch. He held out his palm.

"Ragtime isn't free."

Faust fished the wallet out of his tweed jacket, slipped a few bills into Sumac's hand. He blew the good doctor a kiss.

"A wealthy man, older, owns his own business, knows how to take care of a lady," Sumac said. "I just might have to marry you."

Sumac pulled the alembic components from the coffin, setting them on the floor between them. He attached the silver pipes to cast iron balls, opened the valves, set to work building the boiler and pipe venue in the coffin. He attached a central bong and placed it on a stand.

"Another light?"

Doctor Faust cranked his lighter and ignited the burner beneath the bong.

Sumac slipped a leather bag from a concealed pouch in his dress bust and held it before his eyes.

"Essence of life—the passage to death. I am your priest. Do you accept?"

"He trusted me," Faust said.

"Ground from the dried frontal lobes of our war dead, neurotransmitters regulated in small dosages—too much and madness, addiction. The gift of the gods, a taste of paradise, but only a taste so you're desperate for more. Will you drink the wine of the dead?"

"I drink in the name of my son, for Wilhelm Faust."

Sumac fed the crimson powder into the boiler and flipped several valves. The fluid in the bong popped and sputtered and buzzed. The pipes expanded from the pressure. Sumac worked the gears, a master at his craft. He let the alembic boil and cook.

"My poor disgraced physician," Sumac said. "Not even the war office wants your madness."

Sumac folded back his pant leg. He ran his finger along the aluminum, moaning as he fondled the gears and wheels and springs, smearing his hand in oil.

"Your handiwork?" the drag queen asked.

"That's the only reason the ministry doesn't toss me in the Tower. I craft replacement parts for our soldiers. I own a company. This is an advanced model, doesn't require a boiler attachment to power it. I'd build more for the wounded, but the Ministry won't shell out the extra money. There's a war on, they say."

Sumac pulled the final piece from a compartment in the coffin bottom. The silver mask glowed in the dull light from the gas wall sconces. A hollow shaft ran from the lips. He attached it to the bong.

"Wear this face over your mask."

"Anoint me," said the good doctor.

Sumac pressed the cool metal to his face, a perfect fit in the contour of its cheeks and brow and chin. The drag queen wrapped a leather strap from the edges around his head and tightened it in a buckle. The metal cut the circulation from his face.

"A sacrifice," Sumac said. "It burns away the tadpoles of your taste buds, but you'll no longer care. Food will do little to satiate you after your first dose."

Sumac set his hand on the steam, release valve. "Trust me?" the transvestite asked.

"Of course not."

Sumac twirled the valve. A jet of boiling vapor shot up the shaft, striking Doctor Faust in his mouth. He yelled from the searing steam, burning away the mucus membrane, his gums, the surface of his tongue and roasting his throat. Then the pain ended.

He floated, bobbing in low, ocean waves. The doors in his head opened simultaneously. Circuits connected. Valves turned. The vivacious essence of his thoughts in synergy with the plasma of his soul flowed in pleasurable current to the muddy parts of his mind.

"The fog lifts?" asked Sumac.

"I am a god."

Sumac grinned, pleased that he'd poisoned another mind. He worked his art with pride, pleased to unleash his chaos into a world obsessed with spurious order.

"Darling. You are Anubis, the jackal."

When the high court had stripped his medical license, had decreed him a monster, a hack, for his work, Doctor Faust buried the files of his reanimation research in his mind's cellar. The boiling steam pouring into his blood cracked its hinges. It could be done. It must be done. This is why he'd been woman-born, sent to this world to save the savages from death, to lead them on the road to divinity.

"Now I understand why my son had to die," he said.

"You're going to cover the world in darkness," Sumac said. "I must love you."

"All the equipment is still in my home, the cathedral. With

sound, vibration I will renew, invigorate. I will tell him how proud I am, how wrong I was. He will wrap his hands around my neck and kiss my cheeks. I will make him immortal."

Sumac clapped like a child, pleased by the clowns in the show.

"How terribly cruel," he said.

The transvestite wrapped his legs around his waist, pulled up his dress. Doctor Faust, panted from the ragtime. Swamp sweat drenched skin, soaked his tweed pants and jacket.

"Drill a hole in me. Fill me with your insanity."

Doctor Faust wore the silver mask as they made love.

Across the broken road in the low south end of the city, Doctor Faust watched a lithe lady dancing in the jaundiced light of the gas lamps. He gazed upon the shadow puppet twirling on the surface of the brick buildings, watching through the shattered torso of a silvery-blue angel, depicted in the stained glass portals of the derelict cathedral.

The price of the vaulted, stone church had come cheap after the Preacher's faith had been named the British national religion. Many of the grand buildings had been torn down to make way for cheap apartments. At night, Doctor Faust would stare up to the arches holding high the stone buttresses, now the nest of bats and fouler night things, and he'd marvel in nature's perfection, the arch bearing its load without a whimper, devised and set to a purpose by a mathematician's rites.

The enemy ships had exhausted their bombs an hour since, leaving the streets in an orange glow from buildings burning like torches. Crews fought with mechanized pumps to suck the oxygen from the fires, depriving them of sustenance, but the city continued to burn.

When at last the dancer's shadow faded into the darkness, Doctor Faust strolled the aisle past the broken pews, to the ancient altar, thick with dust and tarnish. There, he had laid out Wilhelm's body, nearly in pieces, held together by thin tendrils of flesh. They'd stripped him of his gray, uniform tunic, to be recycled and given to a new soldier.

"Forgive me, son," he spoke to the vapid flesh. "Tell me you forgive me, my son. I must know."

The lips refused to spin. The eyelids declined to part. The body looked right somehow, sans animation, as if life was the aberration. Death was the goal, the cure from this sickness. Still, Doctor Faust would infect him.

He lifted the body in his arms, carried him as he had a sleeping child to his bed. He rolled out the body onto the back of the pipe organ. In his previous work, shut down by the Ministry, he'd fused the keys with gold electrodes. They alternated in negative and positive charge.

The crown of pipes rose overhead from the organ belly, climbing two stories, shrinking in diameter as the pipes reached the higher rows, feeding through the stone walls. He'd welded lodestones to the pipes, fed iron powder into the bellows below. Beneath the organ in the church crypts, a machine waited all these years, a generator designed to harness and enhance magnetic fields at specific frequencies, to match those in the body, the brain.

The Ministry of War had deemed his work a perversion of nature, and he had recanted as any good son seeking the love of his father. Then the Preacher began this war, and the doctor understood. Whitehall desired to be the only body to hold power over life and death.

He understood the pragmatic condition of matter called life, its secrets, the fields and electrons that composed it in specific equation. Life was his. Life was ragtime.

He examined his son's body. The lung would be easy to replace, either with a pristine organ or one of his machines. Pumps were simple. The bone in the hip could be crafted from plaster. He could replace the eyes with lenses, improve the boy's sight. He'd waited to examine the head. The fine wires of the brain resisted duplication and could never be replaced precisely. The back of the Wilhelm's head hung like a flap from his neck. He turned the body over, prodded around inside the head with a tweezers. The medulla was smashed beyond repair. Bits of the cerebellum still clung to the sides. The frontal lobe looked intact. The primitive parts of the brain could be replaced. As long as the frontal lobe had not been damaged, his son, everything that he ever was, ever could be, could return to this world.

"I will rebuild you," he said. He threw a switch on the wall. It sparked, and electric lighting illuminated the shelves behind the altar at the head of the cathedral. His array of mechanical organs and limbs jump and pulsed, steam pouring from their valves: mechanized legs danced and kicked; hearts pounded in silver skin and rising airbladders; arms waved hello and goodbye. The special model he'd designed even loaded a rifle and pointed it, which it repeated as part of the demonstration. Less animated were the brain components that could replace the inner mechanisms. He'd not perfected them, and the machines though tiny still required a connection to a boiler to power them.

It wouldn't do. Too much of his son's brain had been left in the trenches, food for foxes. To replace all the mechanisms, his son would need to be attached to a substation, a steam engine. He'd be allowed no mobility, and thinking through metal and wire and steam impaired the mind. Though the brain functioned, the personal essence was lost.

Doctor Faust could replace the parts with fresh components, flesh components. He couldn't go to the Ministry though, to harvest the parts of dead soldiers. They'd deem it desecration of the dead.

No. He'd have to go out into the world, to harvest and borrow and replace. He loathed the idea of mutilating the healthy. The Ministry would surely burn him alive if he was caught. But would anyone notice? London bled with injured. Bricks and glass buried people, hiding their bodies. It must be done. His son deserved his freedom.

He carried his son's body into the crypt and wrapped it in a blanket. Then he opened the ammonium freezer and placed the body inside. He kissed his son's cold forehead and shut the lid. Then he laid on top and tried to sleep. Tomorrow, the grim work of harvesting would begin, and it weighed heavy on his mind.

He'd always at least had the solace of knowing that he was a healer, repairing the damaged. Now, he would become a butcher.

Doctor Faust banged on the backdoor to the Pink Lion. On the third knock, Poison Sumac answered, wearing a pink satin robe with frills along the neck and a pair of black panties beneath, showing through the sheer garment.

"You come late," Sumac said, inviting him in.

"Just a little to clear my head," he said. "A little of that old ragtime. I have grave work ahead. I'm selling my soul."

Sumac led him through the back passages behind the stage, into his temple. He'd set a wrought iron table, adorned with metal sculpted roses and two chairs. The ragtime alembic waited, already setup and boiling.

Sumac waited at his chair. He pulled it forward, and the drag queen sat, crossing his bare leg over his thigh. He lit an ersatz cigarette.

"Men are such fools," Sumac said. "You no longer have a soul to sell. You're full of ragtime now, better than a soul. A soul is a debt from God. Cast it off. You'll be free."

Sumac held out his hand.

"Sans a soul, I've only my body to sell."

Faust dug for his wallet, fetched some notes and proffered him the money.

"Oh no darling," Sumac said. "That won't do it all."

"It's all the money I have."

Sumac's lip curled into a grin.

"There are other ways to compensate. You have a thriving business."

"Never," he said.

He found his top hat, got up from the table. His legs filled with cement. He couldn't lift them to walk out of the dismal pit. He couldn't face the daylight, especially with the task ahead.

"I can sell you a few shares," he said.

"No darling. The whole thing if you please."

"It's all I have," he said. His head bowed.

The alembic popped, gurgled. He heard it like a siren song. A hole ripped in his body, a black hole expanding, tearing the fabric of space-time. He needed the key on his back wound like a clockwork toy.

"What does it matter?" Sumac said. "Your son will come back to you, and you can leave all this behind."

"I had a premonition last night that this will be my end."

"In either case, what does your company matter then?"

He hesitated, trying to push his legs again but failing. He sat back down.

"I have a contract already drawn up."

Sumac held out a fountain pen and slid the paper forward across the table. He signed then snapped the pen between his thumb and pointer finger. Sumac smothered him with the silver mask, the ersatz face that fits all faces.

<◇>

Doctor Faust waved the Union Jack as he walked behind the throngs. People massed on the sidewalks, waving their flags and cheering the parade of fresh soldiers marching through Trafalgar Square, marching to France, to the trenches, to war. The conscripted boys marched in rows of six, carrying their rifles over their shoulders. Each face appeared uniform.

He searched for the right candidate, someone whose absence wouldn't be conspicuous. He searched for the lonely, someone who'd come to watch the parade by themselves, with no one to share it with. He hurried, the ragtime euphoria already thinning. After observing the crowd for some time, he found an obese woman, her shoulders pouring out of her blouse's sleeves. Her hand never reached to touch the people around her. She wobbled a bit, fighting to keep her balance. He sniffed the cloud of liquor floating from her breath.

He took out the capacitor cell from his inside, jacket pocket. He spun the crank on it till his fingers numbed, charging the device. He sensed the act's immorality, but it felt like a dream, beyond his control. He'd numbed himself with ragtime, acted without rational thought, his need made manifest. Like a frog catching a fly with a quick tongue, he pressed the capacitor to her bulbous neck. She dropped into his arms. He nearly went down with her, struggling to keep her up.

"You'll excuse my wife," he said to the curious crowd. "My wife celebrates a little too much. I just need to get her home."

The soldiers marching down the street were replaced by steamtanks. They chugged down the road, vapor shooting from their mufflers. They crawled down the road like hungry beetles, their stubby limbs rowing them forward. The buildings shivered from the vibration from the anthropoid vehicles, the mammoth tanks off to murder and main.

The German Zeppelins and Steamflies relentlessly rained their bombs on London, blowing apart masonry into stone shrapnel.

He dropped her three times on the trip home, struggling to drag her down back alleys. For the next time, he'd bring a cart to deliver them to his cathedral, to ease the workload and harvest more parts to save time. Who would notice pieces missing from the victims of the Godless Huns?

Finally home, he laid her out on the altar and rolled out his tool belt. He'd adjusted the pipe organ into an air pump, and he fed a tube down her throat into her lungs. The bellows on the organ sighed and wheezed, alternating between intake and output.

He gripped his chisel and hammer and aimed at the side of her skull. He cracked the bone in one strike, then he used his pliers to chip away the cracked shell. He sliced away the bits of brain he needed, just part of the medulla. He didn't dare take all the required brain matter. Someone might notice and inform the Ministry. No. His work was far from done this day.

He dropped the brain matter into an ethyl solution, then he inserted a device to replace it. He pushed the walnut machine into her brain and attached a tube to the input valve. He cut away a portion of the bone fragment to make room for the tube, then glued it back onto her skull.

"You'll be right as rain," he said to her, kissing her forehead. "I bet you won't even notice the contraption in your head."

He connected the tube end to a portable boiler, equipped with its own handle and wheels like a wheel barrel. He fed the boiler several coal chunks and lit a fire from his lighter. After several minutes, steam whistled from the muffler at the top. Her eyes shot open.

"I'm so glad you're awake, my dear. You've had a bit of an accident, but you'll be fine. I've patched you up good as new, better than new."

"Accident?" she repeated, studying him with glazed eyes.

"Let me help you to your feet, careful though. You might be a bit dizzy."

"Feet?"

"You just need to make sure your boiler has plenty of coal and that you fill the water tank every morning. Isn't science grand? Look at the marvels we can perform."

He led her to the cathedral gate, pushing the boiler in front of them.

"Musical demon," she sang in monotone. "Set my honey a'dreaming. Won't you play me some rag."

He walked her back to the parade and left her alone to push the boiler herself, attached to it until the end of her days. He searched for more donors, anxious to finish the grim work before the ragtime dissipated in his system. He heard her humming the soulless melody as he merged into the crowd.

The stained glass windows on the western wall blew out. Shards rained down inside the cathedral, blown out by a nearby explosion. Doctor Faust wrapped a handkerchief around his mouth to filter the ashy air, the reek of burning chemicals, the unique odor of crispy flesh that fried and cooked and burned to carbon.

He fused the neurons to the various, purloined brain matter, rebuilding his son's automated nervous system, restoring to his body basic life functions. He worked with a thick magnifying glass lashed to his head with a leather band.

At last he finished. With a hand drill, he bored holes into his son's skull then fed copper filaments into them. He attached the wires to the electrodes on the keyboard. He injected him with the revitalizing solution with a brass syringe, stabbing him deep in the heart and pushing the plunger.

"Aqua Vitae," he said.

A German bomb fell close, screaming as it plummeted. The building across the way exploded, showering the cathedral with brick shards and steel fragments. The old church shook most of it off, and he continued preparing. When it came time, he sat on the bench before the pipe organ, ready to play the electrodes, to harmonize the magnetic fields, aligning them to the precise frequency of life.

He leaned forward and whispered into his son's hollow ear: "Forgive your father."

The steam generator chugged beneath him in the crypt. He could sense it shaking the floor, vibrations suffusing through his body. He set his hands to play but couldn't command them to press a single key.

He wept, tears diluting the grease smearing his face. He fetched his coat and ran into the night, dragging his mechanical leg in the street, not caring to dodge falling bombs. When he reached the Pink Lion, after several close calls, Sumac awaited him at the front door.

"Come for the final dose of my beloved ragtime?" the drag queen asked.

"Don't waste my time with questions you already know the answer to," he snapped.

"Business as usual then," Sumac said, leading him through the empty cabaret. Marlene again kept them company, playing counterpoint with the screeching bombs pulverizing the city. Sumac wore the black gown once again, must have been the only dress in the drag queen's repertoire. He'd already set up the apparatus.

"Why do you live like this? You must have a fortune."

"I am content to live in squalor. I give all the money and property away."

"I'd hate you, but I no longer feel hate," he said.

Sumac giggled, clapping his hands.

"The price has gone up," Sumac said. "But fret no more. This is the last dose. After tonight, you'll no longer need my medicine."

He studied the pipes of the alembic, curious as to its operation; perhaps, he could build one himself and obtain the narcotic's ingredients. Though he didn't have the drag queen's connections—all his lovely boys.

"I have the deed to my property. The land itself is worth a fortune, especially after the war ends when the Ministry will look to rebuild."

"This war will never end," Sumac said, overlooking the deed. "Our beloved leader lives for war, depends on it."

"Everything ends," he said.

Sumac hooked up the metal mask.

"Is your son dancing in the moonlight?" Sumac asked.

"I can't do it. Can't wake him."

Sumac nodded, pulling a cigarette from between his bra cups. He offered the drag queen a light.

"Your property will not cover the bill."

"This is all I have," he said, grabbing Sumac's arm, tugging on it. Sumac pulled away.

"For the third hit, the standard fee is the first born child, signed over to me, subject to my will and whims."

He shot up from his chair, raised his arm to shatter the alembic, knock the pipes and valves and boilers from the table into the wall.

"Evil bitch."

Sumac grinned, his upper lip twisting over, revealing the white membrane in his mouth.

He lowered his arm.

"I have no choice," he said.

"What does it matter? Your son will be alive. I'll keep him for awhile, have my fun. I'll soon get bored and release him to the streets. Better than the alternative. And it won't be dull. Never dull."

Sumac growled like a mythical tiger, his eyes flaring, targeting Doctor Faust. A jet of steam shot from his mechanical leg.

"All my lovely, lovely boys," Sumac said.

He nodded. Sumac slammed the silver mask to his face. As the ragtime flowed, infusing through his lungs, he felt a counterforce, a current, sucking him down the tube to fill the vacuum of released gas. It licked at his soul like a wolf lapping up blood.

"Mine, all mine," Sumac said.

At dawn, Doctor Faust played the electrodes, his fingers tingling from the current until they numbed. He knew each key, all the combinations and symphonies to generate the precise frequency of the magnetic fields, the secrets of life.

The pipe organ hummed and chanted, each pipe a singer in the choir, playing alto, tenor and soprano, weaving the electromagnetic mysteries of the cosmos—but mysteries no more. He'd liberated the knowledge from the gods and would give it to the people, end their mortality and know their praises through all time, loved more than their beloved Preacher.

The wires, diodes, and lodestones draped and fused along the pipes buzzed and sparked. The organ radiated an aureate field, a nascent star igniting to life, warm against his skin.

All the hate fled from his heart. Ragtime had cut out his soul, gutted him like a fish and fused itself to his body. You cannot hate sans soul. Sweet, wonderful ragtime. No more did he require gods to worship. He'd been drained hollow and become a vessel for love, his debt to the divine invalidated.

His son's hand twitched.

"Come home to me. Come back to the bright world. Follow the music."

His son's eyelids peeled back revealing milky eyes, vapid of life yet watching. His boy turned his head, scanning his father, a perplexed look on his face. Crimson flooded his etiolated flesh.

"I've returned you to life," Doctor Faust said. "I know the secret now. Ragtime. Nectar of the gods."

Doctor Faust banged on the keys. His fingertips cracked and bled on the white electrodes. He knew the rage that was coming, his son's first reaction after returning to the world. So numbed, he merely went through the motions, a robot made of gears and springs. He perfunctorily played the keys, waiting for the circuit to complete, for the inevitable to occur.

"Sweet melody," his son whispered through petrified lips.

Tears streamed down the Doctor's numb face.

"Forgive me, my son," he said.

His son, still waking, still thawing, getting used to his muscles again but learning quickly, struggled to lift his arms. They flopped around like a fish dropped in a boat, not managing to hit their mark. Then the muscle memory renewed, and he moved his arms with purpose, aim. He clenched Doctor Faust's throat, pushing his thumbs into his arteries.

Doctor Faust didn't struggle, didn't pull away from his son's hold. His son drove his fingernails into the flesh, cracking his trachea. The doctor's head slumped forward. The son released his grip then scanned the derelict cathedral.

Poison Sumac twirled at the gate. The drag queen twirled in a white dress like feathers with silk gloves to match his outfit. He danced in the nascent light, graceful as a dove, his shadow caressing the weeping boy still clutching the neck of his father. Sumac wiggled his pointer finger, beckoning Wilhelm forward.

"Happy birthday, darling," Sumac said. "Come to mother now."

MINE

Bryan Fields

"Mr. Crozier, the Denver Bank of the Platte is a *bank*. Not a gambling hall. We loan money expecting it to be repaid in full and on time. How shall you do that from within a Dragon's gizzard, sir?" Stanton shook his head. "My advice is to accept the Dragon's offer. The sum in question is fair, based on your productivity estimates."

"Irrelevant!" Crozier thumped his cane on the floor for emphasis. "I've spent four years getting the mine operational, and I shall be damned if some overgrown iguana is going to live on the fruits of my labor! The beast is blackmailing me, sir, and with Mr. Wallace's help, I shall have its head upon my wall for the effrontery."

"I see..." Stanton glanced at Wallace. By dress and demeanor, Wallace could have passed for a lawyer or business executive, but the three Colt revolvers he carried belied that impression. The merciless Bengali sun had left its mark on his countenance, throwing the pale, puckered bullet scar along his jaw into sharp relief. Stanton avoided meeting his gaze; no one wins a staring match with a tiger. "No offense, Mr. Wallace, but Cosmogyral Ecstasiate has stood down scores of bounty hunters, each of whom thought himself equal to the task. I have no doubt as to your skills, sir, but the odds favor the Dragon."

Crozier rose from his chair like a bellicose walrus. "Now see here! I am Jefferson Crozier the Third! Where is the bank manager? I will speak with him directly!" He shook the silver ram's head on his cane at Stanton, punctuating his remarks with sprays of spittle.

Wallace placed his hand on Crozier's arm. "Jefferson, please. Mr. Stanton is the loan manager. Protesting matters will gain us nothing but a demonstration of Mr. Beel's expertise in pugilism."

Crozier glanced over his shoulder. The ogre seated next to the door stared back at him. Without appearing to move, Beel cracked the bones in his neck. Crozier lowered his cane and sat down. "Of course. My apologies, Mr. Stanton. I am... unaccustomed to rejection. I realize our proposal is not without risk, but the Skydancer is worth far more than the sum requested. Why will you not accept it as security?"

Stanton shook his head. "As you pointed out, Mr. Crozier, the mine is unworkable until the matter of the Dragon is resolved. A mine that cannot be worked has no value, no matter how much silver it might otherwise produce. You have been a valued customer of this bank for over fifty years, sir, and as a valued customer, I must recommend that you accept the Dragon's offer. Take the money and allow the mine to lie unworked for the next few years."

"I shall not!" Crozier growled. "Getting the Skydancer to full production was my wife's dream, and I shall see it done. This is the reason I retained Mr. Wallace's services. Killing the Dragon will allow the mine to resume production, whereby the loan will be repaid."

"I understood your plan the first time you laid it out," Stanton replied. "My answer remains the same. This bank will not be lending you any money for this enterprise. Even if we wished to, we could not. You are asking us to bankroll a murder. Any loan we made to you would be improper, if not immoral."

Wallace sighed. "Jefferson, it pains me to suggest it, but perhaps this is to our good fortune. The *Xanadu* is ready to make way. We can be in Pioche in three days. The town is a lawless cesspool of the lowest order, and I'll warrant a good two score men with ready gun hands may be hired for the cost of a barrel of whiskey. They shall keep the Dragon occupied until I am able to engage it directly. What we lack in cannon we shall make up in shot volleys."

Stanton asked, "I take it this... *Xanadu*... is some manner of conveyance?"

"A steam house," Crozier replied. "I purchased it for my

wife, but she was taken from me before it could be delivered. It is my home, as well as a monument to my beloved Molly. It is not an asset to be borrowed against, if that's what you were thinking."

"Of course not. I merely—" Stanton stopped speaking as a bell sounded from inside a box on his desk. He flipped open the box and removed a brass ear trumpet attached to a length of cable. He listened for several seconds before returning the trumpet to the box and closing the lid.

Stanton contemplated the top of his desk for a moment before looking up. "That was the bank president, Mr. Bliss. He will approve your loan, provided that the steam house pass into his possession in the event the Dragon takes your life. You will be required to sign a document stating you understand the bank's conflict of interest in this matter and waive all claims which might arise from it. Mr. Bliss also wishes me to advise you against this course of action. That said, the final decision is yours."

Crozier rapped his cane on the floor. "I'll sign. I shall put paid to the Dragon and repay the funds directly. Damn you, sir, and all bankers with you."

Stanton smiled. "Of course, sir. This way please."

Six hours later, *Xanadu* left Denver behind and began the long climb up and over the Rockies. Even from a distance, the design and engineering of the engine evoked comment, as it was shaped to resemble the body and motion of a giant cat, even to the movement of paws as the drive wheels turned. Smoke poured from angular funnels in the ears, and at night the eyes lit up, casting great, searching rays of light into the darkness. Four Pullman coaches followed the engine: a study, living quarters for the owner and guests, a service car with kitchen, storage, and staff berths, and lastly the armory.

Crozier sat in a high—backed chair at the front of the study, wearing a red velvet smoking jacket and matching fez. He stared out the window at the half-seen trees lining the railway line, puffing on a meerschaum pipe. A smiling mermaid curled around the bowl of the pipe, stained tawny amber by years of use. Crozier's thumb and forefingers were never still, rubbing endless circles against the mermaid's prodigious breasts. He refilled his glass of Glenlivet, offering the bottle to Wallace as he sat down.

Wallace shook his head. "I'll drink when the job's done." He nodded to Crozier's butler, Dortmund. "May I have a coffee, please?" Dortmund bowed, pouring and serving the coffee in silence. Wallace dissolved two thumb-sized bricks of sugar in his coffee, swirling it around the cup before he drank.

Crozier knocked the ash out of his pipe and refilled the bowl. "Having second thoughts, Edward?"

"No. My concerns haven't changed." Wallace gestured to the orange and black rug in the middle of the floor. "A Dragon isn't a simple beast, like a tiger. They are more cunning than men and have the patience of mountains. This one is playing a long game, and the mine is just a pawn on the chessboard."

Crozier lowered his pipe, unlit. "What are you saying, man? *I* am no pawn!"

"From the Dragon's perspective, we are. Both of us." Wallace sighed. "You've never seen one in action, Jefferson. I have. I saw Tempestatem Invicta at Shiloh... I saw what he did to those poor rebel bastards. The sun wasn't even up when he attacked. It took him less than a minute to lay down a wall of fire a mile long, all along their front lines. The rebels broke and ran, even as they burned alive. On his second pass, he hit the powder wagons. The explosions, the screams, the stench of burning flesh... I remember it all too well. The smoke turned the sun blood red, and damn near choked us all. He killed twenty thousand men in a matter of minutes, and he did it because a prolonged battle would have impacted one of his businesses."

Crozier pointed the stem of his pipe at Wallace. "You also said you saw him injured. The great Storm was not so Invincible after all, eh? Not to Enfield rifles, eh? And we've got a damn sight more than Enfields to call on."

"Yes," Wallace replied. "God grant it will be enough."

The next morning, Wallace awoke before dawn and joined the night shift engineers, Elgin and Morris, in the cab of Xanadu's engine. Working the night shift required alert minds and keen reflexes. Good coffee was essential, and both men were masters of the brew kettle. Wallace took his first cup as the engineers did—hot from the boiler and black as the night around them.

Both engineers were old friends of his, as were the men of the day shift. Together, they had survived two years under the Union flag and a fair number of scrapes since then. Even now, fifteen years after Appomattox, they had answered his call without complaint or question.

Wallace refilled their cups, leaving the last measure in the pot. He raised his cup in salute and said, "To seeing another dawn." Elgin and Morris returned the salute. The remainder they emptied out onto the ground as a libation for those who hadn't been as lucky.

Wallace rose from his place by the boiler when the breakfast bell sounded. The *Xanadu* approached Ogden and the engineers were busy bringing the steam house to a stop in order to take on water and coal. This was their area, not his, so he left them to their business.

The train station in Ogden was uninspiring, being a squat reddish building set well out from town in the middle of an insect-filled mud flat. Wallace and Crozier decided to forego eating breakfast on the salon car's verandah and dined indoors.

A rapid knocking on the salon's rear door pulled both men away from their table. Dortmund went to open the door; Wallace stepped in front of Crozier, hands resting on the handles of his Colts.

The door opened to reveal a boy of perhaps twelve. He handed an envelope to Dortmund, who rewarded him with a nickel tip before handing the envelope to Crozier. The boy pulled his cap off and bowed, eyes flitting around the salon. Wallace caught the boy's gaze and shook his head slightly. The boy glanced at Wallace's pistols and developed a keen interest in the floor.

"It's a telegram... from the Dragon." Crozier donned his spectacles. "Violence solves nothing, stop. Rental offer doubled, full value of mine to be placed in escrow pending surrender at end of lease, stop. Will cover all fees, stop. Reply soonest, signed, Cosmogyral Ecstasiate." Crozier shook his head. "This must be a joke."

"You don't think a Dragon knows how to send a telegram?"

"What? No! He's sent them before." Crozier waved his hand, dismissing the question. "I mean doubling his offer. It's far more than the mine would produce under the best of circumstances. If I agree right now, the Dragon is going to be losing money."

Wallace raised his eyebrow. "Dragons don't lose money."

"No, they don't. It makes no sense..." Crozier's voice trailed off. "The only other mineral in there is autunite. The foreman reported hitting several bands of the stuff. It's all but worthless."

Crozier leaned back in his chair, stroking his pipe. "There's something more than silver in that mine. Something we missed. It's the only explanation. There's something of immense value there, and the Dragon wants it."

Crozier scribbled a terse reply on the back of the telegram envelope and held it out to the boy, along with a silver dollar. "Take that to the telegraph office as fast as you can, boy. Keep the remainder." The boy nodded and raced from the salon. Crozier poured himself a large whisky, downing half of it in a single gulp. He refilled the glass, but didn't drink. "Edward?"

Wallace nodded. "Yes, sir?"

"Please see to it that we get underway as soon as possible. Shut the gate on her, Edward. God willing, I would see us in Pioche tomorrow morning."

"I'll tell the engineers, and make sure the water reserves are topped off as well. I'll come see you once we're under way and we can mark out a route south from Palisade." Wallace downed the last of his coffee and went forward to the engine.

Xanadu's engine performed without issue all day and into the night, save for refueling at the Palisade depot. Morning found *Xanadu* racing south, past the jagged majesty of the Humboldt Range. The steam house was running on her heavy steel ground wheels, free of the railroad. Now they followed the Wells Fargo trail, as clear and well-maintained a roadway as they could have asked for. Going overland was slower than rail travel, but if the

Dragon had agents watching the refueling depots, it was their only hope of keeping surprise on their side.

Wallace finished his morning ablutions and whipped up a frothy mug of near-to-boiling shaving cream. The occasional bounce and jostle of their passage over the ground made shaving a delicate matter, but Wallace was determined to meet his Maker as a gentleman, should bad come to worst this day.

The sun was well up as he took his breakfast on the verandah; thick rashers of bacon and buttermilk biscuits covered with gravy that seemed equal parts sausage and cream. He followed it with coffee, made by his own hand in the Arab style, using a gold-chased vessel given to him a decade earlier in one of Cairo's innumerable neighborhood *souks*. He closed his eyes, remembering the heat, the smells of coal smoke and burning camel dung, the incessant clamor, and his first sip of the best coffee he'd ever tasted.

He stayed there for three days, living and praying with the locals while he practiced roasting, grinding and brewing coffee from the raw bean. His teacher, an elderly Bedouin, finally pronounced his technique acceptable and sent him on his way. His parting gift was to push the coffee pot into Wallace's hands, saying, "Take it. No one will drink after an Infidel, anyway." Wallace smiled to himself and raised his cup to salute the old man's memory.

His hand froze, the cup nearly slipping from his fingers. Less than one hundred yards away, a massive shadow covered the ground, racing alongside the steam house. Wallace set the cup down, taking care to make no noise. He moved to the side rail and leaned out, staring past the salon car's roof.

A blood-red Dragon soared above them, well within the range of Wallace's double rifle—which was in his bedroom. *Don't run*, he told himself. *Walk calmly, and arouse no suspicion.* It was still all he could do not to race to the sleeper car's door.

He paused at the door and glanced to his left. The giant shadow was still with them. He stepped inside, leaving the door open. Moments later, he emerged with his double rifle. He pressed his back against the side of the rail car, holding the rifle against his chest.

The shadow was gone.

Wallace shook his head. "Clever beast…" he whispered. He stepped to the western side of the rail car and turned to the rear, bringing the double rifle to his shoulder. The sky was empty. He moved to the other side of the rail car, but the eastern sky was equally free of Dragons.

Wallace lowered the double rifle. "Well, isn't that as fine as cream gravy…" he muttered. He slung the rifle over his shoulder and started up the ladder on the back of the salon car. He peeked over the edge of the roof, but there was still no sign of the Dragon. He grabbed both of the curved handrails at the top of the ladder and pulled himself up until his knee touched the roof. He paused for half a second, then pushed backward and dropped to the base of the ladder.

Razor-sharp talons sliced through the air where his neck had been. Wind blasted down around him, filling the air with dirt and sand. The Dragon banked hard to the left, staying low and fanning up a dust cloud for cover.

Wallace dropped prone; sighting the double rifle through the hand rail's wrought-iron balusters. He put the first round into the thickest portion of the dust cloud, without result. He gave the second a bit more of a lead.

Dirt fountained into the air, accompanied by roars of pain and rage. Wallace ejected the spent cartridges but the Dragon was airborne before he could finish reloading. He got to his feet, watching the Dragon climb into the sky.

Crozier opened the salon door. "Did you hit him?"

"Grazed him, if I hit him at all. He's moving too well for the wound to be anything significant." Wallace entered the salon, placing the double rifle in the middle of the snooker table. He accepted a cup of coffee from Dortmund and added twice his normal amount of sugar to the cup.

"I would say we've counted coup on each other." Wallace sat down and took a long drink. "He's giving us a chance to withdraw with honor. However, I'll warrant that the next time we cross paths, we best let fly in a powerful way. Otherwise, things are going to get hotter than a ten-dollar whorehouse on nickel night."

The next few hours were quiet, and *Xanadu* pulled into the Pioche train depot, back on the rail line—at half-past ten. The yard crew guided her through backing up onto an unused siding, well away from town and surrounded by obsolete rolling stock and broken mining equipment. It took Wallace and Crozier some time to cross the rail yard and enter Pioche proper. It came as no shock that the Sheriff, two deputies, and a blood-red Dragon the size of a house were waiting for them.

The Dragon wore a starched white collar and a black string tie at the base of his neck, a top hat large enough to hold several bushels of corn, and a pair of wine-dark spectacles balanced on the bridge of his snout. His left hind leg had a fresh wound plaster wrapped with linen and secured with a dozen turns of hemp rope.

Wallace tipped his hat to the Dragon. "A pleasure to meet you, sir. I hope that small inconvenience will cause you no great trouble."

Cosmogyral Ecstasiate inclined his head and tipped his hat by raising an ear fin. "The wound is minor, thank you. You have my gratitude for not using fragmentation shells."

The Sheriff cleared his throat. "Mr. Crozier, I'm not here to take sides in this issue. I have advised Mr. Ecstasiate of the same thing I am going to tell you: I will arrest anyone who seeks to break the peace in this town. If you resist arrest, my men will shoot you dead. We have had three major fires in the time I've lived here and I will not have another. Shootouts and brawls between drunken miners are bad enough. Settle this with words, or meet on private property outside of town. That, gentlemen, is an official order."

Crozier nodded. "Understood. The Skydancer is private property—mine! And I give us permission to settle this matter there. I trust the law has no objection to that?"

"With regards to that matter, I have one more offer to tender." The Dragon extended his claw with an envelope held between the tips of two talons. "I think you will agree it is more than fair, and I pray you accept it."

Crozier opened the envelope and read through the documents. "This... this is ten times the Skydancer's value."

The Dragon nodded. "Yes. To be paid in cash or in gold bullion, whichever you desire."

Crozier folded the papers and put them back in the envelope. "I take it this is your final offer?"

"You will not get a better one."

Crozier tore the papers in half and dropped them on the ground. "The Skydancer is mine. I will have it, and be shed of you. That is *my* final offer."

Cosmogyral Ecstasiate laughed, showing several rows of knifelike fangs. "*Molon labe*," he hissed. In a moment he was airborne, turning toward the disputed summit of Treasure Hill.

Crozier looked blank. "What the Hell did he say?"

"It was Greek. He said, 'come and take it'," Wallace answered. "That was Leonidas' answer to the Persians at the battle of Thermopylae."

"Well, I am no scholar of ancient Greek," said the Sheriff. "But, if you're thinking about marching up there with a bunch of hired guns, you should keep that little skirmish in mind. Good day, gentlemen."

The Dragon landed on the summit of Treasure Hill and removed his tie and spectacles, dropping them into his hat and setting it aside. He reared back on his hind legs and roared. The sound shook the earth and sent the miners working the surrounding claims into hysterical, headlong flight. As the echoes faded away, Cosmogyral Ecstasiate unleashed a torrent of flame into the air, wreathing the upper slopes of Treasure Hill in flame and smoke.

Wallace smiled, tapping his fingers on the butt of his pistol. "Well, time to go to work. Sheriff, would you please escort Mr. Crozier to the Mountain Meadows Inn? The owner has been handling some small matters for us and those accounts must be settled."

The Sheriff nodded. "Gladly. Have no fear, Mr. Wallace, Fancher has your ruffians assembled, and God's mercy on you all. This way, Mr. Crozier."

Over the next hour, Wallace disconnected the armory car and had Xanadu moved as far up the siding as they could manage. Only Morris remained in the steam house's cab, charged with keeping the fire stoked and the boiler at full pressure.

Wallace took position on the service car's roof, armed only with a surveyor's theodolite, several pencils, and a detailed map of Crozier's original land patent. Four sets of equations ran down the side of the map, culminating in four simple sets of numbers. Wallace copied them onto a new piece of paper, folding it and tucking it into his pocket before climbing down the ladder.

Wallace's perch allowed him an excellent view of Treasure Hill—and the Dragon basking in front of the Skydancer—but the train yard's equipment blocked any such view from the armory car. The arrangement was all Wallace could have hoped for.

The engineers stood to the side while Wallace inspected their handiwork, both inside the car and out. As he rejoined the engineers, Wallace pulled out his pocket watch and shook his head. "Had I not seen it myself, I wouldn't believe this time. Thirty-eight minutes, gentlemen! The lot of you should re-enlist and show the milk-drinkers how real soldiers perform!"

Elgin shrugged. "Was easy enough, lieutenant. You weren't in here fixing what was already done."

Wallace laughed. "Well, all you had to do was stop doing it wrong." He clapped Elgin on the shoulder. "All joking aside, well done, all of you. Perform as well when the action starts, and we will wrap this matter up quicker than you can boil asparagus." He pulled the paper out of his pocket. "Dennis, start with solution one. Elgin, keep eyes on me at all times. Help Stubbs with the rig if you can, but if this goes bad you'll need every second I can give you."

Xanadu's steam whistle sounded three short bursts. Wallace clapped his hands. "Gentlemen, the curtain rises. Dennis, you have five minutes. After that, drop the walls and watch for my signal. And may Fortune favor the bold."

Wallace jogged back to the steam house and climbed up to his perch. He pulled a naval spyglass out of his surveying bag and trained it on Treasure Hill. Cosmogyral Ecstasiate had not moved, but he was watching Crozier's arrival with keen interest. Crozier had insisted on leading the hired guns himself, rather than waiting in safety as Wallace had wanted him to.

Crozier and his men stopped at the bottom of the hill, hundreds of yards from his property line, and took up large, rectangular shields similar to those used by Caesar's legions. These shields were not covered with steel or hide, however; each of these was covered by a thick layer of asbestos.

With every man so equipped, the group assembled into a passable formation, presenting the Dragon with a well-ordered shield wall. Wallace looked back uphill at the Dragon. He still hadn't moved, but he did appear to be laughing.

"That's right, demon. Laugh at the monkeys," Wallace whispered. "Laugh at the naked apes who don't learn from history. The Greeks and Romans tried this, didn't they?" He lowered the glass and took up a red and white flag. As he raised it, he heard the walls of the armory car drop to the ground, leaving its cargo with clear sky overhead.

Something—perhaps the motion of the walls falling, or the dust it kicked up—attracted the Dragon's attention. He looked to the side, staring right at Wallace. Wallace brought the flag down with a snap of his wrist.

Thunder filled the train yard, shaking the ground and rocking the steam house as the 15-inch *Devastator*-class mortar sent its deadly payload into the sky. Cosmogyral Ecstasiate scrambled to his feet, spreading his wings for takeoff. The mortar shell exploded a hundred feet above him, covering the top half of the hill with thousands of needle-sharp flechettes. Hundreds of them tore through the membranes of his wing sails. Hundreds more slipped through the gaps between his steel-hard scales, sinking deep into flesh and bone.

Cosmogyral Ecstasiate fell to the ground, keening in agony. Blood welled up from under his scales and soaked the ground beneath his wings. He tried to stand, but only one of his forelegs would support any weight. He folded his wings as best he could and managed to push himself into a defensive crouch.

Wallace pumped his fist in the air. "Well struck, boys! Well struck! Come and see!" The engineers left the armory and hurried to join Wallace on the service car's roof. Wallace passed around the naval glass, allowing each of the men a chance to see the downed Dragon.

When Dennis finished, he lowered the glass and asked, "What happens now, lieutenant?"

Wallace shrugged. "God willing, this will convince the beast to move on. Jefferson has a list of demands the Dragon will need to agree to, one of which is not embarking on a vendetta against any of us. If they can't reach an agreement, Jefferson will have to kill him. Even that lot should be up to the job, given the state the creature is in."

"Lieutenant? I think you should have a look at this." Elgin passed the naval glass back to Wallace. "I think there's something in the mine."

Wallace brought the glass up to his eye and focused on the mine entrance. Nothing moved in the darkness, but Cosmogyral Ecstasiate was digging into the ground with his foreclaws, throwing gouts of dirt and sand into the air as he dragged himself toward Crozier and the hired guns.

Why would he be crawling toward *them?* Wallace turned to the right, and spotted Crozier's group perhaps fifty yards down the road from the Dragon. They had stopped, but their attention wasn't on the wounded Dragon. Wallace shifted his gaze to the road and started panning back toward the mine.

He saw something move, half hidden behind a large rock on the edge of the road. "I see something... Did a dog get loose up there?"

Elgin shook his head. "Not unless dogs have wings."

"Wings?" Wallace looked again, and saw a Dragon hatchling emerge from behind the rock. Its hide was a uniform bright yellow, almost the exact shade of a baby duck. It hissed and snapped, stiff-legged and defiant as Crozier approached. Crozier dropped his shield and knelt in the roadway. He held his hand out to the hatchling, offering it a sweet of some sort.

The hatchling scampered backward, well out of reach.

Crozier started forward again. The hatchling puffed up its chest and exhaled as hard as it could. No flames emerged, only a few wisps of smoke. Crozier lunged forward, grasping at the hatchling's snout. His hand closed on air as the hatchling raced back to the mine entrance.

Cosmogyral Ecstasiate lurched to his feet, turning sideways and backing away from the mine entrance. He coughed out a small burst of flame; it posed no danger to Crozier, but he retreated and formed up with his men, shields at the ready. The Dragon took another step backward and roared.

Crozier lowered his shield, waving his list of demands. As he spoke, his men drew their weapons and aimed at the Dragon. None of them saw the gleaming golden Dragoness emerge from the mine's darkness.

Her breath was not the liquid Hell-fire her race was renowned for; it was the descent of Fimbulwinter. The cold knifed through clothes and into blood and bone. Sweat became ice and frostbite ravaged exposed skin. When the arctic winds of her breath dissipated, Crozier and his men were enrobed in an inch of solid ice.

Now the Dragoness emerged fully from the darkness, wearing a steel and leather harness which served as equal parts weapons mount and child carrier. She had a Hotchkiss rotating cannon mounted on each shoulder and a Gatling gun under each wing. Six baby duck-yellow hatchlings perched on padded couches, grasping triggers and crank handles with their stubby foreclaws. The Dragoness braced for the recoil and the hatchlings opened fire.

Wallace closed the spyglass and turned away. He pulled a silver flask out of the surveyor's bag and took a long drink, then passed the flask to Elgin. He packed up the theodolite and reclaimed his flask as the first cannon reports reached them from the slaughter at the mine. He closed his eyes, shuddering, until the echoes of the distant gunfire faded.

Wallace shouldered the surveyor's bag and nodded at the other men. "I think we're done here, gentlemen. Grab your kit and meet me at the Mountain Meadows Inn. I'll have the balance of your pay there, and the first round is on me. Godspeed."

Dennis shook his head. "Shouldn't we be running? The Dragons are going to want blood."

Wallace started down the ladder. "If they want satisfaction, then running will avail you nothing. You'll only die tired."

The Dragons didn't come that day, nor the next. Late in the day word spread through town that the Dragons had departed after sealing the Skydancer with stones, melted and fused together into a solid mass. The Sheriff posted 'No Trespassing' signs, and the neighboring mines made plans to resume work. For Pioche, life returned to normal.

Each of the engineers received a telegram that night, asking them to stay on and operate *Xanadu* for the new owners. Dennis opted to return to his family, but the others accepted. Wallace lingered in the bar all night, but no message arrived for him.

The next morning, his breakfast arrived with an envelope sitting on the tray next to his eggs with black truffles. Wallace set the envelope aside while he ate. Once the waiter cleared his empty plate, he picked the envelope up and opened it.

Inside, he found a bank cheque for the balance of the sum Crozier had promised him, an additional $5,000.00 in cash, and a folded note. The note was signed by Aurora Bliss, president and owner of the Denver Bank of the Platte, and said only, 'What's mine is mine.'

Wallace shaved, donned his best suit, and made his way to the train yard. *Xanadu* was ready to move out, but everyone appeared to be waiting. Wallace found a shady spot, and ten minutes later a stagecoach pulled up. A tuxedo-clad Ogre emerged from the salon car and opened the stagecoach door. It took Wallace a moment to recognize the Ogre; it was Beel, the bodyguard he'd met at the bank in Denver.

A middle-aged gentleman with ginger hair emerged first. A young woman with a mane of golden hair stepped down next, followed by six young children with pale, pastel yellow hair. Wallace watched them enter the salon, followed by Beel and their luggage. After a moment, Beel came back out of the salon and walked across the yard to Wallace.

Beel gave Wallace a slow nod. "From Mr. Bliss, with his complements." He handed Wallace a pawn from the salon's chess set. "He asks you to hold his family harmless, should you feel a need to press your business with him. Their bodies will sleep for three years while they walk the world as dreams made flesh. When they awake, he will be at your service. You have until then to plan your next move."

Wallace looked at the pawn, turning it over in his fingers. "My next move? I don't know what that might be. Tell me, what was the point? What is in there? Why all the deception, the manipulation, the murder? What makes that mine so special? Can you at least tell me that?"

Beel reached into his coat, withdrawing a delicate yellow crystal. "This. Veins of it, deep in the mine. It emits energy the children need to live and grow. The other mines do not have the crystals. All this, Mr. Bliss did for his children."

"Oh, Jefferson, I'm so sorry. I should have reasoned it out." Wallace closed his eyes and sighed. "If he had only explained, Jefferson would have understood. He would have accepted the rental offer."

"That is not the game," Beel replied. "No Dragon buys with gold when they can buy with blood."

Wallace dropped the pawn into his pocket. "What if I choose not to play anymore?"

Beel shrugged. "The pieces change but the game continues. Good day, Mr. Wallace." He walked back to the salon car, closing the door behind him. *Xanadu's* whistle sounded and the steam house moved out of the yard.

Wallace glanced up at the fused rock sealing the Skydancer shut. He shook his head, and started back to his hotel. He never played his best games without a fresh cup of coffee.

THE PROMISE AND THE RECKONING

Andrew Knighton

France was burning. Hundreds of feet below the airship *Shaka's Promise*, the place where Paris had been was a sea of lava, dark points breaking the glowing waves. Smoke streamed from broken peaks, spreading from dense columns to an all-enveloping cloud.

The *Promise* hung beside one of those columns, like a fat date dangling from a palm, its stalk a rubberised tube.

"Faster Jim!" Professor Ondieki bellowed, trying not to gag on the sulfurous air. He watched in anticipation as the smoke curled from the tube into the glass chamber of the condenser, a device of stacked cylinders and spiraling brass half as tall as a man. This was the moment he found most difficult, waiting for the evidence to reveal itself. A few more seconds could prove him right or wrong. This was his life's work. This was science.

A dark layer was settling in the jar, but it was all fine particles, none of the heavier volcanic matter he needed to see.

"Pump faster!" Ondieki yelled. "It needs suction."

Near the open hangar door, his teenage assistant pushed back his cap and set to the bellows with renewed vigor. Sweat and ash streaked his face as a layer of fine yellow crystals settled in the chamber.

The hangar glowed red by the lava's light. *Shaka's Promise* lurched in a shifting air current. Her tail swung away from the billowing smoke, drifting toward the volcano and the magma blazing from its peak.

"That'll do." The professor snapped the condenser valve shut. The crystals fit his theory, but they weren't enough to prove it. He needed one more sample, and that meant it was time to move.

He stalked down the airship, footsteps ringing on the

aluminum floor. The *Promise* shook again, throwing him about like a child's doll, and pain shot through him as he slammed against the corner of a table. He shook it off and lurched to the bridge, long fingers grasping the wheel.

Outside the window, molten rock filled the sky. They were perilously close to fiery death.

"All stowed and ready to go, governor." Jim's voice sounded flat through the speaking tube.

"Then hold on tight." Ondieki spun the wheel and yanked the engine lever down to red. The ship turned, tilting to port as she accelerated away. A loose pan clattered across the floor. He should remind Jim to tidy.

A tongue of lava whipped toward them, one last attack from an angry landscape. Ondieki watched, mesmerized by its bright curve, an emblem of Europe's savage beauty. Then it fell away and they soared on, high into the smoke and safety. To Calais and beyond, for one final sample and an answer to his life's work.

Calais, according to historians, had been an important port even before the Reckoning. The Emperor of France, so the stories said, had been on his way there when the fires came. His final words, before returning to doomed Paris, had been "To the boats! While one Frenchman lives, so does France!"

As Ondieki understood it, the tale of Napoleon's last words was a myth. But it was a myth in which Calais took pride. Above the harbor master's office, the emperor's legendary phrase had been daubed in six foot letters, tar black against the whitewash: *AUX BATEAUX!*

While Jim finished mooring the *Promise*, Ondieki peered over the edge of their pier. Four tiers of air docks lay between him and the harbor below, a giant trellis of salvaged timber and sturdy ropes that played host to half a dozen patched balloons and soot-stained dirigibles. Despite the distance he could see movement on the surface of the sea. The eruption that had threatened them the previous day had been part of a larger tremor, triggering quakes and flows all the way to the coast. Calais's floating warehouses and inns were still coming back in to dock, balancing the threat of further tremors against the risk of lost earnings. Two large barges ground against each other, both trying to fit into a single mooring, sailors brawling on their decks like ants fighting over a sugar bowl.

Ondieki coughed, a rasping bark from the back of his throat. He covered his mouth with a handkerchief, and pulled it away covered in blobs of black phlegm.

"Are you alright there, sir?" The words were French but the voice wasn't, weighed down with an ugly, jagged accent.

Ondieki turned to see three men in worn red jackets. Their buttons gleamed in the constant twilight beneath the Reckoning clouds, and they all bore rifles.

"Docking pass?" The leading man held out his hand.

"You are British, yes?" Ondieki replied in English, scrabbling through the papers in his bag.

"So our mam tells us. Durham Light Infantry."

The man seemed genuine. Relieved, Ondieki handed over his pass. Real Redcoats meant real security, not some Germanic chancer trying to take his documents and a "docking fee".

"Staying long, sir?"

Ondieki shook his head. "A day to buy supplies and visit a friend, then on to your country."

"My country?"

"England!"

The Redcoat raised an eyebrow.

"Maybe you haven't heard in Swahi, but there's no England left."

Ondieki laughed.

"That is why I am going. To view the volcanoes, and sample the smoke of the Thames Peak."

"Good luck with that. There's nowt come out of the Peak in years, and good thing too. When father Thames roars, you'll feel it all the way in Africa."

Ondieki smiled. "I am a professor of vulcanology. I will find a way."

<\<\>>

Chez Gerard was the best restaurant in Calais. That didn't mean meat and fruit, like it would in Mombassa, but Ondieki couldn't afford the best restaurant in Mombassa. Not that he'd have gone there if he could. Fish was as good for the body as meat. Gerard's fish might be a little bitter, but Ondieki would be too if he swam in these waters. The sauce took the edge off it.

"Why always garlic?" he asked, fragments of fish flying from his mouth.

"Grows with little light," Dr Espinard explained, "and covers a multitude of sins. Which round here..."

He waved one fat hand, taking in the fish, the potatoes, the peeling paint and their fellow diners. They weren't the sort Ondieki was used to. They had the weathered features of sailors, but framed by jewelry and once-fine clothes. These were men who thrived on the edges of civilization, far from the civil servants and academics of Swahi's capital.

"God I miss wine." Espinard stared at his glass of boiled water.

"Why not import it?" Ondieki asked.

"We can barely import enough food. We survive. Beyond that..." Espinard set the glass down.

"So what brings you back here? Come to admit I was right about the Languedoc range?"

"Come to prove you wrong." Ondieki swelled with pride as he thrust a sheaf of papers across the table. "Atmospheric analysis from the first tier of Reckoning volcanoes. All except the Thames Peak. Look at the third table."

Ondieki gobbled potatoes while Espinard peered at the papers. The Frenchman skimmed through them once then went back, finger tracing a slow course across the page. Finally he stopped, peering over his glasses.

"You're wrong," he said. "I've spent a lifetime studying this. My tests show—"

"Your tests were done with old equipment, cobbled together in Europe. Mine were carried out with the latest African technology."

"Such a connection between the peaks is preposterous."

"Progress lives in the preposterous. Think of Abura when she described evolution, or Pembe when he launched the first airship. When I bring back a smoke sample from the Thames Peak, and it fits those readings, then you'll see."

Espinard set down the papers, a smile creeping up his face. "I'm afraid that the Thames Peak is dormant."

Ondieki pulled one more document from his bag. A blueprint for a cylindrical device, one end spiked, the rest a mass of pistons and steam chambers. Espinard turned the sheet this way and that, looking at it from every angle. His face furled in bemusement, rolls of flesh crumpling over each other.

A waiter appeared, whisking away dirty plates and replacing them with bowls of steamed skyberries. Ondieki bit one of the grey spheres, sweet pulp bursting across his tongue.

"The Reckoning hasn't been all bad, eh?" He pointed at the bowl.

Espinard ignored him, staring at the blueprint. Suddenly he gasped and slammed it down, rattling cutlery and candlesticks.

"You cannot be serious," he said. "This will set off an eruption."

Ondieki nodded. The only thing more satisfying than one's own genius was having it recognized. "A small one. Enough to gather data."

"A small one? What about the tremors? The tidal waves? When England shakes, Normandy drowns."

"Unlikely. The Thames Peak has been dormant too long. And this will allow us to understand the eruptions. Predict them. Control them."

"But if you're wrong you'll ruin half of Europe for nothing."

"If I'm right, I'll ruin you."

Espinard stared, open-mouthed.

"It's a joke," Ondieki said. "You're like me. Well respected, tenured. You'll develop new lines of research."

"I won't, because I'm not wrong." Espinard threw the papers in Ondieki's face. "You're wrong. This device is wrong. Your research is wrong."

He grabbed a fistful of the berries.

"This whole damned world is wrong."

He flung the berries down in disgust and stormed from the restaurant.

It could be hard to see your work undone, and Ondieki pitied Espinard the experience, but there was no need to be childish. He turned, oblivious to the glares of the other diners, and raised a hand.

"Bill please."

Looking out across Calais from the bridge of *Shaka's Promise*, it seemed as if the night world had been turned on its head. Below, a sea of glittering points. Above, nothing but black.

This was Europe, a place of darkness and inversion. Many of its inhabitants had died in the first days of the Reckoning, swallowed in fire and buried in stone. The rest had fled if they were smart, knuckled down to survival if they were determined. Few took an interest in why their world had changed. What mattered was what it had changed to, and how they could survive.

To Professor Ondieki there was nothing but why. Why volcanoes? Why here? Why then? Why was the Languedoc range still active while Denmark lay dormant? Why was Germany ruined but Portugal intact? Why was the ash from one plume black, another grey, a third sickly brown?

From questions came facts, from facts understanding, and from understanding would come control, the ability to master the world through science. What could be more exhilarating than to see the world shift to your design?

Ondieki scribbled in the margin of a chart, resting on a flat part of the steering console. The walk from *Chez Gerard* had gotten his blood pumping, triggering a whole raft of ideas. Espinard's worries about the Thames Peak had been baseless, but they opened up new questions about the connections between the peaks, the boundaries of their influence, the limits of their impact. It was all fuel to the fire of inspiration. But the thrill of discovery made him impatient to get moving.

He tapped the engine pressure dial.

"Are we ready?" he asked the speaking tube.

"Nearly, governor," Jim replied, his voice followed by the rasp of shoveled coal.

Outside, someone was shouting. Ondieki glanced through the window to port. Half a dozen figures were striding along the docks, lit by the acid-green flare of chemical lamps. Brass buttons and rifle tips glittered in the gloom. At their head waddled a fat figure, pointing excitedly at *Shaka's Promise*.

"Time to go." Ondieki wasn't letting anything interfere with his plans. He pulled a lever and the Promise's mooring ropes dropped away, an emergency measure installed after an incident in Kongasso. He turned the drive gauge up to full, and at the back of the gondola twin propellers whirred into action.

"Um, governor, we're not really—"

Jim's objection was cut short as bullets ricocheted off the gondola's armored sides. The shouts were getting louder, as Espinard and the Redcoats rushed to stop them from getting away.

The *Promise* began to move, building speed as she drifted along the dock. The soldiers were running, one ahead of the rest, long legs driving him on. He caught up with the gondola and leaped, thumping against the rear panels. There he clung, feet planted on a mooring rail, one hand scrabbling at a window.

Ondieki stalked irritably down the bridge, grabbing a broom from the tool rack. He stared through thick plate glass into the Redcoat's eyes. The man was stern, determined, not an ounce of fear on his face. They had left the dock and the other soldiers behind, but he was unphased. He had his task and would stick to it.

Below them, the lights of the harbor twinkled.

"I'm sorry," Ondieki said, opening the window, "but science must prevail."

He jabbed the broom handle into the soldier's stomach. The man grunted, lost his grip and fell, tumbling toward the sea.

Ondieki closed the window and stowed the broom,

suppressing a twinge of guilt. The man had only been doing his job. But you shouldn't stand in the way of progress, and at least he'd land in water.

<<>>

The Thames Peak rose like a thorn from England's fossilized skin. The air around was hot and sulfurous, thick with the vapors seeping from its cracked sides.

The *Promise* hung above the Peak's southern ascent, floating at the end of a long anchor rope. A second rope creaked as Ondieki passed it through the pulleys by the hanger door. It was good rope, but a little frayed with age, much like Ondieki's clothes. Funny how time crept up when you weren't paying attention.

"Slower!" Jim's voice rose from the miasma. "Slower!"

Ondieki halted the rope while he gathered his thoughts. Then he began to ease it out again, letting Jim's weight drag him down.

"I'm there, governor," Jim shouted from the ground. Ondieki leaned out of the hangar door, peering at his assistant amidst the rocks below. Jim untied the bulky cylinder of the trigger device from the line, shouldered it and set out across the broken landscape, his footsteps tentative, one hand stretched out in case he fell.

"Try up there." Ondieki pointed at the gap between two frozen lava flows. "And remember, on a crack."

"Right you are, governor." Jim shifted the device to his other shoulder and continued his halting ascent.

Ondieki poured himself a cup of coffee and prowled impatiently around the ship, staring out through each window in turn. Gas supplies were running low, and he couldn't afford for the *Promise's* balloon to be damaged by the ragged, sharp-billed birds that nested in this wasteland. It was one thing to study the fiery peaks of the Reckoning lands, another to find yourself marooned among them, stranded and starving in a waterless wasteland. He would do most things for science, but he drew the line at dying.

He preferred to avoid killing, too.

Something was coming from the south, a circle that tapered away into an inverted teardrop. Through the magnifying lenses of the telescope it resolved itself into a hot air balloon, old and patched, its basket carrying half a dozen red-coated, rifle-wielding men.

"Ready yet?" Ondieki shouted through the open door.

"Getting there." Jim had almost reached a gap between the lava flows. Ahead of him was a jagged crack.

"Get there faster."

"Bloody smoke, governor." Jim turned to face the ship. His voice, still distant, had become angry. "You want it done quick, how about you be the one hangin' on a rope, danglin' over a chasm or fallin' over rocks. I'm scraped, I'm knackered, and I'm too bloody short to climb these boulders, so just give it a rest, or you can find a new assistant."

"What?"

"You heard."

"I give you a place to live, food, purpose, and now you give me this?"

"I cook the food. I clean the ship. I do all the leg-work for your research. You want me to stop?"

Ondieki glanced nervously round. The balloon was approaching fast, carried on the same southerly wind that had brought them here. For once, the maelstrom of British weather had held steady for a few hours, just long enough to land him in trouble. It was one thing to flee the authorities, any academic did that once in a while. It was quite another to fight them off. He didn't fancy the danger, the blood on his hands, or the awkward social and legal consequences.

"Just keep going," he called. "We can discuss this later."

"No." Jim sat down. "I ain't going no further 'til you show me some respect."

"I'm sorry! Now get moving."

A distant shout reached him from the balloon. Distant and angry.

"Get moving what?" Jim retorted.

"Get moving the trigger? Get moving yourself?"

The shouting was becoming clearer. Ondieki distinctly heard the word "shoot".

"Unbelievable." Jim shook his head. "All this palaver, and you can't even say please."

A bullet whistled past the *Promise*.

"Get moving yourself, please?"

"Well, alright then." Jim rose. "But this ain't over."

For the first time he saw the balloon over the surrounding rocks.

"Oh." He shouldered the trigger. "We in trouble?"

"Yes!"

"Right then."

A bullet clanged off the gondola. The Redcoats weren't firing much yet. Perhaps they didn't want to kill Ondieki, just to keep him busy until they could board. Perhaps they didn't believe he could really trigger the volcano. Perhaps they were having trouble loading in the cramped balloon. Whatever the cause, Ondieki wasn't complaining.

He grabbed his own gun and peered down the sight at the approaching Redcoats. He was no soldier, but Europe didn't have space for real wars any more, and he probably got as much target practice as they did. His gun was better too, more modern, more accurate, better range. He could pick most of them off before they reached him. But then he'd have to face the others up close, and the English were experts at brawling.

Besides, he didn't like killing people.

He aimed at one of the balloon's ropes, and fired.

Crack.

Nothing. A miss.

Rope whirred from the docking bay winch as Jim hurried toward the crack. He was almost there, scrambling over a last ridge of jagged, shattered rocks.

Ondieki fired again. This time a rope parted, ends flapping in the wind. The Redcoats ignored it as they rummaged for something in the depths of the basket. One of them was still looking his way, and Ondieki recognised the sergeant who had greeted him at Calais docks. The man looked far less friendly now.

The winch fell still. Jim had reached his goal and was priming the device.

Ondieki ducked as a bullet pinged off the window frame. Another whistled past his head. He peered out, trying to show as little of himself as possible. Half the soldiers were firing at the *Promise*, keeping him busy while the others fired gas-propelled grappling ropes. Two fell short of the *Promise*. A third skimmed the edge of the dirigible but didn't catch.

This close, it was getting hard for the riflemen to miss. Ondieki wouldn't have long to take his shot. He waited for a break in their shooting, then rose, aimed, fired, and dove to the floor. A bullet raked him as he dropped, red-hot pain flaring through his shoulder.

Pressed against the cold aluminum plates, he squinted out through a bullet hole.

The rope he had aimed at twisted, frayed, and snapped. One end of the basket jolted and sank, throwing the Redcoats off their feet. They grabbed whatever they could, trying to stay aboard. Their burner, no longer pointing into the balloon, shot a jet of blue-green flame and blazing air to starboard, sending the vessel lurching away from the *Promise*. As Ondieki scrambled to his feet, the Redcoats were frantically hurling their grapples upwards, trying to replace the ropes and right the balloon.

"All done!" Jim yelled from the ground.

Ondieki yanked a lever. There was blood on the lever, blood on his hand, blood all down his arm. Dizzyness swept through him.

"Governor?" Jim cried as the engines growled, propellers spinning into action. "Still down here!"

Ondieki set the wheel and turned the docking bay winch. His beleaguered assistant yelped as he was lifted from his feet, rising like a fish on a line.

Below, the trigger device whirred into life, plunging a spike of hardened steel and explosives through the volcano's crust. The

Thames Peak groaned, shook, and spat molten lava, first from the trigger point, then along the crack, up the side of the peak and out. Jim screeched in panic and scrambled up the ascending rope, gobs of magma and slithers of rock hurtling past him.

A sheet of fire burst into the sky, cutting the Promise off from the Redcoats' balloon. The air was thick with smoke, dark with the promise of revelation.

Jim hauled himself over the lip of the hangar and lay, soot-stained and trembling, on the deck. A smoking furrow darkened the peak of his cap.

"To the pump!" Ondieki exclaimed as he slumped against the condenser. "We have a sample to gather."

He smiled as he prepped his equipment. Smoke curled from the pipe and into the jar, settling in layers as Jim, exhausted but obedient, pumped the handle. First fine ash, then a layer of tiny yellow crystals, exactly as Ondieki had predicted. The distinct trace of the reaction fuelling every peak of the Reckoning, proof of his hypothesized connection and the first step toward a solution. He felt a sense of triumph, as the world span around him.

"Come on, governor," said a distant voice. "Let's get you bandaged up. Again."

Outside the window, England was burning, but now Ondieki knew there was an end in sight. Nothing could stand in the way of science.

ONE MILLION MONKEYS, LTD

George S. Walker

"The *Falcon* is the only vessel swift enough to rescue the Countess before harm befalls her," said Sir Conrad, his face red with anger. "Or worse, before she betrays England."

Seated in his firm's library, Ian Donaldson drew on his pipe and exhaled. "I sympathize with the unfortunate lady's plight, but my firm is in no position—"

"You have a racing steamship," Sir Conrad interrupted.

"*I* do not possess a steamship. My firm has been engaged by the proprietor to test her seaworthiness and performance limits."

"But because of the Egyptian imperial patrols, Mr. Donaldson, there are no British warships in the Mediterranean!"

Ian took off his spectacles and rubbed his eyes wearily. "Despite the name of my firm, we do not possess one million monkeys. We have in our care nearly a hundred African and Indian monkeys and a few dozen apes. Though they serve well for their trained tasks, they are not an army of men. You ask the impossible."

"Impossible? You've taken the *Falcon* to sea! Before the telegram from London, I watched your monkeys maneuver her expertly in the harbor."

"You've seen me and three of my men supervising a number of apes like Aphrodite here." The chimp, polishing a brass candlestick on the floor, looked up, regarding Conrad warily. "Though trained to operate the *Falcon*, they're not fit to undertake a rescue mission from Gibraltar to Alexandria, Egypt."

Conrad scowled at the chimp. "I can supply officers from the border force for the rescue itself. It is the *Falcon* and trained crew that I require."

"Then you must understand this: A Chinaman is a man. An

Egyptian is a man. Even a savage Apache is a man. My apes are not men. I have discovered an elixir that raises them closer to the intellect of a man, but we are as gods compared to them."

"And yet I have seen them smoking pipes as men."

Ian sighed. "The vices of men are not what distinguish us from beasts."

"Dammit, sir! They can be wild dogs, so long as they get us to Alexandria in the span of a week!"

The queens' paddlewheel barge descended the placid Nile toward Alexandria.

Ada, Countess of Lovelace and daughter of Lord Byron, fanned herself. The sovereign twin sisters, Cleopatra XIV and Cleopatra XV, had servants to do that for them. In the heat, Ada's scalp prickled beneath her bound auburn hair; her European dress was damp with perspiration. She felt homely in the presence of the queens' beauty and would rather be alone, reading.

The queens sat in the salon's twin thrones as servants combed their black hair. Brightly colored hieroglyphics embroidered their gowns, and gold bracelets like vipers snaked around their forearms. One of the Cleopatras spoke to a servant, who handed her a wooden box.

Ada inhaled sharply. *My cards.*

The queen unlatched the box and lifted its lid. She removed a punched card from the box, holding it toward Ada. "What will this do?" she asked in Latin.

"It is a Jacquard card," Ada replied, also in Latin. "A set may be used to operate an automatic loom."

The queen hurled the stiff card in her face. "Do you think us simpletons?!"

Her hand shaking, Ada picked up the card. She opened her mouth to speak, but no words came.

"Give me the card!" commanded the queen.

Ada handed it to her.

The second queen spoke quietly, "We are not so different,

Countess, you and we. Save that my sister and I have the blood of Pharaohs and Roman emperors in our veins."

"And I..." Ada tried to keep her voice light, "I have the blood of mathematicians and poets in mine."

"That and a beggar's bowl may gain you a crust of bread in the streets of Cairo," snapped the first queen.

Ada felt her cheeks grow hot.

The second queen smiled kindly. "We three are all educated women, traveling to the greatest library in the world. On the library grounds is being constructed a great clockwork mechanism your Professor Babbage calls an Analytical Engine. And your cards?" She looked at the countess expectantly.

"Are for the Engine," said Ada in a resigned voice.

The queen looked at her sister triumphantly.

Aphrodite clung to the branch that stretched from the front of the floating forest, feeling the warm sun on her fur, inhaling sea air. Perched above the water, she watched fish flashing beneath the waves.

Behind her, the huffing, clanking monster at the heart of the floating forest belched clouds of smoke. The god ape, Ian, had chosen her for this journey, along with five other chimps and Hercules, the gorilla. One task of the chosen ones was to feed the hot hunger of the monster. Now was not her turn in the fire room, though.

"Aphrodite!"

She turned at the sound of her name.

Ian made the sign that he'd chosen her for a task. She clambered back onto the deck, where Ian stood with Sir Conrad beside a wooden crate.

"This should put your mind at ease about the Egyptian Navy," Conrad said to Ian.

The words were too jumbled for Aphrodite to understand. The god apes were looking at the crate.

Ian signed for her to pry it open. For all their powers, the god apes had weak hands and arms. One by one, she ripped away the boards to reveal a shiny piece of god machinery mounted on wheels. She sniffed. *Inedible oil.*

Ian looked puzzled. "What is it?"

"A Gatling gun," said Sir Conrad. "A new weapon from British America. With a strong man turning the crank, it fires six hundred rounds per minute."

"Bullets, you mean?"

Sir Conrad smiled. "Should we be stopped by an Egyptian warship, this will transform my little squad of five border officers into an army of hundreds." He clapped Ian on the back. "Feeling better about our odds now?"

The god ape Conrad looked happy. Ian did not.

<◇>

Ada set down her mathematics book.

In the bustling harbor at Alexandria, Egyptian workers rushed to tie up the royal paddlewheel barge. Through a porthole, Ada looked out at irrigated gardens and rich buildings. On the front of a temple was a huge statue of the jackal-headed god Anubis. A week ago, captive aboard an airship from Rome, she'd seen nothing of Alexandria.

A servant entered Ada's cabin and gestured for her to follow. The woman spoke no Latin. Ada tried to convey to her that if they were leaving the boat, her books must follow. The puzzled servant finally nodded, herding her off the boat and along the dock.

People were waiting for the queens to disembark. The hot midday sun beat down on Ada, and she had no parasol. The thick hem of her dress dragged in sand beside the street. In the harbor floated Egyptian oil burners, Greek and Roman steamships, and older sailing ships. Ada heard the crack of whips mingled with the shouts of Egyptian foremen. Ibises foraged at the water's edge. She smelled Arabian horses fidgeting in the harnesses of carriages that looked just like those in London.

People bowed down as the queens emerged from the parlor

deck of the river barge with their servants. The foremen's shouts ceased. The harbor grew so quiet Ada could hear locusts. She lowered her head, but did not kneel. The servant beside her, nearly prostrate, hissed and tugged at Ada's dress. Ada swallowed her fear and remained standing.

She heard hollow footsteps of the royal party approaching on the wooden dock, heard the whinny of a horse behind her, and kept her eyes on her feet.

"Countess," commanded a queen.

Ada looked up, meeting the Cleopatras' dark eyes stoically.

The queen on the left shook her head in cold amusement. She said something in Coptic, and the servant at Ada's feet leapt up. The royal party dispersed to the carriages, and the servant jabbered, pulling Ada by the hand toward the queens' carriage.

The queens got in and sat down. The servant pushed Ada from behind. Ada held back, but a Cleopatra gestured for her to sit on the fabric-covered seat across from them.

A guard closed the door, sealing in the heat.

"You will stay in our palace," said a queen in Latin.

Ada nodded her acceptance. "I shall require my books."

The second Cleopatra raised her hand to strike Ada, but her sister stayed her hand. She gave an amused laugh and murmured, "The English..."

The carriage rolled bumpily through the streets, part of the train of carriages. Soldiers on horseback guarded them on both sides. Hooves clopped against sandstone. There were no people along the street. Soldiers ahead of them must have cleared the way.

"Tomorrow, you will see your Analytical Engine."

Aphrodite squatted on a hatch cover beside Hercules, the gorilla. He struggled to light his pipe by scratching lightning sticks. The god apes did it with one quick, magical motion. She sometimes thought Hercules as clever as the god apes, but not at this. He picked out some of the charred leaves, offering them to her to taste. She wrinkled her nose. Ian had given him the pipe, and he was fond of it. Aphrodite couldn't comprehend why. *The only thing that stinks worse than charred pipe leaves is smoke from the fire room's rocks–that-burn.*

One of the god apes shouted.

Ian, drenched in sweat, swung open the door of the fire room, where he supervised the chimps on duty.

"What is it, man?" he called. "A ship from Tripoli?"

"Use my spyglass, sir."

To Aphrodite, the sounds the god apes made might as well be the buzzing of bees. Ian accepted the small club the god ape handed him, sticking it against his eye.

"An airship! Sir Conrad! I shall damper the engine!" Ian ran back inside the fire room.

The other god apes looked excitedly in the air. *What do they see?* Aphrodite smelled nothing new.

Abruptly the clanks of the monster machine slowed, and the huffing of the floating forest changed to a long wheeze.

The fire room door burst open again. Ian emerged.

"Raise sails! Let them think we're a slow cargo ship!"

He signed to Aphrodite and the other apes: "Chosen" and "Re-leaf the forest."

This was Aphrodite's favorite task. She raced to a trunk and climbed, reaching a branch and deftly unwrapping vines. As the giant skin fell free and billowed, she moved to the next branch.

More skins caught the wind, and trunks and branches creaked. Aphrodite swung through the forest of vines. A gull swooped past her. Below, Ian and the other god apes pulled on vines, tightening them. The entire floating forest swayed in the wind.

Ian sank onto a hatch cover, panting from exertion. Aphrodite swung down from a vine and dropped to the deck nearby. She wasn't winded at all.

Sir Conrad joined Ian. "Slow travel this way."

"Safer not to be seen racing to Alexandria." Ian paused for breath. "That airship will be out of sight soon enough: off to Rome, I wager."

"'Tis a pity it came no closer. I'd have given it what for with the Gatling gun. That would have been glorious!"

Ian looked uncomfortable. After a moment's hesitation, Aphrodite clambered onto the hatch beside him. She probed through his hair with her long fingers, looking for mites.

The god ape Conrad's lip curled, and he walked away.

<<>>

The Egyptian engineer sweated profusely, and not just from the heat. Looking even more uncomfortable than Ada, he stood stiffly before one of the queens, who lounged on the divan carried into the building by her servants. The other Cleopatra walked elegantly beside the clockwork machinery, touching shafts and gears. Servants fanned both sisters, but none of that breeze reached the engineer.

Ada couldn't pronounce his name. In fact, she followed little of his speech, though he was giving it in Latin at the queens' request. He mangled declensions, tenses and moods, and his accent was so thick that at first Ada thought he was speaking Coptic.

Relieved that the queens' attentions were on the engineer, Ada stared in awe at the Analytical Engine. It filled the hall behind the engineer, nearly the size of her house outside London. There were polished brass barrels with pegs, levers and gears: she recognized everything from Charles Babbage's drawings. She also smelled Arabian oil. The Egyptians had replaced Babbage's plan for a coal-fired steam engine with an oil combustion engine. She tried to imagine the clockwork in motion, like a giant music box, but playing her program instead of music. *Such a racket it would make!*

"You say it can solve any riddle," said the queen on the divan, pulling Ada back to reality. The Cleopatra was apparently responding to something the engineer had said. "Countess, how would you ask it the riddle of the sphinx?"

"That is an allegorical riddle," Ada explained cautiously, "not a mathematical one."

"A riddle is a riddle," said the standing queen, peeved.

Ada looked at the engineer for support, but his gaze was riveted on his feet. She saw that the Cleopatra on the divan held the wooden box with Ada's program.

"If you open that box, my lady, you will see that there is nothing written on the cards, only holes representing numbers and operations for the computing mill. The machine only understands the language of mathematics."

The queen opened the box and looked at a few cards. "There are numerals written on the backs," she observed.

"That is in case the cards are dropped. The mill requires that the cards be entered in order. In the same way that a cook follows the steps in a recipe."

"And Professor Babbage has taught you all his recipes. His recipes of holes."

Ada hesitated to correct a queen who knew little of mathematics. "I create my own recipes," she said finally.

"But before, you had no place to cook them. Now, by the grace of our cooperation with Professor Babbage, you are free to do so."

"I am not free," she said, barely audible. "And Babbage did not cooperate with you."

The standing Cleopatra strode dangerously close to Ada. "If you think yourself a slave, you have not seen how we whip them in the streets! And how do you think the Analytical Engine was built, if not with Professor Babbage's aid?"

"He was raising funds to have it built in England."

"Where it *never* would have been built in his lifetime!"

"He would not betray England," said Ada.

"Science is not a genie to bottle inside one empire," said the reclining Cleopatra calmly. "You will come to realize that, just as he."

Rocking in deep twilight, the floating forest was at rest. After days of ravenous hunger and activity, the clanking monster at its heart had finally gone to sleep. Besides the god apes, only Hercules and Aphrodite were awake. *What do they want us for?*

"Sir Conrad, your plan is madness," said Ian.

"Only to your non-military eye. I've no doubt the Egyptians have the countess chained to the Analytical Engine. Enslaved to the machine and made to operate it. My lads and I will row the longboat ashore, enter the hall of the machine, unchain the countess, and time permitting, perform some mischief on the machine itself. Then we return to the *Falcon* and steam home. Simplicity itself."

"She is the daughter of an English lord!" Ian retorted. "I dare say they will lodge her in the royal palace!"

"You do not know these Egyptians as I do."

"They are reasoning men, not beasts!"

"What would you have me do? Storm the palace? We are outnumbered by an army of Egyptians."

"Someone should... inquire, at least."

"What?" asked Conrad. "In English? Who is mad now?"

"I speak a little Coptic. A few words."

"Then that should be *your* task, while we are engaged with my plan. Or are you not man enough to step ashore?"

Aphrodite saw anger in Ian's eyes that she had not seen before, even when he punished the small long-tailed thieves.

"I shall come."

Sir Conrad raised an eyebrow. "Then you'd best bring someone with you. That Jerome of yours is a good man if there's a fight."

Ian shook his head. "If I don't return, you'll need him to manage the apes for the *Falcon's* return."

Other god apes were using vines to lower the floating forest's child onto the dark waves. One by one, Conrad and the five god apes of his tribe climbed down onto it. Aphrodite heard a hollow scrape as the child rubbed its parent's flank.

Ian signed to Hercules: "chosen," and gestured for him to join the god apes. Hercules lowered himself onto the floating child with a grace that belied his size.

"Bloody hell!" shouted Conrad.

"You told me to bring someone," Ian called down.

Hercules squatted on the middle of the forest child as the god apes eyed him with mistrust.

Ian signed to Aphrodite: "chosen."

She was glad Hercules had gone first. She swung down, as from a tree in the forest. But she misjudged the forest child's dance on the waves. She hit its bone-like edge and tumbled into the waves.

Gagging on saltwater, she splashed desperately, trying to stretch her muzzle above the waves. Unlike a stream, there was nothing solid beneath her feet. The water sucked her beneath the surface.

Suddenly a strong hand gripped her shoulder, dragging her from the sea. *Hercules*! He swung her with a thud onto the belly of the forest child, where she lay coughing. The gorilla looked at her in concern. None of Conrad's tribe had moved.

Aphrodite watched as Ian descended the ladder of vines.

"These monkeys will be the death of us," growled Conrad.

She didn't understand his words, but heard his disgust.

Four of Conrad's tribe took straight branches and began stroking them in the water.

Ian lit his pipe. Hercules gestured for his own, so Ian handed it to him, along with the lightning sticks.

"Mark my words," said Conrad. "Once loosed in Africa, that will be the last you set eyes on these monkeys."

As the forest child neared the shore in darkness, Aphrodite smelled the god apes' growing fear. By the light of a claw-shaped moon overhead, nothing looked frightening. Only palm trees and sand. In the distance flickered welcoming god ape lights.

The forest child slid to a halt in the surf. Two of Conrad's tribe jumped out, wading to help it ashore. Aphrodite waited till it was safely on sand to climb out.

As Conrad's tribe gathered palm branches to hide the forest child, Ian pointed inland. "Look there. Three iron airship towers, with two airships moored. Have you ever beheld such marvels?"

"If you've lost your nerve," snapped Conrad, "best stay here with the boat. I'll not share the risk of your clumsy monkeys as my men rescue the countess."

"I said I'd inquire," muttered Ian. "I keep my word."

"Very well. But this boat leaves at 3 AM, with or without you and your monkeys."

Ian regarded him grimly.

Conrad handed him something. It glinted by moonlight.

"A pistol?" said Ian. Aphrodite saw how he looked at the object with distaste. "If I cannot find the countess by stealth, I surely will not by force of arms."

"'Tis not for the Egyptians. If the countess cannot be freed, this is your recourse. Do you take my meaning?"

Ian looked at the god ape Conrad in revulsion.

"Better for her than a life of slavery," said Conrad. He waved at his tribe. "Come, lads. For God and Queen Victoria!"

They marched over the sand, between the palm trees, into the gloom.

Aphrodite heard waves lapping against the sandy shore behind her. From the city came a long whistle she recognized, of the giant metal god-snake that slides along the ground, belching smoke. She inhaled scents of dust and seaweed, palms and fish.

Hercules snuffled, looking around warily.

What does he know of the god apes' plans that I don't?

"Time to see this through," Ian muttered.

Ian had started out trailing Conrad's tribe, but eventually led the apes a different way. And got lost. Aphrodite could tell by his frustration. Dwellings of god apes formed a canyon around them, but they must not be his tribe, for he walked in fear. And muttered to himself.

"There's the Library, with its Eternal Flame atop the dome. And the royal palace just beyond. So we're close, mates, dangerous close. Got till 3 AM." He exhaled a shuddering breath.

Ian led them through dark canyons lined with buildings, constantly checking if she and Hercules were following. Hercules plodded on his knuckles, tensely turning his head side to side. Aphrodite walked close behind, shivering with excitement. Despite Ian's and Hercules' apprehension, she was enjoying this. The canyons smelled of food and animals; she heard chickens, donkeys and goats.

When they reached the end of a canyon, a small savanna lay beyond, a great building of the god apes at its heart.

"Almost there, mates. Inside that wall to the left is the livery, but you'd scare the horses. Royalty's in the center, two queen bees in their hive. That wing to the right, that's the place for us. Find a servant, ask our question, and be done." He shivered. "One way or another."

He paused for a moment, taking deep breaths. Then he started across the savanna. As they got closer to the building, there were more palm trees. Aphrodite looked up longingly. She wanted to climb.

When they reached the wall, Ian began muttering again.

"Gate's barred, but of course it would be. No fools, these Egyptians. 'Cept they didn't plan on apes." He turned to her. "Aphrodite."

She looked up at him, and he signed: "chosen." He made gestures of climbing the wall and doing something to the gate. She understood the climbing part.

The wall was made of stone blocks with hard dirt between them. Aphrodite's strong fingers and toes easily found holds and she climbed to the top quickly. Atop the wall, she looked over. There were trees. Fig trees.

So this was why the god ape had told her to climb over. *My reward!* She descended quickly and climbed the nearest tree. The figs were ripe, and she began eating. Better and more plentiful than the food on the floating forest. Why had the god apes been afraid? And why wasn't Hercules following her? She hooted, calling to him.

The gate rattled, and she heard Ian call her name. She pretended not to hear. Ian continued calling. And muttering. He wasn't pleased. She gathered as many figs as she could hold and walked to the gate. There were cracks between the thick boards, and she spotted the eye of the god ape.

"Put the figs down!" Ian hissed. "Open the gate!"

She didn't understand. *Does he want a fig?* She held one up and tried to push it between a crack, but it was too big, and she succeeded only in squashing it. She licked her fingers.

"For God's sake, Aphrodite! Open the gate. Lift the bar. Lift. Lift. Lift!"

She knew the word. *Lift what?* The gate was too heavy. There was a long club attached to it. *Does he want that?* She set down her figs and tried to pull it, but it was stuck. He'd said to lift, though, so she did. At that point, the gate swung toward her, and she jumped back.

Ian pushed through, followed by Hercules.

"Good girl." His tone of voice didn't mean it.

Contrite, she offered him a fig, which he refused. Hercules gathered up her pile. She knew better than to argue with a gorilla.

"Come! Come!" hissed Ian.

They walked around the fig trees toward the god ape building. A few lights glowed from big holes in it.

The god ape went from gate to gate along the building. She watched. Hercules ate her figs.

Ian opened a gate. "Unlocked. Come! Come!"

She and Hercules followed him into darkness.

"Never thought I'd get this far," he whispered. "Where's a servant to ask? No lights here. A light from that stairway, though."

He began climbing. She and Hercules followed.

Near the top, something startled him, and he called out, "Hercules! Hold!"

It was not a word Aphrodite knew. Hercules, wiser than her, lunged forward. When she reached the top, she saw the gorilla standing erect, hugging a god ape. Not in affection, for the god ape was gasping for breath. Ian walked behind him and knelt down. He sniffed a cup and took a sip.

"Egyptian beer. I'll leave you that, but not your musket." He picked up a long, shiny stick. "Let's try some Coptic: English woman where?"

The other god ape made choking sounds.

Ian pointed the stick at him. "Hercules. No hold."

The gorilla released him, and Ian said, "Show. Woman."

The other god ape coughed, cowering.

"Woman," said Ian, frustrated. "English. Woman."

The other bent slowly, lifting a flame holder from the floor, which shook in his hand. Light danced on the walls.

"English," said Ian. "Woman."

The other god ape nodded unhappily and started up the next stairs, watching over his shoulder. Ian followed with the stick pointed at him. Aphrodite was beginning to share Hercules' apprehension.

When they topped the stairs, the god ape led them through a tunnel to a wooden gate. Aphrodite saw his hand shake as he poked a shiny stick in the gate. It opened.

Another tunnel. Partway down it, the god ape hesitated, then rapped on a solid gate with his fist.

"English?" Ian asked him. "Woman?"

The other god ape nodded. He looked miserable.

"Countess?" Ian called. "Are you within?"

"Who's there?" The voice of an ape goddess.

"Ian Donaldson of One Million Monkeys, Ltd., in Her Majesty's service."

The gate opened partway, and an ape goddess in a robe peered out warily. She, too, held a flame holder. Her eyes took in Ian and the other god ape. At the sight of Hercules and Aphrodite in shadow, her other hand went to her throat.

"Does Her Majesty wish me dead, then?" she said.

"No, my lady. Victoria wishes you well. Our boat leaves the harbor tonight, and we bid you be aboard."

"'Tis a late hour for an invitation. I am not dressed." She looked worriedly at the other god ape. "Do the queens know?"

"They will soon enough, if we continue prattling."

"But I do not know you, sir."

"Time is of the essence. We must leave the harbor in

darkness. Do you wish to return to England or not?"

Aprhodite saw a conflicted expression on her face.

"But... why do you travel in the company of apes?"

"My lady, we must be off!"

She raised her flame holder, regarding Hercules and Aphrodite uncertainly, and swallowed. "I will get dressed."

"Hurry, my lady," he hissed.

She re-entered her room. The gate shut.

Ian fidgeted, shifting his weight from foot to foot. He muttered to himself, "Englishwomen."

Much later, the gate opened. The ape goddess' hair had grown longer, falling past her shoulders.

Ian prodded the other god ape into the room, around the ape goddess. He made him sit in a chair and bound him with vines. Ian gestured for Hercules to pull the vines tight. The seated god ape cried out. Ian set down the long stick.

"Follow me, my lady."

"My books."

"What?"

"I shall not leave my books behind." She gestured to a small wooden trunk.

"You can purchase books in London, my lady."

"Not these." The ape goddess made no move to leave.

Ian stared at her, then lifted the trunk. He sighed, carrying the trunk from the room.

He retraced their route through the building, with the ape goddess at his side, followed by Hercules and Aphrodite.

They went out through the main gate and across the savanna.

"Where are your captain and crew?" asked the goddess.

"I am the temporary captain of the *Falcon*, a private ship. She is anchored outside the harbor for safety. A party of soldiers will row us out to her."

"You are not a British soldier, but a mercenary, then."

"I volunteered my services and my apes. I receive no coin for this."

After a long pause, she said, "I thank you, sir."

"Do not thank me until you are safe aboard the *Falcon*."

Beyond the savanna, Ian led them through narrow canyons. "I'm told the Egyptians captured you because you are a great mathematician."

"A fair one. But I understand how to program Professor Babbage's Analytical Engine better than any man."

"And how is that a threat to the British Empire?"

"Imagine your million monkeys all trained in ciphers, all solving one problem. *That* is the power of the Engine."

"The queens' Arabian oil seems a greater threat. Our own warships run on coal from our mines. Oil is the future, my lady."

Thunder boomed behind them. Aphrodite turned, startled. There was no sign of a storm, but an orange glow lit the side of a massive building.

"That will wake the city," said Ian, alarmed. "Can you try harder to keep up with me, my lady?"

"You are not wearing a dress, sir."

"And you, my lady, are not carrying a trunk."

Aphrodite heard gongs in the distance behind them.

"That fire is Sir Conrad's work," said Ian unhappily.

Aphrodite heard voices nearby and the clatter of pots. Her nose wrinkled from the smell of something delicious. It came from a side canyon. She couldn't resist.

"Aphrodite! No!" hissed Ian. He set down the trunk and ran after her.

She stopped abruptly, knowing she'd displeased him. He led her back by the hand.

Hercules hadn't strayed. Ian grunted as he lifted the trunk, then led them to a wider canyon. He kept them close to buildings, shadowed from moonlight.

"This cannot succeed!" the goddess said tightly.

"We are nearly there, my lady."

Aphrodite heard running boots behind her.

Ian turned and saw god apes approaching at a run. "Soldiers," he gasped. "Six of them." He dropped the trunk and pulled out the object Conrad had given him. As he raised it in one hand, it glinted in the moonlight. "Stand back, my lady! But wait..."

He stepped from the shadows. "Sir Conrad!" he called.

The god apes slowed, panting from exertion.

"What a stroke of luck!" said Ian.

"Are these your soldiers?" said the ape goddess.

"Countess, allow me to introduce Sir Conrad."

"My lady," said Conrad, wheezing. "No time. Egyptian soldiers. Coming."

Ian gave the trunk to one of Conrad's tribe and led them into a narrow canyon. "They may not find us here."

They traveled in single file, Conrad taking the lead.

"Did you find the Analytical Engine?" Ian asked.

"Yes," Conrad wheezed. "Destroyed now. Set afire."

"What?!" exclaimed the ape goddess.

"Not sure we could do it," he gasped. "At first, the lads and I smashed things. Drums, shafts, levers. Then we found tanks. Arabian oil! Spread it everywhere. Then a sulfur match. Glorious!" He laughed.

"It may never be built again," said the ape goddess in despair.

The god apes spoke little after that. Sounds of waking voices came from around them in the canyons. Aphrodite saw faces peer from narrowly open gates that closed as they walked past.

The canyons finally led toward the sea. Aphrodite heard the pounding heartbeat of a different floating forest. Its bright lights shone toward shore.

"Bloody hell!" said Conrad.

"Where is your boat?" asked the countess anxiously.

"Hidden, my lady," said Ian, "but we cannot leave in haste with the Egyptian Navy nearby."

"Yet haste is necessary," said Conrad. "Dawn and soldiers approach."

Ian looked back toward land. Perhaps he would lead them into the canyons in search of food. Or let Aphrodite find food for them. That was what she was best at.

"An airship," the god ape said suddenly.

"By Jove!" said Conrad. "Two of them, still tethered."

He led them away from shore, toward the god-made clouds floating above the trees. When they came to a high wall, they walked till they found a gate. Ian signed to Hercules: "chosen," and motioned for him to tear the gate apart.

They passed through the broken remains: Conrad and his tribe, then Ian and the ape goddess, then the apes. Within the walls lay a savanna, and from it grew three tall god-trees that reflected moonlight. God-made clouds were snagged at the tip of two of them. A building of the god apes stood nearby.

Conrad led the way to the closest tree. The surface of the cloud above it undulated with the breeze from the sea. The tree was a skeleton, and he led them inside its trunk.

"The tower lift is out of action," Ian said. "Do you think you can climb so many stairs, my lady?"

Aphrodite saw the countess bite her lip, looking up at flat branches leading into the skeleton. "I shall have to."

Conrad and his tribe started up through the tree. Ian and the goddess climbed more slowly, followed by the apes.

"I am not in the habit of ascending mountains," the goddess said, panting as she rested partway up the tree.

"We are from Gibraltar," said Ian.

"A mountain," she said, nodding. "One of the Pillars of Hercules."

"The same. A good deal steeper than your London."

When at last they reached the top of the tree, Aphrodite saw an agitated Conrad waiting by a path that led to a cage beneath the cloud.

"Quickly!" he said. "Egyptians are on the field!"

They entered the cage. The path pivoted as the cloud turned with the shifting wind, and Aphrodite tried to back out. Hercules pushed her forward. Once they were inside, Conrad released knobby vines binding the cloud. They fell with clanks onto the tower, and he closed the gate. The cloud drifted from the tree, creaking in the wind.

"You had best start the engine," said Conrad.

"*I?*" said Ian. He looked about the cage. "I thought there would be an Egyptian aboard."

"You operate a steamship," said Conrad sternly. "Surely this is similar."

"No. It is not!" said Ian. "I have read treatises, but never touched an Egyptian combustion engine."

The cloud drifted sideways high above the buildings of the god apes, pushed by the wind. The cage swayed. Ian hurried to the back wall, which looked like the inside of the floating forest's fire room.

"Gears and levers," Ian muttered. "Labels in Coptic. That tube must lead to a fuel tank outside the gondola."

"Hurry!" demanded Conrad. "The lift to the other airship is ascending."

"No burner door," Ian muttered. "Well, of course not: the bags are full of hydrogen gas. This wheel must control vanes outside the gondola. Now what do these levers do?"

The god ape pulled on a club, and Aphrodite felt the cage lift her higher.

"I believe I dropped ballast," said Ian, pleased.

"The wind is taking us toward the city!" said Conrad.

"I have seen it operated," said the ape goddess.

"That scarcely suffices, my lady," said Conrad.

The goddess's mouth gaped. "Englishmen!"

Ian played with objects on the wall, but looked worried. At last he stepped back, bowing to the ape goddess.

She swiftly picked up a bent branch from the floor and jabbed it in a hole in the wall. Grunting as she tried to turn the branch, she couldn't budge it.

Ian signed to Hercules: "chosen" and gestured for him to mimic the goddess. She jumped out of the way, and the gorilla turned the branch. There was a coughing noise, like the waking heartbeat of the floating forest. The goddess turned something on the wall with her fingers and the coughing rose to a clatter. Outside the cage, metal branches like palm leaves swung in circles.

"Glorious!" said Conrad. "I'll steer the airship."

Aphrodite saw Ian look outside.

"The other airship is in pursuit," he announced.

The cage enclosing them began to turn toward the sea.

"Look!" said the ape goddess. "Where the smoke is rising.

The Library is in flames."

Hercules approached Ian and motioned for his pipe. Ian took the pipe and box of lightning sticks from a pocket, then changed his mind. He feigned horror, making a series of gestures Aphrodite tried to understand. *Will striking a lightning match here call down lightning from the sky?* Ian set the pipe and matches on a shelf and signed: "forbidden."

"The other airship means to cut us off," said Conrad. "But if it's a race they want, we shall give them one!"

Conrad turned the same object the goddess had. The cloud's clattering heartbeat stuttered and died. Aphrodite heard the goddess gasp.

"Bloody hell!" said Conrad. He picked up the bent branch, forcing it into the hole in the wall, and turned with all his strength. The goddess turned the smaller object on the wall, and the clattering grew again.

"I fear they will overtake us," said Ian. "This has all been for naught."

"*Steal an airship*, you suggested," said Conrad bitterly. "We'd have had a better chance out-rowing that Egyptian steamer in the harbor."

"What will they do to us?" asked the goddess.

"The queens shall want you," said Ian, "to help restore the Analytical Engine. But it will be the noose for me, I fear."

Conrad looked at the apes. "We'd lighten our load without your monkeys."

"This race is already lost!" Ian snapped.

"The Egyptians will dispose of your filthy beasts soon enough anyway."

Ian balled his fists, advancing on Conrad.

"Stop it!" said the goddess. "Stop it!" Tears ran from her eyes.

The other cloud was almost directly below them now.

Hercules touched the fur of Aphrodite's face, signing furtively: "chosen." He walked slowly past Conrad's tribe toward the gate they had entered by.

"Hercules?" called Ian.

Hercules opened the gate, paused for a moment to regard Ian with a sad expression, then to Aphrodite's horror, leapt from the cage. She climbed to where she could see out.

"Your foolish monkeys are deserting!" said Conrad.

By moonlight, she saw Hercules plummet onto the other cloud, barely catching himself by vines wrapped around it. The gorilla's impact had torn the cloud's skin. He clung by his feet, holding something in his hands.

"He's taken the sulfur matches!" exclaimed Ian.

As Aphrodite watched helplessly, there was a spark in Hercules' hands, which blossomed into yellow flame.

"The other ship is afire!" shouted one of Conrad's tribe. "To starboard, sir! Turn to starboard!"

Their cloud turned slowly from the growing fireball. Aphrodite could no longer see Hercules in the inferno. Its light illuminated the interior of their cage. The other cloud began to fall below them.

"Merciful heavens!" said the goddess. "They are burning alive!"

Aphrodite clutched Ian's hand, but it was shaking.

With a radiant expression, Conrad steered the cloud back toward the sea. "Glorious! We've bested both their queens and only lost a pawn!"

Aphrodite saw tears in Ian's eyes as he watched the other cloud plummet toward the city in flames.

Whatever Ian and his kind were, she decided, they were not gods.

BACKS TO THE WALL

Renee Stern

Brakes screamed as the train slammed to a stop, jolting Elbert Runion nearly off his feet. He leaned out the doorway just ahead of the freight cars and peered forward. They should have gone all the way up to the mine, not stopped down here by Sanger Fork's plain wooden shacks and clapboard houses, but a section of missing track blocked their way.

A contingent of company guards commanded by a fussy little man fanned out from a house to block the single street, half of them by the vital engine and the rest at the train's far end, protecting the precious freight cars. Beyond the guards' lines a throng bigger than one coal camp could produce stood shoulder to shoulder with determined faces.

"Because this job wasn't going to be hard enough," Elbert muttered to Jack, his second-in-command in the Pinkertons, wedged into the door beside him. Elbert had never wanted to return to West Virginia, and the bright summer sun didn't make the scene any more appealing.

"That's some welcoming party, boss," Jack said in a voice as flat as the prairies outside Chicago. "It'll be luck like we've never seen before to manage this without bloodshed."

Elbert shook his head tightly. "They're stubborn bastards down here, always have been." He hopped down onto the packed dirt street and Jack followed. "Their backs are at the wall now."

He blew two short bursts on his whistle, sending his squad of Pinkerton agents out to stiffen the guards. He needed some breathing room to figure out how to transport the coal company's automatons the remaining five hundred uphill-yards to the mine—without trouble from the workers the hulking machines were here to replace.

The mines were among the last industries to change over

from human workers to the automatons, heralded as mankind's great revolution; they'd had to wait for the perfection of the spring technology that made the machines safe for underground work, where stray sparks might set off explosions. The spring-driven automatons could work days straight with only a few breaks here and there to wind them up, grease their joints and sharpen their tools.

With every factory and mill changed over to the labor of automatons, the ranks of the out-of-work swelled, fertile ground for union preaching and revolution. But Elbert had fought his way out of the grinding mountain poverty into a good job, proof enough that following the rules granted reward. You didn't need to overturn society.

A woman's voice rang out, sounding tinny from the megaphone that lifted it over the hum of the crowd. "Rise up for freedom, boys!" she cried, a hint of Ireland plain in the sound and rhythm of her words. "Don't let the bloodsucking pirates who own the mines condemn your children to starvation and slavery!"

Elbert choked off a groan.

Jack's eyes widened. "Is that—"

"We knew Mother Jones wouldn't miss a chance like this, but the boss assured me they had her safely contained."

He should have expected the white-haired widow—the picture of genteel womanhood until she opened her mouth to spew her radical firebrand poison—to escape her Pinkerton watchdogs and sneak through the coal companies' cordon around the state. To the politicians and industrialists and anyone who cared about order and law, Mary Harris Jones was the most dangerous woman in the country. To the strikers, union agitators and revolutionaries who adored her, she was their angel, a grandmotherly protector of working men and their families.

Elbert just wanted her to shut up and leave Sanger Fork and the whole damn state, even if it meant shipping her out on the train in a pine box.

He took a deep breath. *No, not that.* A dead Mother Jones would be a martyr to her misbegotten cause, a red banner to set the hills and hollers running knee-deep in blood.

"Ignore her, but be ready for trouble," he told Jack. "Pass the word."

His Pinkertons shouldn't need the reminder. They'd proved themselves under his command, putting down union unrest from Chicago to Pittsburgh; even the Homestead disaster last year hadn't broken their determination. But he didn't want another black mark—or death toll—on his record. Too many men were hungry for his job.

Algernon Blaylock, the leader of the engineering crew responsible for the automatons, emerged from the train, making a show of brushing off his sack coat. Elbert strode over to work out a plan but was intercepted by the man who'd led out the company guards.

"Floyd Cummings," he introduced himself in a clipped accent that proclaimed he was no more local than the ocean or the moon. "You're the head Pinkerton?"

Cummings was the mine superintendent, a man on the rise, posted to Sanger Fork not quite a year ago. Dedicated to his job and his family, in that order, according to Elbert's briefing.

Blaylock joined them with a sour face. "How in tarnation did those people manage to tear up track in the center of this God-forsaken place?"

Cummings bristled. "Perhaps if *they*"—he jerked his head back at the crowd still entranced by Mother Jones' speech—"hadn't gotten wind of our plans somehow or if I'd been sent all the men I requested, I might have done more. They've turned the church into their headquarters and they took over the company store last night. They're well-supplied now, the thieving rats."

"I'm sure you did the best you could." Elbert needed them all pulling together, not fighting against themselves. He shaded his eyes to peer along the tracks to the tipple and other structures that marked the mine three-quarters of the way up the hill. "How are we going to move the automatons into place? Any chance we can drive the crates up there on wagons?"

Cummings snorted. "Any wagons, carts, mules *or* horses are hidden away so well we'd need bloodhounds and the Army to find and take them."

"That's what I thought." Elbert didn't much care for the idea of forcing a way through all those angry people, especially relying on easily spooked animals. But they had few options with the mine uphill. "Can we set up half the automatons to carry the rest of the crates, Mr. Blaylock?"

The engineer studied the land between them and the mine, frowning and shaking his head. "Better to set them all up and march them. The ground's too rough and steep to carry that heavy and unbalanced a load, and has far more obstacles than we've ever tested them on."

The superintendent puffed up like a bantam rooster. "You can't just give up. My company paid good money for those machines *and* for the best security around to deliver them in working order."

"We ain't running, Mr. Cummings." Elbert jabbed a finger at him. "Pinkertons don't run, and I sure as hell don't quit." He turned to the engineer. "Have your boys break out all your machines and wind 'em up. We'll march on out of here soon as you're ready."

Hearing the mountain accent he'd scrubbed so hard from his voice creeping back in, he clamped his mouth shut and stalked back onto the train. The tracks ran right along the edge of the thin river that gave the camp its name, with a matching set of logged-out slopes rising even steeper on the opposite side. It discouraged the miners from surrounding his men completely, but it wasn't an impregnable obstacle.

Jack stood with the company guards, introducing himself and priming them to follow his lead if needed. That was one of Jack's strengths.

Elbert detailed the two closest Pinkertons up to the train roof as sentries and, after a quick word to Jack, sent a message to Mother Jones asking for a parlay. He didn't expect success but he owed it to his men to try.

Cummings flushed nearly purple when the messenger returned to escort Elbert to the church. "You can't deal with these rats and radicals, Runion! You can't trust a word they say—unless you've turned your coat."

Elbert reminded himself of the contract and promised bonuses rather than answer the insults. "Pinkertons always get the job done," he said in a tightly controlled voice. "I want to make sure these people know exactly what they're up against."

Then he checked the draw of his Peacemaker and pulled a steady bohunk everyone called Skee, for simplicity, to accompany him.

They met Mother Jones and a bull-necked miner in the plain church whose unadorned walls and rough-hewn benches were twins to Elbert's boyhood church.

"We won't be persuaded from our course, Mr. Runion," Mother Jones said immediately after the introductions. "These boys here and all up and down this land are fighting for bread to feed their children and for their very future."

"And what future will any of them have if you and your boys force us to fight our way up to the mine?" He held her eyes with all the honesty and sincerity he could muster. "My orders are to move our cargo, no matter what. My men are well-armed and well-trained, but I don't want to spill a drop of blood here today on your side or mine. I'll do whatever I have to, though."

She sized him up with shrewd blue eyes that seemed to see everything. "You think you're on the side of the angels, Mr. Runion, but you know as well as I that the devil is a fallen angel full of tricks. I pray you don't discover that too late."

Elbert shook his head at her fanciful talk. He'd expected more from a woman so many feared and hated. "Stay out of our way and no one will get hurt. You can't stop what's coming, even if you throw away every life under your command."

She laughed. "I'm no general, Mr. Runion. I don't give orders. But we won't start any violence, I can promise you that." Her smile fell away then. "We won't lie down meekly either. Strike us and you'll see the full measure of our resolve."

That was the most he'd gain, Elbert knew. "We understand each other then. Good day, Mrs. Jones."

"I'm not so sure you understand yet, Mr. Runion, but I hope when the scales do fall from your eyes you're not sorely wounded."

How was he to respond to *that*? She was sincere but misguided, a true believer in her cause leading her converts straight to ruin. He headed back to the train, Skee beside him looking troubled.

"We fight over scraps," Skee said in a soft voice. "But scraps is better than starving."

Elbert stared at his man. "Shake off her spell, Skee. You have a good job that's in no danger."

That reminder ought to be enough. Self-interest was a better motivation than belief. You could change your mind at the snap of a finger, but you and yours still had to eat. Ideas didn't pay the rent or fill your children's stomachs.

The problem was that Mother Jones' boys had nothing left to lose.

By the time the machines were ready to go, most of the afternoon had run out. Elbert tried to limit his pacing, but he had to bleed off the impatience and agitation building up like steam in a boiler.

No matter how he tried, he couldn't shake memories of Homestead. The mob of strikers there were all men, standing against him and his squad in the shadows of the giant steel mills and furnaces rather than this shabby coal camp filled with families. The wide, murky Monongahela held back the hills there, a far cry from the swift, rusty-orange Sanger Fork. But the buildings in both places were the same shade of desperate gray, and the air everywhere thick with smoke and dust.

Here, though, the automatons were safe. Their enormous, powerful springs wouldn't—couldn't—explode under fire as the steam boilers had at Homestead. Shards of twisted, hot steel wouldn't slice through flesh like scythes; jets of boiling water wouldn't leave scalded ruins of the slowly dying.

Elbert swallowed bile at the memories. He and Jack somehow had escaped serious injury, shielded by the corpses of their comrades and their foes, but they'd been trapped long hours in the stinking, screaming carnage until the fires cooled. No idea, no cause, was worth a death like that.

As he signaled Jack to move their squad into formation, Cummings ushered his wife and three little girls out of their house onto the train. Safer to put anyone not marching up to the mine there, ready for a quick escape back down the track to Bluefield. Despite Mother Jones' promise, any crowd could turn into a bloodthirsty mob.

He pulled Cummings aside. "I'd like to leave at least five of your men here, sir. You're welcome to accompany us or stay here to guard our backs."

Drawing himself up to a height that still barely reached Elbert's chin, the red-faced superintendent sputtered, "I'm no coward, Runion. It's my mine and you can be blasted certain I'll be there, especially after your foolish talks with the criminals out there failed."

Elbert held up his open hands in a placating gesture. "I meant no offense, sir. Many a man would naturally be concerned about leaving his family's safety to others."

If anything Cummings grew hotter. "You keep your ignorant hillbilly nose out of my concerns, Runion, and concentrate on what *is* properly your business. If you fail me again, I'll go all the way up the Pinkerton line to the top man himself."

Elbert focused on his breathing, muttered an apology as close to groveling as he could stand, and backed away. Now he had someone watching every damn move he made, no doubt looking extra-sharp for any blame he could shift onto someone else.

His job and his men's jobs would be safe if he just finished this assignment, same as any other he'd brought in successfully. Homestead was the single glaring exception. But Sanger Fork wouldn't go that way. That fussy bastard Cummings would end the day on a fine meal of crow, feathers and all.

He wound up by Blaylock and his team. The chief engineer mopped sweat off his neck with a grimy cloth. "We've just finished setting up the commands, Runion." They'd settled on a double line of the machines sandwiching Elbert's men on the march, the Pinkertons ready to fire out through them if they were attacked. "A three-foot gap between each automaton isn't very much. If we run into obstacles they may not hold the configuration."

Elbert stared at the stiff hulks, statues of steel gleaming with a fresh-from-the-factory shine that wouldn't last a day in the mines. They were disturbingly manlike, but with thick, rounded humps instead of heads. Instead of feet they moved on plated tracks turned by wheels. Extra-long "arms" ended in clamps to hold whatever tools the job required; on their own the empty clamps could break bones and smash skulls.

Reminded again of Homestead, he studied the back where the crucial winding mechanism lay. It was barely visible, folded flush now that it wasn't in use. *Clever.* If the mechanism stuck out permanently, it would be too vulnerable to accidental or deliberate damage.

But that wouldn't help keep the automatons on course and protected from attack. "I'll warn my men to watch for the lines stringing out too much. They'll be ready."

"I'm more concerned with the automatons running into each other." Blaylock swiped at his neck again. "We haven't perfected commands to avoid some obstacles but not others."

"And you didn't think this was something I needed to know about?"

The engineer glared back. "It wasn't an issue when we had everything in place to set them up *in* the mine. Once we lost that, what other choice did we have?"

"I need those machines in working order," Cummings said. "I don't care what it costs."

By the steel in his eyes, Elbert knew he wasn't talking about his company's funds. Elbert had few objections when it came to strikers and other criminals, but his men were a whole other story. He'd be damned if any of them took harm just to make this bellyacher look better.

Still, though he didn't understand the ins and outs of Blaylock's work or the complexities of the automatons, even he could see that a machine stationed in place on a factory line or patrolling a set path designed for it was a far cry from negotiating the steep, rocky path ahead of them.

"We know our job," he said. "We'll fulfill our contract, no need to fear on that account. That's why you hire Pinkertons."

Jack took up his post at the end of the line and Elbert moved up to the head. Blaylock positioned himself right behind Elbert, but the rest of his team filed onto the train.

"They'll only get in the way," he explained. "They're better used to defending the train if need be."

It made sense to bring at least one engineer in case the automatons needed adjustments to start work. Elbert pulled out his Peacemaker. "I sure hope you're carrying a gun of your own and are willing to use it. You heard Cummings: We're here to protect your machines before anyone else, even you."

Blaylock made a show of resting his hands on his hips, pushing back his sack coat to reveal his lack of weapons. "The day is coming soon when brutes with guns are as superfluous as those miners out there and the factory workers before them." His slow smile had too many teeth.

A chill crept over his flesh, but Elbert forced himself not to react. "Keep your head down then and stay out of our way." After one last surveying glance, he raised his arm and sliced it down. "Move out."

Blaylock darted over to the first two automatons and slapped a raised patch on their backs next to the winding key. A rough whine broke out, then a steady hum, and the tracks began to turn in a slow, steady crawl.

The engineer had already dropped back to start the next pair. Elbert hadn't thought in any detail about how the machines actually worked, but clearly you couldn't shout an order at something with no ears and no mind.

His fear of being replaced by an automaton fell away. No matter what Blaylock threatened, no one with any sense would set a machine to catching crooks or enforcing security. You needed judgment for that, a sense of right and wrong, and knowing just how far to go and when to stop.

They held their pace to the automatons' crawl as they left the hard-packed street for a softer side path between Cummings' house and a twin that no doubt housed the foreman, mine engineer or another of the coal camp's upper crust. Elbert wondered briefly where they were, whether they'd fled or were among the men guarding the train. He let the thought go as quickly as it came. Unless they were in his ranks now, they weren't his concern.

The guards at the barricades funneled into his line, all but the last five who fell back to the train. The people packed into the street let out a roar like an enraged beast when they spotted the automatons moving out.

Yet even over their yells and the grind and clank of the machines, Mother Jones' voice rang out clear through the megaphone. "Hold steady, boys. This is the call to judgment! We'll show these ticks and parasites in their fine houses that your blood and sweat built, that the working man won't lie down meekly any longer under their boots."

Elbert swore one blistering oath after another in his head. Despite her promise, that sounded awfully close to an incitement to bloodshed.

"Stand your ground, boys," she continued, "but remember, our hands will not be the first raised in violence here. Despite what they say of us, we will not sully our cause. Let the company's hounds show their true colors."

This time the crowd's shouts echoed off the hills caging the narrow valley.

"Don't give them cause, not if you can avoid it," Elbert reminded the men around him. He moved down the line, ignoring the unarmed Blaylock, until he reached Jack.

"I have a bad feeling about this, boss." Jack drew Elbert's attention to Cummings, safely stowed in a knot of his own men.

"We do what we can with what we have," Elbert said with a resigned shrug.

The miners rushed up the hill, curving ahead of the line of machines and men moving at a slow angle across the slope. They dropped debris in their path, logs and barrels and even battered furniture, creating a barricade of their own strung along the route to the mine.

Clever bastards. Elbert hurried back to Blaylock, wondering how they'd known about the automatons' weakness. "I hope you have a plan."

Blaylock looked at him with scorn, as if the answer was obvious. "Send your men out there to clear the way. That's why they're here."

Should've known he'd consider us expendable. Just another tool in service to his damn machines. That tendril of unease for his future tried to unfurl again, but he ignored it as he ordered half his crew along with the mine guards out beyond the automatons. The rest—his best marksmen—he moved up to cover them.

The miners didn't give up that easily. As he'd told Jack from the first, only the stubborn and unyielding survived the hardscrabble mountain life. They retreated a little, some of them managing to rescue parts of their barricade to set up in a new spot.

Before his men could advance, three keg-sized rocks tumbled down from the top of the hill. His anger at not foreseeing that obvious maneuver powered his warning shout, and then he could only hold his breath and hope.

Two missed the machines through lucky chance, one rolling between the gaps in their line, the other deflected by a stump. The third clipped an automaton, skewing it around to point more downhill as it teetered on its tracks.

Blaylock ran to shore it up as best he could, feet braced on churned-up leaves and timber debris.

Elbert shoved his revolver in its holster and ran to help, grabbing one of the O'Keefe brothers for extra muscle. Somehow they managed to keep the machine moving while guiding it back on course and avoid a collision with another of its kind.

Blaylock hunched over and walked alongside it in what Elbert assumed was a check for damage. But he had no time to spare for the engineer. Cummings was ordering men up the hill after whoever had launched those rocks—a deadly mistake.

"Back in line!" Elbert shouted, then lowered his voice to an insistent hiss at the superintendent. "Out here, I give the orders.

The mine may be your concern, but leave getting us there in one piece to my experience. Splitting our forces only gets our men hurt or killed."

Cummings stared back for a long moment, impassive. Then he nodded. "Of course, Runion."

Elbert hurried back to the front of the line, even more uneasy yet unable to pinpoint why. But he had to set it aside. His men clearing the way were under attack, if only with fists and clubs. They were all too close together for even his best sharpshooters to find a clear target.

He'd only just reached them when some damned fool opened up with a rifle. Elbert ducked his head instinctively and looked back at Jack and the others. Another shot cracked through the air—but not from his lines. Someone was shooting into the miners from behind.

From the mine.

The miners realized it an instant before he did. Their mass split, half surging forward into his men with a new fury, the rest swarming back to the fences that protected the workings.

Cummings' men. That tight-mouthed little weasel.

"Fall back!" Elbert didn't trust Cummings' shooters to have any care for the Pinkertons' safety, and for damned sure he didn't want to be cut off.

An explosion down in town drowned him out, one blast followed quickly by three more.

The men fighting around him stopped practically in unison, creating a disturbing similarity to the machines still crawling toward them. Flames licked out of three shacks at the far end of Sanger Fork. Bits of burning tar paper and cloth fluttered down to the ground, starting their own little fires. The people left in the street—women, children, worked-out miners—ran around like ants from an overturned hill, their screams and wailing faint to his ears after the deafening blasts.

He looked for Jack, but spotted Cummings first. A sly, triumphant smile twisted the superintendent's face before it disappeared, wiped clean. Elbert wasn't sure whether the man wanted to provoke violence to justify harsher measures, or simply wanted to evict unneeded workers as a distraction, but the reason didn't matter now. The miners up here drew knives, heating up the fight.

The advancing automatons were nearly on them, raising a whole new threat. Elbert dragged Skee, still grappling with a broken-nosed miner, out of the path of the lead machine, and a handful of the more alert fighters from both sides followed. The automatons' outstretched arms knocked down other men, and one unlucky bastard didn't yank his leg out of the way fast enough. His agonized shrieks were nearly lost in the ruckus.

The brawling stopped, at least temporarily, in favor of escape, while the strikers inside the automatons' column darted back to their comrades.

Cummings nearly popped with outrage. "After them!" He grabbed Elbert's shoulder and pointed at the running men. "What are you waiting for? Shoot them down!"

Elbert loomed over him, trusting Jack to keep everything else together. "Hush your damn fool mouth—sir. Who are you working for, the company or that woman down there? You're playing straight into her hands, don't you see that?"

The superintendent stabbed his finger into Elbert's chest. "Then make sure she stays quiet. Silence them all if you have to. They're nothing but obstacles to progress."

Elbert ground his fist around that finger, ignoring Cummings' squeals and attempts to break free. "Listen here, you little tin-pot maniac. We're here to move those machines into your mine in working order. You think it's any easier with bullets flying every which way or houses blown to Kingdom Come? Both of those have your signature all over them—and if I can tell, you can bet everyone else here can too."

Cummings stiffened in silent outrage. Elbert ran out of words, let loose of Cummings' finger, and stalked over to Jack before the superintendent could respond.

"We need a new plan, boss." The tension in Jack's shoulders as he scanned the hill above them and ahead of them undercut his mild tone.

"I'm fresh out of ideas. Turning tail for home's not on the

table."

They shared a grim smile. "I don't see how they'll stop us reaching the mine in the end," Jack said. "The only question is how many bodies we leave behind us."

"I don't think that's a particular concern for some folks. Nothing in the contract about that, I noticed—and that's all we're paid to consider." Elbert ran a frustrated hand through his hair, then froze. *The contract.*

The coal company had hired Pinkerton to deliver the automatons to its mine. That's what the job boiled down to. If men like Cummings and Blaylock were the future, Elbert didn't see any reason to go one inch farther than he had to. Mother Jones had been only half-right; his sight *had* cleared, but he was still whole and fighting.

Jack's eyes glinted. "I know that look. What do you need me to do?"

Elbert's relief at clearing the mine fence shattered as he took in the bodies of miners and guards sprawled in bloody clumps. Mostly injured, granted, rather than dead, and the fierce fighting here had eased their own way. But the miners who were left in their wake, an obstacle now to their return to the train, would fight them all the harder.

He ordered his men to the fence, ostensibly spelling Cummings' remaining guards. The more attention turned outside the fence, the better for his plan.

Blaylock was too focused on shepherding his machines the last steps into the mine portal, while Cummings concentrated solely on inspecting the outer workings for damage. Another black mark against the man, that he cared more for profit and loss than his people, but Elbert had come to expect nothing else. It worked to his advantage, letting him and Jack proceed without interference.

Another explosion from the coal camp froze everyone but the automatons. Elbert hunted for sight of Jack, his breathing easing back to normal when his lieutenant sidled, hands full, out of the storage bunker under the tipple. He looked over at Cummings next, certain the superintendent had ordered more attacks on his surplus workers.

But the man rushed to the fence, almost panicked, and everyone but Blaylock and the wounded joined him there. Jack took the opportunity to pass him the bundles of dynamite he'd extracted from the bunker, and Elbert hid them in his coat pockets. No one was paying close enough mind to him now to notice.

Instead they gaped at the mangled mess of tracks leading back to Bluefield and safety. The train itself was well clear and untouched, but the streets, ominously, had emptied completely. Mother Jones was *finally* silent, not that Elbert counted that as a victory now. He could only hope that stranding the train meant the miners had no need to attack it.

More reason to proceed with his plan. A big enough distraction might let him lead his men safely out of Sanger Fork, even if they had to walk. He hoped Mother Jones would see it as a fair trade.

He slipped away, before he lost this unexpected chance. No one would miss him just yet with Jack there to cover for him.

By now the last two automatons had disappeared into the mine's black mouth. Blaylock was still in view, half-shadowed as he fumbled with a safety lamp. He looked up in surprise at Elbert's approach. "Is there a problem, Runion?"

The engineer would never go along with Elbert's plan; he cared only about the triumph of his machines. "They blew the tracks out of here," Elbert said, walking closer. Then he laid Blaylock out with a hard punch, and pulled him free of the mine into the shelter of the spoil tip.

The automatons' tracks ground and groaned against the rough floor, echoing out of the mine: still moving forward as commanded, probably until they hit a wall or their springs wound down.

His skin crawled like ants covered him when he ducked inside, breaking the promise he'd made himself when he left home; he gritted his teeth and set each bundle of dynamite in place with an eye to doing the most damage to the portal. He was no engineer, but he'd grown up around miners and explosives.

It wasn't an ideal or even long-term solution, simply the best he could manage. With luck no one would pin the cave-in on him. Only Jack and Blaylock could link him to it, and what was the engineer's testimony against a Pinkerton with his long record against strikers?

Elbert was all for progress, same as he was for rules and order. But they had to be fair rules, and progress had to make room for everyone.

He lit the fuses and hurried back to the fence. Unlike the automatons, he could choose to stop or continue. Sometimes clean hands and a clear conscience weighed heavier on the scale than a full belly.

EOLOMANCER

Aleksander Žiljak

"Sell me a wind, woman!"

Katka shivered—not too obviously, she hoped. She kept stirring the soup with a ladle. She was cooking for the next day. It was summer and days were hot, too hot to cook. Evenings were the time to do it, when it was cooler. She tasted the hot soup with the tip of her tongue. *Good indeed*, she decided and removed the pot from the fire. She covered the pot with a lid, wiped her hands on her white apron and looked at the stranger.

"You hear what I say? Sell me a wind!" Mingan was sitting at the table, not taking his eyes off Katka. He threw a leather purse on the table, several gold coins scattered from it, jingling. Katka looked at doubloons, gleaming in the light of an oil lamp. The pirate studied her with his leaden gray eyes under the strong eyebrows. His aquiline nose and thin lips gave him predatory look. He was gray-haired, too young to be white with age. His hair was neatly clipped, his moustache and goatee carefully trimmed. He was muscular, wearing dark trousers tucked into high boots and a white unbuttoned shirt, its sleeves rolled up. His hairy chest showed. He had laid his tricorne on the table. He had placed his *shamshir* with an ornate scabbard and ivory handle within easy reach. Katka did not miss the knives pushed into his boots, one in each. And a revolver, tucked into his purple silk waist sash.

"What will you do with a wind, Sir?" Katka asked. The doubloons were the cursed coins, she knew, minted of gold dug and robbed in blood across the Ocean, in the mountains reaching all the way to the clouds and vast jungles. And whatever Mingan wanted, she had heard enough about him to know it could only mean more blood.

"I need it to defeat the Golden Armada." Mingan grinned.

A beastly gleam flashed in his eyes. Katka trembled. "I need a wind, woman, you hear? A storm to sweep the corvettes, to scatter the frigates, to bring down the treasure ships from the sky."

"It's a strong wind indeed, Sir." *At least as strong as a* bura, Katka thought. Perhaps as strong as a hurricane. She had never summoned a hurricane.

"Don't tell me you can't do it," Mingan leaned back in the chair. "You're an aeolomancer. You summon winds. I know well you raised the *bura* that smashed the Serenissima fleet against the cliffs of Krk. Never before and never since did people see such a *bura*. How much did the Captain of Nehai pay you, woman?"

"Some things are not done for money, Sir," Katka lied, wiping her hands against her apron absentmindedly. There was blood on her hands. The entire fleet sent by the Serenissima against Senj, with all hands. She had not heard of anybody surviving. Mingan pointed at the purse.

"There will be more, woman. This is just to show you I mean it."

Katka raised her gaze and crossed her arms with determination. "No, Sir. I don't sell wind anymore."

Mingan measured Katka from head to toe. After several moments, he just shrugged. He rose, picked the gold coins, took his *shamshir* and put his tricorne on his head. *So easy?* Katka wondered. She had expected angry persuasion and threats. Mingan headed for the door to leave. He opened the door and stood there, framed by the stony frame. He faced Katka.

"You have a daughter, right? Fourteen-fifteen years old? Life is before her, you should think about her future."

Mingan left into the night, leaving Katka standing next to the table, pierced by fear, holding herself so as not to fall down.

<><>

"Who was that, mother?" Rashelka asked. She descended the stairs into the kitchen, dressed in a nightgown. Her brown hair was disheveled, traces of disrupted sleep in her green eyes, just like her mother's.

"An evil man, my daughter. He wanted me to sell him a wind." Katka took off her apron and hung it on a hook next to the stove. *Bava* was blowing gently outside. Dark sea. Clear sky. Katka drew the green-painted shutters and closed them tight. She closed the windows, too. She wanted her house properly shut tonight.

"What did you tell him?"

"I sent him away," Katka smiled and caressed Rashelka's cheek. "I don't think he'll come back," she lied. She locked and barred the door. She yawned. Cooking tired her. And Mingan? Perhaps she should go to the port master's and report? Or should she simply keep quiet about him? Mingan's sinister reputation had spread far. But Mingan was pillaging across the Ocean, by the shores of Brasilia and all the way north to the West Indies. Nobody ever spotted his airship in the Adriatic Sea, nobody offered prizes for his head here. What was he doing here? Did he fly all the way across the Ocean just for her? Who knew if the port master would believe her? And would he do anything at all?

"Come, Rashelka, it's time to sleep. We must hit the oars tomorrow, to check the fish-traps."

Katka lay in her bed. Despite her tiredness, sleep wouldn't come: Mingan drove it away. She stared into darkness, remembering Senj and the Fort of Nehai, and the invading air fleet in the sky. She was seventeen, already a mother, and already wearing black of a widow. Katka closed her eyes and memories rushed in, still vivid and horrifying after all these years...

Katka stood on the wall of Nehai, madness in her eyes, arms spread toward the sea. The wind was throwing her hair across her face, carrying away her black kerchief. *Bura* was in her fingers. Katka wove the wind as if working the lace from the island of Pag.

With her hands, Katka brought the *bura* down from the Velebit—the breath of the stony dragon asleep above the coast—

and made her whistle above the fort, howl in the pines beneath the walls, roar over Senj and to the cliffs of Krk. Frightened people were taking shelter in their houses of stone, closing their doors and windows. Shutters slammed, roof tiles smashed. Once unleashed, summoned from her mountain throne, the *bura* knew no mercy, carrying away innocent and guilty alike.

Katka was flogging the sea with wind, whirling *fumarea*, blurring the horizon. Above the sea, a gray reconnaissance corvette struggled to stay on course. And then a squall hit the airship and tossed her, breaking her wooden frame like a spoiled child tearing a toy apart. Her back broken, the airship tumbled down. And then, an explosion and fire engulfed the entire corvette. Tiny dots falling from the flames. The crew, greeted by the calls of gulls as they jumped to their deaths, escaping the heat of burning hydrogen and explosions of gunpowder and grenades.

More gray airships in the distance, approached. They must have seen the flames, but the corvette's demise did not stop them. The Serenissima had raised her fleet against the Fort of Nehai. Corvettes and frigates and ships of the line, armed with machine-guns, cannons and grenades, to deal with the impudent *uskoks* of Senj and their Captain. Katka waited for them to come closer and then, bare-handed, she cast gusts at them, each stronger than the previous. The engines ran at full steam, but the unbridled *bura* was stronger, whipping at the ships, scattering them, breaking their battle formation and smashing them against each other. Explosions and flames as far as eyes could see: From Nehai, the sea and the cliffs looked as if they were made of fire.

The Captain looked through his telescope as fires devoured the pride of the Serenissima. And when it was all over, when the sky above the Velebit was free of invading airships, he roared with laughter of victory and shouted to his men and they cheered in joy and celebrated and fired shots in the air. On the walls, exhausted Katka fainted, suddenly hammered by all those distant deaths, and the *bura* stopped—once there was no-one to drive it—as suddenly as it had started.

Later, when she came to her senses, somewhere within the

protective walls of the Fort of Nehai, a leather purse greeted her on a cabinet next to her bed. It was full of looted Venetian *scudas*. A purse of silver coins for the *bura* to destroy the cursed Venetians.

Because, Katka was an aeolomancer. Katka was selling wind.

Until the deaths she had brought that day with her own hands made her realize the true price of her power.

<<>>

A scream tore Katka out of her sleep. *Rashelka!* burst through her drowsy mind. She jumped out of her bed and rushed out of her room. In the dark, dark shapes were dragging Rashelka down the stairs. She was screaming and struggling, but strong hands wouldn't let her free. Then her screams fell silent, her mouth pressed by a palm.

"Let go of her, you trash!" Katka bellowed and ran after them, wind growing in her hands. And then, something hit her across the back of her head—a revolver butt—and she collapsed to the floor, stunned, helpless, on the edge of fainting. She felt someone lifting her. She recognized those hands through the dark, that smell of a wolf. Mingan dragged her downstairs into the kitchen and out. Somebody was in front of the house.

"Shall I burn?" that somebody asked Mingan. It looked to Katka he was holding a grenade.

"No, Wayne!" the pirate replied, dragging Katka through dry grass. "Nobody heard the screams, the nearest house is half a mile away. But fire might cause people to jump to their feet. Let's go, everybody back to the *Embolon*!"

Night air cleared Katka's mind a bit. She discerned the dark shape of an airship against the star-strewn sky: it seemed as big as a corvette, more than 200 feet long. Rashelka was already onboard. Mingan pushed Katka through the entry hatch on the side of a long suspended gondola. Somebody's hands grabbed her and dragged her down the narrow passageway toward the tail. Mingan and Wayne boarded after her. The pirate barked a command and the ship jerked up. She climbed and climbed. Katka heard the engines running: the steam in the cylinders, the chains transmitting power to the propellers driving the airship up.

Katka shook her head, pain hammering in it. She clenched her fists, feeling the wind gathering in them, surging, flowing into her fingers, tingling under her nails—

"I don't think so!" Mingan jumped after her and grabbed her for her hair, painfully, to break her concentration. He yanked her head up. Their eyes met. "We're at one hundred feet already! Not much, but have you ever jumped from that high? With a burning airship straight above?"

Katka relaxed, sinking helplessly, letting the wind dissolve from her fingers back into her body. Mingan nodded. They understood each other well.

"That's better," he muttered. "As long as you're onboard, you can't touch us. Otherwise, you and your kid will fall with the *Embolon*, got that?"

<>

Rashelka rose from a mat and looked through a porthole. The sea was spreading below her. She did not see a single ship on the sea, a single dirigible in the sky. Neither did she see an island or distant land. Nor birds. It seemed they were flying at three or four, maybe even five thousand feet. Seldom any airship ventured higher.

The confining cabin in which she had awakened must have been a storage closet of a sort, emptied just for her. Empty shelves were along one wall. A metal chamber pot was left for her in the corner. Including the mat covered by a flax sheet, there was barely space enough to turn around. The sliding door was closed. Rashelka tried to open it: of course it was locked. *What did I expect?* she thought.

Suddenly, footsteps! The lock clicked. The door slid aside. Mingan entered the storage space. He was carrying a cotton shirt and loose trousers and fabric slippers. He measured Rashelka from head to toe, and then he threw the clothes and slippers on her mat.

"There, put this on," he ordered. "So nobody gets any funny ideas should they see you in the nightgown."

"Where's my mother?" Rashelka leaped after Mingan. The door slid shut and she hit it with her fists. "I want to see my mother!" she yelled. Clicking of the lock was her only answer. Rashelka grabbed the pot, hit the door with it, once, twice. "You hear me? I want to see my mother! Open -"

A curse. Unlocking of the door. The door slid open and Mingan stormed in, his face contorted in anger, and slapped Rashelka. She staggered, the pot fell out of her hand and clattered into the corner.

"I need you alive, babe," Mingan snarled. "But there are different ways one can be alive. Got that?" Rashelka nodded, her cheek stinging.

"Glad we understood each other," the pirate growled and slammed the door and locked it again.

Rashelka cursed after him. Then she took the chamber pot and used it the way it was meant. She took her nightgown off and put the trousers on. She tightened them with a waist-string. The shirt was too big for her. She tucked it into the trousers, rolled the sleeves up and put the slippers on. She sat back on the mat.

Her stomach growled with hunger. She wondered when would they bring her something to eat.

"What did you do with Rashelka?" Katka hissed.

"She is where she belongs," Mingan replied nonchalantly, finishing his supper. "She doesn't sleep on bare planks, I gave her clothes, fed her, emptied her pot, she's under lock and key so nobody touches her. What else do you want?"

"Perhaps to be returned home, Sir?"

Mingan roared with laughter. "Oh, you're good, woman!" He was watching her and nodding. "I see I won't be bored with you."

Katka was sitting in a comfortable upholstered chair facing Mingan, in his cabin in the tail of the gondola. Sunset was burning through the starboard windows, painting the cabin in gold. *We're flying south*, Katka deduced. What is there on the south? Or perhaps Mingan would cross the Ocean at its narrowest? She would not ask him anything.

The captain's cabin was entered through a wooden sliding door. The pirate's bed was alongside the starboard wall, drawers beneath it. A narrow clothes closet was next to the headboard. A toilet with a sink was in the corner, separated by a folding screen. A desk was alongside the port wall, charts spread on and above it. A barometer on the wall above the desk. A chronometer, a sextant placed in a box, a compass, folded charts, several heavy volumes. Books on a shelf. Voice tube mouths. There was a heavy antique-looking globe next to the desk. Arms, repeating rifles, three revolvers, and a flare gun chained and padlocked. Katka doubted those were the only weapons onboard. Besides, she never fired a shot.

On the table where they sat—surrounded by windows giving them a view of the sunset above the sea—expensive plates made of the finest Bohemian porcelain, silver cutlery, crystal wine glasses. Bare chicken bones, some potato leftovers, wine. Mingan had dragged Katka from her locked cabin and then he dumped her into the chair, at the table already set. Her nostrils twitched at the aroma of roasted chicken and potatoes... She realized with anger how easily she succumbed to the pirate's hospitality. Although, she could not miss a wooden club within reach of Mingan's hand, next to the knife and fork. Nevertheless, she did not resist when the pirate poured her the first glass of wine. She was hungry. So hungry she forgot about everything else. Even Rashelka.

Mingan wiped his mouth with a napkin and pushed the plate away from him. He poured himself another glass of wine. He offered Katka, too. She waved her hand away. She'd drunk too much. She wanted to rise.

"Sit down!" Mingan barked.

"But Rashelka—"

"I said she misses nothing! Don't worry, I'll walk her from time to time. Although, the less my gang sees of her, the better. You'll manage."

"How long shall we travel, Sir?" Katka knew it would take at least five days to cross the Ocean east to west. Less in the opposite direction, depending on the winds.

"As much as it takes. Depends when will the Armada start."

Katka sat back into the chair. "It must be a special convoy, when you went all the way to the Adriatic Sea to kidnap me."

"It is," Mingan grinned. "More gold and silver than you can imagine. Your job is to stir the storm, to drive away and destroy the escort. Then, you will bring the treasure ships down, or at least damage them. My *bombardellas* and machine-guns are not enough to attack the Armada openly. They'd sweep us from the sky before we'd get within firing range. But you will have to obey me, got that? I don't want them brought down at high seas."

"But how will you recover the treasure, once the ships are down?"

"That, woman, is my worry."

Mingan pushed the chair behind him, rose and approached Katka. She did not like the gleam in his eyes. He touched her cheek. She pushed his hand away, but there was nowhere she could go. Mingan touched her cheek again. "How old are you, woman?"

"That... That is something a well-mannered gentleman does not ask a woman, Sir", Katka whispered. Mingan's palm on her cheek would not give her peace.

"I'm asking you!"

"Thirty. Last May."

Mingan nodded. "You gave birth young. Almost a girl."

"I also married young, Sir. And was widowed."

Mingan laid his hand on Katka's left breast. She pushed his hand away furiously.

"I had a good supper," Mingan snarled. "And the wine was good. And now I want a woman, to warm myself in her."

"Let me go, Sir, let -"

"Or should I go for Rashelka? Perhaps she would be more willing, who knows?" Mingan grinned. "And send you to entertain the crew? What say you, woman?"

Mingan laid his hands on Katka's breasts again. He was kneading them through her coarse shirt. Katka did not try to push his hands away this time. She closed her eyes, took a deep breath through her teeth, and surrendered to the pagan feeling stirred by Mingan's fingers on her nipples, in the rhythm of the engine driving them south across the Ocean.

<◇>

Rashelka peeked through the porthole, the airship was resting peacefully just a few feet above the water. The sea was calm, they had settled in a deserted bay of an island that rose into a high volcano peak. The Sun-scorched gray soil was covered by tough plants struggling to survive. *Islas Canarias?* Rashelka wondered.

An unusual vessel was anchored away from the airship, her hull somewhat plump, of a horn-like stem, with eyes painted on her iron-spiked bow and folded lateen sail set on a forward-raking mast. Suntanned sailors were overloading a large bundle made of burlap and tied with strong rope from the vessel into the *Embolon* boat. Mingan was overseeing them personally. A sailor scooped a pail of water from the sea and spilled it on the bundle, wetting whatever was inside. Rashelka was puzzled. *What could it be?*

When the bundle was finally overloaded, Mingan threw a purse to the captain of the vessel. He caught it, measured its weight in his hand, opened it and looked inside, smiling with satisfaction. He waved to Mingan while his men rowed back to the *Embolon*.

Ten minutes later, Rashelka heard heavy Mingan's steps. And his men following him, straining as they were carrying the heavy bundle along the passageway.

"Careful," Mingan warned them. Rashelka heard keys jingling, a door sliding aside. *The cabin next to mine*, she

~ 243 ~

realized. "C'mon, on the floor! Unwrap her!" Mingan was giving orders. *Unwrap? Whom?* Rashelka heard the inhuman scream, struggling, trashing on the floor, curses.

"Hold her, Goddamit!" Mingan bellowed.

"Watch it!" somebody else yelled. "Don't let her go!"

"Hold her!" Mingan repeated. "Good, that's it! Let's go, put 'er in the water!" Rashelka heard the water splashing, and then hinges screeching and clanking, as if a heavy grate was lowered, and chains jingling, and locking. And then hits, strong and fierce.

"Damn, she'll smash it!" somebody said worriedly.

"No, she won't!" Mingan replied. "She'll calm down. Hmmm... I've got an idea!"

Rashelka heard Mingan's boots. He rushed out of the cabin and stopped before her door. The keys jingled, the door slid aside noisily, pushed by a frantic hand.

"Come here!" Mingan grabbed Rashelka by her neck before she could make a sound. "So you won't be a dead weight!" Mingan dragged Rashelka out of her cell and brought her among his men. Four of them were standing lined along one wall. Along the other...

Rashelka held her breath. A large box, a bit larger than a coffin, was placed along the other wall. It was made of glass panes in steel frame. The whole box was sealed watertight. The box was covered with a heavy iron grate, locked with a padlock. And in it...

She squeezed the bar tight with fingers of her right hand, shaking the grate, once, twice. In vain. She glared at them savagely. She would kill them all if she could. Then her green eyes paused on Rashelka. As if she sensed the girl, too, was a prisoner on this ship, her gaze softened and she relaxed a bit. She removed a lock of black hair from her face. Rashelka could not look away from her face, just like the face of any other girl, and her sound body turning beneath her navel into a... gray *body of a dolphin*, Rashelka realized. She had a small dorsal fin and a tail, just like dolphin's.

A womanfish! That damned Mingan had a womanfish caught and was now keeping her imprisoned in that confined glass cage and -

"She's your responsibility now," Mingan startled her. "You feed 'er, you change her water! You'll get a bucket and a hose. And fish. Got that?" At first, Rashelka did not answer, still stunned by the unusual creature before her. "Got that?" Mingan yelled and shook her.

Rashelka merely nodded. Who knew why Mingan needed the womanfish, but she realized that maybe she had an ally before her.

The *Embolon* was cruising the sky, driven by her steam engine. Rashelka looked through the porthole, the Ocean beneath them spread as far as eye could see. She saw a small dark spot in the distance and smoke rising from a funnel. It must have been a paddle steamer sailing east. Did they spot Mingan's airship? Did they recognize her as a pirate dirigible? After all, who knew whose colors the damned Mingan hoisted?

Rashelka returned to the womanfish. She had eaten the mackerel she had given her. "More?" Rashelka asked.

The womanfish just nodded and Rashelka took the fish by its tail and lowered it through the grate. The womanfish took it with both hands and bit into the head. Rashelka studied her as bones crunched under the strong teeth. "What does Mingan want from you?"

The womanfish looked at Rashelka with her green eyes.

"I think I know, my daughter," Katka murmured. She sat on a folded blanket, leaning against the wall as she watched Rashelka feed the womanfish: the unusual creature had quite an appetite. It was the fourth mackerel she was devouring.

"Say what, mother?"

"When the Golden Armada airships fall..." Katka lowered her voice almost to a whisper. Rashelka sat next to her. The womanfish appeared to have pricked her ears. "They'll tumble into the sea. Shallow, I guess, a lagoon or some shallow cove, but still. And then the treasure chests will have to be recovered from whatever remains of the ships." Katka and Rashelka looked at the womanfish.

"But those are heavy chests, she's not that strong," Rashelka objected.

"It's enough she just dives to them and attaches the rope. Then they can pull them out with an engine, using pulleys. I've seen Nehai men recovering machine-guns and cannons from a Venetian ship that way."

"They also had a womanfish?"

"No," Katka smiled. "They paid some sponge-divers."

"I wonder if she understands us," Rashelka whispered into her mother's ear.

"I hear you and understand you," a slightly rustling voice replied through the grate. Katka and Rashelka started and looked at the womanfish. She smiled at them, their embarrassment apparently amusing her. "I am Nirveli."

The *Embolon* was floating above the spreading white cloudscape. The Sun on the azure sky pierced the eyes, making Katka blink. The clouds below them veiled the ocean. Mingan was observing the sky above the clouds with his telescope, looking for a reconnaissance corvette, ready to order the ship to dive into the clouds at any moment. The helmsman held the course. Two more spotters on the bridge were watching the sky. The machine-gunners stood tensely behind their multi-barreled weapons.

"Nothing in sight," one of them reported. Mingan looked at him and nodded. The Armada was close, he had told Katka the evening before. *He has well-informed spies*, Katka was certain. He knew when they departed, which course they took, where they would be and when. And now, he was patrolling the sky above the clouds, waiting for them.

"Lower Branduff!" Mingan commanded.

"Aye, aye!" was heard from behind. Katka took a look: three men took to their stations in a hurry. One of them—Branduff—

buttoned his jacket up to his chin, and then he put his leather aeronaut's helmet and gloves on. Goggles protected his eyes. The other two were preparing the car. It resembled a small airship, painted pale gray (*harder to spot it*, Katka realized), some twelve feet long, with a single seat behind a small windshield. Branduff sat in the car, strapped himself in, and gave them a thumb up. The other sailor pulled a lever and the floor below the car opened. He pulled the second lever and the car slid from its cradle, suspended on a steel cable. The sailors took to the winch. They were lowering the car slowly through the floor and beneath the airship, into the clouds. Little fins on its end stabilized it in the slipstream: it followed the *Embolon*, hanging under her.

The car disappeared in the clouds. Katka glanced at the chronometer. Some twenty minutes passed before clicking of a telegraph register was heard. The car was connected to the bridge by a telegraph wire. That way, a spotter could report what he saw, while the *Embolon* remained safely above the clouds. Mingan tore a piece of paper tape, read what Branduff signaled and commanded the sailors to stop lowering the car. He typed something back and received an almost immediate reply.

"Now we wait", he said through his tight lips and caressed his gray goatee.

<><>

"If that scoundrel thinks he will force an abducted womanfish..." Nirveli hissed with anger and stirred in her cramped box. Water splashed through the grate and spilled on the floor planks. "As soon as he releases me back into the sea..."

Rashelka looked at the blue sky through the porthole. They sailed above the clouds that spread as far as eye could see. The shadow of the *Embolon* swept across those clouds. *What is mother doing?*, she wondered. Mingan had burst in and taken her without a word. Hours must have passed and she still did not return.

"And if your mother is as powerful as you say," Nirveli went on, "how come you haven't freed yourselves already?"

"But how?" Rashelka replied, desperation in her voice. "If she destroys the airship, she'd kill us, too!" The girl sat gloomily next to the box. The days on the airship seemed like eternity. Waiting. Locked in the confined cabin with a mysterious sea creature. *At least I'm not caged,* she thought.

"I think... I think Mingan is using me to make mother obedient." Nirveli studied Rashelka carefully, then thought it over and nodded. She removed a lock of hair from her face angrily. Rashelka looked back at her. Mingan certainly did not kidnap a womanfish without knowing how to deal with her. "I'm afraid he'll find a way to make you, too, do whatever he says."

The sun painted the clouds in the late afternoon gold. Hours have passed. And then, the telegraph jumped to life, the register started writing dots and dashes on the paper tape. Mingan pulled it, reading as the code was revealed, his lips moving mutely. Behind him, his crew stared intently. Then the message came to its end and Mingan tore the tape off and raised it triumphantly.

"The Golden Armada, lads! It's here!" he shouted. "Three treasure ships!"

"As many as three!"

"Three, I tell you! So says Branduff, and he has the eye of a falcon! The *Santissima Madre*, the *Algeciras* and the *San Juan Nepomuceno*. And the escort, they're spread five miles long and three miles wide."

"The *San Juan Nepomuceno*... That's a lot of cannons," a machine-gunner said.

"And a lot of treasure!" Mingan replied, grinning, gleam in his leaden eyes, as if he was about to snarl. He looked at them all, cheering them with his stare, beckoning them to follow. Katka watched silently the gold-madness spreading among them, passing from one to another like plague. She watched the glitter of gold and silver and gems clouding their minds. *If they weren't like that,* she knew, *they wouldn't be what they were.* And then her eyes met Mingan's. She was the source of his confidence, the key to the bloody riches in the three large airships. She was his secret weapon.

"The usual battle formation?" Wayne asked, as if he wanted to scatter the spell possessing the pirates. Wayne was Mingan's second-in-command, the pirate captain's most trusted man. The man who wanted to burn her house down.

"By the book," Mingan nodded and looked at Katka. "Box formation, 1500 feet high, with three corvette finger-fours as vanguard." Mingan studied the chart pinned on the wall and read the tape once again. He was nodding. "Just what our informer told us. Devil may take him, that greedy swine was worth every doubloon he squeezed out of me. They're cutting across the sea toward the Grenadines." Mingan tapped the chart with his finger.

"Course oh-five-seven," he ordered the helmsman and he turned the steering wheel. The nose of the airship headed starboard, dashing as if she herself was lusting for blood and treasure.

"Support?"

"Nobody to come to their aid anymore. Habana is far away. The Santo Domingo and Maracaibo detachments will be grounded by the hurricane. And we'll jump them above the Grenadines: there are reefs and lagoons there. Shallows." Mingan looked at Katka. She shivered before the bloodthirsty gleam in his eyes. "That's where you come in, woman! That's where I need your wind!"

"What if the English cut in? They're near," Wayne asked.

"Ha!" Mingan grinned. "The English to protect the Spaniards! We only have to be quick lest *they* rob them first!"

Suddenly, another message came in. Mingan and Wayne looked at each other. Mingan read the tape, his lips tight. He frowned.

"What's the matter?" Wayne asked.

"Funny," Mingan muttered. "Another airship. Out of formation, appearing briefly below the clouds, three miles behind. And she entered the clouds right away, too fast for Branduff to see the type."

"Perhaps a ship from Paramaribo," Wayne suggested. "And

yet, she's too far west. Who can it be?"

"She's no Dutch, you can bet on that," Mingan murmured, watching the sky above the clouds through the window. Then he shrugged and faced Wayne. "Maybe she's just passing by. We stick to the plan and shadow the Armada!"

<<>>

"The Joy-of-Sea?" Rashelka asked, whispering. Her face was next to Nirveli's, separated by the grate.

"A pearl," Nirveli whispered. She did not dare speak louder. In the evening, Mingan had burst into their cabin, cursed Rashelka out into the passageway and locked behind her. Rashelka had heard him talking to the womanfish in a quiet voice, nearly a whisper, she could not discern what. He had exited after quarter of an hour or so, grabbed the girl by her hand and threw her back into the cabin. The womanfish had been quiet, clenching the grate, her thoughts wandering. She had not uttered a word throughout the evening. Only after the pirates had brought them supper—a bowl of porridge for Rashelka, three mackerels for Nirveli—and left them alone, and when Rashelka had made certain that the *Embolon* had sunken into the night watch routine, she had dared to ask the womanfish what had Mingan told her.

"The greatest pearl human eyes ever saw," Nirveli showed her clenched fist. Only their breathing and the monotonous running of the steam engine driving them across the sky were heard in their cabin. "The Spaniards looted it from our Queen seventy summers ago. In the waters of the island you know as Jolo."

"I don't know where it is."

"The Pilipinas," Nirveli hissed.

"But that's the other side of the world!" Rashelka objected. "The other ocean!"

"The other ocean to you, perhaps. The one and the same sea to us," Nirveli replied. "They stole two pearls from us. And they killed many of my sisters. The Tear-of-Sea was lost in the abyss of the trench ploughed next to the Pilipinas. No-one, but no-one, can reach it now. Maybe for the better, it was an evil pearl. We thought the Joy was also lost for good: we spent years searching for it. But it found its way here. If Mingan is to be believed, the Spaniards were hiding it in a vault in the city you call Lima. And now, they're taking it across the Ocean."

And then Nirveli grabbed Rashelka by the collar of her shirt. The girl felt the hot womanfish's breath as she was whispering in her ear. "I must return the Joy-of-Sea, you hear? I must return it to our Queen! I must bow to Mingan. The Joy-of-Sea is the pay he promised me!"

"And you trust him?" Rashelka tore out of the womanfish's hand angrily. Nirveli's eyes shone with deadly glitter. She nodded and grinned.

"It doesn't matter. What matters is whether Mingan trusts me. So I'll be obedient to him. Until the pearl is in my hands..."

Katka dreamt of the Tower. The octagonal tower: they had left it behind, across the Ocean, in hot Athens. The Tower of the Winds and eight wind deities sculptured in its stone. The north wind god Boreas, the northeasterly Kaikias and Apeliotes blowing from the east. The southeastern Euros and the south wind god Notos. And the southwestern Lips, the westerly Zephyrus and the northwestern Skiron. The winds of the ancient Mediterranean sailors, turned to stone a long time ago by somebody's chisel.

The eight winds did Katka dream of, and herself on the top of the Tower of the Winds, the mistress summoning them and selling them. And she dreamt—sweaty and struggling for air in the stifled cabin—of Mingan, the wolf. He was laughing, whipped by the eight winds. He defied them and laughed, madness in his eyes, a knife under Rashelka's throat. The shiny blade rested above her jugular vein. It took but a slight move to make blood gush, to pile her bleeding body lifelessly before his boots. Katka did not doubt his threats for a moment.

The airship was carrying Katka across the Ocean. And the

winds of the New World blew in her now. She felt them in her dream, throbbing in her body and coursing through her hands, tempting her to try them. *Knik* and *matanuska* and *taku*, winds of the Alaskan winter. Fierce *squamish* raging in the fjords of the British Columbia. The strong sharp barber, carrying freezing sleet across the sea of ice. Nor'easter storming off the coast of New England. The wet *Chinook* warming freshly plowed fields in the Pacific Northwest. The warm dry *snow eater* descending the slopes of the Rockies. The savage tornado ravaging the prairies. The strong hot Californian *diablo* and Santa Ana and sundowner.

And the violent summer *chubasco* thundering along the west coast of Central America, and *coromell* blowing from the sea in Golfo de California. The hurricane-strong *cordonazo*, the Lash of St. Francis, whipping the west coast of Mejico. The dry cold *norte* and the furious *papagayo* and *tehuantepecer*.

Bayamo, roaring along the southern shores of Cuba, bringing rain. Puertorican *brisa* and Cuban *brisote* and the squally *brubu*. The trade winds, swelling the sails of the conquistadors. And the hurricane itself, the unbridled beast born along the shores of the Dark Continent and spiraling and traveling—driven by the trades—across the Ocean to unleash its wrath at the coasts of Americas.

On the beaches of Brasilia, *abroholos*, a summer squall. Far down south, south of the mighty Rio de las Amazonas and vast rainforests, all the way to grasslands and snow-capped peaks of the Cordillera, and shores on which millions of birds call and thousands of seals wallow: the cold showering stormy *pampero*; and the hot, dusty, stifling *zonda*; the wintry *suestado* bringing agitated sea and rains, sometimes even snow; and the strong dry *terral*, and *puelche* and *virazon*. And—on the very southern tip of Americas, in the Estrecho de Magallanes—a sudden *williwaw*.

And Katka longed for the winds of her Adriatic Sea, the sea she had come to with her late parents from the hilly Bohemia when she was three years old. She had taken it for her own and its winds had embraced her in return. The early morning *bonaca*—the calm—and the sea as smooth as oil, a bass leaping with a loud splash. *Bava,* just a breeze blowing gently above the water. *Maestral,* blowing away the sultry day sweat from the forehead. Katka loved the *maestral,* raising and going to bed with her. She also loved *levant,* the short-breathed east wind, bringing sudden snow, and *ponent,* the west wind crisscrossing the sea. Katka enjoyed the southern *jugo,* too, driving the dark clouds and making waves and smashing them against the rocky coast, foaming water surging and then pouring down the cliffs. *Lebich* and *tramontana* were her friends, too, all the small boats seeking safe haven before them. And *bura*! Cold mountain breath, carrying the sea dust in gusts, that would not let you walk, howling in pines, bending cypresses, whipping olive trees. And Katka standing firm, embraced by the *bura*—just a breeze to her—and laughing as it whistled in her hair.

Katka dreamt of the winds of the ancient sailors. She listened to the winds of strange names. She longed for the winds of the sea she grew up by.

And in her dream, the hurricane was howling ever louder. The beast was being born. It would not fall back, no matter how much Katka hushed it down. It claimed and demanded, spoilt, hungry; blood-thirsty. It made Katka put a leash on it to sell it to an equally hungry monster laughing above the body of her Rashelka.

The sea went wild, crisscrossed by the roaring winds, through the tattered clouds two thousand feet below. Waves dozens of feet tall were smashing into each other. From the gondola, it looked to Rashelka the snow-capped mountains were colliding. The blue was laced with foam, an artwork of an insane lace-maker. Rashelka craned her head up, the wall of clouds whirled miles high, an amphiteathre surrounding the eye of the storm. And in it, in the center of the hurricane, the *Embolon.* She sailed in peace amidst chaos, sunlit, driven by her steam engine: the source of the storm roaring and trampling and tearing and devouring everything in its path.

Katka stood in the middle of the bridge, her eyes closed, her hands limp down her body. Her mouth moved silently, as if she was speaking to the hurricane without voice, just by thoughts. The gathered pirates watched her with horror in their eyes, in reverent silence, pale, only then—surrounded by the wall of clouds, angry sea beneath them—realizing the full awesomeness of Katka's power. The helmsman clutched the wheel, afraid the airship would escape his grip and ram herself to be swallowed by the clouds. Wayne, ordered by Mingan to keep Rashelka at gun-point, lowered his pepperbox revolver. He was saying his rosary, praying for absolution for making a pact with the devil herself. Only Mingan was grinning, his leaden stare full of madness, exhilarated by the hurricane surrounding them. When the storm passed, he would be rejoicing, there would be nothing left of the Golden Armada.

Rashelka knelt, her eyes darting from her mother to the storm outside and back. She knew the way Katka summoned the wind. She used to call it when they were left becalmed on the sea, their sail limp, or to drive away the scorching heat, or when clothes left hanging needed to dry faster. But those were all breezes, old friends always ready to help. And now, before them, Katka was taming the monster, controlling it, telling it whom to pound to pieces and whom to merely whip.

"Look!" Wayne shouted suddenly, pointing up with his finger in horror. Rashelka looked. A frigate hit the western side of the wall. The wind tossed her some five hundred feet down, like a toy, then it hurled her up, and then her wooden structure could not take the forces any more and the airship disintegrated. The hydrogen exploded and they were all lit by the fiery blaze. And another one flashed through the clouds, the monster swallowing another ship.

"That's the way, woman!" Mingan bellowed, leaning above the chart, his face sweaty. He seemed to be following the hurricane's path, where Katka drove it, where would it strike. "Bring them down! Wipe them out, but watch the treasure ships! Careful where they fall!" Katka apparently did not hear him, lost in a trance, bewitched by the roar of the hurricane, the child she had raised. Out of the sun, to warm it up. Out of the sea, to wet it. Out of the wind, to drive it. Out of the Earth, to spin it. Miles away, by the wall, another airship went down in flames. "That's the way, woman! Do it! Sell me the wind!"

They spotted them through the clouds. Mingan commanded the car to be retrieved. Branduff pulled out of it, taking his gloves and goggles and helmet off as he moved. The machine-gunners watched the sky around the *Embolon* tensely, lest somebody jump them. The barrels gleamed in the sun. Katka and Rashelka spotted the airships, too.

"There's the *Santissima Madre*," Mingan declared, watching through his telescope. Perhaps the Spaniards could have seen them, but Mingan did not care anymore. Their escort was scattered and destroyed, the treasure ships were left on their own. Undefended. But not harmless. "And the *San Juan*. The *Algeciras* is... She's damaged. She's down!"

Katka and Rashelka looked through the pane. The ships were resting in a bay like three silvery whales. One was maybe fifty feet above the water, above the coral reef protecting the turquoise lagoon. The other one was above the shallows, close to the shore. And the third one, the *Algeciras*, was lying beached with her nose in the middle of a sand beach, a narrow white curve separating the sea from the hills covered in unspoiled jungle.

"They weathered well," Wayne noticed. "Two can still fly."

"Don't be afraid, they're not going anywhere," Mingan dismissed it, folding his telescope and leaning above the chart. He took another one and spread it. He studied it for several moments, his eyes skimming across the marked elevations. "Not until they transfer the treasure and men from the *Algeciras*." He called Wayne above the chart. Without a word, he made a circle across it, going from the lagoon all the way around the island. Wayne looked at the chart. Only one glance at the island beneath the clouds was enough for him to understand. He grinned and nodded.

"They don't see us," Rashelka whispered so no pirate could hear her.

"I'm afraid they're not even looking," Katka replied gloomily. She was exhausted, drained, drenched in sweat.

Wayne pushed the helmsman away and took the wheel over. He turned it and steered the *Embolon* starboard, belling full ahead to the engine room. The bridge shook as the engine sprang to life and the airship, still hidden by the tearing clouds, sped forward, following a wide curve around the island, keeping out of sight of the Spaniards.

"Won't he attack?" Rashelka asked quietly, tension in her voice.

"I think I know what he's up to," Katka murmured. "It's too dangerous to attack from the sea. Headlong against their cannons."

"Gunners to battle stations!" Mingan roared. Just what the crew had been waiting for! The lids slid aside noisily. The coordinated gunners grabbed their *bombardellas*, three at each side, and swiveled their barrels out. They were taking the already prepared charges from the storage and started loading the *bombardellas*. Everybody was working in silence, without a further command. In less than a minute, all the gunners pointed their thumbs up. The *Embolon* was ready for battle.

Followed by the tense stares of the pirates, Wayne steered the airship around the island. The Spaniards were left behind their tail. Their airships remained motionless: they were still unaware of the presence of the *Embolon*.

"Altitude three hundred," Mingan ordered, and Wayne swiveled the propellers and vented some gas. The *Embolon* sank, and then she leveled and continued above the sea. At Mingan's signal, Wayne pointed the airship to the island, belling half ahead at the same time. The airship slowed. It was only then Rashelka understood Mingan's plan.

The tallest peaks of the island were above the *Embolon*. Rashelka trembled, the jungle-covered hills were approaching. Katka held her hand. On the chart, the island resembled an arm bent at the elbow under a right angle, forearm pointing west. The bay sheltering the Golden Armada airships was on the shoulder, opened to the north.

The *Embolon* flew over the southern outer reef, the huge shadow sweeping across the lagoon and the white beach. They flew over the narrow "forearm" and found themselves above the turquoise lagoon made by the crook of the "arm". And then Wayne turned starboard a bit and the ship, more maneuverable than she looked, slipped alongside a valley between the two hills. The treetops were speeding right beneath the gondola. Rashelka spotted a flock of green parrots flying from one tree to another, startled by the monster sweeping above them, bringing infernal fire into a paradise.

"Hoist the Jolly Roger!" Mingan yelled.

"Aye, aye, Sir!" Wayne replied with joy. He released a lever and the black skull-and-crossbones pirate flag unfurled, to drive fear into the bones of the Spaniards that barely survived the hurricane and did not even suspect an even greater danger loomed ahead.

Wayne followed the contours of the hills skillfully, all the time keeping the *Embolon* hidden behind the forest green. It took great skill to steer clear and safe of the trees, Katka realized. But the *Embolon* was readily obeying Wayne's wink, every flick of his hands on the wheel.

And then the hill was no more, falling all the way to the beach, and the lagoon presented before them. Wayne ordered full speed ahead and the *Embolon* leapt like a cat upon a mouse. They flew over the helpless *Algeciras*. People disembarked on the beach looked up in confusion, pointing with their hands, scurrying about. Some even waved, thinking help had arrived. Then they saw the flag. Several sailors and passengers ran for the forest, officers yelling after them. Mingan ignored them all: he would deal with them at the end. The *Algeciras* cannons were harmless: he was in their blind angle. The machine-gun posts on the *Algeciras* top were unmanned: the Spaniards did not expect the raid.

"Between them!" Mingan barked and stormed among his gunners. Wayne needed no command, skillfully maneuvering the *Embolon* straight between the *Santissima Madre* and *San Juan Nepomuceno.*

"He's mad! He's heading straight before their cannons!" Rashelka screamed. She already saw the pirate airship caught between the two Spanish dirigibles, muzzles of their cannons spewing death, shots to tear them apart in flames -

"No!" Katka grabbed her arm and pulled her back and pointed with her finger. "Look!" And Rashelka understood. Mingan's surprise attack succeeded fully! He jumped the Spaniards unprepared, exhausted by the storm and attempts to stay together. Without their escort, driven away by the hurricane, they enjoyed some safety only by protecting each other with cannons and machine-guns. But Mingan tore into them like a wolf into sheep. Quickly, suddenly, screaming for blood.

By the moment the first lids on the silvery Spanish treasure ships—their luxurious gondolas embellished with gilt carvings and painted wooden figures—rose, revealing the muzzles of the *colubrinas*, the *Embolon* was already between them, spreading even more confusion. Because, Rashelka realized, the Spanish gunners could have easily missed the swift pirate dirigible. And then, they would destroy each other! She spotted the gunners taking their positions on the top and mounting their machine-guns and removing covers from them hurriedly. Too slow! And the *Embolon* was too low for them. In the meantime, Mingan's gunners were already taking their aims: one side at the *Santissima*, the other at the *San Juan.*

"Give'em Hell!" Mingan roared merrily and their *bombardellas* fired in unison! Not waiting to see the results, the gunners reloaded and fired again. And again! Deafening thunder made Katka and Rashelka press their ears with their palms. The shots hit and exploded and tore the gondolas into a deadly shower of split decorations and planks and broken glass and splinters. Steam burst out of the *Santissima's* pierced boiler and ducts, scalding everything in its path. Ballast water spilled, the *Santissima* started to rise. Somebody fell out of her gondola and splashed in the sea. Several more Spaniards jumped, they had greater chances of surviving the fall into the sea than remaining in the gondola shred to pieces by Mingan's *bombardellas.*

And then, the thundering detonation shook the *Embolon.* Katka and Rashelka looked behind them. A chain of explosions was ripping the *San Juan Nepomuceno* like a toy, spreading from one hydrogen cell to the next. Fire was devouring the aluminum dope-painted envelope and soon, the proud airship was but a burning wooden framework disintegrating in the sea.

Cheers broke among Mingan's crew. Katka became sick. Her ears covered by palms, with tearful eyes, Rashelka witnessed the death of the Golden Armada. A new salvo tore the rear part of the *Santissima's* gondola away from the hull. It fell to the sea. More men jumped from the airship. Rashelka saw a woman, her skirt flapping around her as she was falling. And another woman. Down, in the foaming sea, the survivors tried to swim as far as possible, lest they be buried by the doomed airship.

"Move over!" Mingan yelled, pushing a machine gunner away. He grabbed the weapon, pointed it down and turned the crank. The machine-gun rattle broke through the cannonade, the barrels turned and spewed the lethal hail on the survivors. *He'll kill them all,* Katka realized. *Nobody will survive, he'll kill them all.* It was no battle. It was a slaughter. Cries called toward Heaven, spread arms begged for mercy, but Mingan showered them with bullets, laughing in madness. The sea was painted in blood, bodies were left floating on the surface, lulled by waves.

Somebody pushed a piece of white cloth through a window of what was left of the *Santissima's* gondola. Mingan spat and bellowed: "Finish them!" Another volley from his *bombardellas* showered the *Santissima,* and then she too erupted in conflagration towering half a mile high. Only the burning skeletons—like bones of dead leviathans—were left of the once glorious treasure ships, the pride of the Golden Armada.

"Excellent! Now for the *Algeciras!*"

Wayne turned the *Embolon* at the last airship. They flew through the smoke of the burning *San Juan,* leaving a gray whirl behind. Several frigatebirds flew left of them, agitated by the slaughter above the lagoon. And just like a predatory frigatebird, the *Embolon* pounced on the *Algeciras.*

There was almost no-one left on the beach. Katka saw only several sailors. Commanded by a young officer, they mounted a machine-gun on a tripod. A sailor fetched an ammunition box from the stranded dirigible. And there was a young woman at the edge of the forest, calling. The officer gestured her to run into the forest, but she would not. *An officer's wife?* Katka wondered. *Why else would she stay?* And then, a machine-gun rattle was heard. Katka screamed and threw herself over Rashelka. Glass shattering. Bullets drumming inside the bridge. Wayne cursing and turning the airship. The machine-gun was firing from below the *Algeciras's* top rudder. A rear defense machine-gun post was there.

The bullets riddled the *Embolon's* gondola. Somebody screamed, hit. And then, Mingan barked a command and the starboard *bombardellas* fired at the *Algeciras*. The next moment, the ship was devoured by explosions and fire, tail to nose. Katka looked up. The burning wooden framework collapsed to the beach and the shallows, burying everyone beneath it. Only the woman was screaming at the edge of the forest.

"That's about the end of you!" Mingan spat. He aimed the machine-gun at her.

"No!" Katka screamed and leapt, but too late. Mingan turned the crank, the machine-gun rattled and mowed the woman down. Katka held her scream. The woman collapsed to the sand, under the trees, in the shade, and remained still.

"There! Done," Mingan muttered through his teeth and pushed Katka off him, without even looking at her. "Damage?"

"Nothing of importance here," Wayne replied. Wayne called the helmsman back and he took the wheel to bring the *Embolon* safely away from the wreck of the *Algeciras*.

"Roy was hit," somebody reported from behind.

"Just a scratch, Boss."

Mingan nodded. He was watching the burnt skeletons of the Golden Armada and the bodies lulled by the sea and the smoke above the lagoon with satisfaction. "That's the way you do it," he murmured to himself, grinning. "That's the way you do it."

And then he faced his crew. "Now for the treasure, lads!"

A triumphant roar bellowed through the *Embolon*. "Get the womanfish!"

<<>>

Nirveli splashed from the boat into the sea.

She dove deeply into the turquoise blue of the lagoon, taken by exhilaration, her body washed by the sea after days spent in the stagnant water of her glass cage. All the Rashelka's efforts in changing the water made her captivity only a bit more bearable. Still, she felt gratitude to the girl and her mother. They were just like her, prisoners. *And without them*, she thought, *I would have lost my mind.*

Nirveli stretched, flicked her tail, rushed playfully down to the sandy bottom. She turned around, stirring the sand with her tail. The *Embolon* and the boat were above her. She escaped their dark shapes and swam above the bottom, flicking her tail and pushing herself through the water with her hands. Then she stopped abruptly and remained still to let a shark pass. The cold eye measured her, the jaws filled with sharp teeth opened and closed menacingly, and then the big fish swam on, attracted by the commotion some hundred feet away. Sharks were going frantic over a body. They twisted around it, biting the chunks off and devouring them. Small fish around them struggled for remains. Nothing is wasted in the sea. There were more sharks around. Nirveli did not fear them. The womenfish bewared of only the biggest ones. Before her, several spotted eagle rays glided peacefully above the sand, as if flying.

Nirveli looked toward the surface. Mingan's men rowed after her. The *Embolon* was following them. She surfaced, waved to them, inhaled and dove back. She sped toward the *San Juan's* frame. It rested on the sandy bottom, collapsed, its polygonal ring-like transverse frames joined by longitudinal girders. Nirveli knew the first severe storm would smash the skeleton completely. Whatever remained would be covered by sand: soon, there would be nothing left to indicate a Golden Armada airship had sunk here.

Nirveli slipped in between the girders amidships. She felt tiny within the collapsed structure. She was swimming above the crushed and dismembered gondola stretching beneath the airship. *This must be the front engine-room*, she thought. A boiler. A steam engine, cylinders, tubes. A condenser. Transmission chains torn loose. A propeller was resting in the sand, one blade broken.

She looked back. Facing the tail, she saw *colubrina* barrels under girders: the main battery, never having a chance to fire a single shot. Mingan directed her to head for the nose. A flick of her tail and she sped ahead. She saw a burned body captured beneath a girder. Another one a bit further. Passenger cabins torn into pieces, smashed berths, gilt wooden statues of womenfish and tritons holding lamps, broken off and snapped and burnt. A girl's body dancing among them, swayed by the water. Nirveli was swimming through the tomb, making her way carefully through the remains of the gondola. Officers' cabins. The captain's cabin. And then, what she was looking for!

Three fire-resistant chests under girders and planks and carvings. Nirveli dove to them. She looked carefully, everything appeared more or less firm, and then she squeezed herself under the girders. The chests were intact, singed by fire, but Mingan claimed the contents were completely safe inside. Each was locked with three locks, requiring codes to release the bolts. Mingan had explained to her all that carefully. No lock would stand his nitroglycerine, he had said. Whatever was that nitroglycerine...

Nirveli's heart trembled. The Joy-of-Sea was in a chest like these! Her pay for all that death around her. For a moment, she felt dejected. But then Nirveli dismissed the feeling of guilt. Anyhow, death is a way of life in the sea. And, after all, what did humans mean to her? And their ships, those on the sea and those in the air? What did they mean to her and her sisters? Nets, dolphin harpoons, clubs, barbs, hooks... Menace, danger, death. That was what humans meant to womenfish! The more they kill each other, the better!

Driving away the horror of all those bodies with these

thoughts, Nirveli wiggled quickly from beneath the girders and swam up. She surfaced right before the boat's bow. She inhaled and yelled to the men in the boat: "Three chests!"

The pirates rejoiced. One even patted her shoulder. Mingan waved to her from the *Embolon* bridge and ordered the ship closer. Nirveli took the steel rope she would tie around the first chest, so that Mingan and his men could recover it by a winch.

Three small simultaneous explosions tore the locks open. Mingan leapt through smoke and raised the heavy lid of the chest. Gold flashed before the pirate's eyes, enchanted by the fiery yellow glitter of the coins. His face sweaty, a greedy gleam in his eyes, Mingan took a handful of doubloons. He let them spill through his fingers, enjoying the coolness and tinkling of metal. Then he grabbed a heavy gold chain and raised it for everybody to see and threw it back. He was overturning the golden chalices and reliquaries and crucifixes adorned in emeralds, heliodores and fire opals. Finally, he opened a small compartment within the chest and took a cloth purse out of it. Under the tense stares of the pirates, he spilled diamonds into his fist. Nobody dared utter a word.

Katka and Rashelka seemed enchanted, too, and then the woman shook and tugged at her daughter's sleeve and they looked at each other. They understood each other without a word, there was no way it could have been different. Not for those who had lived honestly on the stone, of fish-traps and nets and hoe, on poor soil walled in stony dry wall, scorched by the sun, whipped by the wind, salted by the sea. The land that was their home.

The treasures in the chests were not meant for Rashelka and Katka. There was too much blood and evil on them. Evil to steal them from land by slavery, blood to loot them from the airships of the Golden Armada by slaughter.

Strange silence settled on the beach. All the chests were opened, all the treasures in them before Mingan and his pirates.

But it looked as if nobody dared touch them. As if the first one reaching for the doubloons and chains and chalices would spark the all-out rapine and grabbing and slaughter. Mingan saw the tension among his men. He knew them, he knew them well. But there was no time to stand there, bewitched. They should run! Mingan opened his mouth to give a command, to have the treasure loaded on *Embolon* and -

"Pay me what's ours, Mingan!" a rustling voice cut the silence. Nirveli was propped on her arms, her tail impatiently foaming the sea washing the beach. "Give us back the Joy-of-Sea!"

Mingan looked at the womanfish. Then he ran to one of the chests recovered from the *San Juan Nepomuceno*. He took a pearl out of it, as large as a fist, of pink overtone, and raised it with his left hand for all to see. It was almost painful to watch it in the sun.

"This what you want, womanfish?" Mingan shouted to her.

"Yes!" Nirveli replied. "The Joy-of-Sea! That's what you promised me!"

"Indeed?" Mingan grinned, his brow raised, and looked at his men, as if it was all a good joke. He lowered his right hand within reach of his revolver. He was approaching Nirveli in casual steps. "Maybe I did... Maybe I didn't... And maybe I don't care!"

He looked at his pirates. They all burst into laughter. Mingan drew the revolver from his sash.

"No!" Rashelka screamed and leapt after him. She grabbed Mingan by his hand and turned him. His face contorted in fury, he whipped her with the stare of a beast and swung his gun and hit her. The barrel cut Rashelka's skin on the top of her head, blood gushed down her brow. Stunned, the girl collapsed to the sand.

"All three of you forgot," Mingan bellowed, his eyes skimming from Rashelka under his feet to Katka to the womanfish, "I don't need you anymore!"

"And you forgot," Katka replied in icy quiet voice, "we're not on your ship anymore."

Wind coursed through Katka's body and surged into her fingers like tide. Her anger boosted it from a breeze into a *bura*, and she lifted her hands and dropped a strong gust on Mingan. The squall felled the pirate. Katka spun around herself, the wind was howling around her and roaring and knocking the pirates down. She thrashed them like twigs, whirling them, breaking them like rotten trees.

Mingan cursed. He tried to rise, but Rashelka pounced at him. He pushed her with his leg into the water. He leaped to hit her, but Nirveli snatched him and brought him down. Mingan raised his gun. Rashelka caught his hand again and pushed it up and the revolver fired into nothing. Nirveli grabbed Mingan by his throat, strangling him. He pushed her away with one strong kick of his knee against her chest, and hit her in the head with his boot and the womanfish fell into the waves and disappeared beneath the surface.

Unaware of anything except the *bura* in her hands, Katka scattered the pirates, lifting them in the air. The wind carried them, throwing them everywhere. They screamed and yelled for help, cursed and swore, victims of the unbridled wrath, but she did not hear their cries anymore. In several gusts, the beach was clean of Mingan's gang.

A machine-gun burst broke from the *Embolon*. Bullets buzzed around Katka, she raised her hands and cast a gust against the airship. The strength of the wind tore her from the anchor, carried her across the lagoon, and then a new gust whirled her and ripped the gondola away, steam hissing out of the boiler. Something burst into flames and the next moment the triumphant *Embolon* was a torch diving into the lagoon with everybody onboard.

A revolver shot thundered on the beach. At the same moment, peace settled on the lagoon. Katka collapsed to the sand. Pain in her chest. Dark. She twitched her head, everything was blurred before her eyes. She tried to focus back. She felt her entire power draining out of her hands, slipping through her fingers just like the *doubloons* from Mingan's fist. *No!*, she cried, trying hard to keep her consciousness and summon her power back.

"Oh yes, woman, you're really something! I knew I wouldn't be bored with you!" Mingan stood above Katka, barrel pointing at her. He was just a blurred shape to her, a grinning monster, a shadow of imminent death. "And you think you did me harm? The *Embolon* was junk anyway. And the crew?" Mingan burst into laughter. "I won't have to share with anybody! It's all mine now! Mine! You hear, you damned thing?"

Somebody screamed, Katka heard the cry in the darkness she was sinking into. Rashelka! The thought of her daughter alone with the monster drove her to seek the last bits of strength in her. She strained and felt the wind rising anew in her, coursing and getting stronger, the last breath she would ever draw out of her body. She knew: with one more gust of the *bura*, life would blow out of her, too.

"Let's finish it," Mingan growled, lifting his revolver and aiming at Katka's head. Rashelka screamed and ran out of the waves, bloodied, tears running down her cheeks. She was running at Mingan, swearing and cursing his dog seed.

"Oh, you are a pain!" Mingan muttered and turned and aimed at Rashelka. Just a little squeeze of the forefinger and—

A shot! A bullet hit Mingan straight in the head, he flew several feet back and dropped, leaving behind a trail of bloody drops whirling through the air. Rashelka fell next to her mother and covered her with her body. But there was no more shooting. *Who fired?* Rashelka wondered. The Spaniards from the *Algeciras* that had escaped into the forest?

And then, an airship descended above the hill to the beach! She flew a yellow-blue-red flag, Rashelka did not know it. The unknown ship approached them, and below her, armed men stepped out of the forest. Rashelka counted a dozen of them. They were armed with rifles, *pistolas* and revolvers, swords and scimitars and machetes at their belts. Most were dressed in pale coarse fabric trousers and opened shirts with sleeves rolled up, their heads bound in bandannas or under broad straw hats. One was wearing a red sleeve cap.

They were led by a bearded man with curly hair. He held a repeating rifle, ready to shoot. Rashelka realized these were not regular troops. *Another pirate gang?* she wondered with trepidation. But the men were passing the chests almost without looking at the gold in them: that was no way bandits would act. Rashelka looked at the airship once again and decided that perhaps she could have been the very same one seen by Branduff when he first spotted the Golden Armada, the same mysterious airship quickly hiding in the clouds.

A tall strong dark-skinned youth approached Katka and Rashelka cautiously. He, too, had a rifle and a *pistola* at his belt. He could not have been much older than Rashelka, but all the same, she was afraid of him a bit. She heard sailors talk about the black men on the shores of Africa and the New World, but she had never seen them in her life. And he, as soon as he saw the bloody stain spreading across Katka's dress, yelled: "Ernesto!"

One of the fighters replied. The youth pointed at wounded Katka and Ernesto ran to them. Something in his melancholic gaze filled Rashelka with trust and she let him examine Katka. *That man has known sorrow and misery*, she thought. *He cannot be bad.* Their commander followed him, the youth and Ernesto addressed him as *Comandante.*

"You are her daughter?" the *Comandante* asked. Rashelka nodded. "Come, this is not a job for us," he led her aside. "You need your wound cleaned, too. Don't be afraid, *companera,* Ernesto was studying for a doctor. And if you ask me, I've seen fighters living through worse."

Rashelka was watching the sea and the sky, burning with sunset. The frigatebirds made black shapes with pointed wings against the red sky, returning to their night roosts. The *Granma,* the bolivarists' airship, rested above the beach, secured with ropes. Peace returned to the lagoon, only the remains of the four airships and the crosses on the freshly-dug graves testified to the slaughter three days ago.

The *bolivaristas* erected a camp at the edge of the forest, fires lighted them as they cleaned their rifles and ate, preparing themselves for rest. In the distance, sentries patrolled the beach: the *Comandante* left nothing to chance. The treasure had already been transferred to the *Granma* and well locked and guarded with machine-guns. Stolen from the people and returned to the people, thus had Ernesto said when they had been loading the last chest. The escaped Spaniards from the *Algeciras*? Some fishermen would pick them up, the *Comandante* shrugged.

"*Hola, companera!*" Rashelka turned. Camilo was standing behind her and smiling with his big eyes. They looked even bigger in his dark face lit by the flame of the sunset. She was not afraid of him anymore. He had helped Ernesto dress Katka's wound skillfully—the bullet had passed through her lungs—and they had carried her together from the beach into the shadows of the trees. And they had made her a place to rest, Camilo had shown Rashelka how to make a roof out of palm fronds. "The *Comandante* told me to hand you this."

He was carrying a bundle the size of a fist. He unwrapped it to reveal the Joy-of-Sea, the large pearl like a glowing hot sphere in the sunset. Rashelka had been afraid the bolivarists would not give the pearl up, but the *Comandante* and Ernesto had felt they owed the womenfish the treasure they had laid their hands on. And as the *Comandante* had said in the discussion, the pearl like that is not easy to cash.

"*Gracias*", Rashelka took the Joy-of-Sea. She rolled the pearl between her fingers and then she clenched it with her right fist and hurled it into the sea with full force. It splashed some fifty feet from the shore. His sadness barely concealed, Camilo watched the waves swallowing the biggest pearl human eyes have ever seen. And then Nirveli leapt from the waves like a dolphin, holding the pearl and laughing. Her laughter merged with the last calls of the gulls and the murmur of the waves into a joyous song. She leapt once again and then she splashed back into the sea, never to appear again.

"There, we righted that wrong, too," Rashelka murmured. "The Joy-of-Sea belongs to the womenfish. And without Nirveli, the treasure would still be at the bottom of the sea. Come, it will be dark soon." She headed for the camp and her mother, recovering under Ernesto's watchful eye and careful nursing of one of the girls that disembarked from the airship. Camilo looked at the waves once again, and then followed Rashelka.

When the Andean *reconquista* crushed the Simon Bolivar rebellion earlier in the century, some of his soldiers escaped and looked for sanctuary in the inaccessible places veiled in legends. Enraptured, Camilo told Rashelka of the hidden city in the mountains where the ancient Incas found shelter before the conquistadors, and of another city, overgrown in the impenetrable jungle. Here the *bolivaristas* built their army anew: maybe Bolivar was defeated, but his torch of freedom was not extinguished. And the more the whips flogged and the tighter the manacles squeezed, the brighter it burned.

But rifles and machine-guns and cannons cost. Revolution is not free, the *Comandante* had noticed last night. Ernesto had been sitting next to him. Together they drafted a manifesto they were to send out to the enslaved and oppressed of the New World. Rashelka quickly realized Ernesto was more than just a doctor. Maybe the *Comandante* was the commander, but Ernesto was the flame of the revolution. And Camilo had been sitting next to them, absorbing every word they said. But, every so often, his gaze would wander to Rashelka. The girl had not missed that. And she liked it.

Revolution is not free, the *Comandante* repeated. And Mingan's informer had doubled his pay. Armed with his information, the bolivarists set the airship to follow Mingan, knowing how his raid would end, and using any opportunity presenting itself.

"Will you come with us?" Camilo asked, catching up with Rashelka. The bolivarists saw Katka's power in action. They spoke with her, they knew she broke the Golden Armada. They wanted her with them. Rashelka knew her mother did not want to kill anymore. But they both also knew what kind of evil was being born in the New World, in its forests and rivers and mountains. They witnessed that evil. It gushed out of earth, burning in the glimmer of gold and silver and precious stones, spilling everywhere, threatening the world. Only the flame of freedom could burn that evil, and drive the beasts in human shape away, and heal the wounded land, and wash all the spilled blood and wipe all the cried tears.

"We must take off tomorrow, we're not safe here. Will you come with us? Your mother and... you?"

Rashelka paused, hope was shining in Camilo's eyes. She looked at the camp. Her mother. Camilo.

"I know how your mother feels... About killing and all, I heard her. But... We need you. The people need you. The revolution needs you..." Camilo looked at Rashelka. And she remembered what her mother had said after the bolivarists left her to rest. Not every wind is a monster. It didn't take a killer to damage moored airships, scatter fleets across the sea or drench marching soldiers in shower.

Ernesto spoke of hope, of fight, of revolution. Of chains cast off. Of freedom and justice. The rebels listened to his words, exalted, the flame was burning and spreading, unstoppable, across the entire New World.

Rashelka offered Camilo her hand and he took it. The warmth of his hand awoke something new in her, something she never felt before. *Perhaps it's really time for the New World*, Rashelka thought as they walked on the beach, led by Ernesto's words, interrupted by applause and cheerful shouts.

TWO COUNTESSAS AND AN UNWELCOME DIVERSION

Rhiannon Louve

On my first night in Senegal, I saw a flying monkey. It flitted instantly out of sight above my window in a once-French *palais* in Dakar, largest port city of the United Senegalese Sovereignties.

I dismissed the winged primate. Unfamiliar with local wildlife, I assumed I'd seen some odd-looking bird, not a monkey. Only one woman knew how to breed flying monkeys—at least, the sort with feathered wings—and she jealously guarded her technique. As I had no reason to believe the infamous Contessa di Casoria had left Italy, a case of nerves seemed more likely. Our trip had been hardly uneventful, between the air pirates and the clockwork dragon we'd been forced to shoot down. Terrible shame, really. It was lovely craftsmanship.

More concerning than any such adventures was, of course, tomorrow's Luncheon. Officially, my brother Frederic and I were here as attachés to the British embassy, bearing gifts to strengthen England's friendship with Senegal. Unofficially, however, I was here to meet Jean-Richard's parents.

Jean-Richard Mbodj was my charming, handsome suitor of nearly a year now. We got on famously, and he even shared my staunch belief that the fairer sex should be trained to combat as well as leadership. For once, I agreed with my parents on someone's suitability as a fiancé.

But though he'd been fostered in England, Jean-Richard's family lived in Africa. As I could hardly become engaged without an introduction to my betrothed's mother, when Father confided he'd granted Jean-Richard permission to beg for my hand, I'd insisted on a trip to Senegal.

As a Duke's daughter, closer to the throne than any other unmarried young lady in England, naturally this drew attention.

Jean-Richard, for his part, was a prince of the Waalo, one of ten kingdoms in Senegal's Council of Monarchs. The parents I'd come here to meet were Ndate Yalla II, elected High Queen of Senegal by her fellow council monarchs, and an educated freedman war hero named John Richard, who'd returned to aid his heritage nation against impending French conquest.

With such a rich family history, how could I not be nervous to meet them? And, of course, two whole nations waited with baited breath on our Luncheon's outcome. The upcoming English-Senegalese friendship ceremony might prove entertaining, but the much more important matter to anyone *I* talked to, was whether our two nations could soon look forward to a Royal Wedding!

The thought churned my stomach. Fond as I was of Jean-Richard, I squirmed to prepare for so personal a decision while the world donned lorgnettes to watch me. I stared out the broad windows of my sumptuous sitting room. Despite the modified French architecture of the *palais*, it was plain from everything my eyes touched that I was far, far from home. Suddenly I felt lonely, rather than excited.

As I gazed out at the city with its jumble of forbidding French structures alongside the newer indigenous cottages and thatch-like roofs, my mind raced over what I might say at lunch tomorrow, and everything that could go wrong.

For example, there was that incident on my birthday to consider. One Reginald Hammond, claiming to be a time-traveler, had helped rescue me from an ogre assassin in impossibly-advanced power armor, sent by a man I'd never heard of—Stalin. It seemed most unlikely that another assassination attempt awaited me at the Luncheon, or that Hammond had the slightest idea what role I would ultimately play in the course of history.

But if there *was* a time machine—if Hammond really *did* know my future...

Well, England's queen-in-training had to expect the

unexpected.

At precisely that moment, in the streets below, I saw Hammond. He strolled through Dakar in loose-hanging local garb, as if he never wore anything else. I blinked and leaned out the window for a better look, but by then he had vanished completely.

I chuckled to myself. Not every Englishman in native garb, assuming I'd truly seen anything of the kind, was a time-traveler in disguise. I had myself so worked up about tomorrow, and about my prospective future with Jean-Richard, that I was seeing things. I took a deep breath and forced my mind to other avenues.

Was it any wonder, then, that I dismissed the flying monkey? In retrospect it seems a foolish inattention on my part, but at the time it did appear more plausible that I'd imagined the thing.

Besides, not long after I saw it, and "Hammond", I heard footsteps behind me. I turned to see my Aunt Diana, Father's much-younger sister and my chaperone for this adventure. Mother had been scandalized by Father's choice, since Diana was childless, relatively young, and unmarried, but Diana was technically a widow, and I'd insisted on a woman schooled in combat to escort me. After the chaos of my birthday, and because he doted on his younger sister, my father had agreed.

"Still up, Evelina?" Diana asked, concerned. "We've a long carriage ride to the High Queen's new country villa in the morning."

I nodded. She was right. I needed to rest. "I'm just so nervous," I said.

Diana waved away my concerns. "Jean-Richard knows his own mind," she insisted, "and this is a good political match, no matter what his parents think of you. England and Senegal need one another right now. With the world in chaos, we civilized nations have to stand together."

I found myself pacing the floor and sat, forcing my hands to relax in my lap. I was braver than this.

"I'll send for a hot toddy," Diana said, approvingly. "I'm sure they make something of the sort 'round here. Now go to bed."

I sighed and gave as meek a nod as could be hoped for from Evelina of Grafton.

"You'll do fine," my Aunt Diana promised, and went to find the maid.

<◇>

Our carriage, the next morning, was of European style, another remnant of the French occupation. When asked, the driver informed me, Diana, and my brother Freddie that our vehicle had been designed for the *gouverneur*'s daughter, for maximum shade without holding in the heat.

Especially impressive were the whirring little ceramic-and-wood air pumps near the ceiling. They were connected to complex devices on the roof, complete with polished bronze clockwork and elaborate glass-shielded wiring. The pumps created a breeze inside the carriage, and did indeed seem to suck the hot air right outside. I almost needed a shawl.

Freddie opened the carriage's front window and asked our driver how they worked.

The driver shrugged, saying only, "Our engineers have had generations to learn about heat. The French lady wanted to travel in the cold, so we learned to make cold."

The open window let in hot air from outside, but I enjoyed the warm breeze, to counter the increasingly excessive cool from the pumps. The air pumps' hum, and our driver's soothing chatter about Senegalese inventions, lulled me finally into the sleep I never had managed well the night before. I leaned against the carriage wall and closed my eyes, while Diana stared out in wonder at the local vegetation and wildlife. Unadventurous of me, perhaps, but I was later glad that I'd managed a nap.

<◇>

I awakened to Aunt Diana's voice, murmuring low to Freddie, her words slicing through my nervous dreams to drag me back to wakefulness.

"...could have sworn I just saw a flying monkey," she said. "The wildlife here is amazing, isn't..."

I cut her off. One flying monkey I could ignore, but not two, especially not if I'd really seen Hammond last night. "Weapons out," I snapped. I didn't care if I were over-reacting. "We're about to be ambushed."

Freddie normally takes my instincts seriously, but in his defense, I'd just woken up from a nap.

"It was a dream, Evvie," he assured, laughing softly. "Everything's..."

The coach rolled slowly to a stop.

We all stared at one another. We heard nothing strange from outside, but we couldn't see the driver. The little front window had been shuttered while I slept. Diana had her side window wide open, but all we saw out that way was virgin wilderness, tall grasses interspersed with shady baobab trees, lushly green in wake of the recent rainy season.

Other than the breeze, and a few ordinary-looking birds, nothing moved. We spotted no monkeys, winged or otherwise.

"I saw a flying monkey last night," I said, to explain my alarm. "I dismissed it at the time, but..."

Freddie's eyes widened. "Now that you mention it," he admitted, "I spent an hour dicing with our ambassador's guards last night, and I did hear di Casoria's name. She was seen traveling through Marrakech a few months back, with a small, pale-skinned woman who frightened everyone. I took no interest, but if rumor is true, and she continued south, she could have reached Dakar by now."

I drew the elegant stiletto I'd hidden in my hair. I always wore at least three blades while traveling, but small is best for tight quarters. The other weapons lay in their sheaths on the empty seat, with Freddie's and Diana's swords.

"We'd best check on the driver," Diana murmured, drawing a slim dagger from her bodice. "We've been stopped several minutes."

As if in response, the background hum of the air pumps

wound slowly down to silence. We still heard nothing outside.

"Right," Freddie said, squaring his jaw. He pulled out a blade of his own, and, weapon at the ready, drew back the shutter between us and our driver.

He was nowhere to be seen. Freddie closed it again.

"You ladies stay here," he said. "I'll go scout, see where he's got off to."

Diana raised an eyebrow at him, and I rolled my eyes in sisterly exasperation.

"Frederic of Grafton," I said. "We're all trained fighters in this carriage. We'll face any dangers together."

Diana watched him pointedly and waited. Outnumbered, Freddie relented. He's supportive of our views on a well-armed femininity, but I think he prefers an appreciative audience when he's being brave.

Nevertheless, he values the advantages of comrades in arms. With one last check out her window for safety, Diana opened her carriage door for us. Freddie and I, in a coordinated leap that only siblings could possibly have bothered to rehearse, dove from our horse-drawn transport as one, somersaulting to our feet in a defensive back-to-back stance, angled to survey the carriage, and take stock of any threats.

We saw nothing unusual. The carriage appeared unharmed. The horses placidly cropped grass at the edge of the dirt road. Our driver remained missing, but with no signs of struggle.

Several yards away, a hot air balloon drifted by, piloted by two women in European dress. Non-rigid balloons have limited combat applications—too easy to puncture, and too big for aetheric defense fields—so they're mostly used as air carriages, for casual transport in safe locales. This one was gaily appointed in pastel flowers. Wherever our possibly-imagined threat originated, it couldn't be the balloon. I signaled it to come closer. Perhaps those inside had seen our driver leave?

Diana stepped lightly down to join us, each of us straining eyes and ears for any sign of danger or explanation. We saw nothing but the balloon—not even a flying monkey.

"Perhaps our driver felt the call of nature?" Diana suggested, halfheartedly.

"If he were behind a tree with his trousers down, we'd have noticed some sign by now," I said.

My mother would have fainted to hear her daughter utter such words. Even my brother looked slightly pained, but Aunt Diana only smirked.

"Well," Freddie said, "I can drive a carriage. Perhaps we should..."

A small, glass vial sailed through the air toward us. Not knowing what it was, we jumped aside to let it fall. It shattered on the ground at our feet, instantly filling the air with ugly brown smoke and a rotten smell. I'd heard of such things, jars of compressed aether, infused with inhalants to spread them quickly upon release.

I tried to hold my breath, but it was too late. I already felt dizzy, and my knees buckled beneath me. As I fell to the ground, my mind processed the vial's trajectory arc.

It came from the hot air balloon. Of course. Balloons were all but silent, and everyone would dismiss their occupants as harmless fellow travelers. Clever.

One of the women in the basket adjusted a few ropes and pulleys. The balloon responded more quickly than typical, moving in our direction, and I saw that it sported lovely technological enhancements, for greater maneuverability. I supposed that technically made it a kind of dirigible, despite its traditional balloon shape. One frets about the strangest details while falling unconscious.

As Frederic and Diana fell beside me, the balloon drifted closer. The gay flowers adorning its silken envelope seemed monstrous in their newfound incongruity. I blinked eyelids grown heavier than stone, managing only one last glimpse of the waking world before the poisoned gas claimed me.

The balloon had drifted quite close by then. I could hear the quiet hum of its piloting gadgetry now, and the occasional hiss from its burner. I looked up at the two women in the basket, just as a cat-sized, winged monkey scrambled excitedly onto the shoulders of, I assumed, the Contessa di Casoria.

But she wasn't the one who terrified me. The other woman was a petite creature, pretty enough, of matronly age and modestly attired, with ordinary dark brown hair and perhaps an Eastern European cast to her features. Her face was unusually pale, and her expression nearly blank, save for a slight smile to blood-dark lips, but even that wasn't what frightened me.

The last sight I remembered as unconsciousness claimed me was the woman's eyes: dark, fathomless, and old. They reminded me of Hammond's eyes, in their out-of-place mystery, but Hammond never frightened me. No, these eyes were something I'd never encountered before, not face to face. These eyes were evil.

I awoke strapped to a table, in what appeared to be a laboratory. I saw an assortment of glass tubing, incomprehensible wires, and a few Bunsen burners. Something I didn't recognize buzzed and crackled in one corner of the small, white-walled room, letting off occasional sparks and powering (or powered by?) some clockwork device I couldn't identify. The room was lit by expensive clean-burning aetheric gas lamps, and had only small ventilation windows high in the walls. All I could see outside them was a sliver of bright daylight sky. Inside, the room had a cool, basement feel.

I didn't feel I'd been unconscious long enough to have traveled far. I guessed it was still the same day as the ambush, and not yet evening. I wondered what Jean-Richard and his parents thought of my failure to attend their luncheon. Or had they realized yet that I was missing?

I appeared to be alone in the laboratory, though I couldn't crane my neck far behind me from this position. If the room had a door, I couldn't see it, but one stone wall was extensively bedecked with heavy steel clockwork. I heard no sounds beyond the crackle and hum of the electrical device in the corner. Certainly, I saw no sign of my aunt and brother.

Tugging experimentally at my bonds, I found them most

admirably crafted and frustratingly sturdy. I could move a little, but not to appreciable effect, and I certainly couldn't pull free. My left wrist-cuff felt somewhat looser than the right, perhaps because my right arm is stronger from all the swordplay. I narrowed my left hand as best I could and attempted to work it free of the cuff. If my efforts worked at all, the process would undoubtedly hurt, but since I'd been kidnapped and bound as, apparently, some sort of science experiment, I surmised that an injured hand would probably prove a worthwhile sacrifice in the cause of escape.

I hoped Diana and Freddie were well, wherever they were. Until such time as I found them again, I focused on saving myself. My hand squeezed and twisted in its cuff, painfully scraping my skin. I didn't let that slow me down. I had to get free.

Unfortunately, before I got far, I heard and saw the heavy grinding of the far wall's huge gears, and a piece of said wall detached itself. It slid forward on some sort of track, and then to the side, revealing a dim opening to another room. From these shadows stepped la Contessa Desideria di Casoria, or rather, a handsome, Italian-looking woman with a flying monkey on her shoulder. I knew of only one person likely to match such a description.

To my discomfort, but not surprise, she was closely followed by a second woman, the petite creature from the balloon, with the dark, terrible eyes. I looked away from this second woman's face, not wanting to meet her gaze ever again. She saw as much, and her delicately age-lined, dark lips curved upward in a small smile. I shuddered.

They entered and closed the big, stone door, and di Casoria went to a small armoire and retrieved two lady-sized laboratory smocks to cover their light, southern Italian style clothing.

The woman with the dreadful eyes accepted her smock without a word, and watched me eerily as she donned it. I noted that my mouth was dry, and that my bodice felt nearly as constrictive as my restraints.

I didn't try speaking to them until the Italian scientist— renowned equally for her advances in biological understanding and her mad, aborted attempt at an Italian war of conquest—turned once more to face me. Despite everything I'd heard about her, she frightened me far less than the smaller, older woman at her side.

"Contessa," I began, keeping my voice steady and respectful, and speaking in Italian. "I must ask you..."

"Which of us do you address?" purred the unknown woman. She had a cultured, notably Hungarian accent. "We are both Contessas in rank."

I hesitated. Had I heard of any terrible Hungarian countesses? I couldn't recall. Von Gottshalk's clockwork monstrosities had made communication with Eastern Europe rather spotty of late, but surely a woman as terrifying as this one would have caused a few continent-spanning rumors.

Both women smiled at what must have been my puzzled expression. Only di Casoria's smile showed true mirth.

"Forgive me," she said, in excellent English. "I'd forgotten that we've never met. Lady Evelina of Grafton, I am, as you seem to have guessed..." She paused to pet the winged monkey on her shoulder. It leaned into her caress like a cat, and ruffled its remarkable brown-feathered wings. "...La Contessa di Casoria. This," She indicated her unsettling companion, "is my friend Erzsebet, Countess of Ecsed. You've heard of her as Elizabeth Bathory."

I blinked. Elizabeth Bathory, the murderous Blood Countess? She'd lived centuries ago!

I remembered Hammond's words at my birthday ball. *Let's just say I'm from the past.* Was it possible this was the real Elizabeth Bathory?

She certainly looked the part—through the eyes at least. I didn't know what to say. I didn't mean to glance her way again, but I did, and I immediately wished I hadn't. Her smile was demure and pleasant, as if we shared introductions at some charity gala. The smile didn't touch her eyes. They hung like gems of distilled cruelty, and I don't truly believe they saw me—not as a person.

More frightening still, she looked eager for something,

anticipatory.

I was a young woman strapped to a table in front of her—a murderess who'd killed hundreds of young women, possibly to bathe in their blood.

Di Casoria's claim stretched my mind's credulity, but my stomach felt certain of my peril. I swallowed hard.

"How is that possible?" I asked, trying to sound calm and curious. I needed time to think, to find some way out of this. If nothing else, I had to stall in hope of rescue. Asking questions seemed like somewhere to start.

My voice only wavered a little, but Erzsebet heard it and offered a distressingly kind smile. Very softly, she answered me. "I came here through a magical portal called a 'time machine'," she explained, without the slightest irony.

Given her native time period, I supposed that wasn't surprising. She had a reputation for horror and death, but hardly for scientific acumen.

She went on. "A man named Joseph Stalin asked me to come kill you, and to be sure you knew who sent me." She gave another horribly compassionate smile. In a voice as soft and sweet as a young girl's she concluded, "I told him it sounded like fun."

Stalin! The armored ogre at my birthday ball had been sent by the same man. No one I knew had ever heard of him, with the exception of that Hammond fellow. What did Stalin have against me? And why was it so important I know his name? I'd learned it meant "steel" in Russian. Was that supposed to be a clue?

And, of course, now was not the time for puzzling over such matters. A time-traveling Elizabeth Bathory wanted to kill me. Joseph Stalin could wait.

"Are... you going to bathe in my blood?" I asked. I didn't want to know the answer, but I did want to keep these women talking, and it was somehow the only question that sprang to mind.

Erzsebet laughed in delight. "You know, I only did that the once," she said mildly, as if admitting to stealing sweets from the baker. "How one's reputation does grow, over time. Gratifying really. And it did give my dear friend Desideria the idea for what we *do* plan with you." This time her smile was predatory, and her terrible eyes glittered. "I'm told the process will be quite painful."

"Yes," di Casoria agreed. Did I detect a certain impatience in her tone? "I may have discovered a way, by running a subject's blood through an enhanced-potential distillation-rejuvenation process, to extract from it a serum of eternal youth. It's quite logically sound," she assured me, "within the new understandings of theoretical bio-physics." As if I should find that comforting.

"Ah," I replied, as calmly as I could. And then, because everything about this notion bothered me, I couldn't help but add, "Beginning to feel our years, are we, Desideria?" Since I wasn't yet eighteen, and the Contessa would be near thirty at least, it was... probably not a clever thing to say.

Erzsebet chuckled, but Desideria di Casoria frowned tightly.

"I wouldn't expect a willful little English *swordswoman...*" She said it as if it were a bad thing! "...to grasp the true Consequence of my contributions to Modern Science, but while you're strapped to a table in my laboratory, let's refrain from petty insults, shall we?" She and Erzsebet both smirked at me. Desideria went on. "I can always make the process *more* painful."

Erzsebet's smile deepened happily. I shuddered again.

"And now, dear," the Italian Contessa said, turning to her time-traveling Hungarian counterpart, "I know how bored you get with the technical bits. Why don't you wait in the drawing room, while I prepare our subject?"

"Of course," said Elizabeth Bathory, with perfect courtesy. "Just be sure to tell me when it's time for the... experiment."

"I will," di Casoria promised.

The Blood Countess retreated through the retractable clockwork wall, and Desideria di Casoria went to one of the tiny, high windows. She stood on a stepladder to open it, and lifted her winged monkey from her shoulder.

"Out you go," she said. "Must have a clean work environment."

The monkey chittered playfully and hopped out the window, feathered wings spreading for flight. I reflected upon the tragedy of such delightful genius wasted on a woman turned mad and cruel by ambition.

The Contessa shut the window and returned to carefully soap and wash her hands in a nearby basin. As she worked, she asked idly, "Tell me about this Stalin of yours. He must be quite a Scientist, to have invented a time machine."

I sniffed. "Why not ask your friend the Blood Countess?" was my reply, though I did endeavor to sound civil this time. "She works for him."

Desideria dried her clean hands and shrugged. "Erzsebet lacks what one might call a *scientific* outlook," she said delicately. "She believes Stalin to be a sorcerer, and is bored by my questioning. All she could tell me was that he's collecting a team of historical villains to aid him in a bid for power, but he must be doing so in secret. No one's ever heard of him."

Historical villains! I struggled to keep the surprise from my face. Clearly, di Casoria knew more about Stalin than I did, but the longer she found me interesting, the longer she might put off torturing me to death for Science.

"Well," I offered, feigning contemplation.

Desideria continued to busy herself, collecting fine rubber tubes and other oddments, as well as an assortment of large, shiny needles. I avoided looking closely at the needles, since every time I did, I lost my train of thought.

I didn't want to be bled to death.

"I wouldn't wager on Stalin's scientific genius," I said carefully. "I've been informed that the time machine was," or rather 'would one day be', but I didn't want to confuse the issue, "a woman's invention. Stalin only uses it."

I extrapolated a bit from hints Hammond had offered, assuming Hammond wasn't simply spinning a wild tale.

"Ah," said the Contessa, as if my words were only predictable. Then she turned to me sharply, in the middle of connecting long rubber tubes to the many slim, cylindrical openings in the laboratory's complex glass arrangement. "But the machine is real? Erzsebet speaks the truth of her origins?"

So, di Casoria had seen no hard evidence either. I shrugged as best I could in my bonds. "She's quite convincing as a murderous madwoman, either way," I said.

"Stalin has shown you no proof of his claims?" Desideria persisted.

"I wouldn't say, 'proof', no." I tried to sound mysterious, though of course I had nothing further. "Why? You wish to join his organization?"

Before I could read her expression, the Contessa turned away from me and fussed with several complex apparati of the weird machine that dominated her laboratory. Apparently, even the strange electrical device in the corner was part of whatever she meant to do with my blood.

When she finished fussing with her machine, Desideria turned back to face me. On a tray before her lay seven thick needles, each one tightly bound to a rubber tube that fed into the machine.

I felt sick.

Desideria di Casoria caught my expression and smiled cruelly. "Doesn't everyone sometimes wish she had a time machine?" she purred.

Indeed. And where was that bloody Hammond this time? Or Freddie, or Jean-Richard! Anyone.

Desideria pulled the lever for the big, stone door, and called through the resultant opening, "Erzsebet, dear! Would you like to apply the needles?"

Countess Elizabeth Bathory appeared in the doorway. Despite the lines of her face, and the subtle aging of her skin, the Blood Countess managed to seem like a little girl who'd been promised a sweet.

Anyone *else*.

I think of myself as a brave woman, but tears sprang to my eyes in that moment. Erzsebet was that unnerving to be near, especially when one is bound to a table and threatened with the total and painful extraction of one's life-blood.

Fortunately, before I could make a sound, both my captors

were startled by a huge crash from somewhere above us, followed by shouts and what sounded like an army trampling overhead. The two countesses stared at one another, and rushed together from the room, leaving the door wide open.

Mere words cannot describe the depth of my relief at that moment. Without delay, I set myself once more to freeing my left hand from the leather strap that bound it. I found myself even more motivated to speed than I had been before, and though I did scrape my skin quite raw in several places, my hand slipped free with remarkable alacrity. The effort left me bleeding a little, as well as bruised, sore, and with a strained thumb, but all of that would heal.

Working furiously, I forced my hurting hand to unbuckle the opposite wrist. Just as I got myself free, I heard soft, light footsteps returning toward the laboratory.

I hoped it was my Aunt Diana. She was that small, that quiet when she moved. I didn't gamble on rescue though. The footsteps could just as easily have belonged to someone else—someone terrible, and mad, and sent to kill me.

The strap around my right hand still looked mostly buckled, though it was loose enough now for my hand to slip free at will. I hoped Bathory wouldn't notice. As for my other hand, much as it hurt, I shoved it back through the left hand strap. It went in easier than it had come out, but it still hurt enough to make me gasp.

The Blood Countess heard my sound and laughed. She stepped back through the door, into the laboratory.

"I'm not much with fighting," Erzsebet said to me. "Women weren't trained to the blade in my time, at least, not for combat."

"Oh?" I asked. I let my nervousness show in my voice. I wanted her to underestimate me.

She nodded happily. "So while Desideria deals with that bit of bother upstairs, I thought you and I could get started without her." She moved toward the abandoned tray of needles, pondered it briefly, and moved on through the laboratory, opening little drawers and cupboards under the counters until she found what she wanted. When she turned back to show me, her pale, oval face was as delighted as if she'd picked a pretty flower.

In her small, pale hand I saw a scalpel: new, sharp, and gleaming. I eyed it warily.

"You see," Erzsebet explained, "I *am* interested in transmuting your blood to a serum of eternal youth. It's an excellent notion. But what I really want to do is hear you scream." She smiled and stepped closer. "Desideria has a strong stomach, and is turning out to be a wonderful friend." The Blood Countess paused, running her dark, awful eyes over my supine form as if weighing her options. "But she has little sense of fun."

Elizabeth Bathory selected her target. She struck.

I was faster.

I slipped my right hand free of its loosened strap, and caught the other woman's delicate wrist in a grip made strong through swordplay. Erzsebet tried to wrench free, but I was much stronger, and her hand barely moved.

Straining every fiber of my free arm and hand, I worked my grip up over Erzsebet's small fist, until I held the scalpel between my fingers.

Elizabeth Bathory slipped free then, but she had to release her weapon to do so. Bound as I was, I couldn't afford to let my enemy dodge back out of my reach. I struck only once, hard and fast.

I'm not the sort of person to aim for the kill. Much as I love fencing, I must admit that I prefer not to hurt people.

For the countess of Ecsed, I made an exception. My blade struck true. Her hands flew to her bleeding throat, surprise and terror naked in those terrible, black eyes. She crumpled to the floor.

I fought down bile and went to work unbuckling my other straps.

Just as I loosed the last one and swung my freed ankles to the floor, five people rushed into the room, swords naked in five hands, each blade bearing signs of recent use.

Panting and staring at the strange tableau I must present— bloodied and rumpled in the crackling laboratory, with the dead countess at my feet—stood Freddie, Diana, my dear Jean-

Richard, and two handsome folk of middling years, a man and a woman in fine Senegalese clothing, both of whom bore a marked resemblance to my dashing African suitor.

I wasn't sure whether to laugh or weep. I dropped the scalpel I hadn't realized I still held.

"Di Casoria?" I asked helplessly, fumbling for something to say.

"Arrested by the guards outside," Freddie assured me. "We had a devil of a time with three of her larger monkey-hybrids, but finally caught them all unharmed." Seeing the room secured, he sheathed his sword.

Somewhat to my relief, the others followed suit, but silence continued to stretch, with me wondering what terrible first impression I must have made on the High Queen and her consort, and whether Jean-Richard would ever forgive me for so ruining our Luncheon. Freddie and Diana, they each informed me later, felt awkward to intrude on so momentous a meeting, and Jean-Richard said he had his heart in his throat, waiting to see how his parents would respond.

Eventually, to everyone's relief, Jean-Richard's father broke the silence.

"Lady Evelina," John Richard said in an American accent that shouldn't have surprised me. "We apologize for your gross mistreatment within our borders, and are glad to find you well." His voice was as rich and lovely as his son's, and his tone held nothing but genuine concern for my welfare.

Then Queen Ndate Yalla II cracked a wide, bright smile. "Indeed, the Lady Evelina is better than well," she said, in a beautifully cultured accent. "We come to her rescue, and instead find her victorious!" She moved to kiss her son on the cheek, and then to clasp my uninjured hand in hers. "It would appear," she said, "that my son has good taste."

I settled then on laughing and weeping both at once, and embraced the startled Queen like a long-lost aunt. Perhaps a royal wedding might glimmer on our horizon after all.

<><>

As for Hammond, I chanced upon the cheeky scoundrel in the Dakar marketplace, eight days later. He bumped me in a perfume-seller's stall, and somehow drew me aside without Freddie, Jean-Richard, or even Aunt Diana noticing.

I fixed Reginald Hammond with something of an icy stare and waited to hear what he had to say for himself.

He chuckled at my expression, and even stammered a little, in defiance of his usual smooth charm. "I wanted you to know," he said, "we restored her body to her cell in Ecsed. I know it means little to you, yet, but your self defense hasn't polluted the timeline. No one will reveal that she was found with her throat cut. They won't risk investigation into the penetration of her bricked-up chamber. You did well."

I eyed him coolly, his words, indeed, meaning little to me. I did, however, take note how very different from Elizabeth Bathory's his own dark, hypnotic eyes now seemed to me. Hammond had none of her cruelty, and a thousand times her wisdom, despite his persistently dishonest air.

"A team of historical villains?" I asked him. I did feel I was owed an explanation. Who on earth was this Joseph Stalin?

"Ah," he said softly. "As to that..."

Another man in the shop noisily knocked over a rack of perfume, catching it just in time so that only one bottle fell to shatter most fragrantly on the cobblestone floor. I barely glanced at the upset, barely took my eyes off Hammond for a heartbeat, two at most.

When I looked back, he was gone.

I still didn't know if time travel were truly possible, but at that point, I began to believe most firmly that I was against it.

ABOUT THE EDITOR

Irene Radford has been writing stories ever since she figured out what a pencil was for. A member of an endangered species, a native Oregonian who lives in Oregon, she and her husband make their home in Welches, Oregon where deer, bears, coyotes, hawks, owls, and woodpeckers feed regularly on their back deck.

A museum trained historian, Irene has spent many hours prowling pioneer cemeteries deepening her connections to the past. Raised in a military family she grew up all over the US and learned early on that books are friends that don't get left behind with a move. Her interests and reading range from ancient history, to spiritual meditations, to space stations, and a whole lot in between.

In other lifetimes she writes urban fantasy as P.R. Frost and space opera as C.F. Bentley

In June of 2011 Irene returned to fantasy with a new series, *The Pixie Chronicles.* "Thistle Down." and "Chicory Up" followed by *The Silent Dragon, Children of the Dragon Nimbus* in February 2012. The re-release of her masterwork series "Merlin's Descendants" is now available at the Book View Café http://www.bookviewcafe.com

Most recently, Phyllis has taken on the role of editor for The Book View Café and Skywarrior Books as well as freelancing for independent authors. Her first non-fiction books, *Magna Bloody Carta, A Turning Point in Democracy* is an examination of the historical document in context to the times, and *So You Want to Commit Novel,* is a collection of writing advice essays for beginning writers.

*

ABOUT THE AUTHORS:

Jennifer Rachel Baumer lives, writes, and runs in the Northern Nevada desert, a couple dozen miles from the mountains where the Comstock silver rush occurred in the 1800s. Her work has appeared in Nevada's Danse Macabre magazine, in Lady Churchill's Rosebud Wristlet, in Sky Warrior Books' Healing Waves charity anthology, and in a variety of genre anthologies and magazines. She's ghostwritten 14 nonfiction books for experts, and is marketing her own novels. Jennifer shares her desert life with her husband Rick and an abnormal number of cats, both indoor types and the feral pack that's adopted her.

*

David Boop is a single father, returning college student, part-time worker and author. He has one novel and over twenty-five short stories to his credit. He's published in several genres, most notably weird westerns and sci-fi/noir. A former journalist, he's added MC and Toastmaster to his résumé. His interests include film noir, anime, the Blues, and Mayan history. You can find out more at Davidboop.com, or his facebook fan page, Facebook.com/dboop.updates.

*

Bob Brown is a Health Physicist and one of eleven children deposited on the earth in the wilds of Central Texas during the Eisenhower administration. Ever since his early days he has excelled in the application of the shovel and the hoe, both of which are necessary to garden, something he does well, as did his grandparents who kept victory gardens at same time that Eisenhower was defeating the European Hun.

Bob has been writing ever since the Nixon administration, which was the same year he planted his first garden. He grew radishes. As he and his writing both matured he entered into a relationship with Northwest Public Radio where he served as a commentator for seven years. During this period he documented the Clinton era and the childhood of his daughter, Cheyenne in detail for the amusement of Northwest Public Radio patrons. He still resides in the Pacific Northwest, where he continues to work as a Health Physicist.

*

Ellen Denham is a multidisciplinary performing artist and writer currently teaching voice and pursuing a doctorate in music at the University of Illinois Urbana-Champaign. She is a 2006 graduate of the Odyssey Writing Workshop. Her previous publications include works in *Daily Science Fiction, Hypersonic Tales* and *NewMyths.com* and her written works for the stage have been performed by the Butler Ballet and the Indy Convergence. Not content to keep her writing and performing life in separate boxes, Ellen likes to hang out in the dark alleys where artistic genres and disciplines intersect. Her performing career has encompassed everything from opera and oratorio to barking Mozart as a dog, turning internet memes into a comic soundscape, and tap dancing in a Santa suit. You may find her online at http://denham.virtualave.net.

*

T. Fox Dunham resides outside of Philadelphia PA—author and historian. He's published in over 100 international journals and anthologies and was a finalist in the Copper Nickel Annual Short Story Contest for his story, The Lady Comes in the Night. He's a cancer survivor. His friends call him fox, being his totem animal, and his motto is: Wrecking civilization one story at a time. http://www.facebook.com/tfoxdunham

*

Bryan Fields spend his days performing percussive

maintenance on Babbage engines and his nights spinning tales of high adventure. He grew up reading classical authors such as Verne, Burroughs, Wells, Haggard, and Lovecraft, often in conjunction with large doses of Monty Python, Wild Wild West, and Hee-Haw. His current influences include *Dr. Who*, *Girl Genius*, and the computer game *Arcanum*.

Bryan began writing professionally as a member of the content design team for the *MMORPG Istaria: Chronicles of the Gifted*. His first short story appeared in the anthology, *The Mystical Cat* in 2012. He finished his first fantasy novel in 2012 and is currently looking for a publisher.

Bryan lives in Denver with his wife and daughter. The three of them can often be found prowling around Istaria, Wizard City, and the wilds of Azeroth. Bryan also makes occasional side jaunts to scavenge bits of ancient technology in the radioactive ruins of the Grand Canyon Province.

*

Sylvia Kelso lives in North Queensland, Australia. She writes fantasy and SF often set in analogue or alternate Australian settings. She has published six high fantasy novels, two of which, *Amberlight* and *The Moving Water*, were finalists for best fantasy novel of the year in the Australian Aurealis genre fiction awards, and short stories in Australian and US anthologies. Her most recent work is the short story "At Sunset", in *Luna Station Quarterly* September 2012, and the contemporary fantasy duo of Blackston Gold, *The Solitaire Ghost* and *The Time Seam*. She lives in a house with a lot of trees but no children, cats or dogs.

*

Andrew Knighton lives and occasionally writes in Stockport, England, where the grey skies provide a good motive to stay inside at the word processor. When not working in his standard issue office job he battles the slugs threatening to overrun his garden and the monsters lurking in the woods. He's had over forty stories published in places such as Murky Depths, Redstone SF and Steampunk Reloaded. He blogs about his latest stories and writing in general at andrewknighton.wordpress.com.

*

Rhiannon Louve's steampunk influences include *Girl Genius, Pride and Prejudice and Zombies*, Abney Park's musical oeuvre, "The Next Doctor" (among other recent *Doctor Who* episodes), and the various legends of Baron Munchausen. She has previously published scholarly essays on contemporary Pagan thea/ology, as well as numerous role-playing game supplements, particularly in Sword and Sorcery Studios' d20 *Scarred Lands* setting. She hopes to soon sell her first novel. Rhiannon provides vocals and keyboards for a geeky metal band, has taught World Religions at the college level, speaks French, co-runs a volunteer organization, and has personal experience with inter-planar airship combat.

*

Nancy Jane Moore's most recent book is *Flashes of Illumination*, an ebook collection of short-short stories released in August 2011 by Book View Café. Her other books include the collection *Conscientious Inconsistencies*, published by PS Publishing, and the novella *Changeling*, available in print from Aqueduct Press and as an ebook from Book View Cafe. Her short stories have appeared most recently in *Postscripts* and in the military SF anthology *Best Laid Plans*.

*

Renee Stern is a former newspaper reporter turned freelance writer whose short fiction has appeared in Beneath Ceaseless Skies, Black Gate, Aeon Speculative Fiction and the anthologies Human Tales and Sails & Sorcery: Tales of Nautical Fantasy.

Her story "Backs to the Wall" comes in part from the stories of mining disasters, coal barons and union struggles found all over West Virginia, where she grew up surrounded by friends and classmates from mining families. She currently lives with her husband outside Seattle, where she is working on several projects, including a historical fantasy novel set in medieval Spain.

*

George Walker is an engineer working in Portland, Oregon. He has written numerous science fiction and fantasy stories, appearing in Steampunk Tales, Digital Science Fiction, Ideomancer, Mirror Shards, Comets and Criminals, Science Fiction Age and elsewhere. Links to a number of his stories are available at http://sites.google.com/site/georgeswalker/

"A Chinese steampunk fairy tale, just like the ones Confucius used to tell."

Of course, Confucius would be rolling over in his grave at how the princess in my story behaves :-)

*

Cliff Winnig's short stories appear in several anthologies, including Footprints and The Aether Age: Helios (both from Hadley Rille Books), as well as Cinema Spec, Retro Spec, Jack-o'-Spec, and Spec-tacular (all from Raven Electrick Ink). His extremely short stories appear in the twitterzines Outshine and Thaumatrope. Cliff is a graduate of the Clarion Science Fiction and Fantasy Writers' workshop and a three-time finalist in the Writers of the Future Contest. When not writing, Cliff plays sitar, studies martial arts, and does ballroom dance, salsa, and Argentine tango. He lives in California with his wife and twin daughters and can be found online at http://cliffwinnig.com

*

Aleksandar Žiljak was born and lives in Zagreb, Croatia. He graduated on the Electrotechnical Faculty in Zagreb, and received a master of computer sciences degree there. Since late 1990s, he has worked as a freelance illustrator, writer and editor.

Beside Croatia, he publishes stories in several European countries, as well as the USA. He has two story collections- "Slijepe ptice" (Blind Birds, 2003) and "Božja vučica" (The Divine She-Wolf, 2010)-as well as a book on cryptozoology in print. He has also won 6 SFera awards for SF art, stories and editorial work. The SF magazine "UBIQ", which he co-edits, was voted the best European SF magazine in 2011.

BOOKS PUBLISHED BY SKY WARRIOR BOOKS

Purchase them through online resellers and better independent bookstores everywhere. Visit us at www. skywarriorbooks.com for news and upcoming books and promotions.

Alma Alexander

2012: Midnight at Spanish Gardens (E-book, Trade Paperback)

Embers of Heaven (E-book, Trade Paperback)

S. A. Bolich

Firedancer (E-book, Trade Paperback)

Seaborn (E-book)

Windrider (E-book, Trade Paperback)

M. H. Bonham

Daemons and Shadows (E-book)

Prophecy of Swords (E-book)

Runestone of Teiwas (E-book)

Samurai Son (E-book)

Serpent Singer and Other Stories (E-book)

John Dalmas

The Signature of God Part 1 (E-book)

The Signature of God Part 2(E-book)

Soldiers! Part 1(E-book, Trade Paperback)

Soldiers! Part 2 (E-book, Trade Paperback)

The Second Coming (E-book, Trade Paperback)

Deby Fredericks

Seven Exalted Orders (E-book)

Carol Hightshoe (Editor)

Zombiefied: An Anthology of All Things Zombie (E-book)

Gary Jonas

Acheron Highway (E-book)

Modern Sorcery (E-book, Trade Paperback)

One-Way Ticket to Midnight (E-book)

Quick Shots (E-book, Trade Paperback)

Frog and Esther Jones

Grace Under Fire (E-book)

Michael J. Parry

The Oaks Grove (E-book)

The Spiral Tattoo (E-book)

Phyllis Irene Radford

Healing Waves: A Charity Anthology for Japan (Editor) (E-book)

Gears and Levers 1: A Steampunk Anthology (Editor) (E-book, Trade Paperback)

Gears and Levers 2: A Steampunk Anthology (Editor) (E-book, Trade Paperback)

Gears and Levers 3: A Steampunk Anthology (Editor) (E-book, Trade Paperback)

Lacing Up Murder, A Whistling River Mystery (E-book)

So You Want to Commit Novel (E-book, Trade Paperback)

Dusty Rainbolt (Editor)

The Mystical Cat (E-book)

Deborah J. Ross (Editor)

The Feathered Edge (E-book, Trade Paperback)

Laura J. Underwood

Ard Magister (Book One of Ard Magister) (E-book)

Dragon's Tongue (Book One of the Demon-Bound) (E-book)

The Hounds of Ardagh (E-book)